PRAISE FOR *EMILY*

Burying The Honeysuckle Girls

"Storytelling in the Southern gothic tradition at its most darkly neurotic and tantalizing."

—Kimberly Brock, author of *River Witch*

"A hell of a thriller with language as lush as its Southern setting."

—Benjamin Percy, author of *Red Moon* and *The Dead Lands*

"Emily Carpenter weaves a masterful web of family drama and spine-tingling mystery."

—M. J. Pullen, author of the Marriage Pact Trilogy

The Weight of Lies

"Searing murder mystery . . ."

—*Kirkus Reviews* (starred review)

"Fascinating . . . An unputdownable read."

—*Publishers Weekly* (starred review)

"A gripping, heart-pounding murder mystery/gothic thriller sure to give readers chills."

—*RT Book Reviews*

Every Single Secret

"A true psychological thriller that will leave you breathless."

—Wendy Walker, bestselling author of *All Is Not Forgotten* and *Emma in the Night*

"A knockout."

—Kimberly Belle, bestselling author of *The Marriage Lie*

"Heart-stopping, exquisitely plotted . . ."

—Wendy Webb, bestselling author of *Daughters of the Lake*

Until the Day I Die

"Chilling . . ."

—*Publishers Weekly*

"Twisty, jaw-dropping . . ."

—Heather Gudenkauf, *NYT* bestselling author of *The Weight of Silence* and *Not a Sound*

"Carpenter's skill for brilliant and twisty storytelling will have you gasping in surprise."

—Hank Phillippi Ryan, nationally bestselling author of *Trust Me*

REVIVING THE HAWTHORN SISTERS

ALSO BY EMILY CARPENTER

Until the Day I Day

Every Single Secret

The Weight of Lies

Burying the Honeysuckle Girls

REVIVING THE HAWTHORN SISTERS

A NOVEL

EMILY CARPENTER

This is a work of fiction. Names, characters, organizations, places, events, and incidents are either products of the author's imagination or are used fictitiously. Any resemblance to actual persons, living or dead, or actual events is purely coincidental.

Published by Lake Union Publishing, Seattle

www.apub.com

ISBN-13: 9781542016193
ISBN-10: 1542016193

Cover design by Damon Freeman

Printed in the United States of America

For those who believe, for those who don't, and for everyone in between. May we all be happily surprised in the end.

Dove

This was how she knew the end was near.

At nighttime, after she'd gone to bed and begun the welcome voyage toward sleep, her friends would appear. They fluttered the curtains and stirred the dust, bringing with them the smell of long-ago, faraway places.

When she was young, she would've thought them ghosts, but at the clear-eyed age of ninety-five she knew better. They were only memories, flickers of her past. The stories she'd kept hidden for so long that she almost didn't recognize the players when they reentered the stage.

The visits (she liked to think of them as visits) had started in the summer when she still lived at the Alabama house across the road from Pritchard Hospital. In July, she'd seen her mother, the Major, and Dell. Then in August, Ethel and Erma and Jimmy Singley. Also, Old Steadfast and Arthur showed up. Come that September—when the business with the Honeysuckle Girls came to a head—Jinn, Collie, and Trix arrived, laughing and fiercely beautiful. They filled the room with the smell of wine. It was her first night back in California that brought the most welcome guest—her greatest friend and staunchest ally, Charles. He sat on his side of their bed and sang to her, and she kept her eyes on his strong, safe profile until sleep descended.

She was glad to see them all. Their presence brought her comfort. When they were alive, some had not treated her well; some had even been cruel, but she didn't mind now. That was one of the many blessings of old age. This softening of memory, the melting away of grudges. Forgiveness was no longer something to strive for. Now it entered her room through an open window.

One chilly night toward the end of October, Dove was awakened by a dream she couldn't remember. She looked at the clock, but she'd left her glasses outside and couldn't see the time. She could see the shadow man who sat motionless in the slipper chair beside her dressing table. He watched her with eyes that glittered.

"You," she said, her voice filled with wonder and the edge of a memory she would have rather not revisited.

"You shouldn't have run, Ruth," the shadow man said. "You brought so much sorrow by doing that. So much pain."

"I'm sorry."

It was all she could think to say, although she knew it certainly didn't make up for what she'd done.

He rose then, letting the faint light fall over him, and when he held up a length of faded pink ribbon, it seemed to glow in the light of the moon.

"You belonged to him," he said. "You always belonged to him."

It wasn't true, but she knew it was pointless to argue. He'd spoken with the zeal of a convert, and that was a thing she was well acquainted with. As soon as she realized this, she also realized something else, something she should have known sooner, from the first moment she'd opened her eyes.

The figure in the dark wasn't a ghost, or an ephemeral memory from her past, but a real flesh-and-blood man. And he hadn't come as a friend. He'd come for revenge.

Chapter One

Tuscaloosa, Alabama
Present

The narrow black ribbon of asphalt unfurled before me like a road to an unknown land. I pointed the nose of the rental car down its path, between the alley of hulking oak trees, and with grim purpose, slammed my foot on the accelerator.

I'd been fearful and fretting about this night for months, and I was more than ready to lay my eyes on the building at the end of this drive. Nothing was scarier than the thing you couldn't see.

Right now, all I could see were trees. In the soft early-summer twilight, the ancient oaks looked like the horror movie version of the drive leading to a psychiatric hospital. Knotty branches twisted into nightmarish appendages. Tormented limbs, entreating an unseen, uncaring God. But these trees, bark spotty and covered with spongy moss, were the real deal. And so was the institution that remained maddeningly out of sight at the end of this road. **Pritchard Psychiatric Hospital,** the elegant metal sign had read. So it had to be there.

"Kudos to Dracula on the landscape design," Danny said from the back seat, reading my thoughts. "Very on-brand." Ray-Bans held back his thick, gloriously unruly red hair, giving him that insouciant devil-may-care look. But looks were deceiving with my brother. His anxiety was a constant hum, just below the glossy surface. It was just part of who he was. Maybe part of who he would always be.

The whole flight he'd been doing his nervous throat-clearing thing. Back out on the highway, when we'd passed the newer section of the hospital, New Pritchard it was called, he'd started up the wrist tapping—an antianxiety technique he'd learned from his own ninety-day hospital stay. Good thing the rental company'd had an adapted car with a spin knob and left foot accelerator. With my condition, driving was always a challenge. But at least it kept me too busy to be nervous.

Now if only Danny and Mom could hang on, at least through tonight's ceremony. I sped up—and also may have muttered something not so nice about my dead grandmother, Dove Jarrod.

I should've been above such pettiness. She'd been dead eight years, and I was a twenty-four-year-old woman who'd made her choices deliberately and with the full knowledge of everything they entailed. Danny, two years my senior, and I both worked with our mother at the family business, the Charles and Dove Jarrod Foundation. Danny was Mom's assistant, and I was the director of fundraising. I'd been there three years, and for most of that time, it had been a safe, steady place to work. Even fulfilling at times—in spite of the fact that I was, in essence, continuously lying to everyone.

But still, I couldn't resist the jab at Dove. The childish impulse to tell her—wherever she happened to be—just how little I thought of her.

It gave me a charge, but not as electrifying as the one I got from thinking about the adventure that lay ahead. Danny had been sober for almost three and a half years now, and Mom's anxiety seemed relatively under control. In fact, recently she'd actually gone on a date with a man from her church, a guy who owned an HVAC company and looked like Ernest Hemingway. Consequently, I'd begun to feel like I might be able to extricate myself, to explore what a future apart from my family might hold. Moving not only felt possible, it felt exciting. Like, at last, I could do something for me. Pull out one Jenga block—me—without toppling the whole structure.

And so, this past winter, I'd secretly applied to Colorado State's occupational therapy program. After two nail-biting months, I had been accepted and was planning on breaking the news this evening after the dedication ceremony. It would be hard, but I hoped they'd understand. I'd head up one more push for the foundation—the documentary shoot that we were wrapping tonight—and then I'd say goodbye to my family, knowing I'd done right by them in every way I could.

This was how decent adult people treated each other, I thought. This was family. *See, Dove?*

"I really appreciate both of you coming," Mom said in the seat beside me. Pretty in a new periwinkle-blue dress and pearls, she wore her honey-colored hair in the same low knot that Dove used to. She was kneading her knuckles, and her gaze darted from me to Danny, then out the window. "You can't know how much."

"The dedication of a creepy, formerly haunted insane asylum in our dear grandmother's name?" Danny said. "Wouldn't have missed it for the world."

"Psychiatric facility," I corrected. "And this event will be great for the foundation, bring us recognition outside just the religious community. The women's program that's going to be headquartered at Pritchard has already been written up in several journals."

"I can't believe she was born here," Danny said. "Can you imagine?" He caught himself. "What am I saying? Of course we can. We've done the time, haven't we, Mom?"

Mom's voice was distant. "Yes, Daniel, we have."

"You know what I can't get over?" he went on, and I sensed an edge in his voice. That old sharpness he used to get when he'd started drinking but was still sober enough to remember the things he was angry about. "That our grandmother was born in a nuthouse and got out by the hair of her chinny-chin-chin. But then, years later, her daughter and grandson end up in places just like it."

"Danny—" I started, but Mom interrupted.

"We should pray." She clasped her hands and closed her eyes, her back hunching. I sighed and checked the rearview mirror. Danny's head was tilted back, eyes defiantly open, but he'd gone quiet. Mom's stalwart, unwavering faith was off-limits. We'd both agreed to that a long time ago. He knew as well as I did what kept her boat on keel.

Mom prayed, "Dear Father, you've brought us so far, and we thank you for all your many mercies. We thank you for Pritchard—both a terrible place and a wonderful one. Dove did love this place, in her own way. She had good memories here, so many gifts . . ."

I checked the mirror again. Danny was staring out the window.

". . . a friend, a boy she played with, remember she told me that once? They used to hide gifts for each other. I always thought that was so sweet. So tender . . ."

Her voice faltered, and I settled in for the long haul. I felt a sharp needle of pity for her. Mom did this every once in a while, lost the trail when she was praying and ended up reminiscing instead. It was just one of her quirks, but also one of the ways I realized that her constant, acute yearning for family had never really been fulfilled.

She said Charles Jarrod had been a doting father, delighted by the baby girl he'd had late in life, but he'd died when she was just a child, and Mom clearly felt the loss. Especially in contrast to the chilly, almost formal relationship she had with Dove. My own father, once a sound tech for Dove's shows, had been a blip on the radar—fathering two children, then melting away into the ether. After that, Mom just stopped functioning. She stayed in her room day and night. Wouldn't cook meals for Danny and me or bathe us. She even forgot to send us to school a couple of times. When they hospitalized her, someone from the foundation came to stay with us.

Then Dove died and left the bulk of her estate for the restoration of Pritchard Hospital and only a pittance to the Jarrod Foundation. The message conveyed to my mother was all too clear. What was important to us—the foundation—didn't make a whit of difference to Dove. Her concerns, cryptic and unknowable, took precedence.

But now that we were here, seeing Dove's dream of reopening the hospital to its fruition, Mom seemed to have reframed the situation. She was beaming, almost tearful, and clasped her hands over her heart.

"This place may have been Dove's beginning," she said in a fervent voice, "but by God's grace, it was not the end."

"Amen," Danny said quickly.

"Amen," I echoed.

Mom looked around the car, seeming to only vaguely recall where she was. Then she turned and sent me a bright smile. "Eve, when did you say the film crew would arrive?"

"Our director flew in the day before yesterday. He should've connected with the local team, the second camera person and assistant. I haven't seen any footage yet, but supposedly they got some fantastic B-roll. Tape of the grounds and the cemetery."

She didn't answer. I hadn't realized it, but we'd reached the end of the drive, where the canopy of trees had finally opened up and the exterior of Pritchard Hospital had come into view. She grabbed my right arm, the weak one, and pointed.

"Look! There it is!"

Danny's tapping finally stilled. "Damn."

But a laser beam of setting sun had hit my eyes, blocking my vision. I squinted and flipped down the visor, focusing on making my weak right arm wheel the car around a lacy iron fountain without smashing into it. I only caught flashes of the huge building as I drove past. Red brick, stone, and wood. Belfries, arches, and parapets. All flickering between shafts of sunlight like an old-time film reel running past a projector light. I maneuvered the rental into a reserved spot beside a sleek silver BMW, killed the engine, and looked in the rearview mirror.

Okay. Wow.

Old Pritchard Hospital was a Gothic monster of a place. Formidable and reassuring all at once, if that was possible. Two long brick wings extended out from either side of the center spired tower, each anchored by enormous magnolia trees. The facade was a series of lancet and quatrefoil granite-capped windows. I felt a chill travel along the surface of my skin.

". . . and there's the hawthorn tree!" Mom was saying. "The one Dove used to talk about. Remember, she planted one at her house in Pasadena? And never let us cut any blooms from it? I wonder if that's the same one that was there when she was."

I mumbled something in the affirmative, but I couldn't say what it was, I was so focused on the massive building behind me. Now that I'd seen the place, even if it was just in my rearview mirror, I felt infinitesimally better. That was the thing about fear. It always encroached in the misty, shadowy unknown. Once I had my hands around a situation—whether it involved my own physical therapy, my mother's anxieties, or my brother's addictions—once I could see the threat in broad daylight, the monster lost its teeth.

Even a monster like my grandmother's place of birth.

Chapter Two

Mom pointed past the hospital, across the lawn to a side lot where two guys and a young woman were unloading equipment from a white SUV. "There's the crew."

A different kind of electricity zinged through me. Griffin Murray, the director of the promotional documentary we were creating about my grandparents, stood with Liz and Naveen, his two camera operators. Griffin was tall and solid, with tattoo sleeves covering both arms, and unexpectedly full lips. He wore jeans and a rust-colored retro Rat Pack button-up shirt that flapped open over a white T-shirt. Brown hair jutted out of a black knit beanie, and he sported a brown and ginger scruff. He looked more like a boxer than a filmmaker. An exceptionally lucky boxer whose face had miraculously escaped destruction.

I flashed back to a couple of months ago when I first interviewed him. His qualifications were extensive: NYU film school, a stint at Sundance, and an award for a short on Alabama poverty. The clincher was that one of his relatives had been an itinerant country preacher just like Charles and Dove. He told me that doing work like this would make his family so proud. Apparently, they were fans of my grandparents.

"Honestly, film school was a blow to my dad," he told me wryly. "He was hoping for a doctor or maybe a professional baseball player in the family. But he's been trying lately. He was the one who actually heard about this job."

"That's great," I'd burbled, trying not to be totally dazzled.

"Not that it's all on you to hire me and resolve my personal baggage, but . . . I mean . . . if you want to, I won't stand in your way."

He'd flushed so adorably that I had flushed too. In fact, I was so charmed by him, I'd barely been able to form a coherent question from that point on. At the conclusion of the interview, Griffin—Griff, he told me everybody called him—stood and gave me a brief appraising look.

"You look like her. Your grandmother, I mean." He ducked his head, somehow pulling off the most endearing display of manly sheepishness I'd ever seen. "Yeah, I've already started on the research. Dug up a few pictures, talked to a bunch of people. She had the same straight red hair that you do. The same . . ." He pointed to his own face absently. "You look like you stepped out of a speakeasy or something."

The past few months, he and his small crew had been traveling all over the country, documenting the history of Charles and Dove's ministry and meeting with people who'd experienced—or claimed to have experienced—a brush with God's healing through them. As a result, we'd only talked on the phone since that initial meeting. But the calls were always fun, full of easy banter and inside jokes, so to say I was looking forward to seeing him in person again was a massive understatement.

I checked my makeup in the visor mirror and swiped smudged eyeliner from under my eyes. "You guys go on in. I need to brief the crew."

"Oh, is that what they're calling it these days?" Danny said.

I gave him a sisterly *eat-dirt* look as we climbed out of the car, but he winked at me and took Mom's arm. They joined the crowd that was streaming toward the entrance of the hospital. I straightened my all-purpose black dress and made my way toward the white SUV. Griff met me, PMW-200 camera in hand, on the lawn beside the hawthorn Mom had pointed out. Its branches were studded with long, sharp thorns and wreathed in lacy white blooms. A bird cooed from some unseen top branch.

Griff's white tee revealed exactly three chest hairs. And although I wanted desperately not to have noticed, I couldn't help staring. I also wanted not to be enjoying how good he smelled, like coffee and old books. How his grin made me grin immediately, like a reflex.

He broke a small bloom off a branch and handed it to me. "Nice to see you."

I took it in my left hand. My right arm, the bad one, twinged the slightest bit. Nerves, probably. I tucked it behind my back.

"You too," I said.

I knew I shouldn't hide my arm. It was an illogical response, but I always had a hard time resisting the impulse. Just like using that term, *bad*, was illogical. Constraint-induced movement therapy taught me that arms weren't bad or good; they were just appendages. Instruments to help us dress ourselves, brush our hair and teeth, write or cook or touch a loved one's face. I'd gotten in the habit of doing almost everything—opening the fridge, brushing my teeth, blow-drying my hair—with my right. Still, I couldn't write with it. And it always felt like there was a neon sign on it, blaring its differentness. So at times, I gave into the urge to keep it out of sight. I didn't want Griff to notice my arm, at least not yet, and that was all there was to it.

"You hear that?" He broke into a delighted grin. "The bird? That's a dove."

"Seriously?" The scent of the flower, sweet with an edge of decay, was giving me a headache. It pulsed at my right temple.

"It's a sign. It's got to be." Suddenly, his expression shifted from delight to frantic worry. He patted himself down. "Oh, great." He yelled over his shoulder, "Liz! Get my phone, will you? I think I left it in the console." Then he turned back to me. "Probably subconsciously lost it on purpose. My dad's obsessively calling, practically every ten minutes, wanting a look at the footage."

I wrinkled my nose. "He is?"

"Oh yeah. Remember? My parents are Dove and Charles superfans."

I lifted a shoulder. "It's kind of sweet."

"Or annoying, depending on who you talk to. So, shot list?"

I scanned the property with a businesslike squint. "You don't need to get anything from the newer part of the hospital. Just the old place here. You got the grounds, right?"

"Check. Cemetery, outbuildings, spooky underground passage Dove escaped through. We already got lots of the interior too. One of the administrators let us in this morning. Hell of a haunted house."

"Psychiatric facility," I said, although I'd seen the pictures from before the reno and he wasn't that far off. Life here for the patients, for Dove, must've been a true nightmare. "People should feel sympathy for where Dove came from," I went on. "A connection to her. But we don't want to go too dark or serious; we want to keep things upbeat and inspirational. This is a sales tool, not a hard-hitting investigative piece. We don't want to bum anybody out."

"That'll be a feat of spin. This place is terrifying, even on a sunny day."

"Later, I'll introduce you to Darrell and Margaret Luster, our newest donors, and we can do an impromptu interview. Sound good?"

Griff was staring into my eyes, and I could've sworn his thoughts weren't wholly related to the Luster interview. Or at least, it felt that way. But maybe it was just my wishful thinking. I was moving to Colorado, and it was kind of cart-before-the-horse to imagine a long-distance thing when we hadn't even had our first date. When we'd never so much as held hands. Or kissed.

"Griff!" Liz yelled from the SUV, shaking me out of my romantic reverie. "No phone in the console!"

He groaned. "Shit."

"Buy a burner at Walmart," I said. "You can expense it when we get back. Find me during Mom's speech, and we'll wrangle the Lusters." I left him and, telling myself to snap out of it, headed toward the hospital.

I walked up the steps. The massive front door was propped open, but even though people continued to brush past me, I couldn't seem to propel myself past the vestibule. Goose bumps rose on my arms and all I could do was stare into the huge entryway.

The place was more opulent, more overwhelming, more . . . everything than I'd expected. The marble floors had been honed and buffed to a rich glow. Wainscoted walls gleamed, leaded glass windows sparkled, and in every corner fat ferns burst from atop ironwork pedestals.

A red-carpeted double staircase split and soared around a brass chandelier that cast constellations of light across the coffered ceiling. My gaze rose to the upper balcony that ran along the second floor. Nestled between two stained glass windows was an oil portrait of my grandmother. She stood with a hand on a simple wooden chair, light-blue caftan falling in folds to the floor. It was exactly the way I remembered her. Delicate bones, translucent skin, pure white hair smoothed back into a bun, just like Mom's. And the red lipstick. Always the red lipstick.

I could practically hear her voice. *I'm not the one who can give you your miracle* . . . and I looked away. But still I felt those eyes on me. That enigmatic smile an invitation, almost as if she were physically drawing me toward her across the threshold. And so I looked back.

We did that for a moment, her regarding me and me regarding her back, and in a lightning flash, I understood the message she was sending. She was inviting me in. Daring me to venture into her territory. She was taunting me to learn all the secrets she'd kept from me and Danny and Mom. But I wasn't interested. I didn't want to know any more of my grandmother's secrets.

One was enough.

Chapter Three

My grandmother, Dove Jarrod, the prominent evangelist and faith healer, died at a ripe old age—eighty-nine, ninety-five, or ninety-eight, depending on who was telling the story and when they were telling it.

At the time, she held a place of honor in certain religious circles. She was regarded by her faithful followers as a miracle worker who could heal any ailment that afflicted a body. Many said that under her touch, asthma and diabetes submitted to the perfect will of God and disappeared. That in the presence of the glory of the Almighty, stunted limbs grew and tumors shrunk. She was a faithful saint, a revered elder, and everyone agreed that living to Dove's age was a reward for being an obedient servant of the Lord.

But even back then, when I was just a kid of sixteen, I knew better.

My grandmother wasn't a saint. She wasn't even one of the good guys. She was a con artist and a liar, and she told me herself, straight out, two years before her death. She might've been known as a worker of miracles, but she was a fraud. The humbug behind the curtain, the Professor Marvel working the levers, putting on a show for the gullible crowd. And being a coward as well, she chose to reveal this information only to me.

She and I were never close, but she wasn't close with her own daughter, my mother, either. She'd gotten pregnant later in life, as had my mom, both in their early forties. And sometimes I wondered if, in my grandmother's case, she'd meant to at all. At any rate, she lived in Alabama my entire childhood and every year dutifully sent my brother and me extravagant gifts for birthdays and Christmases. A couple of times, we all three flew to Alabama for visits, but the stays were always brief and rather formal. Even as a kid, it struck me as odd that she'd chosen to live so far away from her family.

"She was born down there," my mother told me. "In a psychiatric hospital of all places. She has very close ties to many of the people there."

Apparently, many years ago, my grandmother had gotten mixed up in some trouble with the women in a family down there and felt responsible to stick close and try to help them. I wondered how she could feel more duty toward people she wasn't related to than us. When I was fourteen—old enough to access my mother's travel account and book myself on a flight—I went to Alabama and found out. It wasn't that Dove loved those people more than us. It was that she could be her true self with them. And she had to lie to us.

Here's what I figured out. Pretending you're someone you're not for a couple of days is doable. But lying all day every day to the people you love is unbearable, and Dove couldn't do it. Additionally, she knew that for her daughter, my mother, faith was everything. It smoothed the rough edges of her depression and anxiety, got her out of bed each morning. I think my grandmother understood that if she had been around more—if she'd made the effort to be closer to us all and somehow the truth came out—my mother's faith would've shattered.

So Dove stayed in Alabama. She kept up a regular and cheery, if somewhat superficial, correspondence with us, and Mom stayed safe in her make-believe world and all was well. Until it wasn't.

When I was sixteen, Dove decided rather abruptly to move back to Pasadena, into the stately gray-shingled home she and her late husband had bought back in the forties and that the foundation had maintained for her during all her travels. Almost as soon as she was situated, she called and asked me to lunch. I knew what she was up to. She'd chosen me as the keeper of her secret—and now that she was back, she wanted to make sure I wasn't going to betray her.

I told her I had to study. It was an excuse, but it was for the best. If my grandmother had looked me in the eye, she would've seen the truth—that I was ashamed to be related to her. That I believed she had ruined my life. That I would keep her secret, but I hated her.

A few weeks later, on a chilly October night, she passed. *Went to be with the Lord*—was how I put it to Mom's colleagues at the Charles and Dove Jarrod Foundation when I phoned the next day. Mom had started to make the calls, but when I found her, she was sitting on the side of her bed, holding the receiver, trembling and staring into space. I hung up the phone, gently tucked her under the covers, and finished the job myself.

I relayed the news: Dove went peacefully in her sleep, in the privacy of her home. At eight o'clock the next morning, she was discovered by her housekeeper, who called 911. A deputy ME from Los Angeles County arrived, and after a cursory examination of the body, notified the funeral director, releasing it to the care of Arroyo Valley Mortuary.

Two days later, Dove was laid to rest at Forest Lawn in Glendale alongside my grandfather, who'd died back in the late seventies. The graveside service was private but dignified, befitting a minor celebrity of her stature. Just family and a few foundation employees in attendance. Danny was in one of his bad cycles of drinking back then and hadn't answered any of my phone calls, so it was just Mom and me.

That morning, I gave Mom a pill, then dressed her in one of her trim black pantsuits. I helped her apply mascara and her favorite coral lipstick and then put up her hair. I drove us to the cemetery and handled the greeting of the mourners as they arrived. She didn't utter a word the whole time.

In fact, my mother stood dry-eyed throughout the pastor's message. It was only when he said the benediction that she finally turned to the small group gathered around the open grave and spoke.

"The girl has not died but is asleep."

Everyone froze. Chills raced up my spine. Her voice sounded so strange. Like it was coming from someone I'd never known.

"Matthew 9:24," she said, then lifted one finger and sliced it back and forth across the crowd. "You all know the scripture. She isn't dead. So stop crying. Stop crying!"

I turned cold, the reality of what was happening dawning over me.

"She can see us all." Mom's voice was now a full octave higher. "Every one of us, right now, right here. And she is watching what we do. The foundation is all we have left of my mother. Of Dove. It is our duty to keep up the work. Until the trumpet blows. Until the glorious day of resurrection."

I glanced at the others, desperate for help, but they were hanging on to my mother's every word.

"We keep up the work," she went on. "We keep up the work or I will . . . I will die too . . ." At this she let out a long, shrill, keening sob and collapsed on the ground.

The pastor raced to help her up and together we bundled her into my car. "It's up to you now, Eve." He patted me gently on the shoulder. "You're the keeper of the flame."

I know there were other things said to me that day, but his were the words that burned into my brain. Because he was right. My mother was so fragile, helpless. If she was to keep the foundation going, someone would have to keep her going. With Danny out of commission, that person was me.

And I was up to the task, I knew it. I could keep Mom going in a way that Dove, who ran and hid from her family and the foundation, had never been able to. I would stay and take care of the people I loved. Build them up and protect them. Everybody may sing Dove's praises, but I would be the one they could count on.

And I would shield the foundation from her lies. If anyone so much as dared to suggest Dove Jarrod wasn't everything she claimed to be, I'd shut them down. If anyone even considered slandering my grandmother, I'd make sure they regretted the words before they even left their mouth. I'd see that Dove's legacy endured intact. For my mom. For my family. This was all that mattered.

The next day, I started working at the Jarrod Foundation. I was only part-time, but I knew as soon as I graduated from college, I'd take on a full-time role. And I did, sinking my fingers into every aspect of the organization. I saw to it that the foundation did valid, lasting work—after-school programs for at-risk children, aid for sex workers, jobs and education for abused women. I helped people, got us good press, and pursued donors with the tireless zeal of a true believer.

Even though that was the furthest thing from who I was.

What I believed in was being prepared. In a locked drawer of my desk, I kept a prepared official statement that addressed any claims that Dove was not exactly who she said she was—a woman with a gift of healing. I also had a vague plan to fly us all off to Hawaii or St. Lucia to hide from prying eyes when and if the truth actually came out. Over the top, maybe, but I'd seen the havoc a scandal like this could wreak.

Aside from a nominal sum of money, the gray-shingled three-story Pasadena house was my mother's only inheritance. The day after the funeral, Mom, Danny, and I moved out of our condo and into the spacious home. It had 5,500 square feet of furnished rooms, a kidney-shaped pool, and a gnarled hawthorn tree by the back terrace. My new bedroom, originally a guest room, was done completely in ivory. The first night there, I had a muscle spasm in my weak arm and spilled Coke all over the carpet.

I didn't clean it up. Instead, I lay down on the fluffy white bed and stared up at the ceiling. I flexed my fingers out, then curled them into a fist. Open, close. Open, close. As I worked, I chanted a litany.

Intrauterine stroke, upper extremity hemiplegia, permanent nerve damage in my right arm . . . Intrauterine stroke, upper extremity hemiplegia, permanent nerve damage in my right arm . . .

It was my private affirmation of reality. I'd been diagnosed soon after birth. When I was a toddler, my mother had flown us down to Alabama. She told me that Dove prayed for me—for hours. Apparently, I'd cried my eyes out the whole time, but nothing happened. My tiny arm still hung limp.

Mom doubled down and in the ensuing years, dragged me to church visits, tent meetings, and healing conferences, all in her quest to fix my arm. Eventually, when I wasn't healed, she persuaded herself that my arm must be a gift given to me by God. When it ached, she claimed it was a sign from Him. When it twinged, she said a miracle must be just around the corner.

But I grew impatient with divine signs and lackluster wonders. All I wanted was an arm that worked well enough to pass a driver's test. So one bright spring day, without my mother's knowledge, I bought myself a plane ticket, flew down to Alabama, and demanded my grandmother give me the miracle I'd been waiting for. The miracle I deserved.

I didn't get it. Instead, I got a big dose of the truth.

Dove's terrible secret.

That first night Mom and Danny and I spent in Dove's Pasadena house, I lay in the guest bed and lifted my arm straight out in front of me. I studied it closely, taking note of the developing muscles, the smooth skin and light strawberry-blond hairs. It was a nice arm, I thought. An arm any sixteen-year-old girl should be proud of.

I rotated my palm, slowly, deliberately, in each direction. Then I carefully, one by one, curled each finger of the right hand inward with my left. Thumb, index, ring, pinky—until only the middle one was left sticking straight up in the air. I held the finger there, tall and proud. It may take two hands to get the job done, but it could be done.

"Rest in peace, Dove," I said to the ceiling. Then I rolled over and went to sleep.

Chapter Four

Tuscaloosa, Alabama
1930

In the hours since breakfast, Ruth Lurie had come up with a doozy of a plan.

No one would've thought it, the way she was meandering aimlessly across the east lawn of Pritchard Insane Hospital's grounds, weaving around the patients and attendants like she hadn't a care in the world. But she did have a plan, and she considered it to be a good goddamn gravy one, if she did say so herself. If all went well, by this time tomorrow, she'd be gone.

Over her faded blue-and-white checked cotton dress, she wore one of the aprons from the kitchen, which was a mite unusual for her, if anybody'd had a mind to notice. Another oddity: she'd come outside to the hot yard for recreation time, even though she usually stayed in the cool to play gin rummy with Eunice and Ethel, the sweet old twins, epileptics both, who cried whenever one of them happened to beat her. But nobody noticed the apron or the fact that she was outside instead of in, and that gave her courage.

In the sunbaked yard, a handful of patients flitted here and there, like a swarm of listless flies. Dell, a boy her age who'd been born here and was now motherless like her, played marbles alone on the patch of dirt under the boughs of a hawthorn tree. The tree wasn't big, but it was leafy and provided a cool spot. The low branches were still loaded with tiny bright-green thorn apples, which would be good for jam when they ripened.

Beside Dell, the Major sat on his chair, singing snatches of his favorite marching song from the War, the parts his addled brain could remember. He'd been wounded at the battle of Spanish Fort when he was a young boy and had never quite recovered, so his family had put him in Pritchard. He couldn't possibly have been a real major, but that's what all the attendants called him.

"Sittin' by the roadside on a summer's day," the Major sang to no one in particular. *"Talkin' with my comrades to pass the time away. Lyin' in the shade underneath the trees. Goodness how delicious, eating goober peas . . ."*

The silly song provided a pleasant distraction. Took her mind off the incident earlier that morning. Just after breakfast, as Ruth had hurried down the corridor of the women's ward on her way to the laundry, Jimmy Singley, one of the attendants, had snagged a fistful of her skirt and dragged her into one of the empty, unlocked dorms. He'd pushed her against the wall and breathed his stinking tobacco and pickle breath onto her face.

"Thirteen years old tomorrow. Happy birthday to you, little Ruthie."

She'd steeled herself for whatever Singley was about to do. Round about spring of last year, the fella had taken an interest in her. He'd started following her wherever she went—down to the laundry and the vegetable garden, to the day room when she played cards. He never spoke except to fling taunts. And his only touches were slaps, pinches, and the occasional hallway tussle that she'd been able to wriggle loose from.

He liked her; she could tell. And she wasn't no dummy. If she was smart and played a gambler's hand, he might prove useful.

"Listen close," Singley said in the half-light of the deserted dorm. "I've got something real serious to talk to you about. I'm going to put you in the nursery, right after supper."

"The nursery? Why? I ain't done nothing wrong." She studied his slicked-back grease spill of hair, the sleepy eyes and rounded shoulders, but they held no clue.

"For safe keeping. Listen. I'm gonna put you in the nursery, then right at midnight, I'll let you out and take you to the auditorium."

"What's in the auditorium?" she asked, suspicious.

His lips parted in a smug grin, and she felt another blast of his stinking breath. "A birthday present for you. What do you think about that, Little Miss Priss?"

"What is it?" she asked.

"What is it?" he mimicked her, then laughed. "Can't tell you that, little gal, or it wouldn't be no surprise."

She edged toward the door. "I have to go."

He put an arm out, blocking her. "Now wait a minute. Just hang on."

"What?"

"Let me get a hug before you go." He bounced on his toes in anticipation. "Just one little hug. I promise I'll be sweet."

He reached for her, but without even thinking, she slapped his hand away. He caught her wrist and pushed her back. Hard, cracking her spine against the wall. She'd been lucky up until now, always managing to get away from him. But today Singley seemed possessed with a new determination. He pressed against her, determined and quite a bit keyed up, judging from the thing poking into the side of her stomach.

"It's fine work, holding on to your virtue," he said, releasing her. "But I'm telling you . . . one day you're gonna have to mind me."

She mustered up a saucy look and gave it to him, even though she was quaking inside. "Well, all right then. Get on with it."

He ducked his head, suddenly shy.

"I said get to it, pecker! Give me that hug."

"Don't you be giving orders to me. I give the orders." He kicked the doorjamb. "Anyways. What I come to say is my uncle Robert from Enterprise has come to visit for a few days at my mother's house. And what do you know, turns out he's a preacher!"

"What about my present?" There was no doubt that whatever he had up his sleeve wasn't good, but she thought it was better to know sooner rather than later. So she could be prepared.

"Hold your horses, gal. We were having supper the other night at my mother's house and I ask him, 'Do you only do preaching?' And he says, 'That's what preachers do, ain't it?' And I say, 'Preachers do weddings. Do you marry folks?' And he says, 'Why sure, now and then.' And then he says, 'You figuring on getting married, Jimmy? You got yourself a girl?'"

Singley laughed a nervous laugh, and Ruth got cold all over.

He puffed his chest. "So I say, 'Sure I do, I got a girl prettier than you ever seen. She's got hair like red silk and eyes like the sky. I say, you ain't never seen nothing like my girl, not in all the places you've traveled.'"

She might've been cold, but Singley felt like an oven. He felt like a radiating sun, shooting out molten tongues of burning hot fire.

"And then he says, 'Well, Jimmy, she's gotta be a grown woman. She's gotta be of age or I can't marry you.'" Singley could barely contain himself. His lips split into a wide, gap-toothed grin. "And you are! You're of age—thirteen years old, as God's my witness. So your birthday present, Miss Ruth Lurie? Well, it's the Reverend Robert T. Singley, right here at Pritchard, declaring us man and wife."

For the first time since she'd been a bitty little girl, Ruth felt pure terror. It wiped her mind clean and locked up her limbs. And for a moment, she believed she was going to piss the floor right where she stood. But she hadn't, and eventually, Singley let her go.

Now, out in the hot yard beside the bloom-wreathed hawthorn tree, the Major was still mumbling his song. Ruth gave the old man's shoulder a reassuring pat and squatted down beside Dell. The boy knuckled down with his big blue shooter, squeezed one eye shut, and surveyed the marbles in the circle of dirt.

"Put 'em up, dead duck," he said.

The shooter clacked, making two marbles spin out past the line.

"Couldn't find nobody to play?" Ruth asked.

He grinned over at her with his one open eye. It was the exact color of the shooter, a soft cornflower blue. Just like hers. When she was younger, she used to pretend she and Dell were brother and sister. She'd let him crawl up in bed with her and scratch his back. To get him to sleep, she'd describe the house where they would live together one day. *A room for you and next door'll be mine.* But that had stopped, in time, as the attendants didn't let the boys and girls mix past a certain age. She missed him, especially on cold nights. His little body had been hot as a furnace next to hers.

Now he waggled his eyebrows at the hollow knot in the tree behind him, just a few feet up from the roots. It was where he hid the marbles he won off other patients. It was also a place where they liked to hide little gifts for each other and the Major: A wrapped toffee from Ruth. A broken celluloid comb from Dell. A double acorn from the Major.

"Couldn't find nobody else who wanted to lose their aggies." He looked up at her. "You want a go?"

"Aw. I don't reckon I feel like making a little boy cry today."

He stuck his tongue out at her. "Skeered," he muttered and went back to his game.

The Major kicked a foot over his knee. "Better watch yourself, girl. He'll be taller than you next week."

"And I'll thrash you," Dell added.

"It's a date." She ruffled the boy's hair and went off to find another attendant, Mackey, who was watching a group of men play horseshoes.

"Can I pick blackberries?" she asked him.

He glanced at her, disinterested.

She held up her apron. "I won't go far. Just around the edges of the wood. I'll take 'em straight to the kitchen."

He grunted an assent, and she ran around the far edge of the building, toward the kitchen door. She slipped in, past the bustling cooks and patients in charge of chopping onions and washing dishes, and let herself into the laundry. The room was clouded with steam and rang with the chatter of patients and the clanking of the metal wringers. She sidled to the big glass-paned door that led out to the corridor and untied her apron. With her teeth, she tore one string and stuffed it into the hinges of the door. Then she turned back, leaving the way she'd come.

Half an hour later, back in the yard, she found Betty hunched over the Major. Betty liked to smear her poop on the windows, and now she'd removed the old man's cap and was in the process of poking her crusty fingers into the crater on the top of his head where a Union ball had smashed into his skull. Ruth marched up and pushed her away. Betty howled, but Ruth didn't pay her any mind. She carefully smoothed what remained of the Major's white hair over his ruined scalp and replaced his cap.

She kissed his cheek. "Goodbye," she whispered.

Chapter Five

Tuscaloosa, Alabama
Present

"There are things known and unknown, and in between are the doors."

I turned to see a woman in her late thirties standing behind me. She wore a strapless blush sundress and there were freckles across the pale skin of her chest and arms. A dark braid hung over one shoulder, secured at the end with a brass and ivory barrette in the shape of a bird.

She looked flustered for a moment, then she laughed. "Sorry. Sometimes I just blurt out whatever comes to mind. It's Jim Morrison, I think. Or it sounds like the kind of dippy shit—oops—" She grimaced. "—*stuff*, he would say."

Her accent made me think of every Flannery O'Connor and Eudora Welty short story I'd ever read in school. Pure Deep South. I smiled at her.

She offered her hand. "Althea Cheramie. I knew your grandmother. Sorry for the cursing."

The name caught me, but only for a half second, and I recovered. This was one of the women from the family Dove had stayed in Alabama for.

"It's fine." I shook her hand. "Eve Candler."

"I know." She pulled me into a hug. I smelled cold water, like the smell of a creek, sweet flowers, and rich, dark earth. I felt dizzy for a moment, caught off guard by the embrace and the overwhelming sensation of being transported somewhere else. Somewhere old.

"I've looked forward to meeting you for so long," she went on. "I only knew Dove for a short time, but she was very special to me. I named my daughter, Ruthie, after her."

I nodded, trying not to let my feelings show. It wasn't this woman's fault, but what my grandmother had done for Althea Cheramie was more than she'd ever done for me. But that was Dove, through and through. Ready to go to the ends of the earth for a stranger.

"I have a box of Dove's things for you in the car," Althea continued. "There were some odds and ends, things she left in her house in Tuscaloosa when she moved back to California. The new owner just recently found them in the attic. I haven't gone through it, but I think there's some interesting stuff. Pictures and newspaper clippings."

"Great," I said. "The foundation has catalogued and archived most of her belongings. But they're always happy to have more."

"I could've mailed it to you—I've had it for months now, but I don't know . . ." She paused. "I guess I sort of hoped I could give it to you in person."

Someone jostled me, and I stepped aside to let them pass.

"Go. Do your thing. We can catch up later." Althea waved at a broad-shouldered man in a tan suit who was herding two small children, a girl and a boy, up the walk.

I let myself be herded into the grand reception room and absorbed by the well-dressed crowd, then found a quiet corner to review my mental notes. The people here were the movers and shakers of Alabama. Politicians, business owners, and even a smattering of coal, timber, and iron ore heirs and heiresses. There was more money and political influence squirreled away in this state than anyone suspected. My job was to get it out of their pockets and into the foundation's coffers.

Just as a server in crisp black put a flute of champagne in my hand, Mom appeared at my side with an older couple in tow. "Eve, I'd like you to meet the Lusters," Mom said. "Darrell and Margaret. I was just asking them if they'd allow you and Griff to interview them for the documentary. Maybe after the dedication?"

"That would be perfect." I shook hands with the silver-haired couple. "So nice to meet you."

These were the big fish—Margaret and Darrell Luster. Darrell had started a successful commercial construction company back in the sixties. Margaret was the sole heiress of a fried chicken franchise out of Birmingham, now all over the country. The couple had all but signed on the dotted line agreeing to give the Jarrod Foundation over seven million dollars spread out over the next five years. Hooking them had been a huge relief, for me especially, but now my stomach dropped just at the sight of Mom commandeering them. Sweat slicked her temples and her hands danced at the woman's shoulders.

I switched the flute I was holding over to my right hand and concentrated on a steady grip. My mind immediately calmed in response to the small action of therapeutic habit, and I felt the rest of me relax too. "We're so grateful for your interest in the foundation, Mr. and Mrs. Luster. And for your incredible generosity. And yes, I'd love to get something on tape, if you're open to being on-camera talent." I turned to Mom. "You should head to the dais. They're probably looking for you."

I gave her a gentle push and she disappeared into the crowd. When I turned back to the Lusters, Margaret was staring intently at me. A birdlike woman wrapped in a sculptural pantsuit with a pair of enormous earrings that looked like welded hardware dangling from her lobes, she took my free hand in hers as if we were the only two people in the room. Her watery eyes laser-focused on mine.

"I've listened to every one of Charles Jarrod's sermons," she said in an even more syrupy accent than Althea's. "Even a couple of bootleg tapes from the 1930s."

I tried not to let my discomfort show on my face. She was one of the Dove and Charles super-groupies, as Danny and I used to call them (before Mom heard us and put a stop to it). Harmless, mostly, if you didn't count the handful who'd broken into our house in the years since Dove's death. They'd only ever done it when we were gone. And only taken cheap mementos—photos of Dove, a pair of her earrings, a scrapbook of her old pamphlets. These items were talismans of their hero. And in their world, one that operated not on logic and reason but on incomprehensible divine magic, a piece of Dove meant a piece of God.

But these folks were also our bread and butter, so I knew what to do. Suck it up and fawn.

I smiled. "Looks like we have a true-blue fan here."

Margaret Luster shook her head, impatient. "What I'd really like to get my hands on are the *other* tapes. Dove's earlier tapes."

"I'm not sure I know what you're talking about." I glanced over her shoulder. Her husband had vanished, and suddenly I fiercely wished for his return. The hand holding the champagne flute had started to tremble just the slightest bit.

"Good afternoon, staff, friends, and honored guests."

On the makeshift stage behind me, a young woman in an elegant white pantsuit stood at a podium. She wore black-framed glasses, nearly obscured by a curtain of neat twists, and gave the microphone a few taps.

"Are we on? Welcome to the official dedication ceremony for Pritchard Hospital's new Dove Jarrod Building."

A polite smattering of applause rippled through the crowd.

"And thank you to Bryant's Catering for the refreshments."

Margaret was still focused on me, her nostrils flaring determinedly. "The missing ones from the early days. When Dove was ministering with that other young girl. They called themselves the Hawthorn Sisters. They preached right here in Alabama."

The moniker—*Hawthorn Sisters*—sent a strange electric thrill through me. I was used to hearing the groupies tell me about their encounters with Charles and Dove, but I'd never heard anything about any duo called the Hawthorn Sisters. Margaret must be mistaken. Or thinking of someone else. Dove had always been very clear about how, after escaping Pritchard, she'd come straight to California where she'd met my grandfather.

Up at the podium, the woman in the white pantsuit was still talking. "My name is Beth Barnes. I'm director of operations for our newest program, the Bridge. It's a groundbreaking modality we designed to address women's issues in a safe and therapeutic environment. Thanks to Dove Jarrod's personal contribution, we'll have the honor of operating out of this spectacular, historic facility."

More applause and now the clinking of glasses.

Margaret Luster gave my free hand a squeeze. Her eyes glowed with a strange light. "The other girl was from a prominent family up in Florence. Lumber, I think. Anyway, the story is that back in the mid-1930s the Hawthorn Sisters held revivals and performed all sorts of *miracles*."

She whispered this last word, and I gritted my teeth. Hyperbole was part of the deal with these people, and she'd obviously mistaken Dove for some other female itinerant Southern preacher.

"There's so much power in the old ways, you know?" she said. "Those folks preached with such fervor and conviction. Such unwavering faith. Not like the watered-down, feel-good stuff you see on TV now. No, no, no. I tell you, these people had the real fire."

I spotted a server across the reception room holding a full tray of drinks, downed the remainder of my champagne and snagged another.

"In fact, I'll kick myself if I pass up the opportunity while I have you . . ." She pulled me even closer, so close I could see the web of fuchsia lipstick that had bled into the creases above her thin upper lip. "Will you pray for me . . . right now? I have a condition. Myocardial ischemia. It's a blockage in the arteries and can cause all sorts of problems. Heart attack, blood clots, strokes—"

"I'm so sorry to hear that," I stammered. "But I'm not—"

"Just real quick like." Her hands were tiny, warm claws on mine. "We could go to the ladies' room." Tears filmed her bright eyes. "I just feel like the Lord brought you to me, here in the place where Dove's life began. I think He brought you here to bless me in a way I've never been blessed before."

I started to feel lightheaded, the churn of resentment and empathy making me feel sick to my stomach. This woman was facing a potentially deadly diagnosis; she was scared and desperate, and because of who she believed my grandmother to be, she was asking me for help. But what could I do? Nothing. And now my right hand was shaking violently, the full flute of champagne sloshing.

I pulled loose and stepped back, bumping directly into Danny. "I'm sorry. I just can't . . ." I clutched frantically at his arm. "Margaret, would you excuse me? I need to sort out a few logistical issues with the film with my brother."

She extended her hand to Danny. "Margaret Luster. So pleased to meet another grandchild of the great Dove Jarrod."

"Likewise." Danny took my arm.

"We'll catch up later," I assured her as Danny hustled me away. We ended up at the foot of the red-carpeted staircase and, relieved, I put the flute on a small table.

"Who was that?" he asked, eyes wide.

"Our newest donor."

"Are you okay?"

I was sweating, I realized. Trembling all over now. "I'm fine."

He narrowed his eyes at me, but I waved him off and he nodded up at Dove's portrait. "I keep expecting her to step out of that painting and tell us what she saw here, back in the day." He sighed. "I'm going to go look for coffee. Find me after the fun's over."

He left and I climbed a couple of steps toward the second-floor landing. Beth Barnes was now well into her speech.

"Dove Jarrod and her husband, Charles, were perhaps the most well-known traveling evangelists in the thirties and forties, and she continued the work of their ministry even into the eighties. They led revivals in every state in the US and traveled to dozens of foreign countries as well."

Someone in the crowd murmured a soft "amen."

"They met with presidents and kings, dignitaries and even a dictator or two. But they ministered to the common folks as well and were honored with all kinds of awards from religious and charitable organizations."

I climbed a few more steps. Thick carpeting sank under my feet and I ran my fingers along the glossy railing. I looked out over the crowd, then up toward the windows that lined the gallery.

"—but before Dove Jarrod was Dove Jarrod, she was Ruth Davidson, and before that, Ruth Lurie. She had many trials, but she never forgot where she came from. She never forgot the injustices she witnessed here at Pritchard. The abuse and death of her mother. The torture of so many innocent people . . ."

I felt a chill work its cold fingers up my spine. I could see it now. The reason Dove had willed the bulk of her estate to restore this part of Pritchard. It was because the place had been a nightmare—for her and so many others. And Dove knew, maybe better than anybody, that only money, not some miracle from above, could turn it into a force for good.

Poking around online archives while prepping for the documentary, I had come across some pictures of Pritchard in the twenties and early thirties. The photos, even in black and white, had made my stomach roll. Filthy, peeling walls, cornices laced with rot and mold. And then there were the patients. Ragged, dirty. Gaunt and grim. I expect, at one point or another, they had all begged God to save them from the horror. But He hadn't, had He? And Dove had saved herself.

I'm not the one who can give you your miracle. All I can do is tell you the truth . . .

Beth continued. "The Pritchard legacy encompasses so much, good and bad, fine and ugly. Noble and debased. It is a shame to our state, a blot in our history books. And yet, at the same time, in a strange way, it is a triumph . . ."

I turned my gaze from Dove's portrait to the wide hallway and closed my eyes. I could almost see her. A girl, twelve years old, thin from the lack of food, pale, probably, with short burnished red hair. Standing barefoot on that second-floor landing. Smiling.

Smiling. Like she had a secret. A plan . . .

". . . a beacon for all those who struggle with mental health issues and for those who advocate for them," Beth was saying. "As they embark on a journey toward wellness . . ."

I turned to the screen beside the dais where they'd started rolling Griff's footage—a three-minute sizzle reel he'd roughed together back in LA. Stills of Charles and Dove over piano music, a sepia reenactment of an old-fashioned tent meeting. Slo-mo shots of the Jarrods' house, their home church, a few recipients who'd benefitted from the foundation's gifts.

My phone buzzed.

I'm outside getting some exteriors. Can you pop out for a sec?

The reel was still going, everyone watching in rapt silence. No one would notice if I slipped out for a few minutes. I headed down the stairs and threaded my way through the crowd.

Outside, the sky had gone a soft dark blue, the heat finally starting to settle. Cicadas buzzed in a deafening chorus in the dark beyond, but closer to the edges of the gravel parking lot, fireflies circled. And the dove. He was still going at it too, which seemed strange. I thought they only sang during the day.

I stopped at the end of the stone walk. To my right, in the middle of the expansive lawn, the thorny, blooming tree glowed in the moonlight. I scanned the opposite side of the lawn but saw nothing. The parking lot was deserted too, from the looks of it, and beyond that, a field and a line of shadowy woods in the distance.

I walked to the lot thinking I'd take a look in the rusted old iron fountain. Maybe there were still coins in there, thrown by long-ago patients or visitors. Wishing for things beyond their control. Wishing for freedom.

And then a thought occurred to me. Griff had lost his phone and planned to get a burner in the morning. He couldn't have texted me.

Suddenly, I felt a sharp pain on my scalp, and someone yanked me backward by my hair. I gasped and clawed the air, trying to keep myself upright. The person tightened their grip, tilting my head back. I cried out, just as a hand closed over my mouth.

"Hello, Eve," a low voice hissed in my ear. "Welcome to Alabama."

Chapter Six

Tuscaloosa, Alabama
1930

Ruth woke to the sound of a bolt sliding back from the heavy door. She sat up, promptly banging her head against the wooden slats of the crib. She winced and rubbed the spot.

Watery moonlight spilled between the bars of the lone window set high in the wall. The nursery. That's where she was. After supper, Singley had made a fuss about how she didn't clean her table properly, dragged her down here and locked her in one of the wooden cribs. Now she realized the bolt she'd heard belonged to another door, one far down the long hall. She might have to wait an hour before Jimmy came.

The nursery smelled of old baby piss and doo. She'd lived there until she was about three years old. After that they let her stay in a dorm, chained by her leg to her mother's narrow cot. Then her mother hanged herself. That was when she was six or seven; she couldn't quite remember. Memories were strange here at Pritchard. They tended to fade, leaving a gray blank in their place.

The nighttime sounds of the ward floated around her from down the hall. Shouts. Sobs. The muffled *thump-thump-thump* of human bodies hitting walls and floorboards and straw pallets. The last was a sound that had become like a part of her, the music of the inmates as they lulled themselves to sleep by beating their heads.

At long last, Singley slid back the bolt on her door and unlocked the crib. He led her down the hall, and she told herself to keep calm. She didn't know when her chance would come, but when it did, she'd know. If she jumped the gun, she'd end up Mrs. Jimmy Singley, and she'd be good gravy goddamned if she was going to let that happen.

Jimmy looked down at her, his face as red as a tomato. "Let's step lively. Don't want to keep the preacher waiting."

When they pushed open the double doors of the auditorium, she saw a tall, broad-shouldered man standing in the center of the stage. He wore a black felt hat with a rolled brim. It was tilted jauntily to one side. His black suit jacket, vest, and pants had a sheen to them, like they were very old. When Singley deposited her at the man's feet, he swept off his hat and eyed her. His hair was black as coal and gray around the edges, his skin thick and pocked with scars.

His face wasn't badly shaped, and he may have been handsome at one time, dashing even, but his eyes flashed with something dangerous. He smelled like oranges and clove and it nauseated her. The sight of her seemed to take him by surprise.

Singley ducked his head. "Evening, Uncle Robert. This here's Ruthie."

"Evening, miss."

He replaced his hat, but his dangerous eyes never strayed from Ruth. He cracked a large set of knuckles, held out his massive hand, and Singley slapped a wad of bills into it. Ruth's eyes widened. How much money had Singley paid for the man to say a few quick words? That must be some racket.

"James," the man said in a sonorous preacher's voice. "Do you take this woman to be your lawfully wedded wife?" He was still gazing at Ruth.

Ruth stayed stiff as a board. She had a bad feeling about this black-vested, behatted beast, with his glittering eyes, rough face, and hands the size of frying pans.

Singley looked slightly confused. "Yessir, I do. But ain't you gonna say a few words before—"

"And Ruth, do you take this man to be your husband?" The preacher's lip curled into a barely discernible smirk, but he didn't say what he might have found amusing.

Singley's mouth unhinged in shock, and he looked from his uncle to Ruth, then back again. "Hey, now. You can't—"

"It's my turn to talk," Ruth said to Singley, then locked her gaze on the reverend's eyes. "I can't marry this man, sir. Not without telling the truth first. So he knows what he's getting."

The reverend Robert T. Singley reared back the slightest bit, like a horse that had encountered a rabbit. "You don't say?"

"You see, sir, I've been used poorly. By another man."

Singley gasped, a wet, desperate sound. "Ruth! You didn't tell me."

"You never asked," Ruth snapped.

"My goodness." The reverend's eyes burned into her. "What a little spitfire *you* are."

"And a slut, no two ways about it," Ruth said matter-of-factly. "So I figure we better postpone this ceremony until another day. Until we can settle things with the other party. I expect he'll have something to say about who's marrying who."

The younger Singley sputtered and flapped and rubbed his double chin. "She's *my* girl. *Mine.*"

"And that other fella's," Ruth said.

The reverend's lip curled into a smile. He seemed to be enjoying his nephew's anguish. He eyed Ruth, as if a new idea had occurred to him.

"Well, what do you want to do?" the reverend asked in his deep, growling voice.

Singley looked from him to Ruth in confusion. "I can't marry her now."

"Sure, you can, you idiot."

"I can't! She ain't no virgin!"

The reverend laughed, then looked at Ruth, his face gone grave. "Oh, you can, nephew, and you must. She's been soiled and it's up to you to salvage her. It's a man's duty to protect the woman, you know that." He extended a finger and lifted a strand of her hair off her cheek. He then ran it along the slope of her jaw.

That's when Ruth knew it was time.

She turned and ran—up the aisle of the auditorium, through the double doors, and all the way to the stairwell. Three flights down to the laundry, she pushed open the glass-paned door she had rigged earlier that day. She scurried across the room and slipped behind the big sinks, letting herself into the underground passageway that the attendants and nurses used to deliver the dirty linens to the back building. It ran all the way past the fields at the back end of the property.

She ran as fast as she could, barefoot over the packed dirt, her blue-and-white dress rippling as she went. Halfway down, she came to a small crevice between two rocks. She squeezed into it and shimmied her way up a couple of feet, coming to a rotted board. She punched at it until the outside latch sprung open and she could push the trapdoor up. It was just wide enough for her to wriggle through.

She'd done this before, on a few rare starry nights in the summer when she needed to see the sky. Those times, she'd never realized she could've run. Or that she even wanted to.

But oh, how she wanted to run now.

She was only a couple of yards from the blackberry bushes, still heavy with unpicked fruit. She stood for a half second, sniffing the air for the scent of the Warrior River. The bluffs were due south of her. The trusty Alabama sky enveloped her like a blanket. She started running again, the Major's marching song keeping time in her head.

Just before the battle, the general heard a row.
He said, "The Yanks are coming, I hear their rifles now."
He turned around in wonder and what do you think he sees?
The Georgia militia eating goober peas . . .

Chapter Seven

Tuscaloosa, Alabama
Present

Every inch of my skin tingled with adrenaline. I could hear my breath in my ears, shallow and staccato, a counterpoint to the melodic whir of crickets in the trees. I felt sure if I tried to run, my legs wouldn't cooperate. The only parts of me that seemed to be working were my racing heart, lungs, and fast-constricting throat.

And my nose. I smelled cloying aftershave, not like anything I'd smelled on Griff. It was the kind old men wore.

The man chuckled, a wheezy, phlegmy expectoration that sounded more like a cough. "Get up."

He shoved me toward the parking lot, away from the hospital's floodlights and deeper into the shadows. I stumbled toward the line of parked cars, guided by the fist twisted in my hair. He stopped me between my rental and the silver BMW. The BMW's back window was smashed, the glass webbed but still holding together. On the seat was an upended cardboard box. Dove's things.

I must've shivered, because he assured me, "Don't be scared, darlin'. I ain't gonna hurt you. Not as long as you give me what I want."

I still couldn't see him, so I tried to focus on his voice. Had I heard it before? He didn't sound like the people I'd just been mingling with inside, no slow drawl that dripped like honey. This guy's accent was nasally, with a distinct Southern twang. He was from the country maybe. The mountains.

We were past the cars now and in the field. Headed away from the collection of buildings that made up New Pritchard and toward the woods. He prodded me along, and when we finally got far enough away from the hospital, he removed his hand from my mouth. The other remained twisted painfully in my hair.

"Scream and I'll kill you," he said.

"I don't understand," I whimpered, hating how scared I sounded. Hating that he could hear it too.

He spoke in a patient tone. "Dove Jarrod got to be pretty famous out there in California, but down here in Alabama, we weren't fooled. We always known who that bitch was, and Lord, let me tell you, have I ever been waiting a hell of a long time to set things right."

I tried to keep my voice level. "Just tell me what you want."

He laughed again and I smelled tobacco. The minty kind people tucked in their bottom lips. "Two things, darlin.' Just two things. The big Rs. Revenge and recompense."

He stopped and leaned in close, his face pressed against mine. "I want to know where the Flowing Hair Dollar is. The one your grandmama stole from Coe after she murdered him."

Even though his grip was tight, I momentarily forgot about it and shook my head in confusion. "I don't know what you're talking about. My grandmother ran away from this place when she was a kid. She went to California where she met my grandfather and started traveling with him. She couldn't have killed anyone down here or stolen anything."

He shoved me forward again. "Well, sure. Who's gonna tell their own kin that they're a murderer and a thief? But it's true. The old-timers down here—the people who know the secret stories—they been talking about what your grandmama did since 1934."

We were heading toward the far line of trees. Far enough away now that nobody would hear me even if I did scream. As we walked, I tried to formulate a plan, but my brain wouldn't obey. All I could think of was what Danny would do if something happened to me. What Mom would do.

"She didn't go straight to California," the man continued in his wheezy hillbilly accent. "She stayed here in Alabama, for several years in fact. Made quite a name for herself here . . . in addition to killing a man and robbing him blind."

I stumbled a bit but didn't fall, because he yanked me up by my hair. I cried out and he pushed me onward in the darkness.

"She killed him, she robbed him, and after, she hid his body so everyone thought he wandered off. Then the bitch ran off with Charles Jarrod."

My mind raced. None of what this man was saying fit the facts, at least the ones I knew. But I couldn't think of one thing to say in Dove's defense. It was like I'd gone blank inside.

He pushed me up a knoll, toward a filigreed iron arch. We passed under it, and I saw we were in a cemetery. A very old one. Moonlight spilled through the trees, bathing the ground and the rows and rows of iron crosses in watery silver. Then I saw what looked like a plastic milk crate sitting in the center of the graveyard. Terror rippled through me. I did not want to see what was in that crate.

He still held me by the hair, and pulling my head back, leaned close. His voice was a purr. "Down here, lots of folks fell for her pretty lies. *God's gonna heal you, just put your dollar in the bucket. Repent and follow the will of the Lord and you'll be saved.*" He clucked his tongue. "I say she could've prevented a whole heap of suffering if she'd taken a lick of her own advice."

The man cleared his throat like he'd had his fill of reminiscing.

"But Dove's dead and gone. And even though none of us can change the past, I believe you, darlin', can improve my future. Now, if you find yourself in possession of such a valuable item like the coin she took, you basically got two choices. You can either sell it back to the person you stole it from. Or . . ." His minty breath was hot in my ear. ". . . you hide it."

The man pushed me down to my knees. I landed with a thump, and he grabbed a fresh fistful of my hair and forced my head down toward the milk crate. Holding my breath, I forced myself to open my eyes and look. I was surprised by what I saw. A pile of bones with a dirty-looking skull sitting on top. I was oily with sweat and I needed to breathe. When I did, I could smell the bones—the stench of dank earth, decaying organic matter, and, oddly, motor oil. I felt myself sway to one side; the edges of my vision softened and blurred. I was going to pass out.

But the man held me fast. "Allow me to introduce you to Old Steadfast Coe, may he rest in peace. Dove Jarrod murdered him back in 1934, right in his very own bed, and then she hid the body so nobody could pin it on her."

I gulped, trying to force down a retch. "These could be anybody's bones," I said faintly.

"They could be, but they ain't. And I got a signed confession too. From Dove herself, admitting to the murder."

I felt a scream rise up in me. And the overpowering desire to pummel this man with every bit of strength I had. My grandmother may have been a hustler, a showman, and a con, but this man wasn't talking shell games. He was calling my grandmother a murderer.

Above me, he chuckled, a low, evil sound. "Sorry to break the news to you, darlin'. Sorry to knock that angel off her pedestal. But Dove killed this man right here, Steadfast Coe. And now you got three days to give me the coin she stole or the whole world is going to hear the truth about it. I'll call you at this time in three days."

It was Friday. He was giving me the weekend to find something that had been lost for decades.

"Monday at seven-thirty. I'll call and tell you where to bring it. You understand? If you don't hand over the coin at that time, I'm gonna take Old Steadfast here to the police and tell the whole wide world that Dove Jarrod was a murderer."

I started shaking uncontrollably, sweat pouring in rivulets down my back and legs. My vision went spotty, and I tried to catch my breath, but I couldn't. I'd lost control of the situation, and now, I was losing control of myself.

Still I tried to sound calm. "It's not true. And people won't care. Nobody cares what some woman did a hundred years ago."

He tightened his grip on my hair, burning my scalp. "But your family does, don't they? And all those rich folks inside that hospital over there. Dove held out on me, and I can respect that. But you've got no reason to do the same."

"Dove? You saw Dove? When?"

"The day she died, the very same day. I guess you didn't know that. Why would you? Yes. I did see Dove—and then I choked the life right out of her."

Everything around me went still and black. My body was trembling but not from fear. I was flooded, from my head to my toes, with clean, hot rage.

I took a deep breath and clawed my fingers into the dirt. "You sonofabitch," I growled. "I'm going t—"

Suddenly my head jerked back then forward, connecting solidly with the ground. There was a root there, and as my mouth filled with grass and dirt, white, hot pain exploded behind my eyes. My body went slack, sliding out of his grip to the ground. I waited for the next blow but heard instead the rattle of the bones and the *chuck-chuck-chuck* of cowboy boots on dirt. He was running away. The sound diminished into silence, and I rolled myself into a ball, trying to focus. There were no stars visible, just a strange yellow glow muddying the blue.

I felt myself drift.

Murder. A dead man's bones. A stolen coin . . .

"Hey!" I heard across the field. A woman's voice. "Come back!"

Then a man's voice too. "I found her! She's over here!"

I rolled onto my back, arms flopping out on the ground beside me, and groaned. Two people ran to my side. A woman—Althea, I realized—kneeled beside me, helping me right myself.

"Eve? Oh my God! What happened to you?"

Gingerly, I touched my forehead, then winced at the lightning bolt of pain. "Somebody grabbed me. A man. He hit me . . ."

And then the other voice. Griff. "I think I saw him, but he was too far away." He paused. "I was looking for you to set up the Luster shots and . . . Jesus. Eve . . . your face . . ."

Althea fumbled for her phone. "I'm calling 911."

I put out a hand in protest. "No. Please. I'm fine. Really."

My head was reeling, fuzzy and sluggish from the pain, but my brain still screamed at me. *No police! No police!* it warned. And I knew enough to listen. The man had called Dove a murderer and a thief. I couldn't risk anyone else hearing those accusations.

I had to keep this whole thing as quiet as possible until I could deal with the asshole who'd attacked me. And I was sure as hell going to fucking deal with him. This was why I'd stayed at the foundation. This is what I'd always known was coming.

"No police." I stood, with some difficulty, and touched my fingers to my forehead. "I just got a knot, I think. I'm fine."

"What the hell's going on, Eve?" Griff asked.

"I'm not sure." I glanced at Althea, her phone already connected to 911. Ignoring her shocked expression, I took it from her and pressed it to my ear. "Hello?" I said in a shaky voice. "So sorry. Misdial. Everybody's safe here. Everybody's safe."

Chapter Eight

Tupelo, Mississippi
1934

Ruth crouched in the dark corner of the cage, sawdust beneath her shoes. She braced herself between two iron bars. The smell of animal urine stung her nostrils and made her eyes water, but she didn't dare close them. She needed to keep an eye on the shifting shadow in the opposite corner.

She was seventeen years old. Only just a bit taller than she was four years before when she'd run from Pritchard, and barely a brick heavier. She'd never had much in the way of food, and doing the work of two grown men didn't allow for much meat to accumulate on her bones. Still, she was too big to slip between the bars. And no matter what size she was, she'd be the loser if she had to battle with what lurked on the other side of the cage.

Down in Meridian, the town she'd first come to after her narrow escape from Jimmy Singley and his preacher uncle, she'd fallen in with a gang. They'd nicknamed her Annie, after that radio show *Little Orphan Annie*. It wasn't so much that she had no parents—none of the kids did—but more because she fought first, swung hard, and, more often than not, ended squabbles. And her hair was redder than Alabama dirt, that was for damn sure.

The children slept in alleys and barns and sometimes fields with haystacks. The leader, Bug, a giant of a twelve-year-old with a kick of sandy hair right in the center of his forehead and a persistent rash on half his face, liked lording it over the others. But he didn't much like to fight, and even though he was big, he was doughy. He told Ruth she could be his lieutenant because she kept the others in line.

"Swipe 'em," he'd say after sauntering past a café and seeing silver candlesticks on a carved oak sideboard through the window. "And the doilies what's underneath while you're at it." Or "Get that Sutton feller to cough up a few coins for the Orphans' Home, why don't you?" The Orphans' Home being another word for Bug's pockets.

One night, when they were all gathered under a rotted-out dock, Bug suggested a couple of kids waylay a traveling menagerie and steal their lion.

"What you gonna do with a live lion, Bug?" Ruth slurred. She and another girl had nicked a fancy brass cane from the train station and discovered it was filled with moonshine. Ruth had been strutting around with the cane all day like the queen of England, ducking into alleys and tipping back like a fancy chip.

Bug's head wobbled on his shoulders and he imitated her voice. "Sell it off to another circus man, what do you think?"

Ruth eyed him coolly. He could mock her all he wanted, but he should be careful. She had a suspicion that she didn't need him half as much as he needed her, and one day she was going to let him know all about it.

"All right," she said. "Well, I guess I better handle this one on my own. We don't want nobody getting killed." A couple of the filthy, bedraggled children gaped at her. Bug nodded his assent.

Of course, Bug was an imbecile, and she hadn't even considered stealing the gol-dang live lion. What she had done, however, was introduce herself to the owner of the circus and offer to feed and pitch hay for the animals for a dollar a week. After appraising Ruth's skinny but scrappy body, the man said he'd just lost his number-one fellow to some floozy in Tupelo and if she weren't afraid of the occasional nip or stomp, he'd be right glad to have someone new.

She left with them that night.

Dr. Asloo's Wild Menagerie was surely a step up or two from Bug's gang. That is, until just a few moments before, when she'd lugged in the cat's water bucket and the door to the iron cage had swung shut, locking her in. It had happened one other time, years before, but she'd just slipped between the bars. Unfortunately, she'd gotten too big, and now she was cornered in this stinking cage, staring down an ill-tempered lion who wasn't double dosed with Dr. Asloo's special pine syrup like he was before the shows.

At least he wasn't pacing anymore. Ruth shot him a baleful look, catching a flash of orange eyes and a hungry snort in return. Well, if this was where she died, so be it. She didn't have any regrets, and the only two people she ever missed were Dell and the Major. Well, she missed Dell; she worried about the Major.

But she'd made her choice. She couldn't go back. And, likely as not, the Major was already dead. He'd been as old as dirt when she ran and that had been four years ago. She did wonder if Singley was still there and what had happened to that horrible preacher uncle of his. She'd never forgotten the man's oily eyes and smile. The way his face lit up in a leering way when she said she'd been done wrong by another man.

Later, oddly enough, she'd found it to be a handy lie, when embellished just the slightest bit. She told one of the other girls that she'd had relations with numerous men, afterward relieving them of what money they carried and a tiny nick of earlobe sliced off with her knife. The girl had backed away in awed deference. It worked with the others too, keeping them at a distance and making her feel safe. The lying didn't bother her, not at all. What she was—or wasn't—didn't matter one whit.

She might still be a virgin, but she was tough as any whore.

The lion roared, jolting her from her thoughts. Braced against the bars, her arms were aching now, thighs trembling from the exertion of holding so still. Trying not to startle the snuffling shadow, she eased herself down to a sitting position, whispering under her breath the only words that came to her fear-addled mind.

"Sittin' by the roadside on a summer's day. Talkin' with my comrades to pass the time away . . ."

A snort and a whine. Scratching in the soiled sawdust.

She felt a trembling set in. A heat settling over her body as the creature neared. She smelled his sour, filthy smell. But the silly song was stuck in her head now, and strangely it made her feel better. She sang again.

"Lyin' in the shade underneath the trees . . ."

The lion made a sort of mewling noise, an almost mechanical sound that came from deep in his throat. He was closer now. So close she knew she was in trouble.

"Goodness how delicious, eating goober peas . . ."

The lion snuffled and nudged her. Instinctively, she put a hand out, feeling thick fur and wet nose.

And something else. A needle of electricity, like lightning, zapping her body, zinging up and down along her spine. It filled her with a floating sort of peace. *Maybe this is what you feel right before you die.* If so, she was grateful.

She blinked, then looked into the lion's orange eyes. "Come on, now," she said to him. "Step back."

Instantly, the great cat wheeled around and pressed his bony hindquarters against the bars. Ruth watched him for a long while, completely still, barely breathing. When he didn't move either—didn't pounce or tear her to shreds—she let herself lie down on the straw and close her eyes.

Chapter Nine

Tuscaloosa, Alabama
Present

The Embassy Suites was huge and seemed to be hosting a dozen conferences. I wished I'd tried a little harder to find a charming Southern B&B outside of town. A place out of a William Faulkner novel maybe, wallpapered with cabbage roses and crammed with rickety, peeling, homey furniture. A place where a person who'd just had their face shoved in a pile of dirty bones could melt down in peace.

Althea and Griff had somehow managed to maneuver me and the box of Dove's belongings that Althea had brought from the Alabama house through the crowded lobby and up to my room. I texted Mom and Danny that I'd suddenly gotten violently sick to my stomach and had had to sneak away from the ceremony. It was a lame excuse, and I wasn't sure if they were going to fall for it, but it was the only thing my addled brain could come up with in the moment.

Althea had texted her husband, Jay, too, and I didn't know what she told him, but apparently, he was cool with taking the kids home and letting her stay with me. I felt a little better now that we were up in my room, door chained and bolted, an ice pack pressed against my tender temple. I sat on the bed, Althea and Griff on the narrow sofa. After I made them swear not to call the police, I told them everything.

Althea looked from me to Griff, flabbergasted. "You're telling me this guy broke into Dove's house and killed her and nobody knew it? I don't see how that's even possible. The authorities said she died of natural causes, right?"

"Yes," I said. "But he had to be lying. He was just trying to scare me, right?"

Griff dug in his pocket and produced an airplane bottle of Jack Daniel's. He cracked it open and handed it to me. I took it with my left, sipped, then closed my eyes, letting the warmth spread. I offered it back to him, but he waved me off. "All yours." He looked royally pissed, but I was too tired and upset to ask why.

"Okay, I'm confused. Why were you outside in the first place?" Althea asked.

I shifted uncomfortably, my muscles screaming in protest. "I got a text from Griff. At least, I thought I did. I forgot he lost his phone."

"Who's this Steadfast guy he supposedly showed you?" Althea asked.

"I have no idea," I said. "I didn't know Dove that well, but I never heard her mention anyone called Steadfast. But that doesn't mean anything. She knew a lot of people."

"And Dove supposedly murdered this guy, hid his body, then stole a coin that belonged to him?" Griff asked. "That's a lot for a young girl to do all on her own."

"And if she did, I can't imagine she'd sign a confession," Althea said.

"Also, if she stole the coin, why wouldn't she sell it?" Griff said.

"I don't understand any of it." I threw up my hands. "He implied she wanted to hang on to it, I guess for the kick of knowing she'd stolen something so valuable. He called it the Flowing Hair. I'm assuming it's well known. I don't know. None of this tracks."

"You better believe it doesn't track!" Griff spat out. "I've just spent the past three months, day and night, meticulously researching Dove

Jarrod. Reading everything I could get my hands on, interviewing every single person who'd ever had any kind of personal interaction with her and her husband. And not one of them said anything about her spending time in Alabama after she left Pritchard. Not one!" He shook his head, exasperated. "My own parents have followed her career religiously for decades. They're from Alabama, for Chrissakes, and even they didn't know. How is that possible?"

I buried my face in my hands. He was right. But I didn't have the words to tell him how, in some bizarre way, this was the real Dove, the Dove I'd known since I was fourteen years old. The woman who kept secrets.

"I guess Dove really wanted to keep her past hidden," Althea said quietly.

"Sorry, Eve. Not trying to make this about me." Griff glanced at Althea. "Mind if I borrow your phone?"

She handed it over and he started tapping on it, so loudly it sounded like he was going to break the screen. Althea winced, then turned to the coffee table where she'd dumped the contents of Dove's box.

"Okay, let's think. We've got a scrapbook with a few yellowed newspaper clippings, a handful of faded photographs, and an old family Bible. Maybe there's some kind of clue in all this stuff that'll tell us who Steadfast was. We should split it up, go through the articles and photographs."

The newspaper articles seemed to be mostly announcements of engagements, weddings, and births. One was a brief write-up, dated June 5, 1934, about a Mrs. Magdalene Kittle, wife of Mr. Eli Kittle of St. Florian, Alabama. Mrs. Kittle had been taken to the Lauderdale County jail on suspicion that she had caused the death of her middle son, Jasper, age seven, by forcing him to spend three days and nights in the woods. Mrs. Kittle had been repentant, and the judge was inclined to leniency in his sentence. Especially as the woman had eight additional children who still needed looking after.

Althea shuddered and refolded the yellowed paper. "My God. Why would Dove hold on to something so morbid?"

I shook my head. "No idea."

Griff lifted a finger for our attention, then read from Althea's phone. "Per Wikipedia, there are only fifteen Flowing Hair Dollars left in circulation. First dollar coin, designed by a Robert Scot, was minted by the United States government in 1794 and 5. One side has a bust of Lady Liberty. The other side, an eagle surrounded by a wreath. Ninety percent silver, ten percent copper. Last one sold for ten million." He looked at us. "Long story short, it's purported to be the most valuable coin in the world."

We stood, absorbing this in stunned silence.

I looked down at a tissue-thin piece of paper that had fallen out of the Bible. "Listen to this. *Dear Mr. Jarrod, I hope this letter finds you in fine mettle and blessed by the Almighty. I am Miss Ruth Davidson, the girl who sang the alto part on 'Throw Me Overboard' (and other selections) along with Miss Bruna Faulk at your tent meeting in Florence, Alabama, on April 21. There was quite an outpouring of the Spirit that night, which all were heartened to see, and I do believe many were saved. I was in the green dress. Miss Faulk and I have continued with great and blessed success as the Hawthorn Sisters—*"

I paused. There it was. The Hawthorn Sisters. Just like Margaret Luster said.

"Go on," Althea said.

> "*—singing and ministering here and there, managed by Mr. Arthur Holt. However, Miss Faulk and I now find that we have run through near about all west Alabama and east Mississippi, and we would very much like to attach ourselves to someone such as you, in order to travel to further states, especially California.*"

I flipped the paper over, but there was nothing on the other side.

"Missing a page or two," Griff said.

"But clearly she wanted out of her situation," I said.

Althea waggled her phone. "I googled Steadfast. He's either an internet company, a brewery, or a real estate leasing firm. No person that I can find."

"We'll have to look up death notices, I guess." I sighed. "Just add it to the list of things Dove lied about. Or omitted." I inhaled and let my breath out slowly. The adrenaline had ebbed, and I was starting to feel the effects of being roughed up as well as, thankfully, the alcohol. I scooted back on the bed and rested against the headboard.

"What do you think made her do that?" Althea said. "Be so secretive about her life?"

I shrugged. "Dove had my mom later in life, when she was forty. That was the late fifties. She and Charles were still traveling, doing meetings, conferences, seminars. Sometimes, Mom went with them, but mostly she stayed home. I think Dove was better at helping strangers. She had a harder time with the long-term, family commitment stuff."

Althea settled back on the tiny sofa and lifted an eyebrow. "She definitely kept her past shrouded from me. I know a lot of people thought she was the half sister of Dell Davidson."

Griff perked up. "Oh, right. The outlaw from Mississippi. I did hear about him. Maybe that's how she got mixed up in this Steadfast guy's death."

"Maybe," I said. "She never directly admitted she was Dell Davidson's sister, but she didn't deny it either." I shrugged. "That was Dove. She didn't feel any compulsion to set the record straight about anything."

"Not even with your mom?" Althea asked.

"No. Mom acted like those stories didn't exist. Dove was her touchstone. She dedicated her life to preserving her legacy and continuing her ministry in any way she could. I mean, quite literally—she made it her career."

"It made her feel close to her mother," Althea said.

"Yeah. My father left us when I was young. And Dove was already living in Alabama then, and I guess, for Mom, the foundation became a substitute for the real person."

Althea nodded, but she seemed lost in thought. I felt strange, spilling my guts to a near stranger and one of my employees. But who else could I talk to? I was alone. Completely alone. A wave of despair washed over me.

"Eve?" Althea said. "You okay?"

I lifted my chin. "I should tell you. I'm not that surprised that my grandmother might've been connected to some trouble. There's something you don't know about her."

Griff sat up. "What?"

"I had a problem with my arm, something I was born with—and she tried, but Dove wasn't able to heal me."

They were quiet.

"I was okay with it for a while, but then, when I was fourteen years old, I changed my mind. I went to Alabama to see her. Alone. Just booked a flight and . . . went. I was going to insist she try again. Pray or whatever. Finish the job she started and give me my miracle."

I held out my right arm, dispassionately, like it wasn't even a part of me. But it was. It made me who I was. Just an arm, slightly softer and smaller, the muscles less defined than those in my left arm. No one would ever know by looking at it how hard that arm had worked. Still did.

"I was a kid. I wanted to not have to always be thinking about it. Hiding it from people." I kept my eyes down, reluctant to see their reactions. It felt easier that way. And easier not to know if this new revelation was having any sort of adverse effect on Griff. But then I forged on, telling myself that if he was bothered by my arm, he could well and truly go fuck himself.

"I landed in Birmingham. Caught a cab to her house in Tuscaloosa. Knocked on the door. She invited me in, and we had spaghetti and sweet tea and Oreos. We talked. But there was no miracle." I paused. "Then she sent me home. A few years after that, I heard about a specialized type of treatment, constraint-induced movement therapy, and fixed myself."

Althea looked puzzled. "I don't understand. Why wouldn't she pray for you?"

"It's not that she wouldn't. It was that she knew it wouldn't work. She started crying. Confessed to me, all of it, that she'd been a fraud from day one. That she'd built a life, a career, all on a lie. She said any time someone claimed to be healed by her, it was either a plant in the audience or someone who got carried away with emotion and convinced themselves of it. Like a psychosomatic thing. She said she'd never had a gift, never worked a single miracle, and she couldn't do anything for me."

They stared at me.

"How can that be true? I mean, all those people . . ." To my surprise, Althea's eyes had filled.

I clenched my jaw. "She scammed everyone and people let her. For decades. That's how."

"God, what a blow," Griff said. "You must've been devastated."

I nodded. "Basically, in the space of fifteen minutes, my entire understanding of life was upended. The next day, when she dropped me off at the airport, she asked me not to tell my mother. She said she knew it was wrong, letting Mom believe it all, letting her live her life in some pink-cloud la-la land. But she said sometimes you had to do the wrong thing for the right reasons."

"She knew you could handle the truth," Althea said quietly. "She trusted you, Eve."

"Hell of a thing to trust a kid with, though," I said. "Let me tell you, it's really hard to keep a secret your whole life. Add to that the constant worry that the truth will somehow come out anyway and send your family and its only source of income down the toilet. Which, by the way, is exactly what happened tonight."

"What almost happened," she said.

I stood and tossed the ice pack on the desk. "We'll see. But yeah. Bottom line is, I'm not completely shocked that my grandmother was involved in some shady business and didn't bother to tell any of us about it. That was one hundred percent her style. Here's the thing, though. Whatever she did or didn't do, right now, I just need the foundation to stay strong. For Dove to keep being *Dove—*" I waggled my hands, jazz style. "Because that's been the one constant in our lives."

They just watched me.

"I know the foundation probably can't go on forever, and I'm not saying Mom and Danny can't live without it. But . . . for now . . ."

. . . right before I leave . . . escape . . .

". . . I need things not to change. If that guy finds proof that Dove was a thief and a murderer, it will destroy my mom. And I can't let that happen. I just can't. I love her and I can't—" My voice cracked.

Griff shifted his weight. "Maybe you should sit down."

I sat on the edge of the bed, and my resolve finally gave way. I started to cry.

"Sorry," I said between sobs. "I just . . . I've spent my whole life trying to protect them. To keep them safe from anything that could go wrong. And now it's just all shot to hell. And it's all because of Dove."

"You have every right to cry," Althea said. "And we really should call the police."

"Please, no. No police. My brother is a—" I blotted my nose. "He's not the most stable person in the world, and my mom's got panic disorder. It'll completely freak them both out, to an unsalvageable degree. I just need to think. To calm down and figure out how to fix this. Because I know I can."

"Wait," Griff said. "The guy said he was going to take the bones of the man Dove supposedly murdered to the police and say she did it? They might be able to prove it's Steadfast Coe, whoever that is, but there's no way they can definitively prove Dove had anything to do with his death. Not even with this supposed signed confession."

Althea shook her head. "I don't know. It seems bad."

"She's right," I said. "Human bones are an irresistible story. And even if the confession is some kind of forgery, it's going to make enough noise to cause a problem. Accusations like this can torpedo a nonprofit in a heartbeat."

And could send my mother straight back to the hospital.

I suddenly felt so helpless. All these years, I'd thought I had this thing under control. But Dove's lies hadn't lain dormant. They'd germinated and multiplied, sending out a million runners that clung to whatever they encountered, smothering, strangling, crushing everything in their path. And now I was supposed to find one of those curling, pernicious vines and rip it out by the root before it reached my family? I didn't even know where to begin.

". . . that's why we should try to find the coin," Griff said.

I didn't realize he'd even been speaking. "Wait, what?" I stared at him.

"I'm just thinking—your family went through Dove's belongings after she died, right?"

"Thoroughly," I said. "We cleared everything out and the foundation catalogued and archived every single item of significance. There was no coin."

"So if she really did spend some time here in Alabama before hooking up with Charles in California, maybe she hid it here."

"What?" I said.

"Eve," Althea said, sounding excited.

"We could find it," Griff said.

"Sounds like a long shot to me," I said.

Althea piped up. "Okay, yes, a long shot, maybe. But think about it. If you did somehow manage to find the coin, at least you're still talking to the guy. You keep him close. Keep control of the situation. And maybe then, we can figure out what the hell is really going on. Get a real investigation started before he just starts spouting off lies."

"Okay, okay," I said. Then shook my head. "But how in the world am I supposed to find a coin that's been missing for a hundred years?"

"Eighty-six years, to be precise." Griff pulled aside one of the curtains. Outside the lights of downtown Tuscaloosa twinkled. "I've got files and files of notes. Hours of footage. We'll figure it out."

"We?" I said. "No way. No. This is my personal disaster. You guys don't need to involve yourselves in this."

Althea folded the flaps of the box. "You need a local. Somebody who knows their way around. I've been full-time mom-ing lately, and honestly, I think it's driving Jay and the kids around the bend. He'll thank you for getting me out of the house."

Griff planted his hands on his hips. "You hired me to research Dove and Charles, and I have, as much as was available to the public. Tonight, I got some pretty interesting stuff from that woman, your donor Margaret Luster. She's certifiable, no doubt, but she knows a ton about Dove. All that stuff about the Hawthorn Sisters. How they traveled all over Alabama, preaching and stuff."

"Oh my God, that's right," I said. "I'd completely forgotten about her."

"She might have some insider information about the coin," he said.

Althea had already retrieved her phone and was dialing Jay.

"Hey, babe," she said, and she stepped into the hall.

Griff put a hand on my shoulder. "We can do this, Eve. I really think we have a chance."

I raked my fingers through my hair. It was probably just my imagination, but it felt like the fetid smell of minty chewing tobacco and putrid human bones had permeated my clothes and skin and hair.

Griff looked pensive, like he was choosing his words carefully. "I'm not defending Dove for turning you away or for lying all these years about who she was—if that's really what she did. But if she did lie, she must've had her reasons. Right?"

"I guess," I said. Even though I wasn't sure I agreed with him.

The truth was, I had no idea who my grandmother was. Dove Jarrod was a complete stranger to me. But I was about to do everything within my power to change that.

Chapter Ten

Tuscaloosa, Alabama
1934

The Reverend Robert Singley had not enjoyed a full night's sleep in four years—the time that had passed since he'd first laid eyes on the girl. And this night, standing by the well behind his sister's white house and drawing on his dead brother-in-law's pipe, he felt like he might've entered into some kind of lovesick delirium.

He could see her soft red hair around her china doll face. Her smooth skin and cupid lips and those tiny, perfect white teeth, just as if she were standing right in front of him. His stupid nephew Jimmy wouldn't know what to do with a cherub like that. She'd be wasted on that oaf.

But she'd make a dandy preacher's wife.

He'd stuck around in Tuscaloosa mostly because he knew the situation in Enterprise was still rather unwelcoming. But it was also because he couldn't shake the girl's memory. Luckily, his sister, Jimmy's mother, was a docile woman, and uninclined to questions. When Singley had first arrived, his sister's husband was stilling living, and she'd been glad to offer their upstairs room and a nice supper every night at six-thirty.

Four years had passed in a blink. No sheriff had come for him from Enterprise. His sister's husband was buried down at the Baptist church, and Jimmy had persuaded a cow of a girl to marry him. They'd moved to Birmingham, where Jimmy had taken a job at the furnace, leaving the reverend and his sister the only occupants of the house.

At his sister's request, the reverend stayed on, now enjoying an expanded meal plan—breakfast at seven, soup at noon, and supper. She missed her husband, so he allowed her to fuss over him, laundering his shirts and trousers and drawing him a bath each night. Other than the occasional odd job around the house, he didn't work. He didn't have to. His sister's new job at the asylum brought in plenty. He didn't feel much like preaching either, lovesick as he was. Not to mention, the churches around Tuscaloosa only paid preachers in collard greens and live chickens.

He had to admit he liked his life. He liked lazing about the tidy house, arranging their mother's jewels that his sister kept in a silver pitcher. He liked playing with the pearls and diamonds and jet he'd never been allowed to touch when he was a boy. He also liked napping in the wicker rocker on the front porch with his father's big black Bible turned to the book of Hosea and tented over his chest.

"The Lord said to him, 'Go, marry a promiscuous woman and have children with her, for like an adulterous wife, this land is guilty of unfaithfulness to the Lord.'"

The memory of a woman, he reasoned, should always be pleasant, wreathing gently around a man's head like the smoke from his pipe. But it wasn't that way with the girl. Thinking of Ruth physically hurt him. And the last time a woman had hurt him, why, he hadn't taken a shine to that in the least . . .

But that was in the past. And it was dead and buried in Enterprise, where it belonged.

He whistled a long, low hoot out into the night and watched the trees for signs of life. When he was a boy, he could call in the owls so reliably that his mother used to call him Little Daniel Boone, but now the branches stayed bare and bereft. Just like him.

Ruth would be grown now, he thought bitterly. Would she have fallen in with a bad lot? Been forced to offer herself to the men on the byways? He could just see it—his angel, his cherub, lying beneath a monster of a man, dress torn, her pale breast exposed, only a pink nipple showing in the dim light of the ramshackle hotel room. Maybe this was all happening in a barn on a bed of golden hay. Or a cold, dusty train car. Either way, she'd be crying through it all, that precious angel, her face streaked with tears while that nasty brute rutted into her.

Ah, the indignity!

Maybe she would fight. And the brute would have to put a hand around her throat to keep her still. Ruth would only struggle for a minute there, surely, with a rough hand squeezing her throat. There'd be no one to hear her cries.

Reverend Singley had to admit he found the images quite compelling. He clenched the pipe between his molars, unbuttoned his trousers, and plunged both hands inside.

Ruth, Ruth, my backsliding Ruth. She is gone up upon every high mountain and under every green tree and there hath played the harlot. Return, thou backsliding Ruth, saith the Lord, and I will not cause mine anger to fall upon you . . .

He was inspired as he worked on himself. Why, he could be her Hosea. He could rescue her from fornication and bring her back to righteousness. He was a shepherd in search of the one lost lamb, he thought, his breath now coming in short gasps. He'd marry her, saving her from the shame and sin she'd surrendered herself to. And he'd bring her to his sister's house and allow her to work her way back to the piety that befitted the wife of a preacher.

He'd dress her in the best clothes and place his dead mother's pearls around her neck. They'd sleep in his sister's cherry bed, with the wheat and apples carved on the headboard. Sleep there as man and wife.

She would cook him breakfast each morning and serve soup for lunch. After supper, he would read aloud from the Bible. Make her confess to him about the hotels and the barns and the train cars. Maybe he'd even start a new church right here in Tuscaloosa.

He shivered and let out a quavering sigh.

"Robert? Land sakes, what are you doing?"

His sister, hair in rollers with pink wrapper clutched around her, stood before him. He buttoned his pants easily, almost laughing out loud at her shocked expression. He felt an extraordinary calm now. "Sister."

She frowned. Shook her head so that the permed curls vibrated the slightest bit. "Robbie, it's past midnight. And you know the rats are attracted to the smoke. Next thing, they'll be in the house."

He laughed out loud now, and even to his ears it sounded cruel. But then she, silly woman that she was, smiled and giggled nervously.

"What's the joke, Robbie?"

He stepped closer to her. He could feel the damp spot on his undershorts sticking to his leg. Oh yes, indeed, Ruth would look like a picture in that kitchen, standing before the stove. Settled with some embroidery in his sister's easy chair. Stretched out on that feather mattress, smooth and milky and open for him.

He took one end of the pink wrapper's tie and pulled it. His sister's wrapper fell open. He grinned, but she swept the ends of the robe tightly around her. "Come on now, Robert. I ain't decent."

He put a finger to his lips. "No. You aren't." He pressed his hands on either side of her face, gently. His fingers were sticky, and he could see when she recognized the smell. "But don't you worry. I'll make sure to fix you up before anybody lays eyes on you."

She nodded, but he could tell she was confused, her eyes wide and wild. Stupid frump. He leaned forward slowly, ever so tenderly, and planted a kiss on her sour old puckered mouth. She smelled like Sloan's Liniment and the cleaner they used in the loony bin.

"Robbie?" She sounded afraid, which galvanized him. In fact, he'd become quite calm after the good working over and the sight of her fear.

He gently wrapped the tie about her neck, front to back then front again. When his sister made another protesting whimper, he fixed her with a stern look. *"'I suffer not a woman to teach, nor to usurp authority over the man, but to be in silence.'"*

Obediently, she shut her mouth, watching him rotate his fists around each end of the tie and then pull. At that, she must've decided God's commandments didn't apply to this situation and screamed. The tie cut off her air, though, and soon all she could do was claw and scratch at him. It took her a good twenty minutes to quit struggling and he was bathed in sweat at the end.

He went inside to recover, made himself a sandwich and smoked another pipe. Then he went back out to the yard and threw her down the well.

Chapter Eleven

Tuscaloosa, Alabama
Present

At some point later in the night, Danny tapped on the door between our rooms.

I had drifted off while trying to come up with a story to sell him and Mom but roused at the sound. When he opened the door, I rolled over on my stomach so he wouldn't see my battered face.

"You feeling better?" he whispered. "Can I come in?"

"Mm-hm," I said into the sheets.

He settled beside me on the bed, flicked on the TV, and cranked the volume almost all the way down. He'd already changed into pajama pants and an undershirt, and he started the tap, tap, tapping at his wrist. I cracked open my not-swollen eye. *House Hunters International.*

"Bad champagne?" Danny asked.

"Maybe. I'm not sure. Is Mom okay?"

"Oh yeah, she's got her Xanax and Bible, so all's right with the world."

"You?"

"Hanging in."

But was he? Sometimes it was hard to tell with Danny. "Sorry to bail on you tonight," I mumbled into the pillow.

He patted my back. "All good. Nobody even missed you. Well, we missed you, but you know what I mean. The film crew got a ton of great stuff, and Mom was the belle of the ball, and Dove just looked down from that portrait and laughed at all of us."

I groaned. "I love you so much. You're the best."

"I am. And I love you too, sis. Also, by the way, these two?" He gestured toward the TV. "Getting divorced after they move to Bali."

My chest loosened in relief. He sounded completely normal, not at all like he suspected anything. But the bed was shaking ever so slightly. He'd moved on to his chest, tapping the dip between his clavicle bones.

"How are you?" I asked.

"Well, I survived a room full of strangers, and I'm not setting myself on fire and running through the hotel bar naked. Or picking up a drink. So let's call that a win."

I snuggled farther under the down comforter. "Maybe I should start tapping."

"It might be a bunch of mumbo-jumbo mindfulness BS. But it can't hurt." He hesitated. "I felt so . . . wrong being there today. Did you? Did you get that thing today, Evie?"

"What thing?"

"The thing you used to get with your arm. Remember? You said it would tingle when Mom was about to come home and catch us watching Cinemax and drinking her Diet Cokes."

I laughed, but then I thought about standing next to Griff, by the tree with the white blooms. My arm had twinged then, hadn't it? But that was just because of Griff's pretty face and nice body. That was lust, plain and simple.

His voice got softer. "And that time when you just knew something was up and came and got me at that stupid bar? Remember? You said you felt it in your arm right before I started panicking, right before I lost it."

"Danny," I interrupted him before he could unlock that painful old memory. We didn't need to go there right now. One thing at a time. "I know I said all that. And I'm glad I could be there for you. But I was confused back then. About God. About Mom. About my arm."

He was quiet.

"I was following Mom's lead. Wanting things to make sense. For there to be something that connected everything, that made it mean something."

"And you don't believe that anymore? That the Spirit uses your arm to . . . communicate things?"

"It's hard to say," I said, my voice light. I didn't want to get into it, not right then. "You know, sometimes hemiplegia is just . . . hemiplegia."

He huffed lightly. "Of course, you're right. You're totally right. It's just sometimes, I just want there to be . . . something else. I want something bigger than me out there . . . fixing things."

I didn't answer.

"Sorry. Talking out of my ass over here."

"Speaking of me being right," I plunged in, glad we could move on from that particular minefield. "I'm going to need you to fly back with Mom, if you don't mind. I want to stay here for a while. A couple of days, maybe three. So I can work on the documentary."

"Okay . . ." He sounded doubtful.

I held my breath. "I'm starting to think there's more about Dove and Charles that we don't know—really interesting stuff—and I think it's worth trying to dig it up. You can take the rental. Griff's got the van."

He was quiet for a moment, then spoke in a flat voice. "You're a liar."

My throat went dry, the base of my skull pulsed, and then, dammit all to hell, my stupid right arm tingled, then went completely numb. *He knows.*

He leaned over and poked me. "You want to stay so you can bang the hot cinematographer."

I let out an audible whoosh, I was so deeply and utterly relieved.

"I understand." He kissed my cheek and tousled my hair. "And you have my blessing, but only if you tell me everything, *ex post nasto*." He bounded off the bed and clicked off the TV. "Okay, seriously, sis. You had better be back in a week. Because, as you know, Mom and I can't deal without you."

Chapter Twelve

Florence, Alabama
1934

It was now or never, Ruth thought, staring at the heavy double doors of the imposing redbrick house on Court Street. This was her chance to get a job—a good one, if her calculations were correct—and she didn't intend to lose her nerve.

When she'd woken up that morning in the lion's cage, the beast was gone and the door wide open. Probably out on the town with one of Dr. Asloo's men, trying to drum up interest for the next show. She'd slipped away from the small encampment of wagons and trucks and wandered the mile or two into town. They'd have to find another girl. She was done with lions.

Florence, Alabama, was a bustling hamlet nestled into the curve of the Tennessee River, like a babe in its mama's arm. It boasted a busy, gleaming downtown and plenty of grand old stone buildings, not to mention several streets of impressively columned Victorian mansions. Ruth counted five churches in all—First Baptist, First Presbyterian, First United Methodist, Trinity Episcopal, and St. Joseph Catholic—and plenty of shiny cars jamming the roads.

Lots of money, she thought. Even more than in Meridian or Hattiesburg.

After she'd begged a dime and gotten a hot dog at a small diner, Ruth headed to the big stone post office to see what was what. She had nicked a soft gray broadcloth coat with chartreuse satin lining from a closet and spent the last few hours sauntering casually down several wide streets in Florence looking for some kind of opportunity. She found what looked to be a prospect on Court Street, just north of the main business district but south of the college. The second biggest house, an imposing antebellum structure set back off the road.

It was the tree in the front yard that initially caught her eye—a gnarled old hawthorn, blooming in its lacy glory. She got choked up a little bit, seeing that tree and thinking about Dell and the Major. But then she noticed the house was host to a continuous flurry of interesting activity and the tears dried right up.

She parked herself underneath a leafy mimosa on the corner and watched. Every half hour on the dot—according to the bells from the university tower—a different girl, decked out in trim hats and gloves, walked sedately up the limestone steps and knocked on the great front door. Promptly each was admitted into the cool, dark, cavernous interior. Then, precisely ten minutes later, each had reappeared. But they didn't leave like they came. Coming out, they looked like a bunch of cats with their tails on fire, barreling down the steps, then onto the sidewalk, arms folded across their chests, faces aghast.

Job interviews, Ruth had figured after a while. And none gone too well either. Good news for her. If she was quick thinking and didn't let whatever had rattled the other girls rattle her, she'd be in high cotton.

Before another girl could appear, she hurried up the steps and pushed the brass doorbell. The door didn't swing open right away like it had for the others, so she pressed the button again. No sense in letting the next candidate find her here and take her spot.

She heard a lock turn and the door let out a low creak. Then it swung open and Ruth was met by the barrel of a gleaming .22 rifle. She blinked once and gazed down the black tunnel of iron, feeling some strange force take hold of her. Something akin to exhilaration. The barrel began to move—down, down, down—until it was aimed directly at her feet.

A small dimpled girl stepped into the open doorway and swatted the gun aside with a plump, authoritative forearm. "Lordamercy, Grandy! How's that any way to greet a guest? My goodness."

The girl stepped out onto the vestibule, hooked a soft, small hand in the crook of Ruth's elbow and propelled her over the threshold. Ruth flinched, tripping over the warped chestnut boards of the vast foyer and coming face-to-face with the bearer of the weapon. It was only an old man. He shouldered the gun and the young girl addressed him like a schoolteacher would a naughty boy.

"This is Mr. Steadfast Coe, my grandfather. Forgive his rudeness."

Ruth proffered a hand. "Hello, Mr. Coe. Pleased to make your acquaintance."

"I don't need no girl." He turned and shuffled under an archway into the next room. His voice sounded raw and cracked, as if it wasn't in the habit of being used very often.

The girl clucked at him. "Of course you don't. We just got someone to tidy up. And to fix you some soup. Now go put that thing away, for heaven's sake, so Miss . . ."

"Ruth," Ruth said, surprising herself by ditching her nickname. But she was done with Annie, that dirty street urchin, grifter, con. She was going to become respectable, and she intended to do it right. So Ruth it was.

". . . Ruth and I can talk."

Ruth's stomach fluttered. The old man wore a plaid shirt, soft with age and filth. His pants were stained and drooped under his pot belly. And she could smell urine, old and new, as he'd passed by her.

The girl gripped her arm. "You're one of Mrs. Scott's girls?"

Ruth froze, panicked for a moment, then remembered the girls she'd seen. They must've been sent by an agency. As well as she might've been.

"Yes," Ruth said and smiled sweetly.

"Saving the best for last, let's hope."

She maneuvered Ruth by the forearm into the room the old man had entered. He was standing beside an enormous marble fireplace, lifting the rifle onto a pair of brass brackets. Task accomplished, he shuffled past the girls, hands buried in his pockets, without a word or glance directed at either of them.

Ruth surveyed the room. A library or parlor or music room, she couldn't tell and wouldn't have known the proper name if she had. There were both books and smoking chairs and a glossy ebony-and-burled-wood piano in the corner that said *Steinway* on its carved music rack. But the place was a sight. Rather than cool, as it had looked from the outside, it was hot and fetid, the furniture coated with dust and the soaring windows clouded with dirt. Stacks of yellowed newspapers lined two walls. There were ominous lumps along the edges of the Persian carpets, where the richly papered walls met rich baseboards. Dark scatterings that looked alarmingly like rodent droppings.

She sat with the girl, the two of them at either end of a dusty silk-embroidered settee.

The girl sighed. "I'm sorry, I don't remember seeing you on the list. What's your last name?"

Ruth thought fast. Using Lurie, her real name, was out, unless she wanted to risk them tracing her back to Pritchard.

"Davidson," she said.

Boy, would Dell ever bust a gut at that, her using his last name like they were brother and sister. She wished he could see her now in this fine house. This might be the first time in years she'd been this close to him.

"Oh? The Tuscumbia Davidsons? Or the Memphis Davidsons?" The girl looked completely earnest, her eyes wide. She was pretty in a wholesome way—brunette with the rosiest cheeks Ruth had ever seen. She wore a simple but expensive-looking housedress in a sedate brown plaid.

Ruth shifted on the settee. There was a spring directly under her bottom. "Hard to say."

"Age?"

"Seventeen."

"Me too!" The girl seemed to catch herself then, realizing she'd strayed from her composed employer role. She folded her hands again. "You're the youngest they've sent but it's no matter. You seem strong."

"Oh, I am. And I sing too."

"Do you like Cab Calloway?" The girl gave her a wink. *"Hi-dee, hi-dee, hi-dee, hi."*

Ruth grinned and echoed back. *"Hi-dee, hi-dee, hi-dee, hi."*

"Whoa-oh-oh-oh-oh . . ." they sang together in perfect harmony. *"Hee-dee, hee-dee, hee-dee, hee. He-e-e-e-ey . . ."*

The girl giggled. "You like Cab Calloway?"

"I like that song especially." Ruth had only ever heard "Minnie the Moocher" on the radio when she was passing a store or the open window of someone's house. She didn't know Cab Calloway from a hole in the ground.

"Grandy might like you to sing to him. I do it sometimes. You have a pretty voice. Like a dove. And you look like a dove too. Soft and delicate." She pointed to the coat. "And gray."

"I do love to sing." That part was true enough. She'd never minded the mandatory chapel services at Pritchard when the chaplain told them a Bible story and they sang a hymn.

"And your references?"

Ruth dropped her gaze. "Mrs. Scott didn't mention that I needed them."

"Well, never mind that," the girl said briskly. "We'll get back to that if need be. In the meantime, I'll tell you about myself and the job. I'm Bruna Faulk, Mr. Coe's granddaughter. I live a couple of blocks away with my parents, which is why we need a housekeeper, cook, and companion for him." She inclined toward me and spoke in a low voice. "He's gone a little bit soft in the head, I'm afraid. Forgets things, people, his family. And he wanders off, which is a primary concern. The last time, he made it all the way to the bridge. And he had *that* with him." She pointed to the rifle on the mantel. "He wasn't in any war, but he does like his guns."

Ruth took mental note of that. Not that she planned on stealing anything, but it was good to know the old man wasn't afraid to wield a weapon.

"Anyway, you'll clean and cook three squares for him. Our housekeeper, Vesta, will drop off the groceries for you, so you don't have to leave." She took note of Ruth's expression. "You'll have Sundays off. That's the day my mother comes over. We're Jewish so we don't have church. Well, my father's Jewish. My mother used to be Presbyterian. Anyway, you're welcome to go to church, of course. I go to the Methodist church some. There's a boy I know there."

She smiled, blushing even more and pausing briefly. "Or you can take a walk, see a picture at the Shoals, whatever you like." She hesitated. "I know the house is an absolute mausoleum. But he wouldn't let the last girl do anything with it. And he won't let Mama clear out the old furniture or buy him any new. I just want you to know. It's not that we don't care for him. We do."

After the long speech her face looked so bereft that Ruth felt she had to say something. "Probably he just likes things how he likes them," she offered. "Old folks are like that."

"I told them I could stay here, to cook and clean for him, but my parents said—" She stopped abruptly.

"It was beneath you," Ruth said. She could see Bruna was from money. That dress was made of expensive wool and cut well.

Bruna made a flustered sound. "I don't know why. I like to cook and clean and I have all the time in the world. What difference does it make, as long as Grandy feels loved?"

Ruth nodded.

"I graduated from Mount Vernon Seminary and Junior College last spring and was hoping to go on to Smith, but my parents didn't . . . it didn't work out." She fell silent. "Have you done this sort of work before?"

Ruth considered fibbing, then thought better of it. "Truth be told, I'm not one of Mrs. Scott's girls. I just took leave of my employment at Dr. Asloo's Wild Menagerie. I watered the animals, mucked out the cages, and tried to keep from being eaten."

Bruna didn't seem bothered at all by her confession, but she was gaping at her all the same. "I've heard of him! The man who puts his head in the lion's mouth!"

"The very one."

Her eyes shone. "You work for him? What a gas!"

Ruth eyed her skeptically. Was the girl pulling her leg?

"Why in the world did you quit?"

"I didn't, not exactly. Last night, I accidentally got locked in the lion cage."

"With the lion? Jiminy!"

"I prayed, though. Declared the Word of the Lord over him and said I was a daughter of Eve and he better listen to me. And then he fell right to sleep—and I did too."

Bruna let out a shocked sound. "Well, what do you know. A miracle." She blinked. "You got a fellow?"

"When I was a little kid." Ruth wouldn't say Dell's name, but she couldn't resist telling Bruna about him. "We used to hide presents for each other in a hawthorn tree at the . . . out in front of my house.

Where I lived." Then she remembered she was there for business. "And the pay? What would that be?"

Bruna's hands drifted down to her lap and folded demurely. "Five dollars, every two weeks. Minus expenses."

Ruth didn't have any idea what kind of expenses she could possibly incur, living in this grand house, having food delivered right to the front door, but she was so elated, she nearly screamed out loud.

"Are you all right?" Bruna asked.

Ruth nodded, and Bruna stood. Ruth stood too.

"Well," said Bruna, looking immensely pleased and relieved. "If you agree to it, it looks like you've got yourself a job. As long as you don't mind the . . ." The girl looked around the room uncertainly, then finally at the mantel and the gun. "And the . . ."

"When do I start?"

"Right now, if you're agreeable."

Ruth was more than agreeable, and after they shook hands, Bruna gave her a tour of the house. Ruth saw the drafty upstairs consisting of four bedrooms with four-poster beds, two tiled bathrooms, and a central hall the size of a gymnasium. The downstairs had an identical layout: massive hall, library, sitting room, dining room, and kitchen. The ceilings soared. They were punctuated by finely painted murals and a half dozen plaster medallions that dangled crystal chandeliers—but everything below was ruin and rot.

Bruna said the house locked from the inside as well as out. She showed Ruth where they hid the house key—behind a loose brick at the edge of the porch—and told Ruth not to tell Steadfast or he'd take it. Vesta, the maid, would be by first thing in the morning with groceries, but in the meantime, perhaps Ruth could persuade Steadfast to have some toast and tea for his supper. Ruth said she'd try, then walked Bruna to the door.

She put a hand on Bruna's arm. "If you don't mind—what happened to the last girl? The one who watched him before?"

Bruna's face took on a pained expression. "Well, now . . . that was an unfortunate thing. And not entirely my grandfather's fault. He is soft in the head, you know."

Bruna looked uncomfortable, but Ruth took her hand. "I'd just like to be prepared, you see, for all eventualities. Something I learned from working with the animals."

Bruna nodded. "I understand, I do. But you must promise you won't let it color your opinion of my grandfather. He's a good man. A kind one, just not himself these days."

"No, no. Of course not."

Bruna flushed and her hand felt damp. "Well . . . I'm sorry to say that the last girl . . . Well, he shot one of her toes clean off her foot."

Chapter Thirteen

Tuscaloosa, Alabama
Present

I was the first one downstairs in the hotel's bustling red-leather and stacked-stone restaurant the next morning, fogged with exhaustion and fear. The night before, I hadn't slept for longer than thirty minutes at a stretch when finally, around five, Mom came into my room to tell me she and Danny were leaving for the airport.

I buried my face in the pillow. She kissed me, and my nerves felt so raw, I almost changed my mind about everything. But she seemed unusually jovial, buoyed by the success of the previous night, and I let her go without a word.

The light of day—along with the throbbing headache and giant purple lump over my eye—brought everything into sharp perspective. I'd gone to work at the foundation because I'd been determined to take care of my family, to protect them from whatever fallout might result from Dove's big lie. But the reality of that had always been a bit murky in my mind, a vague, unformed threat that, like an old-time Hollywood press agent, I would handily dispatch with a public statement and an overseas getaway.

Never once, in all that time, had I considered Dove's lying in a broader sense. If she'd lied about one thing, there was the strong possibility that she'd lied about more. Not once did I dream that she actually could've committed real honest-to-God crimes that would have lasting consequences on a larger, life-shattering scale.

I hadn't given my grandmother enough credit, apparently.

Though truth be told, I think on some level I'd always known this day was coming. One way or the other, there was always retribution for a person's sins—and that was why I'd stayed. To fight the fallout. So now I had to stay. For my family, I had to see this Steadfast thing through to the bitter end.

I swallowed two Advil I'd bought at the hotel shop and nursed a cup of coffee while Althea and Griff circled the breakfast buffet. Althea was in head-to-toe black: yoga pants, sneakers, and a zip-up hoodie, a grimy olive-green backpack slung over one shoulder. Griff, wearing an ivory-colored beanie and heathered T-shirt, sat down with a plate loaded with scrambled eggs, grits, and every conceivable kind of breakfast meat, but all I could focus on was how kind and compassionate his expression was each time he looked at me.

They both started in on me again about the police. So to shut down that line of conversation, I promised I'd report it after the three days had passed. At this point, I said, I couldn't risk anyone contacting Mom and Danny or word getting out and affecting the foundation in any way. Griff and Althea weren't happy about it, but they conceded that it was my choice.

We split up for a couple of hours—Althea to square everything away with Jay and her kids, Griff to finish up with Liz and Naveen and buy a new phone, and me to wander through the aisles of Target, stocking up on extra clothes and toiletries. At noon, we regrouped at Dreamland, a tiny barbecue joint on the outskirts of Tuscaloosa that Althea said was to die for. I ordered racks of ribs for the group, while Griff and Althea both excused themselves to make calls. Althea's expression when she returned told me the news wasn't good.

"So that was Beth Barnes at Pritchard. I made up some BS story about Griff misplacing his phone last night. She said the hospital installed security cameras during the reno, but they haven't been connected yet. So no tape of your guy."

"Shit," I said.

Griff returned then. "Naveen and Liz will return the van and the rest of the equipment and wait for my call. I don't know if you want me to film any of this, but I'll have my camera, just in case."

I rolled my eyes. "I have a feeling whatever it is we're about to find is going to be less than upbeat and inspirational."

"It'll be real," Althea said. "Maybe that's better."

Real—whatever that turned out to be—would probably not encourage donors to open their wallets. At this point, the most important thing was to shut down the real stuff, if it turned out to be bad. To lie, in other words. I sighed, my head throbbing.

Althea nodded at my plate of untouched food. "Forgive the mama bear routine, but you really should eat something. You're going to need your strength."

I picked up the rack of ribs in front of me and she nodded approvingly.

"What's our first move?" Griff asked.

"Margaret Luster," I said. "Our first and only move, at this point."

Althea raised her eyebrows. "Can you call her? See if she'll meet with you—us?"

While they obliterated the plates of ribs, coleslaw, and white bread, I wiped my fingers and scrolled through my donor contacts. I dialed Margaret and pushed my plate away. The smell of the place was making me queasy and the throbbing in my head had become unbearable. I didn't know how I was going to make it through an interview with this woman.

"Hello?" Margaret Luster said on the other end of the line.

I set my jaw. "Margaret, it's Eve Candler from the Jarrod Foundation."

"Eve! I'm so glad you called. I tried to find you again last night, but your mother told me you were under the weather."

I touched the lump on my temple and smirked at Althea and Griff. "Yes. Something really hit me out of the blue. Margaret, I have an unusual request."

"Sounds interesting."

"I've decided to dig a little deeper, try to get to know more about my grandmother's time in Alabama when she was young. If I was to drive over to Birmingham today, would you be available to answer some questions?"

"I'd love that." She sounded excited, giddy even. "Maybe we could figure out where those bootleg tapes are as well."

"Maybe so. But mostly I'm interested in any stories you've heard about Dove when she was in Alabama . . . what she did here . . . and who she did it with."

"Well, that's my favorite subject, you know," Margaret said in her rich-lady drawl. "We're just wrapping up Bible study here, but after everybody clears out, I'm all yours."

"Thank you," I said. "I'll be bringing a couple of friends. And if you don't mind, could you keep our meeting just between us? I'd rather not broadcast what I'm doing."

"Oh, honey, I get it, I really do. The Hawthorn Sisters were full of the anointing. They made quite a splash back then, and I expect folks did whatever they could to get close to it." She hesitated, lowering her voice. "The fire of God is like a magnet, Eve. It draws both sinner and saint. But it also attracts another kind. A wicked kind. I've lived a long time, and believe me, I've seen what some people—a certain ruthless type of person—will do to get ahold of that fire."

She paused a moment, then spoke again. "This might sound silly, but . . ."

"What?"

Her voice was kind. "I think you should be careful, Eve. That's all."

Chapter Fourteen

Florence, Alabama
1934

As it turned out, Steadfast Coe did indeed harbor a strange animosity toward human toes, both the male and female variety. He continually railed against barefoot dandies in the park, barefoot ladies on the banks of the river, and barefoot children any place at all.

There were a variety of other things he didn't like either: being awakened at any hour of the morning, flowers of any sort, dogs that lacked the skill to hunt, undercooked toast, overcooked toast, the smell of lemon verbena cleaner, singing, conversation, rainy days, cloudy days, overly sunny days, Yankees, Anabaptists, Republicans, Democrats, beef stew, oatmeal, fresh air coming in through open windows, Aimee Semple McPherson, the *Music by Gershwin* radio show, and most especially his eldest daughter, Edith, who had dropped out of high school to marry a Jewish atheist.

None of this bothered Ruth, especially not the toe matter, as she had no desire to walk unshod through the swales of dust bunnies, rat pellets, and various puddles of mysteriously congealed goo that covered the floors of the Coe house. She was happy enough to keep her shoes on at all times and retain her digits, fully intact.

The first night she was in the house, after Mr. Coe had retired to his upstairs bedroom, she stayed up into the wee hours cleaning. She worked her way through the entire first floor with a mop, bucket, and scrub brush, starting with the parlor, the room where she and Bruna had first talked, and ending with the wide central hall. She swept, mopped, dusted, wiped windows, shook out curtains, polished brass, and scrubbed floors. She decided to ask Bruna if the heavy Persian rugs could be sent out for cleaning. And perhaps she could even convince Mr. Coe to let his daughter repair the torn upholstery and order new curtains. The family seemed to have plenty of money.

She had proof of it now. As Ruth moved through the house, she'd discovered a closet of chinchilla coats, fox capes, and mink stoles. Silver tea and coffee services, trays, and serving dishes were haphazardly stacked in several large buffets and sideboards. There was a glass-fronted cabinet of tiny Chinese men carved into jade. And a treasure trove of coins that Ruth found hidden in the darnedest locations all over the house. Every time she found one—in a fireplace grate, or between the pages of a book or two floorboards—she'd drop it into her pocket. She found a crystal jar with a silver lid that sat on a dresser in the mint-green bedroom and poured the coins from her cupped hand into the glass. They made a beautiful tinkling sound.

Later, Bruna would explain that the coins were the result of mint errors—pennies, nickels, and quarters that'd been double-struck or struck off-center or had the wrong planchet on their face. Apparently, it drove Old Steadfast to distraction that some things that wrong and mistaken were floating around in the world, and he felt compelled to hide them away. They had some value, Bruna thought, but she wasn't at all sure what it amounted to.

But even without the coins, Ruth felt sure Steadfast Coe had to be one of the richest men in Florence.

Tackling the second floor proved a much more daunting task, and one she didn't accomplish until later in the week. For one, she had to devote more time to cooking Mr. Coe's meals and seeing to it that he didn't escape the confines of the house in the daylight hours. She repeatedly had to drop whatever she happened to be scrubbing or polishing or sweeping and rush out the back door to wrangle her charge.

Every time she steered the old man back, he struggled and showered her with curses, but, for the most part, he was weak and no match for her. As for the colorful language, Ruth had certainly heard worse, most of it from her own mouth.

At night, after Mr. Coe had his glass of whiskey and regular dose of pine syrup and was safely snoring in his bed, Ruth would creep back down to the maid's room where she slept. It was cramped and jammed between the kitchen and the side porch, and it smelled of tar and coal smoke and whatever she'd cooked in the kitchen that day. Cleaning through the night was out of the question. She was so exhausted, the moment she fell into bed, sleep took her.

But all in all, she felt that fate had landed her in a pretty place.

This particular night her room was especially hot, so she pushed open the window, just a crack, got undressed, and lay on the narrow iron bed. She closed her eyes, letting the smell of the Tennessee River and the demure north Alabama spring waft over her.

Sometime later she woke, sensing a presence in her room. The window was open all the way now, rainwater on the worn floorboards. She held her breath, although that was probably the wrong thing to do if the culprit was in her room. A dead giveaway that she was savvy to his game.

"Ruthie, you up?" came a voice from the shadows. A voice somewhere between man and boy. "Ruthie, don't be scared. It's me, Dell."

He edged out of his hidey-hole into the pale light cast by the bright moon. Handsome, with a head of tousled hair like straw and a green bandanna that kept it off his fine forehead. Tall and solid, carrying with him the faint aroma of manly things like smoke and dirt and motor oil.

He wore a button-up shirt that gaped open, showing a smooth chest reddened by the sun, and brown pants cinched by a too-big, worn belt.

"Dell! Goddamn you!" Ruth said.

He froze. "Goddamn me?"

"How'm I not supposed to be scared with you hiding in my room?" But she couldn't suppress a grin. She felt something more than relief or the simple pleasure of reuniting with an old friend. It felt more like the warmth of the sun or a hot bowl of grits or the gift of a soft bed.

And to tell the truth, she had been thinking a lot about Dell lately.

It was usually while she was cleaning and listening to Mr. Coe's radio. The songs made her think of Dell, and as she worked, she tried to picture the way his face would look now. She took the boyhood image burned into her memory—cornflower-blue eyes and a lightning-flash smile—and, building upon it like a sculptor might, layered on a man's defined jaw, brisk stubble, and broadening chest. The image that'd resulted in her mind had made her draw in a quick breath.

Now she realized he was even more handsome than she'd imagined.

"I'm sorry." He looked around. "This is your room? Gee, Ruth. Is this slick."

She sat up straighter. "Yes, I'm employed by Mr. Steadfast Coe now. But I'm guessing you know that since you climbed in this particular window. Who told you I was here?"

"I have my ways." He waggled his eyebrows and whistled. "Boy, howdy, this is sure some sweet setup." He sat on the edge of her narrow bed, keeping a safe distance between them. "I'm really sorry about scaring you, Ruthie. I've been in Florence a couple of weeks, sniffing around, seeing what's what, and I did get wind of you—and your situation."

She raised her eyebrows, hoping to look stern but failing miserably. His deep voice carried a certain timber that stirred her up and made her stomach flutter without ceasing.

"But I didn't tell the boys, in case they got any ideas. We won't try nothing here, I swear to you. We got a job here and then we're off to Texas."

Her heart sunk.

"But I couldn't leave without seeing how my old friend was doing."

Ruth spoke as evenly as she could manage. "I'm getting by."

"Good, good."

"And you?"

He shrugged, and she understood immediately without anything more being said. He bent the law the same way she had since the day she left the asylum.

"I've missed you, Dell," she admitted.

He brightened. "I missed you too, Ruthie. I hated it when you left. I can't tell you how lonesome I was. But I was glad, also. Mackey told me what Singley tried to do, making you two get hitched . . ." He hesitated.

She waited. Whatever he meant to say, she was not going to say it for him.

His voice got even lower. "If I'd have been grown, I'd have flat killed him."

"Good thing you were a scrawny kid, then." Ruth couldn't help but smile. "Where'd you meet up with these boys you're running with?"

"Over in Georgia. At a hotel south of Macon. I was handing out towels to naked folks who smelled like rotten eggs." He touched her hand. "Ever since I heard you were in town, all I could think was how I had to get to you. How I had to see you before you got away again."

She could hardly believe her ears. "Really?"

He nodded, his lips parting. They were so beautiful, his lips. Full and pink and perfectly formed. And without thinking, she leaned forward and pressed her mouth to them. He returned the kiss. His shirt was damp from the rain, but she didn't care. She let him wrap his wet arms around her and lower her to the bed. He tasted like tobacco and the spring rain, and he made a small whimpering sound as they kissed. She pressed her body against his.

As their arms and legs looped and held each other, their breathing got faster and louder. Ruth was glad the house was so big, and Mr. Coe wouldn't hear them. She felt hot all over—on fire. The way she felt kissing Dell Davidson was a force bigger and stronger than anything she'd encountered before, even that ornery, half-starved lion. The smell of this boy, the feel of his skin against hers—she didn't have the words to describe how good it felt. How surprising and wonderful and delicious.

Then, when Dell's hand moved under her nightgown, along each leg, then between them, she spread them a fraction wider, capitulating to whatever he wanted to do. He didn't have to do much. Almost as soon as he began to touch her, she started quaking against him, gasping with her head thrown back.

He put a finger to her lips. "Shh. I don't want you to get in trouble."

She blinked at him, dazed and limp. After a few moments, he scrambled off the bed, straightening his pants. He was red in the face, eyes cast down at the floor.

"That was ungentlemanly of me," he said. "My apologies."

She covered her mouth with her hand, but behind it she was smiling. He was everything she remembered—home and comfort, light and laughter. And now this new feeling. This wild, rugged desire. This perfect, unexplainable joy.

"You better not apologize again," she said. "Or I'll sock you."

He stared at her a moment, then rubbed his brow, a smile transforming his face. "I'd let you."

She smiled back. "What's the job in Texas?"

He scuffed his shoes on the floor.

"Tell me," she said.

"A bank," he said.

She absorbed this, surprised by the way the words filled her with worry. She stuck her chin up. "Well, don't you get shot."

He nodded.

"Will you come back?"

"I will if you want me to."

"I do."

He stared at her for a moment, but this time he didn't smile. He looked deadly serious. "You bet I will. You bet your beautiful baby blues I'm coming back for you." He hauled himself over the windowsill, then turned back to her. "I'm going to marry you, Ruth Lurie."

She felt her skin go to goose bumps. "I go by Davidson now. Ruth Davidson."

He didn't answer, but his smile said all she needed to know. Then in an instant, he was gone, dropping out of the window, down to the grass below. By the time she was able to untangle herself from the sheets and fly to the window, all she could see was his retreating form, disappearing into the moonlit elderberry hedge.

Chapter Fifteen

Birmingham, Alabama
Present

Margaret Luster's house was located off a winding road in Mountain Brook, an upscale suburb just south of Birmingham. The modern house sat at the end of a long, leaf-strewn drive, a low steel and glass series of connecting boxes that nestled into the rocky hillside.

Margaret swung open her front door. She was clad in a watercolor caftan and enormous coral jewelry and gathered us into the soaring glass foyer like a mother hen. Then she got a closer look at me.

"Your eye!" she gasped.

"Shower door at the hotel," I said. "I'm fine."

She led us through a long hallway hung with colorful abstract paintings to a library. It was lined with books and furnished with four identical green-leather chairs circled around a low marble table. She offered the leftover spread from her ladies' Bible study—iced tea and chicken salad—but we declined.

Griff hefted his camera. "Do you mind if I get some footage of you talking about Dove?"

Margaret smoothed her hair. "Of course not, darlin'. I feel like I'm practically a pro after our interview last night. Sit, everyone, please."

Margaret, Althea, and I sat while Griff positioned himself behind us. I could sense him lining up his shot, adjusting settings on the camera.

Margaret turned to me. "I believe I owe you an apology for yesterday, Eve. You know, for the prayer thing." One perfectly manicured hand drifted up to her coral necklace. "I'm embarrassed, I'll be honest. I haven't handled my diagnosis well. I try to be strong for the young women who come here, wanting me to impart words of wisdom from all my years walking with the Lord, but lately, I haven't had anything for them. They don't want to hear that I'm full of doubt. They don't want to hear how I stay awake at night remembering the moment the doctor told me I may die." She pressed her lips together. "That I'm *going* to die."

Althea tilted her head, lips pursed in sympathy. Griff shifted his camera off his shoulder.

"I saw you yesterday and . . . you just looked so much like her. And I had this wild, nonsensical thought that maybe you were gifted in the same way she was . . ." She sat back in her chair. "Anyway. My husband thinks I live in a fairy tale, and I know he's probably right. But it's a comfort, isn't it? To believe? I mean, really believe that the order of things can somehow be reversed, and in the end, the day can actually be saved?"

I didn't know what to say. It was the same question Danny had asked me. And the answer was yes, I had believed that once, when I was a kid. Then Dove had ended my innocence and belief and I'd had to rely on myself.

Margaret stood. "But you wanted to hear about your grandmother, not me. So, with that in mind, I'd like to show you something."

She left the room and when she returned, she was bearing a sleek silver laptop. She angled it toward us on the table. On-screen was a graphic of an audio tuner. I felt an unaccountable flutter of anticipation in my stomach.

Margaret's voice was breathy and dramatic. "About ten years ago, a friend of mine stumbled on an estate sale over in Tuscaloosa. It was nothing to speak of, small house, mostly junk. But in the middle of the mess, she found this suitcase full of dozens of old wire and magnetic recordings of Charles Jarrod's meetings. Chock full of them, for less than twenty dollars. Of course, knowing I was such a nut about the Jarrods, she bought the whole kit and caboodle. I found this wonderful Dutch man, an expert in digital transfer, who put it all on the computer for me. There's this one . . ."

She clicked on the red "Play" button, and a young girl's voice filled the room. I realized the sound was emanating from a variety of speakers concealed around us.

"There's a treasure hidden," the girl said. "And the Holy Ghost says it's yours to find."

Her voice was twangy with that old-time Southern lilt. But affected, too, in the way that old movie stars used to talk. Goose bumps ran up my arms and over my entire scalp.

Dove. The voice of my grandmother.

"No matter your lot," Dove's small voice said. "Almighty God will always care for you!"

Griff sat forward, body taut and head tilted, adjusting the lens of the camera to get both Margaret and the laptop in the shot. I lifted my eyes to meet Althea's. Like me, she'd gone completely still.

"You must look with new eyes at everything around you, and He will provide," the girl sang in a clear voice. *"If you cannot cross the ocean, and the heathen lands explore, you can find the heathen nearer, you can help them at your door."*

The singing—her voice, soft and sweet and pure—startled me. It was as if, by singing, she'd reached inside me, around my defenses, and poked at something soft and vulnerable.

"If you cannot give your thousands, you can give the widow's mite; and the least you give for Jesus will be precious in his sight." She sang

the chorus—*"Hark! The voice of Jesus crying, 'Who will go and work today?'"*—then Margaret paused the audio.

"This was one of the first meetings Dove and Charles did together. I don't know what year it was. But she was so young, you know. Only seventeen or eighteen. But I don't know . . ." She hesitated for the first time since we'd gotten there. "They never struck me as much of a match."

"Why not?" Althea asked.

"He was much older than her," Griff said. "Twelve years."

"Not so unusual back then, though, right?" Althea said.

Margaret gave a small head shake. "It's more than that. I've listened to these tapes over and over." She leaned forward, her coral necklace clacking. "Dissecting every word and every sentence, hoping that I'd find my miracle in their voices. And in all that time, I couldn't get over the feeling . . . that . . . I don't know how to describe it . . ."

Griff cut in. "Is it that Charles and Dove never interact with each other in an affectionate way?"

Margaret jabbed a finger in his direction. My head swiveled to stare at him.

"I mean, I've only heard a few of the old recordings, but I noticed it too. They don't seem like husband and wife. Like lovers." He glanced quickly at me and I felt myself go warm in the face. "It's more business-like, detached and professional. Almost like collaborators, like . . ." He searched for the word.

"Partners in crime?" I said dryly.

"I agree with you, Griff," Margaret said, but I could feel her watching me closely with an inscrutable look in her eye. "Something in the dynamic between Charles and Dove in these early tapes has always felt off to me. Too perfect and brittle, I suppose, for a couple who were newlyweds."

I realized my leg was jiggling, my mind obsessing over the time that was rapidly ticking away. I didn't want to be rude, but I didn't need to hear Margaret opine on Charles and Dove's onstage chemistry. I needed to find out about Steadfast Coe and the stolen coin.

Margaret clapped her hands. "But I think we're getting ahead of ourselves." She bustled to the shelves and drew out a large leather album. She laid the book out on the marble table, opened it, then rotated the album toward me.

"Before Charles and Dove Jarrod paired up," she said reverently, "Dove was one half of the Hawthorn Sisters."

Affixed to the pages of the album were two bills. Advertisements, brittle-looking and faded to a faint sepia. *Hawthorn Sisters Healing Revival!* the one on the right proclaimed. *Holy Ghost Preaching, Prayer for the Infirm, Word of Knowledge in Operation.* Below that was a grainy photograph of two young girls on a stage, holding hands and wearing matching frilly dresses. One of the girls was plump and pretty, with long dark curls and a Judy Garland sparkle. Beside her, Dove looked like a child—an ethereal elfin creature with luminous skin, straight bobbed hair, and a gleam in her eyes.

"She really does look like you," Althea said, looking over my shoulder.

"Exactly like you," Griff said from behind the camera. "It's uncanny."

"Are you okay?" Althea put a hand on my arm.

I wasn't sure. It was all so much. My grandmother had escaped the hellhole that was Pritchard Insane Hospital only to stay in Alabama. But why? And why hadn't she told her family the truth about this period of time? What did she have to hide?

Margaret beamed at us. "Another friend of mine found those bills in her attic, in her parents' things. Two of only a few remaining advertisements for the Hawthorn Sisters, from 1934. The one on the left is from a Billy Sunday revival, where they only appeared as a guest act, but the other was a solo appearance, one of the only ones. And possibly the last appearance before she married Charles Jarrod."

I looked closer. "At the North Alabama State Fair?"

Margaret arched an eyebrow. "Well, that's the South for you. Other state fairs had movie stars and vaudeville shows, but down here we had preachers and revivalists." She sobered and laid her hand on my knee. "Of course, you know she was born as Ruth Lurie to a patient at Pritchard Hospital."

Just over my shoulder, Griff's camera whirred to life.

"Yes," I said. "Then she ran away in 1934 when she was seventeen years old. She went to California. Where she met Charles and married him." My voice sounded so small in the big room. "Only now I'm learning that timeline is a bit off."

"Correct. The truth seems to be that she went to Florence, a town about two hours northwest of here."

Griff cleared his throat, obviously still upset at his failure to dig up this bit of crucial information. I wanted to tell him that I appreciated his dedication to meticulous research, but he had no idea who he'd been up against. My grandmother was a master at pulling the wool over people's eyes, and she'd been at it a hell of a lot longer than any of us could imagine.

"I understand she called herself Ruth Davidson," Margaret Luster went on, her eyes bright. "She told people she was the outlaw Dell Davidson's sister. Is that true?"

I shrugged. "I've heard that but I don't know if it's true. I never heard her mention him. Or Mom. Not that I recall."

Margaret nodded. "At any rate, Florence was where she met Bruna Faulk, the other Hawthorn Sister. Bruna Faulk's mother was from a very prominent local family that made their money in lumber. The Coes."

Coe. I sat up straight, every hair on my body standing on end. Althea glanced at me.

"How would've Ruth and Bruna met?" she asked Margaret. "They were worlds apart, in terms of class."

Margaret chuckled. "Well, this is where my imagination has taken over." Her eyes flashed. "I've developed my own theory about that. Ruth was seventeen and alone in Florence, presumably. She would've been desperate for work, like everybody else during that time. Because Steadfast was a widower and quite elderly, I think she may have been hired for him by the family, either as a housekeeper or cook."

My breath whooshed out of me. If this was true, if Dove had worked for Steadfast Coe, she would've absolutely had the opportunity to kill the old man, giving at least a shred of credibility to the asshole's claim. *Dammit.* I met Althea's grave eyes briefly.

Margaret was still talking. ". . . got started performing together at meetings, I can't imagine. All I know for sure is that Steadfast Coe died in the summer of 1934 and right around the same time was the last appearance of the Hawthorn Sisters at the North Alabama State Fair." Margaret pointed at the faded ad. "From all accounts, that's because Dove—Ruth—left with Charles Jarrod."

"He poached her. Or they fell in love." Althea glanced at me, and I knew we were thinking the same thing: *Or Dove murdered Steadfast and had to get out of town, fast.*

"I'd bet on the poaching," Margaret said. "The Hawthorn Sisters were wildly popular with folks. A big draw, from what I hear."

Griff peered around the camera, also directing his words to me. "Then wouldn't Charles have advertised a former Hawthorn Sister as a new part of his show? But I've seen plenty of old bills they put up around the towns during that time, and Dove wasn't listed on any of them. It wasn't until '35 that her name shows up with his on the bills."

Margaret spoke up again. "But the falling-in-love theory doesn't hold up either. If Charles was just passing through town, they couldn't have fallen in love that quickly. It just doesn't make sense. She and Bruna could've had some sort of falling-out. Maybe over money." She cocked her head to one side. "Even during the Depression, a lot of people gave whatever they had to evangelists who promised them

God's favor, so it's entirely possible that the girls were making very good money."

"Maybe more on a good day than most folks saw in a year," Griff said.

"Makes no sense," I said.

Margaret laced her fingers and leaned forward, her eyes alight. "You have to understand, Eve. In those days, people like the Hawthorn Sisters offered people something of immense value, something more precious than gold."

"Hope," Althea said.

Margaret nodded. "Eve, you should understand that. Because of your work with the foundation."

"I get it, I do. But I don't think Dove left because of a disagreement over money." I leaned forward too, mirroring her. "Margaret, there's something we're not telling you."

She blinked at me.

"There is a reason that we've recently learned about that might've forced Dove to leave Florence and the Hawthorn Sisters to go with Charles."

She sat very still, her hands twisted together, eyes fastened on mine.

"Did you ever hear that Dove . . . that Ruth Davidson may have had anything to do with Steadfast Coe's death? And that she might've possibly stolen a valuable coin from him?"

Her eyes widened. Both hands rose, fluttering up to her chest. "Absolutely not. That's horrendous." She glanced from me to Griff to Althea. "Who would ever dare accuse Dove Jarrod, such a wonderful woman, of such a thing?"

Griff hefted the camera behind us, his tone casual. "Just some gossip we got wind of. Gossip we hope to disprove."

She shook her head. "I warned you, Eve, didn't I? To be careful. Wicked people always seek to destroy the Lord's anointed." She sent pleading looks from Althea to Griff, then back to me. "Who is it? Who's saying those horrible things about her?"

I smiled thinly. "The source is not important."

"Well, it's slander, is what it is. Although . . ." She sat back, a faraway look in her eye.

I leaned forward. "What is it? Is there something you remember?"

"I did hear something about a coin. Not too long ago. Now, what was that story . . ." Her eyes lit up. "That's right. I remember now. The Coe family heir, a young man up in Florence, is running for governor. He's not Bruna's grandson, but one of her brother's, I believe. Anyway, the local news did a piece on him a while back, and he was showing the reporter around his house. I'm not sure, but I think it was actually Steadfast Coe's former home."

My skin rose in goose bumps. If she was right about Dove working for Steadfast, it could've been Dove's home too.

"He gave the news crew full access, showed them every room, top to bottom. Which I thought was . . . bad form. The place is . . ." She wrinkled her nose. "Overdone, in my opinion, more new money than old. Anyway, if I remember correctly, there was a coin collection he was particularly proud of."

Althea, Griff, and I locked eyes. A coin collection. We'd actually stumbled on a lead.

Chapter Sixteen

Florence, Alabama
1934

Saturday morning Ruth had a full breakfast on the dining room table by the time Steadfast lumbered down the stairs. He hooked a suspender over his bent shoulder and eyed the table. It gleamed with china, crystal, and silver all laden with fried veal, oatmeal, poached eggs, and coffee.

Steadfast studied the table and then sat, tucking the monogrammed napkin into his collar. He held up a delicate teacup printed with roses and let out a grunt. She hurried to his chair, poured coffee from a silver pot, and watched him slurp deeply.

She beamed. "There was a little braised chicken left from the other night, but I thought you might prefer the veal." She jumped up. "Oh, I plumb forgot." She ran to the sideboard and fetched a sterling pitcher bursting with white lacy blooms that she'd cut from the hawthorn tree beside the front walk. She placed it in the center of the table and sat.

"There we go." She smiled.

His face hardened and he went still.

"Sir?"

His eyes clouded, and his brows lowered, gathered like thunderclouds.

"Shall I—" she began.

Steadfast pushed back his chair and it clattered to the floor. Quick as a rabbit, she leapt out of hers. He lumbered out of the room and across the front hall. She stood a moment, waiting for what, she didn't know exactly, but all remained quiet. She chewed at her cuticle. He'd looked angry, really angry. Could it be that the sight of a meal all laid out like that made him think of his long-lost wife?

Then she filled with indignation. Steadfast Coe might not get out much, but he knew how folks were suffering. How dare he thumb his nose at a good hot meal when there were so many who went without? He was a monster, that's what. More of a monster than Bug or Asloo or even that lion that had come close to tearing into her flesh for his breakfast.

Steadfast was a coward and a bully, and it might've only been a week, but she'd just about gotten her fill of his nonsense.

She huffed back to her place, reached over, took his plate, and heaped double portions of everything onto it. She topped off his coffee cup, good and black, and gulped it down. Then not bothering with a napkin, ate ferociously. She stopped only when the pitcher on the table exploded.

The blast was not from the old .22. This one came from a shotgun. A veritable cannon, shredding the silver pitcher into ribbons with a deafening clang and filling the air with a shower of white petals and shining water droplets. The pitcher hit the red marble mantel on the far side of the room and Ruth dropped off her chair. She didn't scream. She just cowered under the table, holding on to a leg.

When there was no subsequent shot, she crawled across the Persian rug, through the pantry, and into the kitchen. She ran out the back door, letting the screen door slam behind her, and hid in the elderberry bushes. Coe didn't follow her out. In fact, the house remained so still, she began to worry.

What was he doing in there? Was he pointing the gun at his head now, readying himself to pull the trigger a second time? What would become of her then? Surely Bruna and her family would blame her. Maybe even have her thrown in jail for not watching the old man.

After about twenty minutes, she thought she could detect a series of muffled thumps from inside the house. Then all was quiet again. Should she risk going back? Maybe. When he escaped, he usually did so out the back, and there were enough obstacles—a shed, a clothesline, an old well, and the elderberries—that he never got too far. But if he made it out the front, he could easily make his way down the road, straight into town and all the way to the river.

She crept from the bushes and skirted around the side of the house. She came to a dead stop when she saw him. His suspenders now hanging to his knees, Steadfast held an ax, the head of which was buried in the trunk of a tree just to the side of the walk. It was the hawthorn tree. The tree she'd plucked the blooms from and arranged in the pitcher.

Steadfast adjusted his stance, ripped the ax free, and swung again. But it was awkward work. The tree was low to the ground, and although shrunken with age, the old man still stood at least six feet tall. Because of that, the ax kept missing its mark, glancing off branches and the trunk.

Eventually he must've sensed her presence, because he turned and narrowed his eyes at her. "What's the matter with you? Didn't you have no mama?" he called out.

Ruth felt herself flush hot and her scalp go tight. Now that she was close, the scent of the blossoms and the fresh-cut wood made her head hurt too.

He let out a laugh that sputtered into a cough. "Don't you know nothing, girl?"

She came a few steps closer, keeping one eye on the ax. "About what, sir?"

"You cut off blooms from one side of the tree and it's all uneven. You can cut more, but then it's wrong again, and you have to try again to make it right. You can't just pick a couple of blossoms off a tree like that. It's irresponsible! I used to tell that girl the same thing. Told her over and over, but she didn't pay no mind either. It's got to go!"

He took another whack at the trunk, and Ruth covered her mouth to keep from protesting. It wasn't her place, she knew, to keep a man from cutting down a tree on his own property, if that was what he took a mind to do, but the tree was large for a hawthorn and a sight to behold, covered in snowy white blooms. She felt sure Bruna's mother would not be pleased.

She needn't have worried, though. On Steadfast's final swing, the iron blade hit a knot and bounced back, hitting him square in the forehead. He dropped like a rag doll.

Ruth screamed and ran to him.

When she fell to her knees in the dirt beside him, she saw to her great relief that he hadn't been knocked out after all. There was a lump all right, a great big egg-shaped protrusion that was already turning dark purple and a gash over that spilling blood into the crags and craters of his old face. But he was still clear-eyed, mumbling and struggling to stand.

Ruth tried to get a look at his head, but he shooed her away.

"It's got to come down. You ain't gonna stop me."

She backed away. Watched him struggle to his feet and pick up the ax. He turned so he was facing her. She stood there, breathing hard, and he remained as well, stooped and staring at her with his baleful, unblinking blue eyes, the head of his ax glinting in the sun. He looked like he was considering his options.

And one of them might be murder.

Ruth moved back. One step, two. Then she turned and ran.

Chapter Seventeen

Birmingham, Alabama
Present

I might've only had two and a half days to find the coin, but strangely, all I could think about as we pulled away from Margaret Luster's house was more barbecue. Pulled, sliced, or falling off ribs—I didn't care. I was starving, and I'd barely had an appetite yesterday. All I wanted now was to focus on something other than Dove and the missing coin. Classic Southern smoked meats seemed like a great alternative.

"The best in Birmingham," I said.

Althea wheeled her car onto the highway. "Oh boy, you've been fully indoctrinated, haven't you? That was quick."

"Challenge accepted." Griff leaned between our seats. "What are we talking—Full Moon? Jim 'N Nick's? Golden Rule? Because there's wildly varying opinions on the matter. And when you say 'the best' are we talking the best ribs? Or the best sauce? Because sauce is a whole category unto itself. And then there's coleslaw, okay. We haven't even mentioned coleslaw."

As Althea merged into traffic, I relaxed into my seat. I was happy to be talking about something innocuous for the first time in twenty-four hours. And still. I couldn't help but think about our visit with Margaret

Luster. On our way out, she'd pressed a memory stick of all the Jarrod tapes into my hands. I'd given it to Griff.

In downtown Birmingham, we ate at a place called Full Moon, then headed north on 43. Our destination was Florence, the city where the Hawthorn Sisters had begun and ended their short-lived ministry. And where Jason Faulk lived, Steadfast Coe's only apparent descendant, nascent gubernatorial candidate, and possessor of one TV-worthy coin collection.

In the back with his earbuds in, Griff tapped away on his laptop, loading the footage he'd gotten into the editing software. He'd offered to let me listen to Margaret Luster's tapes of Charles and Dove, but I demurred. The thought of their voices—their secrets and lies folded into every syllable they spoke or sang—filling my ears right now made my skin crawl. I'd leave that part of our amateur investigation to Griff for the time being.

"Okay, so what's our play in Florence?" Althea asked. "We need to be careful. Jason Faulk's running for office. He really could stand to benefit from recovering the coin—and solving the mystery surrounding his great-great-grandfather's death. Setting himself up as hometown hero in order to sweep the election. He might be behind all this."

I took a breath and let it out slowly. "But he's our only connection. I think we definitely pay him a visit but proceed with caution. Somehow—without giving anything away—we've got to confirm the coin is really from his collection and try to get an idea of where it might be."

"On the other hand, if he's not involved, he may be willing to help us find it."

"Possibly. He also may help us set up an elaborate sting to nail the guy for extortion. All the while keeping the whole operation completely under wraps."

She gave me a rueful smile. "Sure. No big deal."

"No big deal whatsoever." I sighed and stared out the window.

Griff leaned forward, one earbud dangling. "Hey, fun fact. Did you know that during the Great Depression when the banks were failing, a lot of folks hid their money and valuables in their houses? Mattresses, doors, false cabinets, and loose floorboards. And the old standby, some of them buried their stuff in a hole in the backyard."

"Makes sense," Althea said.

He put his hand on my shoulder and I shivered involuntarily. "Dove was young and didn't have many resources. Odds are, if she did steal the coin, and she did really live in the Coe house, she could have easily hid it there, where she knew it'd be safe."

"If so, I'm sure the Coes have already turned that house upside down," I said.

"Couldn't hurt to try one more time." He popped his earbud in again and sat back.

I glanced at Althea. "You know, Griff and I can handle this. You can head home. I won't mind. And I'm sure your family is missing you."

She tucked a dark curl behind her ear and snorted. "Listen. Jay's practically giddy to have a couple of days where he can give the kids Hot Pockets, park them in front of his iPad, and watch all the ESPN he wants. He's always on me for not being social enough, for never doing any girls' trips. He says I think I'm human bubble wrap that's going to keep the kids from shattering. And that it's going to backfire on me one day."

"You're a great mom," I said. "That's obvious."

She gave me a wry smile. "Honestly, I'm not. I'm a slightly better than mediocre, highly obsessive mom. I'm just messed up enough from not having a mother that I try to make up for it with my own kids." She gripped the steering wheel resolutely.

"Not much of a girls' trip," I said.

Althea drummed her fingers on the steering wheel. "This is way more fun than lying on the beach with a virgin mai tai and listening to women talk about *The Bachelor*. I mean . . ." She draped an arm across the seat and tilted her head in Griff's direction. "If you think about it, we actually have our own real-life bachelor right there in the back seat. No disrespect to my own darling, sexy husband, but if you ask me, that dude's on the entirely wrong end of the camera."

I snuck a look back at Griff. Earbuds still in and eyes locked on his laptop, he swayed in time with whatever he was listening to. Maybe Margaret Luster's tapes. Whatever it was, he had the look of someone utterly enthralled and inspired by his work. I had to admit, it was ridiculously sexy.

"He likes you," Althea said, dropping her voice even more. "You know that, right?"

"He's a really talented director. We work well together."

She raised one dark eyebrow. "You're all business, Eve, aren't you?"

"Somebody in this outfit's got to keep their feet on the ground."

But she was right. I was all business. And maybe I had been for so long that I'd forgotten how to be human. But as much as I was drawn to Griff, I didn't have time to deal with those feelings or whatever they implied. I had just enough time to figure out how I was going to convince Jason Faulk, a complete stranger, to cooperate with me and help me locate this missing coin.

Althea flicked on her blinker and switched lanes. "So your mom and Danny are true believers, huh? Into the signs and wonders and miracle thing?"

I snapped back to the present and flushed uncomfortably. "Mom is. Danny's hard to read. He's an outsider by nature. I know there are times when he gets scared . . . or feels desperate, and he starts in with the whole God-is-going-to-fix-everything routine."

"But you don't believe that," Althea said.

"I did. At one time. When I was younger."

"Well, technically there's nothing that says you have to believe in order to keep the foundation running as a functional business entity, does it? And even if Dove did some unsavory things in her past, that doesn't negate the good she did later. Right?"

"I don't know." I sighed. "In this case, it very literally might do just that."

She glanced sympathetically at me. "Which especially sucks after all you did to protect your mom and brother."

On the other side of the window, the land had flattened and there were fields with rows and rows of broken brown stalks. Tufts of cotton clung to the stalks. Clumps of it scattered along the side of the road. "It's going to be a hell of a thing if the truth comes out," I said.

Althea looked thoughtful. "Sometimes you've got to tear something down before you can build it back up again."

Was she talking about the foundation or my mother? I didn't know, but honestly, it didn't matter. Not now. I wasn't willing to allow either of them to be torn down. Their survival had become my own.

A few minutes later, the river—the wide singing Tennessee—came into view.

"Ah . . ." Althea flipped down her visor against the setting sun. "Here we are."

I looked across the choppy expanse of blue-black water. There was a long trussed bridge that connected the southern bluff with the rising hills of the northern bank. I could see signs of the town, rows of streetlights nestled in lush trees. What were the odds of us actually being able to find a coin that had been missing for eighty years? What were the odds that I could somehow use that coin to lure the asshole who attacked me and keep him from talking?

They didn't seem good.

Griff leaned over the seat, one earbud out and grinning triumphantly, and said, "459 North Court Street." He handed me his phone. "You're on hold for Jason Faulk, Steadfast Coe's great-great-grandson."

Jason Faulk's crisp assistant came back on the line to politely inform me that his boss was saving his remarks to the press for the event that evening. Before I could correct him, he put me on hold again. By then, we were on Court Street, rolling past the back of the imposing brick house, a Georgian antebellum with a sprawling lawn that appeared to take up the whole block between Court and the next street over. The place was crawling with activity. An ant line of uniformed workers ferried white folding chairs out of vans, up the back portico, and into the house.

Jason Faulk was having a party.

"Hello?" The assistant at the other end of the line.

"I'm here."

"We're asking press to enter in the back and collect their badges in the kitchen. We'll have a brief pool when Mr. Faulk's ready to announce, so you might want to bring cameras."

"Announce?"

The man huffed impatiently. "His run for governor. You are press, correct?"

"Absolutely and thank you so much." I hung up. "Hey, guys. We should find a hotel so we can change. We just got invited to a party."

Chapter Eighteen

Florence, Alabama
1934

Ruth wandered around downtown Florence for a couple of hours until it started to rain. When she returned to the Coe house she stood, staring in stupefaction. The hawthorn tree was now in two pieces—the lower half of the jagged, chopped-off trunk and the top half, which was taking up a good portion of the front yard. The head of the ax was buried in the trunk, just above the roots.

What was Edith going to say when she saw this mess? Ruth would be fired for sure.

Ruth saw a shadow pass in front of the parlor window and, in spite of her worry, felt weak with relief. Steadfast hadn't wandered off. And he hadn't shot himself or dropped dead from apoplexy. But he had to be exhausted. She hoped that meant he'd go straight to sleep.

She crept onto the front porch, retrieved the key from under the brick, and locked the front door. She huddled on the swing, sheltered from the downpour, and waited. Steadfast couldn't escape out the front. If he ran out the back, he'd get stuck in the elderberries.

And the house faced east. The sun would wake her before Edith showed up for her regular Sunday morning visit with her father . . .

Ruth did wake early, before the sun even, and crept back into the house. She cleaned up the cold food and dirty dishes and gathered the drooping remains of the hawthorn flowers. She mopped up water and hid the shredded silver pitcher in the coal scuttle in the kitchen. When Edith arrived, yoo-hooing in the front hall, Ruth was already wearing the purloined gray coat and quaking with nerves.

"Where are you off to?" Edith asked.

"To meet friends." It was the truth. She had been thinking of tracking down Dell.

"At church?" Edith pursed her lips and carefully set her pocketbook on an inlaid demilune table. She was all angles, with carefully curled graying hair and disapproving eyes. Bruna, curvy and soft, must have taken after her father.

Ruth just smiled.

Edith cocked her head, appraising her. "Bruna said you've taken Mr. Coe well in hand. That you have a way with him." She glanced around the hallway. "You certainly have a way with a mop and bucket."

"He's not so bad."

"He's a devil," Edith said. "And a menace. I see he's taken the hawthorn down."

"Yes, ma'am, I—"

"No need to explain. I know why he did it." She glanced up the dark stairs. "He suffers from an anxiety neurosis. That's why he hides those ridiculous coins. But the tree . . . it's such a loss. I suppose the fact that his beloved wife planted it the day I was born wasn't a good enough reason to leave it standing." She huffed and turned back to Ruth. "Be back to the house by six. Be prompt and come back as you left it. Not drunken or reeking of smoke." She sniffed. "And leave any young men you might collect back in town."

There was no sign of Dell or his gang downtown. At the diner, Trowbridge's, she encountered a little boy of ten or eleven, standing on a ladder and holding up a Bible. He was shouting and waving the big black book and had drawn a substantial crowd. The boy reminded Ruth of Bug; he had the same freckles and bad teeth and could've used a good scrubbing. This boy, however, spoke in as sonorous a voice as a person could while shouting.

He told all the people that down yonder, around the corner, in a tent they'd set up that morning, there'd be more preaching by a man named Charles Jarrod. There'd be singing too, he said with a wink, which sent a ripple of appreciation through the crowd.

Ruth was curious. She wandered to the lot where they'd set up the tent. Inside, it swarmed with workers who were setting up long benches made of planks and tree stumps. Straw covered the ground in front of a big makeshift wooden stage at the end of the tent.

"Have you seen him before?" a girl about her age asked.

Ruth turned. "Me?"

The girl nodded. "My aunt saw him in Memphis. She said he's a double for Errol Flynn."

"Well, what do you know," Ruth said, which was about the extent of her knowledge and opinion of Errol Flynn. She'd never set foot in a movie house.

She left the girl and wandered behind the stage. Underneath was a space of about three feet, the dirt layered with straw. It looked warm and dry and cozy. The perfect place for a nap. After her miserable night on Steadfast's porch, that was all she could think about. She crawled beneath the stage, almost to the middle, and shut her eyes. She was asleep in seconds.

She awoke later to a great shaking and crashing. Footsteps, she realized, shaking off the haze of sleep. A lot of them, on the stage above her. She'd slept through the start of Charles Jarrod's service. She crawled to the gap and peered out, but all she could see were feet. Two pairs of shoes, to be precise—a lady's black pumps and a shiny pair of wine-colored leather brogues.

"He's already paid up, so you've got to do it." It was a man, the owner of the brogues.

"I'm all nerves, Arthur. My voice is going to come out shaky." A girl.

"I told you to take a nip. But you don't listen to me. And now look at you."

"I can't do it. There's too many people."

Ruth cocked her head in astonishment. She knew that voice—it belonged to Bruna Faulk. She scooted closer to the gap and tried to get a line of sight.

"Just close your eyes and pretend like it's the heavenly host," said the man. "And if you choke, just pretend you've got the Spirit, run off the stage and we'll git."

Bruna giggled. "Nice way for a preacher's son to talk."

Ruth crawled out from under the stage, shook the straw from her coat, and smoothed her hair. "Oh! Well, hey there, Bruna."

Bruna clapped a hand over her mouth.

The man—a boy actually—looked Ruth up and down. "Who's this?"

Bruna brushed straw from Ruth's coat. "Ruth! What in heaven's name were you doing under there?"

"You steal something, girl?" the boy said.

"Arthur!" Bruna swatted him. "Of course not. She's our nurse. Grandy's nurse."

Ruth smiled at the boy—handsome with curly brown hair that he'd slicked back, well-cut navy trousers, and a mustard-gold tie. She stuck out her hand. "Ruth Davidson."

He shook it. "Arthur Holt."

"Arthur's the son of Reverend Holt over at First Methodist. He signed me up to make some summer money singing for Mr. Jarrod's show."

Ruth grinned. "I'm pleased to meet you."

He grinned back. She liked the way his eyes danced. He looked like a couple of drops of whiskey in a glass of lemonade. Like he could be trouble, but in a good way. She wondered if he was the boyfriend Bruna had mentioned the first day they met.

"What are you singing? Because I know quite a few songs. I'm happy to go up with you. Throw in a little harmony. I used to sing with Dr. Asloo's outfit sometimes. When the animals got too rowdy." She smiled from Arthur to Bruna.

Bruna's shoulders sagged in relief. "You'd do that? Oh, Ruth, that'd be wonderful."

Arthur glanced at Bruna. "We're getting paid for a soloist, not a duo."

"I don't have to get paid. I could just go up with you and move my mouth like I'm singing, if you'd prefer that. I'm used to being onstage."

"You know 'Just a Closer Walk with Thee'?"

"Like the back of my hand. We learned every hymn there was at chapel in Pri—" Ruth caught herself. "Where I grew up."

Bruna took Arthur's hand. "Let her go up with me. Brother Jarrod won't care. He won't even know the difference."

Arthur gave Ruth a cursory glance. "Well, she's passable to look at. I guess if you're off-key, maybe that'll be something to distract them." He winked, but Ruth wasn't altogether sure he hadn't been serious.

They climbed the stage and, after an introduction by a man in a brown suit, sang the hymn. Ruth kept her eyes trained on Bruna, blending her voice in perfect harmony with Bruna's clear soprano. After the applause and a chorus of amens, Bruna started "The Old Rugged Cross."

Ruth joined, her glance alighting on the preacher. Charles Jarrod stood in the shadows on the far side of the stage. He was tall with thick hair, commanding eyes, and a noble chin. If he looked like Errol Flynn, Ruth thought, then she could see why the girls went for the film star.

Jarrod was watching her too. Just her, with a thoughtful expression. The kind of look that made her trip over the next stanza.

Ruth averted her gaze to the rows of benches filled with people. It was dark outside the tent, the inside lit only by blazing oil lanterns set on barrels. It wasn't so different from the way the crowd looked at Dr. Asloo's show. She liked their expressions—mouths parted slightly, eyes wide, faces reflecting the lights from the stage. Now she and Bruna were the lions putting on the show.

And Arthur, Bruna's friend, was standing right in the middle of the crowd filming it all on one of those portable movie cameras. Like they were real film stars.

She sang now without even thinking. She felt only lightness and strength. The words flowed out of her and she felt the air around her turn warm, like a caress all over her body. Her head felt light, her vision blurred, and the people below her went smeary. If only the words of the song were true. If only there were a different life than this one. A life of beauty, of clean things and sweet smells and pink-tinged clouds.

Oh, how she'd love to disappear into that life . . .

A woman near the entrance of the tent suddenly leapt to her feet, her hand thrust in the air. "A feather! A feather! It just fell on me! Right from heaven above!"

Ruth blinked and snapped to attention and both girls stopped singing. The piano music trailed off just after. The woman was pushing her way past the others on the bench, still holding something aloft. She ran up the side aisle, her face shining, and thrust the object at the girls.

"It's an angel's feather," she gasped. "Angels are with us here. Tonight, in this very place!"

Ruth gulped and glanced at Bruna. Then Charles Jarrod strode onto the stage. He took the object from the woman's fingers and held it up for the crowd.

"It's a feather," he said gravely. He laid his hand gently on the woman's head. "The Lord bless you. You are His child, and this is His promise to you." He addressed the crowd. "This is a sign for all of you. The Almighty is here tonight, and He is watching each and every one of you." He nodded at Bruna and Ruth. "The chorus, one more time, girls."

The piano started up, and the girls sang again. As they did, people poured down the aisle to the stage and dropped coins in a silver plate at their feet. Jarrod told them to sing another hymn, and the pile of coins grew.

When the stream of worshippers seemed like it was abating, Jarrod stepped back and stood beside Ruth. Even though he was several feet away, she felt electrified. She could feel the warmth of his body and smell his menthol aftershave. She turned and met his eyes, which were all at once tender and strong, and for a moment, she imagined, also strangely shy.

"Look at you," he said.

She didn't know how to answer. But he didn't seem to mind. He took her hand and, unfurling her fingers, dropped the tiny white feather into her palm. The moment passed as quick as it came, and he was gone, ambling to the far side of the stage.

Later, when they came off the stage, Ruth showed the feather to Bruna.

"I've never seen an angel's feather," Bruna whispered reverentially.

Ruth started to laugh, but then she saw that Arthur and Bruna both appeared as serious as if they'd just attended a funeral. She clamped her mouth shut. She couldn't quite believe it, but they seemed to have taken the whole episode entirely seriously.

Ruth nodded, but let the feather drop to the ground. It was only a bit of common down after all, plucked from under the wing of a goose.

Chapter Nineteen

Florence, Alabama
Present

We got a couple of rooms at the Hampton Inn at the south end of Florence. Althea and I doubled up, and Griff took the room next door. After donning my black dress from the night before and reapplying makeup to the swelling over my eye, I convened with them in the lobby.

We agreed that, while trying to talk to Jason Faulk—the freewheeling bachelor of Florence running for governor—at his party wasn't ideal, we couldn't afford to waste any time. So, less than two hours later, we were casually strolling through the back entrance of Jason Faulk's elegant home, where we snagged a few unclaimed press lanyards from the kitchen table and lost ourselves in the crowd.

It was a raucous gathering, the spacious jewel-toned rooms filled with people knocking back drinks and shouting hellos across gleaming antiques juxtaposed against sleek modern pieces. Althea, Griff, and I positioned ourselves in the wide front hall, which was decorated with massive color-block canvases. It was an oddly large space—in fact, the whole house was, with its soaring ceilings and vast open rooms.

I couldn't help thinking that the man who attacked me could be here, at this very party—watching me and stalking me from room to room as I investigated the mystery Dove had laid out for me. Truth was, the idea freaked me out more than a little bit. That and the knowledge that every minute that passed was putting me, the foundation, and my family one step closer to ruin. I lifted a glass of red wine off a waiter's passing tray and took one gulp. Then another, longer one.

Althea handed me a campaign brochure from a stack spread on a side table. It was a slickly produced one-sheet listing Jason Faulk's many accomplishments: degrees from Duke and Sewanee, the lesser Southern Ivies. A stint at a respected law practice, then for former governor Barnish, who'd been quietly invited to leave office a few months into his administration because of some financial shenanigans.

I considered this. Faulk must not have been tainted by Barnish's misdeeds. In fact, if this party was any indication, he was still a much-loved hometown guy. And from the looks of the impeccably designed house, he was still living high off of Coe lumber money. But obviously, he was not the kind of guy who was content to rest on Daddy's (or Great-Great-Granddaddy's) laurels. He was clearly doing everything within his power to keep himself at the top of Alabama's who's who list. It looked like everybody in northwestern Alabama and their brother was packed into the house.

But I had to keep this in mind: there was the chance that Faulk had been behind my attack at the hospital. He could've picked up some less-than-legal tricks from his former boss Barnish and, figuring he could extort me into finding the coin for him, sent that asshole after me. Like Margaret said, I needed to be careful. But I also needed to find that coin collection.

"Let's split up," I suggested to Althea and Griff. "See what we can find."

They agreed, Althea heading back to the dining room and Griff to the parlor. I moved toward the back of the house, eventually finding myself in the deserted, tastefully renovated kitchen. On the far wall, I opened a door, old and warped the slightest bit, and slipped in.

I pulled the door shut behind me. The room was not a pantry, more like a closet with towers of cardboard file boxes and metal shelving units lining the walls. The shelves held cases of beer and boxes of wine and what looked like a jumble of household equipment. I breathed in the musty, uncirculated air and sighed, feeling the tingling sensation in my right arm again. I rubbed it, taking in the environment. This very well could've been the maid's room. It was just the right size, and close to the kitchen. Which meant, if Margaret Luster's theory was right, Dove may have slept in this very spot eighty years ago.

I lifted the lids of a few boxes, but all they held were files. On the shelves, I sifted through the flashlights, extension cords, batteries, and various pieces of workout equipment. There were a couple of antique items too. A pair of fireplace andirons. A brass spittoon. A shoebox full of rusty, vaguely menacing-looking vintage kitchen gadgets.

I looked out the window. The backyard was flat and, except for the U-shaped driveway, devoid of any vegetation other than grass and the occasional tree. I guess Jason Faulk hadn't gotten around to landscaping yet. I wondered if Dove's view had been the same. Had she felt lonely in this little room? Had she lain in bed, plotting ways to make money? Cooking up her traveling-evangelist act? Planning the big con?

I turned my back to the window, my gaze falling on the door. It was nothing special, just an old paneled door layered with decades of paint and fitted with a simple bronze knob and plate. Below the doorknob was a keyhole with one of those old-fashioned bronze skeleton keys. I stared at it, faintly mesmerized until the door swung open and I jumped.

Griff stuck his head in. "There you are. Find anything?"

"Nope. You scared me."

"Sorry." He slipped in and eyed the file boxes. "You gotta wonder what kind of secrets he's hiding in there."

"Just because he worked for a cheat doesn't automatically make him one," I said, sounding more defensive than I intended.

"Doesn't mean that he's not, either. Be careful."

"I know, I know." I rubbed my arm again absently. It had started doing its tingling, throbbing thing as soon as I'd set foot in this house, I realized. Steadfast Coe's house, where my grandmother might have lived for a time. It was a leap, but what if she'd hidden the coin here? What if somehow my arm . . . what . . . sensed it?

Word of knowledge, the true believers called it. The thing Danny referred to last night. When a part of your body received a message from God or the Spirit or the other side. A word of knowledge might be a sign, but it was also more than that. You were supposed to do something with the sign—heal somebody, impart information. Uncover a secret . . .

I let go of my arm. I was losing it, I really was. Reverting back to old habits and childish superstitions because of all the strain. I needed to focus.

The coin, Eve. You have two days to find it.

Tick-tock.

"I'm going to check out the upstairs," I said to Griff. "Maybe you should cover the first floor."

He nodded. "You got it."

Back in the cavernous hallway, I climbed a sweeping Persian-carpeted staircase. The expansive upper hallway—covered in an ancient paper of grapevines and foxes and smelling faintly of mildew and mothballs—looked like it had escaped Jason's interior design efforts. So, too, did the first bedroom I came to. It was done up in mint green, wallpaper, bedding, and curtains. The room smelled of ancient dust.

Near the windows was a sort of stand with a wooden box resting on top, a display box with a glass lid. I moved closer. Rows of coins winked at me. Gold, silver, and copper, thin and delicate with unfamiliar engravings of Native American headdresses and eagles and women with ropes of braids, the coins were nestled into perfectly matched slots cut into a blue velvet board. Then I noticed something irregular about the display.

One of the slots—the one in the center—was empty.

Chapter Twenty

Tuscaloosa, Alabama
1934

Reverend Robert Singley had a dilemma. What he must do was clear: bring his harlot Ruth home where she belonged. To him. But he didn't know where she had got off to, and he had no idea where to begin his search.

He meditated upon the problem, mulling it over by day as he walked the streets of town, at night praying at his bed on his knees for a divine answer. After seven long days, he concluded that when Ruth ran from Pritchard, she likely needed money. And as generally the only work was in the textile mills, she'd probably headed to one of the many that dotted the state. Possibly the one in Birmingham, the town closest to Tuscaloosa.

Ruth working in a mill seemed altogether reasonable to him. And if there was one thing he knew beyond a shadow of a doubt, it was that his Ruth, his love, was a reasonable girl. Hadn't she confessed to her impurity, her moral corruption, at the moment of her impending marriage to his nephew? This certainly spoke to her having a measure of sound judgment and sensible ways.

He closed down his sister's house, gassed up her car, and drove the fifty-three miles to the city. He got a room downtown at the Thomas Jefferson, had a dinner of steak, potatoes, and scotch, then went to sleep. The next morning, he drove to the mill and asked to speak to the foreman.

The foreman, a dyspeptic-looking man wearing a crushed-felt hat and a sour expression, hadn't heard of Ruth. Nor had any of the women or little boys and girls he pulled aside at quitting time. One older girl, dressed in striped overalls, two greasy pigtails hanging down her back, caught his eye. When the coast was clear, he waved a dollar at her and ushered her into his car. Once there, he issued two quick slaps across each temple to quiet her down. She stared at him with large eyes, though not quite as frightened as he thought they should be.

He patiently ran through his litany again. "She's about your height. Would be sixteen or seventeen by now. Name's Ruth Lurie. Red hair, skin like milk, with a regal bearing. The bearing of a lady. If you saw her, you'd know her. When she's in a room, ain't nobody looking at nothing else."

"Well." The girl made a show of rolling her eyes. "How nice for her. But I told ya. I ain't seen nobody with no *regal bearing* at this place." She chewed on her lip. "Although now that I'm thinking about it, I do know other girls you might like. And they'd treat you plenty nice."

"I'm not looking for a whore." He sat back on his haunches and scanned the length of the girl's dirty overalls.

"They're nice though, these ones. They follow the preachers, the tent men that go up and down setting up meetings. These ladies is cheap and clean and don't cause no trouble. They cater to the Lord's men." She straightened. "As a matter of fact, there's one in town now. Brother Comer, from over in South Carolina. Plenty a ladies along with him with milky whatnot, I can assure you. I can take you, if you want. He's set up just over in Pell City, if I remember correct."

"I don't want a *whore*. I'm looking for my wife!" He struck her hard, this time with his fist, so she'd get the message loud and clear.

But truth be told, after discussing Ruth's many admirable physical attributes, not to mention being in such close quarters with this girl who smelled of cotton lint and kerosene, he'd gotten himself an itch. *The* itch. He held his hands up, and she scrambled back, bumping her head on the window behind her.

"Would you like a present?" he asked affably.

She narrowed her eyes. "A present?"

He removed his black hat and pointed to the brim. Tied there was what looked like a narrow pink satin ribbon. "This would look nice on the ends of those pigtails, don't you think?" He unwound the pink satin ribbon, the tie from his dead sister's robe, and held it between his hands like an offering. "It's plenty long enough."

And indeed, it was.

Chapter Twenty-One

Florence, Alabama
Present

I lifted the lid of the coin box, slowly so it wouldn't creak, and leaned in for a closer look. Coins of all sizes and colors nestled snug in their slots. But they were dull and clouded. No one's cherished possessions, from the look of it. Clearly, they hadn't been cared for in a long while.

And then there was that empty slot.

"Trying to clean me out?" a man said behind me. I turned so fast I knocked the box and it wobbled on its stand. My arm shot out, the right one, and I caught it just in time.

He didn't seem perturbed by my gaffe, just kept his appraising eyes on me. "Or do you just happen to be a random numismatist who crashed my party for a closer look at my exceedingly rare coin collection?"

He had a deep voice softened by a honeyed accent. His face was grown-up-frat-boy handsome with premature wrinkles around his eyes, probably from too many poolside summers and Aspen winters. He had artfully mussed blond hair and TV-ready teeth. Handsome in a way. Like central casting's idea of a young upstart governor.

"I'm so sorry," I blurted. "I didn't realize anyone was in here."

He glanced at the box. "They're error coins, struck on the wrong metal or stamped off-center. One's a mule. Nickel on the front, dime on the back."

He opened a dresser drawer and drew out a small silver flask. He held it out, but I shook my head. "During the renovation, I moved them up here, even though any thief worth their salt wouldn't bother to steal them. Altogether, they're probably only worth a few thousand. Now the missing one . . ." He gestured at the empty middle slot. "That one was priceless. Or so the story goes."

My heart nearly shot out of my chest. "No kidding."

He knocked back a slug from the flask. "Mm, yeah. The Flowing Hair Dollar. Exceptionally rare coin. Minted in 1794 and modeled after the Spanish dollar. In 2013, a Flowing Hair of lesser quality and value than my great-great-grandfather's coin sold at auction for over ten million. I've been told that Steadfast's would probably go for fourteen to fifteen. Which would mean, if we could find the damn thing, I could finally afford to renovate the rest of this house."

He chuckled, but I was full-on shaking now, nerves getting the best of me. "It's lost?"

"So the story goes. People around here have been gossiping about what happened to it forever, but it's impossible to separate fact from fiction. Sometimes I think my great-great-grandfather made the whole thing up. Like he never owned it to begin with." He narrowed his eyes. "You're into coins?"

"I'm not a numa . . . numa—" I faltered.

"Numismatist. Yeah, I see that now. You're press." He dropped one hand in the pocket of his slim-fitting gray wool pants. Gestured with the flask. "So, you're just plain ol' snooping."

"No, actually." I looped my badge over my head and tossed it on the dresser. "I'm not press either."

His body tensed, eyes locked on mine. I could tell he was bracing himself for bad news.

"My name is Eve Candler. I'm the granddaughter of a woman who I think may have worked for your great-great-grandfather, Steadfast Coe."

He slumped. Gave me another look, then let out an incredulous laugh. "Wait. What?"

"Her name was Dove Jarrod, but she went by Ruth Davidson back then."

He shook his head. "You know, they said running for office would bring the cranks out of the woodwork, but this is one for the books." He caught himself. "Not that you're a crank. That I know of. It's just . . . the one thing I didn't expect was anyone showing up with a family connection. Most of my family are . . . not interested in affairs such as these," he concluded weakly.

I just stood there, twisting my fingers. Anything I said in response to that would definitely be wrong.

"You're from California, correct?" he asked.

I straightened. "How did you—"

"Oh, I know of Dove Jarrod," he said. "A.k.a. Ruth Davidson, a.k.a. one half of the Hawthorn Sisters. And you're right. She did work for Steadfast, for a short time."

In response to my stunned look, he gave me that photo-ready young-governor look. Recovered already, apparently, from the shock of finding me snooping in his coin collection.

"Honey, don't look so surprised. You're on the buckle of the Bible Belt and it's a big old shiny rhinestone one. If there's one thing we're proud of around here, it's our hometown evangelists." He straightened an expensive-looking lavender tie. "Me, I'm a good Southern boy. Got my letter down at First Baptist, walked the aisle so many times I could sing "Just as I Am" backward in pig Latin, and could beat the Apostle Paul's ass at an old-time sword drill until he wept like a baby."

"Wow," I said. I hadn't expected this.

"Jason Faulk. And for the record, I'm impressed you got the number of 'greats' right." He offered his hand and we shook. "To what do I owe this honor?"

I hesitated. My story was ready to go—simple and mostly the truth—but still, now that the moment was here, jittery nerves were muddling my thoughts.

I squared my shoulders and lifted my chin, mustering whatever charm remained in me after the past twenty-four hours. "Actually, Mr. Faulk, I need your help. I'm making a documentary about my grandmother, for our foundation, and I wanted to ask you a few questions about her time here. If you happen to know anything."

He cocked his head. "Sounds intriguing. I'll do whatever I can to help."

"I've heard some rumors—"

"Oh, God. Not those." He grinned. "And it's Jason. Please."

I managed a tense smile in return. "Some rumors about that missing coin . . . and my grandmother."

"That she might have stolen it?"

"That, and that she might have . . ." I swallowed. ". . . actually, been the one who killed him."

He looked thoughtful. "I can tell you the gossip I've heard. But it's just a bunch of old-timers telling ghost stories."

"Anything could help."

He sat on a small silk bench at the foot of the bed. "The older people around here used to talk," he began carefully. "Some of them said your grandmother may have had something to do with Steadfast's disappearance. But I've also heard it was his daughter or my great-uncle. Some people have even claimed that . . . get this, Dell Davidson, the outlaw, passed through Florence back then and while he was here, offed Old Steadfast." He rolled his eyes. "I don't know, honestly. When somebody disappears, people like to talk. Build tall tales. But in the end, that's all it is, talk."

I nodded. None of this helped me really, but his words did set me at ease. Or at least closer to a sense of ease than I'd expected. Maybe I could trust this guy after all.

"The truth is probably a lot simpler," Jason said. "Steadfast probably had some type of dementia, maybe even Alzheimer's, and wandered off. He definitely had OCD. Did you know that?"

"No."

"Undiagnosed, obviously. It wasn't something doctors knew how to treat back then. But my grandfather told me that's why Steadfast collected the error coins. He obsessed over the mistakes, and his compulsion was to collect and hide them, here in the house. At some point along the way, he came across a Flowing Hair, not an error coin that I know of. But my assumption is that he hid it anyway along with the others."

I contemplated this.

Jason scratched his jaw. "In the sixties, my grandfather found two of those coins behind fireplace bricks. And I found one when I was a kid, jammed up under a windowsill in the bedroom across the hall. To tell you the truth, I never thought anyone stole the Flowing Hair. I've always believed it was right here in the house."

I dropped down on the bench beside him. "Are you serious? You really think it's here?"

"Steadfast was nothing if not consistent with his compulsion. I seriously doubt your grandmother had anything to do with its disappearance. Or his death. She was just a girl, right? There's no way she could've killed him and hidden his body."

Relief coursed through me. Jason Faulk didn't believe I had the coin. And it was clear he hadn't sent anyone after me.

I inhaled. "Can I be honest with you?"

"I wish you would."

"Yesterday I was attacked at an event honoring my grandmother in Tuscaloosa. I couldn't see the man who did it, but he told me he had Steadfast's remains. His bones. He showed them to me."

His mouth opened and he let out a brief "huh" of disbelief.

"He said he wanted to ruin Dove's reputation and her foundation. He said that unless I gave him the coin that she supposedly stole in three days, he was going to take the bones—and a signed confession from Dove—to the police and tell them that she murdered Steadfast." I took a breath. "I've got two more days to find the coin or I'm toast."

He looked at the spot above my eye. "So that's where you got that shiner, huh?"

My fingers went to my face and I nodded. "He also said Dove didn't die of natural causes. He claimed he killed her."

No reply.

"Did you hear me?" I said.

He shook himself, yanking loose his expensive-looking lavender tie. "You'll have to forgive me. Tonight, I was prepared to suffer the slings and arrows of trickle-down capitalists and well-meaning homophobes. Not someone who may possibly untangle my fucked-up family history."

I hesitated. "Look, I'm sorry to do this now, at your party. I really am. But can you tell me what you know? If you've ever heard any information—any real information—about Steadfast's death or the missing coin, I'd be really grateful if you'd share it."

"I haven't." He held my gaze. "I'm sorry. No one in my family knows what happened to Steadfast or where the coin went. It's unfortunate, but the truth is just that simple . . . and boring, I'm afraid."

I didn't know what I'd expected—for Jason to possess some long-forgotten tidbit of family lore that would have led me to the coin and some kind of exoneration of Dove? Or maybe, even more preposterously, for him to go full Superman, pull some backroom political levers and save the day for me? I just knew I certainly hadn't expected the avalanche of disappointment that engulfed me.

"Eve." He stood. "A thought, if you'll indulge me."

"Sure."

"I don't think this whole situation has to be a negative. Not necessarily."

I gave him a confused look. "What do you mean?"

"The slickest agency in the world couldn't come up with PR this good. Finding my long-lost ancestor? Blowing up an extortion scheme. It's actually pretty brilliant, if you think about it."

I stiffened, reflexively. "Okay, hold on, though. I understand you're trying to help, but we can't—"

"Just hear me out. You've got two days to find the coin, right?" His lips curled in a devilish grin, an impish gleam in his eye. "God, it'll be so perfect."

"What will be perfect?"

"Just keep an open mind." He grabbed my elbow, the weak one, and hauled us both up. "Would you mind coming with me? We can talk more downstairs in my office. And I really want to loop in a couple of advisers, if you don't have an objection."

I certainly did have an objection.

But we were already moving toward the door. Before I could protest, he guided me through it, and the sounds of the party below—laughter and tinkling glasses—rose up to me. I broke out in a flash of sweat.

"I can find Matt," he was saying. "We'll get Emmett and Eleanor on the phone, then we can get to work. Hash things out."

I pulled my arm from his grasp. "Mr. Faulk—"

"Jason, please."

"Jason," I repeated. "Stop."

He did, his hand still at my elbow.

"All of this . . . everything I just told you is extremely confidential. You absolutely cannot tell anyone. You have to understand. I'm here to stop rumors, not start them."

And then I felt his brown eyes, beautiful and thickly lashed, fasten onto mine. He formed his perfect lips into a smile that highlighted just the right angle of cheekbones. All so mesmerizing. Oh, he really was the consummate candidate. "Look, Eve. You asked for my help and I'm going to help you. But you've got to trust me. I'm not going to let any—"

His phone rang and he pulled it out of his pocket. After a few seconds he barked, "Okay, give me a minute."

A woman's laughter spiraled up from below us. "He doesn't care about your *income inequality*. He won't even let me buy the house I live in from him!"

Jason groaned, looking supremely annoyed. "Yep, right on time. Here to provide the entertainment."

I didn't wait to find out what he was talking about. I started down the steps, nearly colliding with Althea, who was heading up. Jason clattered past us both, a blur, and at the foot of the staircase, intercepted a petite young woman. She was about my age with a crown of spiky black hair and black-winged eyeliner. She wore an old plaid shirt unbuttoned over a purple tank top, and had multiple piercings studding her nose, ears, and sharp arched eyebrows.

She was just reaching for a champagne flute from a passing server, but when Jason took her elbow, he accidentally upset the tray. Champagne splashed and glass shattered.

Jason jumped back, a warning in his voice. "Ember."

But the woman turned toward the crowd. "You all think he cares about you because he lets you into his home. But it's easy to show off what isn't yours. This house was handed to him on a silver platter. Given to him, not earned, like everything he has."

Jason reached for her and she grabbed him back, swinging him around and away from her in a kind of manic do-si-do. A few people laughed like this might be the entertainment they'd come for. Then she spoke again, her voice brighter, but distinctly slurred.

"Steadfast Coe died and left the house and all his money to his two grandsons, nothing to his daughter or granddaughter. Of course."

I watched in horrified fascination. This lady wasn't just fun-drunk. She was ready-for-a-fight hammered. The crowd hushed.

"Ember," Jason said quietly.

An unsuspecting partygoer, edging his way from the uncomfortable scene, passed the woman, and she neatly relieved him of his beer. "But the granddaughter was a wonderful person. She could sing and dance. She was pretty and smart." The young woman turned to Jason. "But she got nothing, did she? Because she was a female. Because she didn't *count*!" The woman's voice slid up an octave. "Her name was Bruna Faulk Holt and she was my Granny Bru! I loved her and she deserved this place!" She pointed at Jason and stared at the crowd. "If you elect this man governor, and he takes everything you have, do not come bitching on my doorstep!"

"You mean my doorstep," Jason said quietly. "My doorstep. I own the house you live in, remember? I bought it with my own money that I made from a job I hold down. Does that sound familiar?"

Silence fell over the room. Somewhere, a door closed softly.

She spotted me at that moment and did an almost cartoonish double take. I noticed then that her winged eyeliner was smudged and there were dark crescents of sweat under her arms. I also noticed Jason's men, the ones in black T-shirts, easing their way through the crowd, closing in on her.

"Hey, I know you," she said, her voice loud enough to reach us on the stairs.

I met her blue eyes and couldn't move. Her stare created some kind of force field that held me. I felt a sudden pang of sympathy.

"You're—" she started to say, then stopped, her face crumpling, mouth contorting in a tragic slash. "Oh my God," she wailed. "Oh *fuck*—"

But then she yelped, a bloodcurdling shriek. One of the black T-shirt guys had snuck up and snagged her around the waist, swinging her toward the front door. Her legs flailed as she reached back toward me, as if touching me was going to change what was happening to her, and I got one last look of a desperate black-winged eye.

Chapter Twenty-Two

Florence, Alabama
1934

Because Arthur Holt's father, the Methodist minister, knew about every tent revival, camp meeting, and sacred harp singing in the Shoals area, Arthur was able to arrange lots of appearances for the girls. The engagements were mostly on Sundays, Ruth's day off. Occasionally, they fell on a Friday night or Saturday, and Bruna had to cajole Edith into watching Steadfast an extra day. This resulted in quite a bit of sniffing and pursing of lips as Bruna's mother thought singing in tents smacked of vaudeville.

Bruna took the position that without school or a job to pass the time, she'd most likely wind up running off and getting married. The unspoken message, Ruth gathered, being that the groom in question was Arthur Holt, far from Edith's first choice for her well-born daughter.

Truthfully, he wasn't Ruth's first choice for Bruna either. Arthur was always giving the girls suggestions to refine their stage presentation and polish up their hairdos and clothes. And before every meeting started, he'd pull Bruna away for a private pep talk. It was just as well

Ruth wasn't invited to their get-togethers. If that puppy tried to tell her how to sing, she'd bust him right in the nose.

At any rate, presented with the choice of her only daughter marrying a Methodist preacher's son or singing at a few revivals and remaining available for a more advantageous match with one of Florence's wealthy denizens, Edith relented, and the girls took their act on the road.

As it turned out, the road generally consisted of a twenty-mile radius around Florence and included the towns of Sheffield, Muscle Shoals, and Tuscumbia across the river. All Bruna and Ruth needed was Steadfast's old ice cave packed with chicken or potato salad or whatever Ruth had cooked that day, and they were on their way.

Early on, Bruna suggested they call themselves the Hawthorn Sisters. "Because of the tree he chopped down," she giggled. Ruth had to admit she didn't mind the impudence of the name. And it made her think of Dell.

It wasn't long before they were doing much more than just singing at the meetings. Sometimes, when she had a particularly captive audience, Ruth would tell the story of Dr. Asloo's lion. How—through the power of the Lord, she spoke to it and closed its mouth. Entranced by the story, the audience was then primed for Bruna. She'd sashay to the edge of the stage and call out whatever might be troubling the worshippers' hearts. Loneliness, family strife, or envy—she named them all, and, convicted by the Spirit, people rushed forward with tears and confessions. The girls would lay their hands on them and pray, pronouncing them healed of their maladies just like they'd seen other evangelists do, and Arthur recorded it all on his small Cine Kodak Model K.

It was during one of these meetings, up in St. Florian, that a man dressed in filthy overalls and a filthier cap brought his wife down front. She wore an apron stained with grease. It appeared the man had dragged her directly from her kitchen in the middle of cooking supper. She hung her head down, wisps of light-brown hair curtaining her face, but Ruth could still see the shadow of a bruise at the corner of her eye, purple and yellow.

The man, his bewhiskered face mottled red, shoved his wife forward. "Lay yer hands on this un," he spat at the girls. "See if the Almighty can fix a willful heart and a stiff neck."

The woman lifted her face. She wasn't crying, nor was the fever of the Spirit high on her cheeks. Her face was blank; her eyes two holes of dead space, framed by that nasty bruise.

"I can't seem to get out of bed in the morning," she said quietly.

"Morning and afternoon and night," her husband's twangy voice rang out from behind her.

Ruth took her other hand. "What's your name?"

"Maggie Kittle."

"You got kids, I reckon."

She nodded. "Nine."

Bruna pressed her lips together.

After they prayed for the woman, the man marched her back down the aisle toward the back of the tent. Just before he reached the opening, Ruth lifted her chin and sang out in a pure, clear voice.

"Steal away, steal away, steal away to Jesus . . ."

The man stopped. The congregation sat frozen on the benches. The Hawthorn Sisters didn't sing spirituals. Spirituals were field songs sung in the black churches, not at white revivals. Furthermore, a lot of people thought that particular song was about a slave who wished to escape to freedom.

Bruna elbowed Ruth gently, but Ruth ignored her and sang the second line. *"Steal away. Steal away home. I ain't got long to stay here!"* The metaphor seemed appropriate enough to Ruth. This lady needed to escape.

The farmer turned slowly, deliberately, his face a study in fury.

"My Lord, he calls me," Ruth belted out across the crowd. *"He calls me by the thunder. The trumpet sounds within my soul . . ."*

Even from where she stood, Ruth could see the man tremble with rage. His sneer turned to a snarl. But this just served to spur her on. Her voice boomed across the tent, stronger and surer than it had ever felt before. *"I ain't got long to stay here!"*

The piano joined in. Then Bruna too. At last, the crowd sang, clapping along tentatively. Ruth, watching it all, grinned. The feeling was intoxicating, like moonshine out of a walking cane. It was only when the man took his wife by the arm and pulled her the rest of the way out of the tent, that she realized she may have gone a step too far.

Chapter Twenty-Three

Florence, Alabama
Present

Jason Faulk followed the phalanx of black T-shirts who hauled his cousin to the front of the house. I gave Althea and Griff the high sign and we made our escape out the back. Back at the Hampton Inn, we changed and reconvened at the indoor pool—or rather, the small adjacent hot tub.

We sat around the edge, dangling our legs in the frothy, suspect water. When Griff peeled off his T-shirt and jumped in, shorts and all, Althea and I both screamed in dismay.

"Oh, please. Water's great, girls. Come on in!"

I shook my head. "Noooo . . ."

"Absolutely not." Althea made a face. "As I tell my kids, Griff, 'we don't play in garbage cans.'"

He laughed and produced two more airplane mini bottles, pouring one into the bubbling white-foamed water before handing the other over to me. "Disinfectant. You're safe now."

I took a sip and made another face. But I was furtively studying his bare torso. He was lean with just the right amount of build, his abdomen and back covered with tattoos. There were so many I couldn't tell precisely what I was looking at. But I'd been looking long enough, so I averted my eyes.

Althea held up her can of Diet Coke in a mock toast. "I'll stick with this. But I notice you always seem to have a supply of those handy little bottles."

He arched an eyebrow at her. "I'll admit I come prepared because I enjoy sharing a drink with friends after a long day of shooting. But it's only because I happen to dislike bars." He found my eyes. "I prefer a place where you can actually hear what the other person is saying."

"Point in your favor from the ladies' team," Althea said. "Right, Eve?"

"I think so. I hate bars too."

"What a coincidence," Althea said, in a coy tone. "You're a gem, Griff, you know that?"

"Ha. Tell my parents that."

"Oh, come on, they've got to be proud of you. Up-and-coming filmmaker."

"My mother is. One of the reasons I go by her last name." His gaze was still trained on me, and it was getting hard not to gaze back. And this other thing, the way he was divulging bits of personal information to me, was really kind of sweet. Like he was interviewing for a different kind of job altogether. "What do you say, Eve. Do I lose my point?"

"A less-than-spectacular parent's nothing to be ashamed of. My dad wasn't great and look at me. I turned out fine."

"Better than fine," Althea said. "I'd say absolutely stellar."

Griff raised his tiny bottle of bourbon. "I would too."

"Griff," Althea said. "Just curious. You're single, right?"

I slapped my knees, businesslike. "We should really get back to business, don't you think?"

Althea just grinned.

"Well, I do. We don't have much time." That came out slightly sharper than I'd meant it to, but whatever. Time was running out.

"Okay, fine. Thoughts on Jason Faulk?" Griff asked.

"Possibly a jerk," Althea said.

"Definitely not on good terms with his cousin," Griff agreed.

"What's your assessment of him, Eve?"

"I'm not totally sure what his motives are, but I think he might be willing to help us out. Let us search his house even. I'm just a little worried about his inability to keep Dove and the foundation out of the news." I let my feet drift through the warm water.

"I think we should talk to Ember first." Althea pulled her legs out of the water and reached for a clean towel. "Besides being Bruna Holt's descendant, she may know something about the coin that Jason doesn't. And maybe she'll be more understanding of our need to be discreet."

"Okay," I said. "We can find her in the morning. My guess is she'll be sleeping off whatever she was on tonight."

"Speaking of discreet," Griff said. "Do you think she's got a problem? Like a problem, problem?"

Althea shrugged. "It's possible. And with that guy as her only family . . ." She rolled her eyes. "Forgive me, but politicians aren't exactly my jam."

"I hear you," I said. "We'll tread carefully. I don't want her getting hurt."

"Yeah, well, people get hurt in situations like these," Althea said. "Family situations, I mean. Collateral damage is almost impossible to avoid."

We all got quiet, then Althea stood up.

"Hope y'all don't mind, but I'm off to bed. I feel hungover every morning just because I'm over thirty-five. Enjoy it while you can." She sent us a wicked grin and made her way to the glass door. "I'm sure y'all won't miss me one bit."

The door shut behind her, leaving Griff and me alone in the humid, chemical-infused enclosure.

"You're not turning in, are you?" He looked at me, forlorn. "Please don't go to bed." He dropped into the bubbling water. "Look at this elegant hot tub we have. We shouldn't let it go to waste."

I inspected my toes. I really needed a pedicure. "I don't know. I've got two more days until my life is metaphorically over." I'd meant for it to sound lighthearted, but my voice had come out ponderous. Grave even. Oh, boy, I really sucked at this. Why the hell couldn't I ever fake nonchalant?

He pushed toward me through the water. "You've done all you can do for now. So you might as well enjoy yourself." He rested his hands on either side of me, tattoos in full view. There was so much to take in—a snowcapped mountain, a tree with blossoms, a series of numbers—I almost didn't notice the name. *Anna.*

"Why do you think she came?" he said.

My head popped up. "Who?"

"Althea. Why do you think she left her kids and husband and took off with us?"

I stared at him.

"I mean, I get that she knew Dove, and they were close, but like . . . what does she get out of helping you find the coin and save the foundation?"

I frowned. "I don't know. I guess she feels like she owes Dove after she helped her find out what happened to her family."

"Okay, I'm just talking here," Griff said. "But what if she's in on it—I mean the plan to get the coin?" His face was as open as I'd ever seen it. He wasn't messing with me. He was truly concerned.

I thought back to the box of Dove's things Althea had produced. She'd said she held on to them because she hoped to give them to me in person, but now I wondered. They were exactly the kinds of items Dove's groupies liked to collect. What if Althea had somehow come into possession of them by some other way—some illegal way—and she'd been searching them for a clue to where the coin was?

The thought of Althea betraying me—and Dove—would have seemed far-fetched a couple of days ago. But today, after seeing Jason Faulk latch on to the missing coin story for his own political PR purposes, the idea was not so easy to dismiss. People were swayed by money; that was the bottom line. It was simple human nature. And with the Flowing Hair, we were talking tens of millions. With that much cash on the line, I wasn't sure anyone could be trusted.

"I don't know if she's involved," I said. "But it would be odd to name your daughter after someone, then try to screw their whole family."

Griff rubbed his jaw. "Yeah, you're right. I'm probably overthinking this."

"But we'll keep an eye on her. If she's up to no good, better to have her close."

He got quiet, and then I realized he was looking at my legs. I drew in a breath, ordering my muscles not to clench. This was usually how things went. A man ventured a touch on any part of my body, and I would be unable to quit obsessing over my arm—when would they get to it and notice its smaller size? What would they think? Would they be turned off in some way? So then I would lock my body away, my mind following close behind, and the moment would pass, never to be recovered.

But Griff already knew about my arm, and things could be different this time. So I ordered myself not to move, not even to think. If nothing happened between us, it was not going to be because of my raging self-consciousness.

Griff slowly ran the side of his thumb down the length of one thigh, and my heart kicked up a rhythm so fast I felt breathless.

"Can I ask you something?" he said.

I lifted my eyes to meet his, allowing myself another quick glance at his bare chest. It was easy to imagine being enveloped in those arms, against that chest. Easy to imagine falling asleep wrapped up in them.

"Sure," I said at last.

He reached for my right arm. I closed my eyes—*just hold still, just hold still*—and let him slowly, gently draw it out until it was fully extended between us. Then he ran his thumb along it just as he had on my leg, right down the side of it, following the line of muscles—biceps brachii, brachioradialis, flexor carpi ulnaris—ending at my wrist. I shivered.

"What exactly happened to it?" he asked. "I don't see any scars."

I opened my eyes. "Fetal stroke. Which doesn't leave a scar; it typically leaves nerve damage. It happened in utero. Resulting in hemiplegia, right-side paralysis affecting my vision and my arm."

He nodded.

"Like I told you guys the other night, when I was fourteen, I underwent CIMT—constraint-induced movement therapy. Now I swim, do a lot of yoga to keep it strong. But it'll never be one hundred percent on the involved side, and technically, I'll always have the brain damage that caused it in the first place."

He nodded. "Makes sense. But it's a hell of an arm, if you ask me. Been through a lot."

"Well, thanks." I realized I was gritting my teeth and ordered myself to release my jaw. Griff hadn't given me any reason to distrust him. I could relax.

"What was the therapy like?"

I studied him. "They cast your unaffected arm, the one you use to do things like brush your teeth and cut your food, and you have to do all those things with the affected arm."

"Doesn't sound too horrible, at least."

"You think? Well, let's see." I took hold of his right arm and forced it, gently but firmly, behind his back. "You're right-handed, aren't you?"

He blinked at me, surprised. "Yeah."

"Okay, now do something with your left arm."

"Like what?"

"I don't know, pretend you've got an eyelash stuck in your eye."

"I've got a better idea." His lips parted. "Let's say you've got the eyelash."

"Okay." I held my breath.

He reached up and tenderly brushed an imaginary lash from just under my eye with his fingers. My skin tingled.

"No problem." There was a hint of laughter in his voice.

But I still held his arm pinned behind him. "Not so fast. There are harder tasks. I just started you off easy."

One corner of his mouth curled up. He was up for the game. Intrigued. And I was . . . well, I was going down a dangerous path. Distracting myself. Inviting more complications—more heartache—for when I finally said goodbye to the foundation and left for Colorado. I hadn't dated anyone for any length of time since I was a teenager. Hadn't developed any deep friendships with other women either. But besides my habit of freezing up around men, there was a reason for that. One with origins in my psyche.

It was hard work, the constant pretending I had to do for my mother and brother and everybody at the foundation. And at the end of a day, it felt like there was nothing left. Sometimes I felt empty, worried I'd lost my authentic self. That the real me had dried up and blown away from sheer lack of use.

But here I was. And here was Griff, and something was holding us here together.

Something worth working for, maybe.

"My hair," I said. "I like to tuck it behind my ears."

With his left hand he reached up and, careful to avoid the lump, smoothed my hair, tucking the errant strands into place.

"Good job." I readjusted my grip on his arm. He angled his body closer to mine.

"One more. Hold on." He carefully removed a hair that had gotten caught in my mouth. "There."

My breath was coming faster.

"The button," I said. "Top button of my shirt."

He followed my directions.

"The next one . . ."

He undid the next three buttons and pulled my shirt open. He leaned over and kissed the spot just below my clavicle bone. When he lifted his head, I saw he was flushed and breathing just as hard as I was. And then he kissed my lips, just once, softly. "What next?" he said.

"Your room," I said. "Then left hand only, unzip my shorts."

Chapter Twenty-Four

Florence, Alabama
1934

In only a few months, the Hawthorn Sisters were the most popular act in northwestern Alabama, and as a result, they'd pulled in a tidy sum of money from the collection basket, all of it divided three ways. Arthur divided the take into thirds and gave each girl her share. Bruna kept hers under her mattress. Arthur hid his in the leg of his mother's piano bench. Ruth tucked hers in the lunch chest, in the narrow space where the ice went.

Things had settled at the Coe house. Edith's husband, Harold, had the hawthorn tree chopped up and hauled off and he'd confiscated the rifle and 12-gauge. The old man seemed quieter in body and spirit after that. Instead of slipping out the back door and searching for an escape route, he spent his days roaming the house, mumbling to himself, touching candlesticks and books and paintings. Sometimes he'd pour the error coins out of the crystal jar and spread them across the mint-green bed.

One morning, when the old man failed to answer her call for breakfast, Ruth went on the hunt, climbing the stairs and searching all the rooms. She found him in the mint-green room, slumped at the dainty dressing table. She stood in the door, watching him. He was staring at himself in the silvered mirror. His mouth worked and a line of spittle ran from the corner around to his chin. Over the age-spotted scalp, his white hair hung limp and tangled—he wouldn't allow Ruth to trim it. He looked like an ogre from a fairy tale, just waiting for some unsuspecting villager to cross his path. All except his face. It was slack and vacant, like he'd gone someplace far away.

"Mr. Coe?" She took a few steps into the room. "Mr. Coe, your breakfast won't be hot for long."

As if he hadn't heard her, the old man placed his hands on his face, peering closer into the mirror. "Where are we?"

She moved closer. "You're at home, in your wife's room."

He didn't acknowledge her. "I don't see him no more. That fella that used to come around for Edie. What happened to him? Probably fell off the bluff and drowned in the river. Doing us all a favor."

She drew close behind his chair. "Look at your hair . . ." She picked up an ivory comb with a silver handle. "If you'd like, I can help you."

He said nothing. With great care, she lowered the comb to his head and gently drew the teeth, forehead to crown, down his scalp. When he didn't protest, she did it again, easing the comb through each snarl and tangle. As she worked, he leaned back and let his shoulders drop. But his face stayed frozen in that blank mask.

After she got out all the knots, she found a jar of pomade in a drawer and smoothed it over the long white strands, tucking the length behind his ears. She rested her hands on his shoulders and smiled at him in the mirror.

"There now. Handsome as you like."

Just then, a small electric charge traveled along her arms and down her spine. She shivered. In the mirror, Mr. Coe's face had tightened, reordered itself somehow, and his gaze was fastened on her face. A tear slipped from the corner of one of his eyes.

"You're a beauty," he said to her. "You know that, Miss Ruth?"

She met his eyes in the mirror. He'd returned to himself. And she saw that he was, in fact, correct. She was a beauty. When had that happened? she wondered. The change? Because there had been one, sure as shooting. She was no longer a ragged urchin but had become a girl of fine and full figure. Her back was straight, neck graceful, limbs long and tapering. Her shiny hair had recently deepened its reddish hue from carroty to a rich auburn and now framed her oval face like a picture. Her face was delicate but strong. Lips full, eyes expressive and wise.

No one could see the blackness of her heart by looking at her.

No one could see her secrets—that she was a liar and a con.

She would always be safe . . . as long as she had this face to hide the truth.

The old man reached into the back of the drawer and pulled out a dull black metal pistol. He pulled back the slide with gnarled, trembling fingers and pointed it directly at her.

Ruth leapt back, nearly stumbling over her feet. "Good goddamn—"

"Oh hush. I ain't gonna shoot you. But there are people who want what I got, and we can't be too careful."

He reached for the crystal jar, removed the silver lid, and fished around in it. He pulled out a coin. It was dwarfed by his large rough thumb and forefinger.

"Well, come on. Come over here."

She inched forward until she was in arm's reach and took the coin. It was the one with the woman with flowing hair. Copper maybe, edged with traces of green.

"The others, you gotta get them out of circulation," he explained to Ruth. "If you don't . . ." He stopped and scratched at his sideburns with the pistol. "Well, the world just won't feel right. And if the world ain't right, I can't quit thinking and thinking about it, all day, every day, till it nearly drives me plumb crazy. I can't have that. You understand?"

She nodded, even though she didn't really.

He held up the copper coin. "But this one. This one's perfect. No flaws, minted just the way it was supposed to be. So I ain't got no use for it. What's the use in hanging on to a perfectly good dollar?"

She managed a laugh. The things he said.

He set the gun down. "It's yours if you want it."

Ruth examined the slim coin. "Mr. Coe. You really shouldn't. I'm sure it's valuable. Your family—"

"Bunch of ninnies," he interrupted. "I don't give a rat's ass what those chuckleheads say. I want to give it to you, so I'm giving it to you." He gave her a curt nod. "Make sure and hide it. Someplace safe where nobody will find it. That thing's dear."

She took it in her maid's room and dropped it into the keyhole of the door, and just like a piggy bank, it fell into the mechanism with a satisfying clink. She hoped when the time came, she could get the doorknob off and dig it out. But for the time being, she rested easy knowing nobody would guess where it was.

Chapter Twenty-Five

Florence, Alabama
Present

Ember Holt's Facebook page was sparse, but it did say she'd graduated from North Alabama and worked over at the Marriott Conference Center on the river. Althea and I left Griff to sleep off the previous night's Jack and headed over to the Marriott.

Althea called Jay, and self-serving though it was, I couldn't help but listen. They talked about the kids, joked about some elaborate school assignment their daughter, Ruthie, had to complete, then some issue Jay was having with the hot water heater. By the end of the conversation, I was feeling like a world-class shit. How could this loving wife and involved mother be after the coin? I couldn't see it.

Ember wasn't at the restaurant, and her flat-faced toothpick of a manager was more than happy to let us know what he intended to do about it. "You tell her this is it," he said when we introduced ourselves as college friends. "Tell her I'm done. One hundred percent done."

"We will," Althea promised. "But could you just . . . she's moved recently—"

He snorted.

"—and we lost her address. Could you—"

"Over on Larimore. Nice little stone cottage with a tree in the front yard decorated like the devil's Christmas tree. You can deliver a message for me. Tell that Sabrina-the-witch-pretending deadbeat that she's fired, okay?" he said over his shoulder, already heading back to the kitchen.

When we swung back into the Hampton Inn parking lot, Griff was waiting for us, camera in hand. As he climbed in the back seat, he gave me a grin and touched my shoulder. I had a sudden pang of fear that Althea would zero in on it. But she just wheeled out of the lot and recounted what we'd learned.

We found Ember's house easily enough. It was a really cute place with what her boss had so accurately called the devil's Christmas tree in the front yard. The tree was a medieval-looking thing, its branches festooned with springtime blooms. Hung among the blooms were glittery black pentagrams, skulls, and goat heads cut from cardboard. A white corrugated plastic sign propped against the trunk proclaimed **FORTUNES BY EMBER ~ SEER, MEDIUM, PSYCHIC** in a ghoulish black font.

I wondered if it was just an act of defiance—a middle finger to her rich, connected cousin and maybe the rest of a family who'd grown tired of all the chances she'd obviously squandered. Or could Ember Holt really tell the future?

Griff left the camera in the car and we knocked on the front door, peeling blue paint and rotted at the bottom. A shirtless kid around nineteen or twenty answered.

"Whoa," he said, rubbing the sleep from bleary red eyes. "Good morning, grown-ups."

"Is Ember around?" I asked. "We need to talk to her."

"She's at work."

"Ah, no, she's not," Althea said. "She didn't go in."

"Then she's probably out back."

"Excuse me?" I asked.

"In the shed. Just go around back and you'll see it." He swung the door shut before I could ask any more questions.

I was already halfway down the steps when Griff called out behind me. But I couldn't wait any longer. Maybe it was the defiantly decorated tree with its hopeful homemade sign. And probably the shabby condition of the house. But mostly, I think, it was the memory from last night. Of Ember Holt's black-winged eyes. The haunted look in them. The sight had shaken me in a way I was having a hard time understanding. I might not let loose with my emotions in the same way, I might gather myself against the world, but I recognized the desperation I'd seen in her face. Maybe we were the same, on some level. Both of us burdened with other people's secrets.

And I had to talk to this woman now.

Situated in a corner of chain-link fence in the postage-stamp backyard was a small whitewashed wooden shed. The roof was aluminum and the door warped. Fingers of rot and moss crept up the walls from the damp earth. The windows were taped over with cardboard and there was another sign, this one hand-painted on a piece of plywood and tucked into the sill.

IT ONLY TAKES AN EMBER TO START A FIRE.

I knocked but there was no answer. When I pushed the door open, the smell hit me hard—dirt, human sweat, and motor oil. I caught a flash of movement from the shadows of the back wall. White sheet. Pale arm.

"No readings," came a hoarse voice from the depths of the shed. "Shop's closed."

Griff gave me a gentle push into the dark, but I grabbed his shirt and pulled him along with me. No chance I was going in there alone. The smell was overpowering, and it was so dark the only things I could make out were an ancient lawnmower, bags of fertilizer, and empty plastic plant containers.

"Come back later tonight," said the voice. "I'll give you one half-price."

"Ember?" I called into the mustiness. "I'm really sorry to bother you, but I need to talk to you. It's Eve Candler. We met last night. At Jason Faulk's party."

A voice frogged with sleep and last night's alcohol cut through the dark. "Oh God."

I heard the rustling of bedcovers and the squeak of springs and she came into view. Her ringed eyes were dark holes of eyeliner and wildly streaked shadow, and her hair was smashed flat on one side. She was wearing a lilac tank top and sweatpants. Tattoos of undefinable patterns peeked out from the neckline and armholes of the tank, petals of roses and the curve of bones. She was diminutive, curvy, and quite beautiful, something I hadn't noticed last night.

"My shift started two hours ago," she said, gloomy.

"Yeah," I said. "We just spoke with your boss."

"So you're my personal pink slip, I'm guessing."

I nodded, apologetic.

She inhaled deeply, then let her breath out in a slow, steady stream. She closed her eyes and shook her head as if clearing the cobwebs. "Okay. Moving on."

She came back to life and studied me. Every detail it seemed, my clothes, shoes, the purse slung over my shoulder. Then finally her gaze lifted to meet mine. Her eyes were clear blue, slightly puffy, and completely devoid of recognition.

"Who won?" she asked, indicating my eye, fully bloomed in its purple glory today.

"Shower door."

"Ah." She looked thoughtful. "Last night's not all that clear. Sorry. Hope I didn't say anything untoward."

The formal word made me smile. "You didn't. Not to me anyway. It's just that you seemed to recognize me."

She nodded, this way and that, like she was trying to recall. She stepped closer. "We haven't met, have we?"

"No. I don't think so. Not formally."

And then her face changed, a lightning shift from curious to alarmed. "Oh. Oh, no."

"What?"

"I'm pretty sure I did something really stupid."

"What?"

She turned away, scratching at her scalp, staring at the floor. It was as if she were talking to herself. "It was so stupid. I should've known my instincts were right. That you were coming. I swear to God, when the hell am I going to start trusting what I *know* . . ."

"Ember. What's going on?" I asked.

She glanced at me. "You're here for the bones, aren't you?"

My mouth went dry.

"So you can clear Ruth's name."

I stared at her, unable to respond.

"The thing is," she said mournfully, "if you are, it's too late. I know I'm such an idiot, but I sold them."

Chapter Twenty-Six

Florence, Alabama
1934

Brother Comer did enjoy his moonshine, that was for sure. Ruth had spotted him as she, Bruna, and Arthur had crossed the railroad tracks on their way toward Sheffield. He was tipping back a jug a good hour before the service and was nowhere in sight when six o'clock rolled around.

This left Ruth and Bruna in charge of entertaining the antsy crowd, which was going to be a hell of a feat from the annoyed looks on the congregants' faces and their discontented murmurs. Even Bruna seemed out of sorts, her face fixed in a grim scowl after her regular private talk with Arthur.

She and Bruna had been singing for over thirty minutes when Ruth finally told the lion story. But after she was done, the girls were running on empty, Arthur scowling, and Brother Comer was still nowhere in sight. They'd have to launch into "God Bless America" if that rat didn't show up soon.

Not that this crew would know the difference. In the one good turn of the evening, the folks had gotten so drunk in the Spirit that they were swaying and sweating, crying real tears and jabbering in tongues.

But Ruth knew that, in the end, they'd really come for Brother Comer, not the Hawthorn Sisters, and eventually they'd turn on the girls if the star of the show didn't appear.

"What about 'Rivers of Delight'?" Ruth whispered to Bruna.

"You can reach those notes?"

Ruth gestured to the listless crowd. "You think they'll notice? We could sing 'The March of the Valkyrie' and they'd sing hallelujah right along with us."

"We should just sneak out the back."

Ruth shook her head. "I'm not leaving until I'm paid."

Bruna sighed. "From the looks of it, we aren't going to be." She glanced at Arthur, fiddling with his tie in the wings. "And Arthur's going to be fit to be tied."

"Let him," Ruth said. "We should do 'Steal Away to Jesus' again. They like that one. But this time the last stanza. Just follow me."

"Oh Lord, Ruth. Are you trying to get us in trouble?"

Suddenly they heard a voice behind them.

"It's gone!"

They turned to see a woman, about sixty or so, with a large hat, half-crushed and sprouting curled feathers, pulled down low over tight gray curls. She was dressed in shades of brown, and an old-fashioned reticule dangled from her wrist.

"The growth is gone." She pointed to her neck. "It was here, right here, when I came tonight. But then you began to sing, and it began to shrink." She clasped her hands over her neck. "Someone call Mr. Foshee. He'll know. He's the one who took me to the doctor in Decatur!"

Bruna's eyes looked like they were about to spring out of her head, and she dug her nails into Ruth's palms. "Jiminy! What do we do now?"

"Mr. Foshee is just down the way," the old woman called out to the crowd. "He promised that he was coming along shortly."

"He musta got waylaid by a blind pig just like Comer!" a man yelled. Laughter rippled through the tent. A blind pig was what folks called a speakeasy.

"I know this Mr. Foshee," Ruth said to the woman. "He's tall, right? Works for you . . ."

The woman nodded, her hand still wrapped around her neck. "At the butcher shop. That's right."

Ruth addressed the crowd. "Then, I ask you, why do we need the word of Mr. Foshee, of any man, when we have the word of a good woman? A kind and forthright woman of impeccable honor and dedication to those in service to her family?"

The woman blinked at her, and Ruth put her hand on the woman's back.

"'Bless the Lord, O my soul,'" Ruth said. *"'And all that is within me, bless His holy name.'"*

Bruna put a hand on Ruth's shoulder. *"'Bless the Lord, O my soul, and forget not all His benefits: Who forgiveth all thine iniquities; who healeth all thy diseases.'"*

Her voice rang out, clear and firm in the tent, and the crowd amened.

"This woman's been healed," said Arthur, rounding the end of the stage. He looked like he'd been surprised out of a nap, tightening his tie, smoothing back his hair, and blinking hard. "Let us praise the Lord and sing him a new song!"

Ruth had the briefest inclination to kick him in the balls, but she was grateful for him all the same. He had a showman's sense of timing, that was for sure. And Bruna had started up another round of "Throw Me Overboard." In seconds, the girls were swarmed, people pulling on their dresses and begging for prayer. Arthur tried to keep a semblance of order, making the people wait their turn in orderly lines. It was near midnight when they prayed over the last person.

"A piano leg's not going to do the trick," Arthur crowed as they trudged back in the direction of Florence. "I'm going to have to find another hiding place."

Ruth, her arm linked through Bruna's and her body wracked with weariness, didn't want to talk about the money. All she could think of was the old woman who claimed her tumor had disappeared. She had been mistaken, there was no doubt, or was out-and-out lying, but now the horse was out of the barn. The Hawthorn Sisters had a reputation.

Bruna leaned her head on Ruth's shoulder and groaned. "I just want to go home and sleep."

Arthur sidled up on Bruna's other side, and Ruth saw his hand snake up behind her, at an angle lower than it should. Bruna yelped and skipped forward, tossing her head, straightening her skirt, and sending a saucy look over her shoulder.

"Fresh," Bruna said.

"Just how you like it," Arthur replied.

Ruth stayed quiet. Eventually Bruna fell back to join Arthur, and the two continued to walk, heads pressed together and whispering things Ruth couldn't hear. Ruth contemplated them with new eyes. She'd known Arthur and Bruna liked each other, even loved maybe, but now she saw the truth. They were sleeping together, sure as shooting. What's more, they were going to get married.

She could see it so clearly now, the simple fact, as if it were a revelation straight from heaven. And understand the implications as well. If Bruna and Arthur got married, they would no longer have any need of her. Surely, they would ditch her, and the thought of that happening, the fear, consumed her. So much so that she failed to notice the tall, thin man standing on the side of the road in a black hat tied at the brim with a pink satin ribbon.

Chapter Twenty-Seven

Florence, Alabama
Present

"It was about a month ago. The guy was waiting for me when I got home from work," Ember said.

"Did you recognize him?" Griff asked.

"Well, I had met him once before, but I never found out his name."

"What did he look like?" Althea asked.

"Like every old redneck around here." She sighed. "The first time I met him, I was hammered, spaced out on Xanax too. I went to a bar in town, Toasties. We started talking there . . . I don't know exactly what was said, but I'm sure it's all"—she swirled her hands above her head—"up there somewhere, in the cloud." She turned back toward the murky shadows. "All I remember is the man acted like he was just one of those Alabama history wing nuts. He said he'd heard I had Steadfast Coe's bones, that he thought the old man's maid had killed him, and he wanted to give me a thousand dollars for them. A couple of nights later he showed up at my house."

"Did you also have a document with them?" Griff asked. "Like an old letter? The guy said he had a signed confession."

"Nope," Ember said. "Nothing like that. Just the bones."

"Okay, back up," I said. "You didn't think that was weird at all? That he wanted some old bones? And he had an opinion about who killed him?"

Back still to us, she peeled off her tank and pulled on a threadbare plaid flannel shirt. I averted my gaze to an old lawnmower, plastered with grass clippings and dirt.

"Believe it or not," she said, "bone collecting's a thing. Naturalists, oddity freaks, people who get off on that stuff. He said he'd been looking for a full male skeleton, and I guess word got out that I had one." She shrugged. "I'm used to it. The religious nutjobs, the loonies who worship the Hawthorn Sisters, asking me for mementos."

She appeared in a weak shaft of light. "It's old-timers mostly. I'm told the Sisters were quite the superstars back in the day. Anyway, my dad had the bones for years. He kept them down in our basement. After he and my mom died, I cleared out their house and brought them over here."

"Not trying to be a smart-ass here," Althea said, "but you knew Steadfast's disappearance was never solved. If you had his bones, why didn't you turn them over to the police?"

She let out a short, nervous breath. "I was a kid when I first found out about the bones. Like, I literally stumbled across them in my parents' basement one day. When I asked my dad, he told me it was my great-great-grandpa Steadfast Coe and that he had found the bones on our family property. In Alabama, if you find human remains on your property, you're not required to report it."

"Why didn't your dad have them properly buried then?" I asked.

"Because he was a jerk." She shrugged. "He told me not to tell anyone. I was twelve; I didn't question him. My dad was not the kind of guy you messed with, if you know what I mean."

"I hear you," Althea said.

"Of course, later, I connected the dots," Ember went on. "Realized that maybe he was protecting somebody he cared about, maybe a family member, from being implicated in something less than legal."

So not Dove. I couldn't help it; I wilted in relief.

She raked her fingers through her short hair. "But if my dad was protecting someone, that person's probably dead now, so why should I give a shit? I could've gone to the cops with the bones, I guess. But why? Nobody around here cares anymore who killed the guy . . . and I could use the cash." She turned to me. "But that's not what I feel so bad about. The thing is, I *knew*. I fucking *knew* you'd show up eventually."

I felt a chill roll through me. "How?"

"I just had a feeling, I guess." She fixed me with an incredulous look. "Didn't you see the sign out front?"

I stared back. "I don't believe in psychic abilities, Ember."

"Okay. Then maybe it was because Granny Bru was one of the Hawthorn Sisters, and I heard the rumors about Dove, and I figured one day it might come back to bite you."

This line of conversation was getting us nowhere. Time was ticking and I needed something concrete to help me in my search.

"So this is your house?" Griff asked.

"No," Ember said. "It's Jason's. He lets me stay rent-free, which is nice, and I appreciate it. My parents are long gone and my launch was what you might call . . . rocky." She shut her mouth, clearly trying to dam the flow of unwanted information.

But the picture was becoming clearer. Jason and Ember had some kind of miserable cycle of family dysfunction going on and I'd landed smack in the middle of it. Navigating it may get sticky, but I had no choice. These people were all I had.

"What about the Flowing Hair Dollar?" I said. "You got that stashed away back here, too?"

"No," she said, wary again. "Why do you ask?"

It was time to lay all my cards on the table.

"Because the guy with the bones thinks I have it, Ember." I pointed to the bruise. "He did this to me, then told me he wants to make a trade. The coin for the bones. If I don't give him the Flowing Hair

Dollar by tomorrow night, he's going to turn the bones over to the authorities and say Dove murdered Steadfast."

Her face crumpled and she put a hand over her mouth. "Oh Jesus. I'm sorry. I'm really, really sorry, Eve."

She moved to place her hand on my arm, but I angled away, just out of her reach. "Then help us now, please," I said. "If you know where the coin is, if you have any idea whatsoever, I really need you to tell us."

Her smile was full of bravado. "I know I must look like I come from the criminal branch of the family, but I swear to you, I don't know anything about the coin. And if I did, I sure wouldn't be living here."

Hopelessness washed over me. Dove had lied about her past, about her work for Steadfast and the accusations that had been leveled against her. And now those lies were gathering into a giant wave. Gathering and cresting higher and higher above me every minute that passed, and I couldn't do a single thing to protect everything in its shadow.

Ember had positioned herself in front of me, her face gone soft with genuine curiosity. "So, Dove's granddaughter. I can't believe we're finally meeting after all this time. You look so much like her, you really do. To be honest, it's really freaking me out. Like, look . . ." She thrust her arm in front of me and pushed up the sleeve. Her arm was covered in goose bumps.

I wasn't about to say it, but mine was too.

"Wait," she said abruptly. "I do actually have something you might be interested in. The reels."

Griff perked up. "Reels? What reels?"

"Old recordings that my Granny Bruna left me. I'd never give those away."

Griff and I exchanged glances. The bootleg tapes Margaret Luster was talking about. Ember had them.

"Would you allow us to take a look at them?" Griff asked.

"I mean, you can *see* them," Ember said. "But not watch them. I don't have the right kind of film projector. They're inside." She turned back to me, a slight smile on her face. "Did you see the tree out front?"

"The decorated one? Yes."

"It's a hawthorn. Kind of our family tree. Did you feel anything when you passed it?"

I tilted my head to one side. "Like what?"

"Like a flash. A picture in your head. Or a particular pain somewhere in your body?"

"No. Not really. Sorry."

She grinned at me. "It's okay. It was worth a try. Anyway, the tree's great because, it pisses Jason off. Treat me like the black sheep of the family long enough, I'll give you the blackest sheep you ever saw. Freakin' black hole, dark night of the soul, after midnight . . . sheep."

"Here, here," Althea said.

A phone buzzed behind us, and Ember dug it out from under a pile of God-knows-what on the cot. "What?" She was quiet for a long time, biting at a ragged nail, her raccoon-ringed eyes, large and white in the gloom, latching on to me. Then she started to speak in low, whispered tones.

I wanted to look away, but I couldn't. What she'd just asked me had piqued my interest. She seemed to be suggesting there was a connection between Bruna and Ruth, her and me, and a hawthorn tree. Which was ludicrous, of course. Absolutely ridiculous. Dove never had a gift. Ember's psychic business had to be a con. And the tree? It was nothing more than a freaking tree.

But that's what these kinds of people did. They planted ideas, stoked secret hopes and dreams. And then, just when their marks were good and vulnerable, they ever so gently relieved them of their cash. And yet, as much as I hated it, I felt myself drawn by Ember's suggestion. By the allure and mystery of it.

I still wanted to believe, in spite of everything I knew.

"Oh God. Okay," Ember said to the person on the other end. "I don't need the car. She's here with me. We'll be there in five. Have coffee, okay?" She ended the call. "Gird your loins, y'all. Little Lord Jason has summoned us."

Chapter Twenty-Eight

Florence, Alabama
1934

The Hawthorn Sisters were deluged with invitations to minister at all the spring camp meetings, from Killen to Waterloo, all the way down to Grove Hill—and two in Corinth, Mississippi, and Lawrenceburg, Tennessee. The most illustrious of all the requests came from the organizers of Billy Sunday's famed tabernacle meeting that was scheduled in Huntsville for a date in June.

Billy Sunday was the most famous evangelist in the country, if not the world, and a song or two on his stage was worth its weight in gold. His famed tabernacle, a wooden structure that resembled a fancy pole barn, was erected on the fairgrounds especially for the famous evangelist's meetings. It was lit from stem to stern with electricity, covered with a thick layer of sawdust, and set out with real chairs instead of plank benches.

In the center, there was a round stage with a carved wooden pulpit and canvas banners painted to look like the clouds of heaven. When Ruth stepped onto the stage, she felt lightheaded. A much bigger crowd would be here, maybe even from as far away as Tuscaloosa. What if someone in the crowd recognized her from Pritchard? Or worse, what if Jimmy Singley decided to come see a Billy Sunday service himself?

Arthur pulled Bruna out behind the tent for their regular pep talk, and Ruth sang her scales and picked at her thumbnail until the skin tore. Bruna really needed to be warming up with her, not listening to sweet nothings whispered behind the tent. Or were they sweet nothings? When Bruna joined her after these talks, she sure didn't look flushed with love. She looked agitated. Distracted. Ruth didn't like it, but she didn't have a say in the matter. Bruna seemed content to let Arthur run things.

The crowd was huge. Brother Sunday himself was a hellfire-and-brimstone preacher—describing the sinner's immoral acts in such graphic detail that it was said in one meeting, twelve men fainted and had to be carried out. Ruth couldn't imagine why people liked him so much, but she guessed it might be the same reason they paid good money at the movies to see things like *Dracula* and *Frankenstein*. The girls had been one of eight acts that went on before the preaching, and their take from the love offering was less than at many smaller camp meetings they'd done. On the ride back to Florence in Arthur's daddy's Franklin Victoria, she said as much.

"I say, let's stick to the small meetings. People know us there, and we make more money."

"Better to be a big fish in a small pond," Arthur agreed. "We could start having our own meetings soon. The Hawthorn Sisters got their own followers now. We don't need Billy Sunday."

Ruth whooped and started singing a Cab Calloway song, the one about the oyster stew. Arthur joined in, and she gave him a surprised look.

"I reckon you don't sound half-bad for a preacher's son, mister."

"You ain't the only one who can put on a show," Arthur shot back.

Bruna giggled. "We can't put on our own show, you two. We don't even have a tent. Arthur practically had to sign away his life to borrow this car, and Mama's not going to want to give Ruth any more days off."

"Besides that, who would we get to preach?" Ruth said.

"You could tell more stories about that lion," Bruna said. "The people really like that one."

"I have a plan," Arthur said. "The Hawthorn Sisters are going to go big. Bigger than Billy Sunday if things go the way I'm planning. But you gotta trust me and do what I say. For starters, you got to be clean and sweet and look like a couple of cherubs sitting on clouds. I'll do the preaching."

Ruth harrumphed.

"And none of that horse-pucky Billy Sunday hollers about people being roasted alive in hellfire." He glanced at Bruna. "When I preach, I'd say stuff that left folks feeling lighter. I'd respect the people that came—the people that are barely making do, who have to scrape and scrimp and go without—and I'd give them something to lift their day. I'd give them some good news. Something to make their everyday lives a little brighter. And we'll do even bigger miracles than Sunday."

Ruth and Bruna were silent.

"You know, I heard that once, John G. Lake's wife got shot by accident. Well, Mr. Lake was halfway across the country, but when he prayed, they say that bullet disappeared right out of her stomach."

"My goodness," Bruna said.

"I heard some people found it later, covered in blood, under the stage at that very meeting."

"He pushed the bullet out?" Ruth said.

"God pushed the bullet out," Arthur said. "I tell you, God the Father is for us, not against us. With Him we can do anything . . . but if the flock don't see it, how will they believe?"

Ruth's insides twisted. She didn't like the eerie cadence of his voice.

But when Bruna spoke, her voice was soft and sincere. "Well, that is nice, Arthur, it really is. I'm sorry for doubting you. I truly am." She smiled at him shyly, and Arthur gave her a supercilious nod.

"Nothing can stop us," he said. "No power, no principality. No law has authority over us, girls. We're God's chosen. We'll get us our own tent and a truck with something catchy written on the side—"

"Repent! Jesus Is Coming Back," Bruna said.

Arthur nodded. "We'll have wheelchairs and crutches lining the stage, all the folks you've healed . . ."

"Who *God* has healed," Bruna corrected.

"We'll split everything three ways. Fair and square." His jaw worked nervously, like he was just barely keeping the lid on the most wonderful secret.

"What?" Ruth said.

"Arthur!" Bruna said. "Out with it."

He hit the steering wheel. "All right. I guess y'all are gonna drag it out of me so I'll just go ahead and spill the beans. I got us our first single bill, main attraction, three nights at the North Alabama State Fair in July. The regular church folk'll be there, but also all the farmers will be done with the harvest. There could be up to two thousand people. It'll be the perfect time to kick off our own show."

Ruth's nerves twanged. Dell was sure to be back by the summer, and the two of them would be long gone. There was no chance she could stay just to keep the Hawthorn Sisters going. She hadn't yet figured how she was going to tell Bruna. And now this.

"Arthur," Bruna said. "You know we go away the whole month of July. We'll be in Palm Beach until the fifteenth and then up to the Greenbrier to see Aunt Venetia."

Arthur gripped the steering wheel but didn't speak.

"I thank you for going to so much trouble getting Ruth and me the job, I do, but we can't possibly do it. Mama won't hear of me missing the trip, and Ruth's got to look after Grandy." Bruna sent a desperate look back at Ruth.

"You said you wanted to be free of your parents," Arthur said, his voice tight. "How you going to do that if you keep taking their charity?"

Ruth reckoned that Bruna going on vacation with her mama and daddy wasn't anywhere close to taking charity, but she held her tongue. There were things she didn't understand about coming up in a wealthy family. And even though Ruth couldn't imagine what kind of misery plenty of food and pretty clothes and fancy vacations could possibly bring, she understood Bruna felt stifled.

What she also understood was the way the air had changed in the car. Arthur was seething. Bruna stared sullenly out the window. Ruth felt a deep pit of fear open up in her. Maybe Bruna marrying Arthur wasn't the worst that could happen. Maybe what was more troubling was Arthur's ruthless ambition for the Hawthorn Sisters—and his determination to see more miracles.

You didn't just make that sort of thing happen.

Chapter Twenty-Nine

Florence, Alabama
Present

Ember retrieved a key from under a brick at the edge of Jason's porch and let us in. We'd barely gathered in one of his elegant front rooms when Faulk swooped in, took the stage, and started in on Ember.

"You literally had our great-great-grandfather's bones *stashed* in a *tool shed*?" he yelled. "And for how long again?"

She opened her mouth to answer, but he cut her off.

"Then, like an absolute moron, you sell them to a complete stranger you met at a bar!" He jabbed a finger in my direction. "That man assaulted Eve, did you know that? He beat her and is currently extorting her for a multimillion-dollar coin that belongs to this family!"

"I know and I'm sorry. But I had no way of knowing."

"Some psychic gift you got there, Ember," Jason said.

Now she glared at him, refusing to engage. I couldn't say that I blamed her. Jason was a formidable opponent. And kind of a jerk, to echo Althea's memorable estimation. Griff, Althea, and I stood awkwardly through Jason's diatribe, eyes trained on the luxurious Persian rug. Only Ember sat, legs crossed in a languid pose in the corner of a purple silk sofa, and kept her gaze on him. Clearly, the cousins had spent a lifetime annoying one another. This was nothing new. In fact, she actually seemed to be reveling in this new disaster. When Jason finally ran out of steam, she stood, stretched her lithe torso, and wandered over to the gleaming, elaborately burled walnut-and-ebony Steinway.

"First of all, Jason, before we go further, I think we should acknowledge that the Hawthorn Sisters are back together again. In a manner of speaking." She struck a single key on the piano. The note sounded clear and loud in the cavernous room.

Jason slumped, his anger energy apparently zapped. "Okay, Ember. Congratulations."

"Secondly, I'd like to set the record straight," she continued. "My dad was the one who found Steadfast, not me. Probably when PawPaw Arthur was in the old folks' home. I'm guessing he started running his mouth about what he did to Steadfast back in the day and where he hid the body, so Daddy did what any good son would do. He went and got the bones before anybody else could. He was protecting our family, Jason. He wasn't about to let everybody know that PawPaw was a stone-cold killer."

She pressed a series of keys softly. *Da-da-da-da . . .* The sequence was vaguely familiar. The opening notes of a hymn. A chill went through me.

"I found the bones in the basement of our house," she continued. "But Dad threatened to whip the fire out of me if I told. So if you want to blame someone, Jason, blame the person who knew where the body was hidden in the first place. The person who might've even killed him—my shitty PawPaw, Arthur Holt."

Jason removed his jacket—a crisp blue houndstooth—and stretched his neck tiredly. "Your grandfather didn't kill Steadfast, Ember. Quit trying to make this into an episode of *Dateline*."

She huffed in frustration. "I'm not trying to make this into anything. You called this meeting, not me. Maybe because you're worried my PawPaw did kill Steadfast and steal the coin and somehow the stink of my family is going to get on you?"

A look of scorn covered Jason's face. "Are you kidding me? I don't care if your redneck-preacher grandpa killed our great-great-grandfather. You know what a scandal like that means for a political candidate these days."

"Means they get elected," Griff said. "And a million-dollar book deal."

Jason pointed at Griff. "And that's for a good scandal. This one just sucks."

"So why are we here then?" Ember asked. "Why did you call?"

Jason looked at me. "You tell her."

"Politicians may not be held to the same standards these days," I said to Ember. "But scandal can still kill a preacher's career. The old-time faithful don't like their heroes turning out to be thieves or tax dodgers or pedophiles. Or cold-blooded killers." I realized I'd been popping my knuckles nervously and folded my arms over my chest. "You know the usual suspects: Jim and Tammy Faye, Ted Haggard, the entire Boston diocese . . ."

Griff interjected. "The media loves this kind of takedown. These guys all see blood in the water—or at least a week's worth of clickbait."

I turned to Ember. "He's right. And a week is plenty long enough to decimate our donor base. What I need is your help finding the coin. By tomorrow night."

"You mean my psychic help?" she asked.

Jason snorted. "No, Ember. We need information. Did your dad tell you anything else about your shitty PawPaw stealing the coin and hiding it with the bones? Or do I have to pony up some cocaine before you'll tell us?"

Althea drifted to the window, looking grim. Griff walked to the piano, twisting in his earbuds. Ember looked like she'd been struck in the face.

I cocked my head at Jason. "Would you mind . . . Could we just keep things a little more . . ."

"Civil," Althea said curtly from the other side of the room.

"Sorry," he grumbled. "I just don't have the bandwidth."

"Well, you got all the Coe inheritance, *Jason*. You couldn't expect to get all the bandwidth too."

"Ember," I said. "I'm the one asking for help. And I'll do anything for it. Do it for me. Please."

She pulled me down beside her on a striped silk loveseat. "Give me your hand," she said abruptly. "The right one."

I offered it, and she closed her eyes for a couple of seconds.

"You have it too, don't you?" she said quietly.

I shook my head, forehead furrowed in confusion. But I knew what she was talking about. I knew damn well.

"You know things. The way I do."

Now she was eyeing me. Something in her expression, the child-like flash of vulnerability, tore at me. The way Jason seemed to consider his flesh and blood both an amusing annoyance—a dog that won't be housebroken—and an irrelevant part of his life seemed so unfair. I'd bet in another time, he'd have her carted off to the asylum. Like I might've been, with my weak arm.

"No," I said quietly, as gently as I could. "I don't know things."

She held fast to my hand. Her face had taken on a peculiar glow. "But you feel them sometimes, don't you? Their presence? The weight of them?"

The nerves in my hand were pinging in a way I hadn't felt in years. Like needles all over.

Ember sang softly. *"There's a land that is fairer than day, and by faith we can see it afar . . ."*

Her voice was easy and professional, with a unique smoke-throated rasp. It conjured up the sensation of sun after rain. Steam rising up from a grassy field. The musty smell of straw and old wood, canvas and human bodies. I heard the piano and the bass, heavy thunder from speakers rigged to poles. Everybody in the room seemed to come to attention. I stared at her.

Ember had drawn closer to me. "Can I tell your fortune, Eve?"

Althea's head turned sharply from the window. She glanced at me, but as our eyes met, I couldn't read her expression.

"Sure, I guess," I said.

Ember didn't speak. Instead she sang again, the next line of that old revival hymn—*"For the Father waits over the way to prepare us a dwelling place there . . ."* She nodded. "You know it, right?"

I realized I was clutching her hand in return now. I nodded back, then sang with her, *"In the sweet by and by we shall meet on that beautiful shore."*

It was uncanny, the way our voices blended—her soprano and my alto hooking on to the other's notes—then broke apart again, like we'd sung this a million times together. Now both Althea and Jason were staring, and Griff had pulled one earbud out.

Ember let go of my hand. "Your arm."

I met her eyes.

"There's something about it, isn't there? Something different?"

I shook my head, pressed my lips together. I could feel Griff watching us, but I wasn't about to volunteer any information.

Ember's forehead scrunched as she concentrated. "Her right arm was hurt too, right? Dove's. I remember Granny Bru told me this story. When they were at the fair—"

"Hey, guys," Griff tapped on his phone screen and pointed at a small white cube tucked behind a plant on a set of shelves. "The funniest thing. Listen."

Out of his phone came the sound of the tinny, scratched recordings. One of Margaret Luster's old tapes on the memory stick she'd given me.

"In the sweet by and by we shall meet on that beautiful shore," sang the voice from the speaker. Dove's.

"What is that?" Ember asked.

Griff spoke over the music. "It's some old tapes of Dove and Charles we were given. When you guys started singing, I realized that was the last song I'd been listening to." His gaze met mine, and once again, I felt my skin prickle. I'd thought he had interrupted in order to derail Ember's questioning about my arm. But in a way, in the strangest, eeriest way, maybe, instead, Dove had done it . . .

Ember turned to me, her hand gripping mine. "It's not a coincidence. It's a sign." Her eyes were wide and shining, and her neck was flushed a deep pink, and I felt an immediate, visceral need to get away from her.

Thankfully, just then, Jason stood and clapped his hands. "Okay! We should get started looking, don't y'all think? We have a little over twenty-four hours before Eve has to engage with this guy. In the meantime, I invite you to turn this place upside down."

Ember walked to Jason and chucked him under the chin. "We can pray to St. Anthony to help you find a lost item. Bet you Southern Baptists didn't know that."

He ignored her. "I'll unlock all the doors to every closet and maid's room and butler's pantry. I'll also turn on all the lights and open all the curtains. No corner, no nook or cranny's off-limits."

"Thanks again," I said.

"No problem," he said. "And here's the deal: For the next day and a half, I won't tell a soul on my staff about this. But if we find the coin and set the guy up, I'm calling every local and national news outlet that exists to be there when he gets busted."

"Deal," I said.

We trooped into the wide hall.

Griff stuffed his earbuds into his jeans pocket. "Check for hidden compartments, behind any built-in drawers or cabinets and for loose boards on stairways. Old houses are known for their creative hiding places." His hand rested against my lower back for a fleeting moment, and normally it would've sent a thrill through me. But I was still off-balance from earlier. The way Ember and I sang together . . . and then her question about my arm.

Where had that come from?

"Let's hope Steadfast made use of those hiding places," Ember said.

"Or Dove," I added. "She could've been the one who hid the coin."

"We'll see," she said with a wink. Then she ran halfway up the stairs, threw out her hands, and raised her face to the ceiling. "'Tony, Tony, look around. Something's lost and must be found!'"

Chapter Thirty

Florence, Alabama
1934

Ruth had always been a light sleeper, but with Steadfast's escapes and the ever-present hope that Dell would reappear on her windowsill, she'd gotten jumpier than Jesse James's watchdog. The night of the Billy Sunday meeting, she woke to the sound of thumping from directly overhead. Sounded like Steadfast's room.

She'd left the window open—she did every night now just in case Dell should happen by—and the night air was April-soft and pungent with the smell of lilacs. But Dell wasn't there and now she heard footsteps. She snatched her wrapper from the hook on the back of the door and flew into the entrance hall. The front door was shut—thank you, Jesus—but there were wet footprints leading from the door to the stairs.

Good goddamn gravy.

A thief in the house? Was that possible? She thought of the black pistol Steadfast kept in the back of the drawer in his wife's dressing table. If she was quiet, she could scoot in there and snatch the gun, quick-like, before the scoundrel caught sight of her.

She started up the stairs, keeping close to the wall to avoid the squeakers. Halfway up, she heard another thump.

Bloody hell. She scampered up the remainder of the steps and flung the door to the mint-green room open, feeling for the gun in the drawer. When her fingers touched metal, she drew it out, shaking, and pulled back the slide.

Her heart thundered and her breath came in short gasps. She crept stealthily out of the room and across the wide upstairs hall to Steadfast's door. She laid her fingertips on the wood, leaning close, but she didn't hear anything. She eased the doorknob to the right and pushed open the door a crack.

The room was dark and stuffy, the way Steadfast liked. All was quiet. She pushed the door open wide enough to slip through and saw the room wasn't entirely dark. It was lit by one candle. The flame stood tall and thin in the airless room. And in the glow, she saw Arthur Holt.

She let the gun drop down by her side. "Arthur!" she whispered.

He was standing by the bed, his hat in his hands. He stepped toward her and gulped.

She almost laughed at the incongruity of seeing him in Steadfast's bedroom. "You scared the devil out of me. What are you doing here?" She glanced at Steadfast, completely still on the bed.

Arthur wore an expression Ruth hadn't seen before and couldn't quite discern. Was it sheepishness? Shame? She couldn't tell. He was still dressed in his navy trousers and white shirt and tie from the Billy Sunday meeting, but now they were soaked. He must've gone back out after he dropped her and Bruna at their houses and gotten caught in the rain . . .

"Ruth. I'm so glad you've come." His voice came out in a rush, and immediately she knew he'd been up to no good. "I just wanted to speak with him. About the fair and our new venture."

She felt paralyzed. She knew she should do something, but she couldn't decide what it was.

"I thought if I explained it," he went on, "he'd surely see clear to giving you the time off."

Arthur spread his hands and sent her a look of desperation. Ruth's heart started back up with its skittery beat, and she felt icy all over. She knew what a lie sounded like, and this was one if she'd ever heard it.

"I was anxious to talk to him, to see if I could make him understand. You have to believe me, Ruth—"

"Believe you?" She looked at the old man again, and this time, she saw that his head was twisted unnaturally, his chin thrust toward the ceiling, his lips parted. She rushed to the bed and, putting the gun on the night table, leaned over Steadfast.

Steadfast's face was waxy and white, and Ruth's warm breath was all that stirred the air between them. She laid a hand on his chest, then his cheek. Feeling a rush of shame and then engulfing sorrow, she turned back to Arthur.

"What did you do?" she screamed.

He'd backed all the way across the room. "He was already like that when I got up here. I swear to it, Ruth! I swear!"

She stalked across the floor, grabbed fistfuls of his wet shirt, and shook him. "You murdered him! You murdered him!"

He let her shake him. Let her scream at him, then he even let her slap him, once, then twice. On the third time, he caught her hand.

"Ruth, you have to listen to me. He was already dead."

"I don't believe you," she cried.

"Do you have eyes? He was an old man! This is what happens to old men. They die, peacefully, in their beds. In their sleep. And that's what happened."

He released her. Mopped his face with both hands. Ruth clamped her mouth shut.

"I'm a Christian man, Ruth. I believe in the Ten Commandments. *Thou shalt not murder.* I wouldn't hurt anyone; I just came up here to talk."

She was still trembling, but she'd begun to settle. Doubt was creeping in. Maybe he was telling the truth. Maybe it was just a terrible coincidence and he was as horrified by the situation as she was.

"What happens now?" She wasn't asking him, not precisely.

He slumped and gave a half-hearted shrug. "Bruna's brothers will inherit all his money, and she'll get nothing—because that's the way the Coes work. And they'll turn you out, I suppose." He inhaled then blew it out. "But it's okay. You girls'll be fine. Because you're the Hawthorn Sisters, and I'm going to make sure you're well taken care of."

Ruth was trembling and Arthur put a hand against her face. His hand didn't feel like it could've snuffed the life out of an old man. It just felt strong and warm, even gentle. Tears gathered in her eyes.

"You touch people, and you heal them, Ruth," he said quietly. "That's a powerful gift."

Tears slipped down her cheeks, but she could only shake her head.

"I don't, not always. They imagine they're healed, or they heal themselves with a positive outlook. It's only sometimes I think it might be real—"

He interrupted her. "Shh. It doesn't matter what happens or why they think it happens. The important thing is that when people see you up there—in the lights, your hair shining like flames—they *believe* you."

She started crying softly, tears raining around her nose and slipping into her mouth. She didn't completely understand why. Steadfast Coe had been a thorn in her side. He'd devised new ways to torment her every day—stonewalling, sulking, and fussing from sunup to sundown. He'd even shot at her, for the love of Jesus, but the last time they spoke, he'd been so different. He'd been tender and generous. He'd trusted her.

She'd loved him, she understood that now.

"And now you'll have all the time you want to minister with Bruna." Arthur let his hand drop gently to her shoulder. "But we have a problem. You see that, right?"

She blinked up at him, wiping her clouded eyes. "No."

"They're all going to think the same thing you did. That I killed him."

"No. No, they won't. Not if you explain—"

He let out a humorless laugh. "He's a rich man. Was a rich man. And I'm a poor preacher's son. They're going to think exactly what you thought—that I killed him, either to get to his money through his granddaughter or because I was angry that he was taking your time away from the Hawthorn Sisters. In fact, they might even think we did it together."

Ruth felt another twinge of doubt. The words came out so smoothly, his logic running a couple of steps ahead of hers.

"I didn't want to say this right out . . ." he continued. "But I've thought of something. A way we can . . . not fix it, of course . . . but turn it around."

"Turn it around?"

He spoke carefully, deliberately, like he was picking his way over broken glass. "If we hide him and tell everyone he's wandered off, like before, no one will question it."

The skittering of her heart stopped. So did her breathing. "If we just leave him in his bed, no one will question it either," she answered in a level voice.

"You're not listening to what I'm saying, Ruth. Everyone in town will search for him, but only for a few days, and only just around here and maybe down to the river. If we hide him good, they won't find him. And they'll just think he did what he's done before, roamed down to the river or somewhere and gotten himself lost."

No. She could never do that to the Faulks. To Bruna.

"I was thinking . . ." He moved closer to her, his face open and alive. "Forgive me for saying this, but this is a fortuitous turn for us. I mean, we could use it for the good, like the Lord promises. Romans 8,

'All things work together for good.' A death is a sad thing, but we can use it for good, to His glory."

"What are you talking about?"

"At the fair, in July, there will be a miracle." His eyes were bright in the candlelight. Alive with a kind of fever. He looked half-crazed now. "A revelation, of sorts."

"Arthur, no—"

"Yes, yes." His brain seemed to be clicking away, his eyes unfocused. "One of the Hawthorn Sisters will get a vision from the Lord, showing her where Old Steadfast Coe ran off to. Where he spent his last moments just before he came face-to-face with his Maker."

"One of the Hawthorn Sisters?" she said.

The candle flickered and the light left his eyes. He straightened to his full height and looked down, studying her with a detachment that sent a bolt of fear into her chest. He smiled then, a strange curling smile, but his eyes had returned to their previous hardness.

"Good Lord, Ruth, why do you have to be this way? Why can't you be easy like Bruna? Sweet and submissive and adaptable like a godly woman should be? Why do you turn everything into a battle?"

She stood very still. Very conscious of the gun she'd placed on the table a couple of paces behind her. She could whirl around, grab it, and shoot him now. Tell the police she'd come upstairs to find him attacking Steadfast.

She could kill him.

But Bruna would be heartbroken. She might never forgive Ruth. And Bruna was all she had. Bruna, even more than Dell, was the one person she couldn't live without.

He went to the old man's desk, pulled a sheet of stationery out, and scribbled something on the bottom. "Come here."

She moved closer. He'd signed his name at the bottom of the paper.

He pushed the pen to her. "Go ahead, sign it. It's our agreement, that we're going to do this together. I'll fill in the rest later. This way, if you ever think about ratting me out, I'll make sure all the right people know."

She knew it was wrong, but she was afraid. So she took the pen and signed her name directly under his. He folded the paper and put it in his pocket. Then he pulled the sheet over Steadfast's head.

His voice took on a brisk, businesslike tone. "Now Ruth, listen close. The plan is, we'll hide him together. Far away from town. Then, at the fair, when it's time for the revelation, the Lord will speak to you and you'll bear witness to the crowd."

"Bruna's going to be out of town." It was the only thing she could say.

"I'll talk to her daddy. Man to man. He'll listen to reason."

Her insides felt as if they were being squeezed, and she couldn't think. There might not be any proof, but Arthur had killed Steadfast, she was now as sure of that as she'd ever been of anything.

"You won't breathe a word of this to Bruna. You will not say a thing. Do you understand?" Now his face looked monstrous in the candlelight.

"Yes," she said. Because she did. She understood that she'd just given her life and her future over to Arthur Holt.

Chapter Thirty-One

Florence, Alabama
Present

We didn't find the coin.

But it wasn't for a lack of trying. We ripped Jason's house apart, top to bottom, pulling out drawers and cabinets, throwing up window sashes and clearing out closets, but came up with nothing. Well, next to nothing. Griff came across an old pistol. It had been stuck down in the lining of an ancient portable ice chest, which was crammed back in the tiny, airless maid's room off the kitchen.

"Vintage Colt 1911," Griff said, studying it with admiration. "Classic World War I. The army sold these after the war. Steadfast probably bought it for home protection."

I felt a chill run up my spine.

Ember motioned for the gun and ejected the pistol's magazine. "Empty." She popped the magazine back in.

Jason took the gun from her. "You know, that reminds me. I heard a story once about Steadfast. Apparently, he shot a woman who worked for him in the foot."

"You're kidding," I said.

"You think he took a shot at Dove, and that gave her a reason to murder him?" Althea asked.

"I just think we need to be open to any possibility," Jason said.

Ember regarded the rest of us. "It's no secret the men in our family were a bunch of oddballs. Jason's granddad Orillion built himself a bomb shelter down in the Dismals Canyon complete with a state-of-the-art arsenal. Our great-uncle James ran off with four different women, but his wife wouldn't divorce him, so he always went back to her.

"The women on the other hand . . ." She ran her fingers over the windowsill, then pushed open the window and leaned out. "Mothers in our family always planted a hawthorn tree when a baby daughter was born. There used to be a big one here, out front, but I think it got hit by lightning or something. My Granny Bruna's tree is still going strong, though, over at the house where she grew up. And there's one across town too. That's my aunt Deborah's."

"What about your tree?" I asked. "Is that the one in your front yard?"

"Nobody planted one for me," she said simply. "That one was already at the house. That's how I knew the place was meant for me. It was a sign."

After we concluded we were done for the day, Althea, Griff, Ember, and I headed out for meatloaf and fries at a restaurant on the main drag. Althea and Griff said they'd go back to Jason's. I wanted to head over to the library to see if I could dig up any old newspaper clippings about Steadfast's disappearance or the coin in the archives. The thought of it filled me with gloom. Research seemed like the last thing that was going to crack this case.

We dropped Ember at her house, then went back to the hotel. I did a sequence of yoga poses, working my arm with a series of stretches, then took a scalding shower while Althea called Jay. When I was done, I sat on my bed, toweling my hair dry, already feeling better from the exercise.

Althea grabbed the remote and muted the TV. "You know, this thing you're doing—looking for the coin. It's really incredible, you know."

"Oh, well. I don't know about that." I tossed the towel over the back of a chair and started brushing my hair with my right hand. It felt good to force it to work again. In all the stress of the past few days, I'd been favoring it.

"That's what family does," I said. "You look out for each other."

"I admire how you do that. The way you're so committed to keeping them safe."

I lifted one shoulder. "I love them."

She propped her head on one hand. "So, here's a question. What would happen if you didn't do it? Take care of them, I mean. What would happen if you let them figure out their own stuff?"

I sent her a rueful grin. "They've got some really serious stuff."

"I remember. Your mom's breakdown. Danny's drinking. How much they depend on the foundation."

She said it so simply. Three short sentences—making my life sound so uncomplicated and clear. But there was more to it, wasn't there? There was my self-imposed isolation. The careful and constant balancing act of lies and half-truths. The crushing weight of feeling—of *knowing*—I was the only one who could protect the people I loved.

If I let my family figure out their own stuff, I'd have nothing left to do but face mine.

She raised a hand. "I get it. None of my business."

I hesitated. "It can be, if you want."

I knew I was taking a risk. If Althea was only on this trip because she was after the coin, this might be one way to get it. Convince me to confide in her, to shift my allegiances from my own family to her. The thing was, she'd already started to feel like a friend. Someone I could trust. Even if she did have ulterior motives, I still wanted to talk to her.

I swung my legs around to face her on the other bed. "What would you suggest I do?"

She scooted against the pile of pillows. "It just seems to me that this belief you have—that Diane's going to curl up and die without the foundation—well, she knows you think that and she's using it to hold you hostage. It may not be Piper Laurie locking you in a closet full of crucifixes, but it's still manipulative. Some people might even call it abuse."

I swallowed, my throat suddenly dry. "You'd call it that?"

"I don't know. I'm just making an observation."

"Well, all due respect, but you don't see everything."

"Okay." Althea's tone was gentle. "I didn't mean to offend you."

"Look. My mother's a fragile person. She doesn't handle life's difficulties well. When Danny and I were small, our father left. Then Mom left, psychologically. It wasn't her fault, and I understand how hard it was for her, but still . . . what she did had consequences."

"That must've been traumatic."

"It was a learning experience for sure." I shrugged.

"Look, I get that I'm inserting myself into a situation where I don't belong. I do that sometimes. Jay says it's my big heart. It's really that I'm plain old nosy."

I sat back against my bed's headboard too. "It's fine. Fire away."

She looked thoughtful. "I just wonder if—as long as you think it's your job to protect your mom from the big bad world, maybe she's going to let you?"

I didn't say anything. I honestly hadn't considered the idea that I may not be as indispensable—in my mom's life, in Danny's, at the foundation—as I thought I was. I'd just assumed that what the preacher at Dove's funeral had told me was an irrefutable truth, that I was the keeper of the flame.

But what if it wasn't? What if all this energy I'd expended on making sure everything was under control at all times, had just been me spinning my wheels?

Althea tilted her head sympathetically. "I'm here to help in any way I can." She hesitated. "You know, I told you at the hospital opening that I'd wanted to meet you for a long time. But I wasn't entirely honest about why."

I straightened, my nerves on alert.

"I never told you this," Althea said, "but when I was looking for Dove all those years ago, I ran across some stories about her. One in particular."

"Okay," I said, cautious.

"Back in the thirties, when she was doing a revival up in eastern Alabama, she took my great-grandmother up to the mountain to see a young girl who'd gotten pregnant. The girl was miscarrying, Dove said, and she prayed for her." Althea leveled her gaze at me. "The baby lived. There was no way she could've known about this girl, Eve. Her pregnancy was a secret. She hadn't told anybody."

"What happened?"

"When the baby grew up, she and Dove became friends. Later on, after Charles died and Dove moved back to Alabama, they were roommates for a few years."

"Wow. I never heard that story." I rose wearily and walked to the window. Peeked to the street outside. It was just a deserted parking lot with one lone bike lying on its side. "But it doesn't change what she told me. That her gift was a lie. All of it. Every healing or miracle she ever did."

"But what if that wasn't true? What if some of it was real? And she just—I don't know—couldn't guarantee it or something, and so she hedged her bets and told you she was a fake?"

I didn't answer, but it made me think. About all those times my arm tingled and then something happened: a math test was canceled, we didn't have to run the mile in PE, Ryan Dekko called me cute, right to my face. And then there was that moment earlier today when Ember and I had harmonized so perfectly, so unexpectedly, on that old hymn—the one Griff had been listening to Ruth and Bruna sing at that very moment.

I let out a caustic, humorless laugh. "Look, I wish I could use some psychic gift and find the coin. But as much as Dove didn't have a gift, I have even less of one."

"But how do you know? I mean, beyond all doubt?" At my silence, she spoke again. "I wasn't honest with you about another thing, Eve."

I felt afraid to look at her directly.

"I came along on this trip because I wanted something from you. Your gift. The thing Dove told you she didn't have."

My heart suddenly felt impossibly heavy, like somebody had aimed a gun and shot it full of lead. Althea had come on this trip because she needed something from me. It hadn't been altruism or friendship or even loyalty to Dove. I was a means to an end.

Althea took a deep breath, her voice raw. "It's Jay. He's . . ." She shook her head. "They don't know what he is. They think maybe it's something to do with his immune system. Maybe Lyme disease, maybe not. Whatever it is, he's not right."

I knew I should comfort her, and part of me wanted to, but I couldn't.

She pinched the bridge of her nose. "It's not your problem. I shouldn't have made it yours. It's just—he's struggling. We're all struggling."

I sat there, silently ruminating. I wanted to be okay with Althea's confession, but I was angry—that she hadn't been honest with me from the start. That yet another person thought I could perform miracles—just because I was related to Dove. And I was tired too, of feeling so goddamn alone.

I folded my arms over my chest. "I'm sorry."

"You're mad too. Which you have a right to be. I'm sorry I wasn't straight with you. I should have told you right off the bat."

I took a deep breath. "It's okay, Althea."

She shrugged, her eyes red and shiny with tears.

"He's with the kids? Jay?"

She shook her head. "My mother-in-law has them. Jay can't drive some days. He can't be in a room with too much light. His legs go numb, he can't sleep. Eve, I'm sorry I wasn't honest, but I'm grasping at straws here. I love him so much. I've loved him since I was just a kid."

"Althea," I said. "I hate that this is happening to the two of you. And I wish I could help you. But I can't. I don't have any magical power."

She nodded mutely.

"If you want to leave, if you want to go home to him, I understand."

She hauled herself off the bed with a groan and rifled through her suitcase. "I cared about Dove and I care about you. If you'll have me—and I swear to tell you the truth about everything from now on—I'd like to stay."

I smiled. "Okay. I'd like that. If it's what you want to do."

"All right. I'm going to shower. Wash off all this grime."

She slung a clean pair of sweatpants and T-shirt over her shoulder, and I felt a pang of envy watching her. Althea had discovered the secrets of her family with Dove by her side. She'd gotten to know my grandmother in a way I never had the chance to. All the more reason I should listen to her. Maybe she'd gotten wisdom from Dove that I'd missed. Or maybe she was just using me. I felt so confused.

"Althea?" I said as she headed for the bathroom.

"Yep?"

"I apologize if I misled you in any way. But I'm not the one who can give you your miracle."

"Don't sweat it. Still the best girls' trip ever." She sent me a wry grin and shut the door behind her.

Chapter Thirty-Two

Florence, Alabama
1934

Edith Faulk might not have been an overly affectionate daughter, but she was fiercely dedicated to preserving the Coe family reputation. As such, she was distraught over Steadfast's disappearance.

She ordered the police out on a search and tried to galvanize the town, but most folks demurred. They murmured that Steadfast Coe was old, gone off on his head, and prone to wandering; someone would probably find him soon enough. Because of this, there was little support for more than a listless walk down to the river and back. And after a week, no one was even talking about it down at the grocery, the feed and seed, or the butcher shop.

In the middle of the hubbub, Ruth visited Bruna at her parents' home. It was the first time she'd ever been there, and she was agog at the place. The house, just a few blocks away from Steadfast's, was as different as the sun from the moon. With its modern design, the low-slung house of red brick and wood was full of angles and corners that slunk along the property like an angular cat waiting for its prey. Ruth had never seen anything like it.

Bruna met her in a large open room with one wall of built-in shelves, another of glass. She rushed to Ruth and embraced her.

"I can't believe he's gone missing," she sobbed into her friend's arms. "I'll never forgive myself for being so mean about him."

Ruth hugged her hard.

"He's a nasty son of a gun," Bruna said. "Even still, I can't stand the thought of him out there, wandering around somewhere hungry and cold."

Ruth patted her arm. "If he's out there, we'll find him, I promise you."

This was the absolute truth. Ruth and Arthur had rolled Steadfast into a sheet and dragged him outside. Then they'd hauled him into the back seat of Arthur's father's car and driven down Gunwaleford Road all the way to the end, where Arthur had tied the sheet to hold the dead man inside. They'd hiked for a mile and a half, each of them taking one corner of the sheet—through rain, over cotton and corn fields, past stands of oaks and pecans all the way to a shallow gorge with a stream.

The narrow trickle of water led into a cave that the locals called Key Cave, where moonshiners were known to hide their wares and pay the police to keep away. They waited there for a whole hour, just to make sure the coast was clear. Then the two of them dragged the old man to the back of the cave and pushed him into a narrow crevice, chinking the opening with as many rocks as they could gather.

"After you have your vision, and we take up a collection," Arthur said, "I'll head out here and pull him back out so it looks like he wandered into the cave."

Ruth had nodded mutely.

Now she was comforting Steadfast's granddaughter. She felt like such a fraud.

"But truly, I'm worried about you. Where will you go?" Bruna asked Ruth in the living room of the extraordinary house.

"Oh, don't you worry about me," Ruth said. "I'll be fine."

"Maybe Arthur can cut you an advance of your share now, and you can get a room in town."

Ruth clasped her friend's hands in hers. "That's a good idea. I'll mention it to him."

"Or you could stay here." Bruna brightened slightly.

Ruth let go of her hands. "I wouldn't want to take advantage. I'll go to town and see what I can rustle up." She gave Bruna another hug and headed toward the front door.

"Ruth—"

Bruna's face was pale and drawn. She was sad, Ruth thought, but she would be okay. The Hawthorn Sisters would have more meetings, put on shows in Alabama and Mississippi, pray over folks and give them words from the Lord to lift them up. She had the coin, but she couldn't very well pawn it off, not this soon after Steadfast's disappearance. That would cast suspicion on her for sure.

So that was it then. She'd stay, for now. Tell Dell that they must put off a wedding until later. Maybe after all this business was done, the four of them, she and Dell, Bruna and Arthur, could go to California. The Hawthorn Sisters could make enough money out there, and each of the girls could take off on her own. Bruna would have what she wanted: Arthur and freedom from Edith and Harold. And Ruth would have Dell.

She just needed to trust that Arthur had everything well in hand.

There was another part of her that knew this wasn't true. Arthur had broken into Steadfast's house and murdered him in cold blood, and there was no getting around it. And he'd done it for nothing but money.

Which is why Ruth knew, as clearly as she knew her own name, that if she crossed him, if she mucked up his plan in any way, Arthur would choke the breath out of her too. And he'd quite enjoy it, she had a feeling. So she had to think quick. To figure another way out . . . not only for her but for Bruna as well.

"I'll see you soon," Ruth said and, after kissing her cheek, left Bruna standing alone in the strange, modern house.

The next week, Bruna and her two older brothers, James and Orillion, and her mother came to clear out Steadfast's house of valuables. There was still an off chance in their view that the old man was just lost, but in his absence, the house was a target for thieves, and something must be done about that.

"Am I being sent away?" Ruth asked Bruna when the brothers vanished upstairs.

Bruna took her hand and pulled her back to the kitchen. "No, not yet. Mother still believes there's a chance he'll come back. They'd like you to stay until then, but I'm afraid they're cutting your pay."

Ruth nodded mutely.

"We'll bring some bacon and cornmeal by—and anything we can from the garden. Hope you like cucumbers." She sent Ruth a pained smile. "They said you can stay here, for at least a few more weeks. At least until Mother's ready to sell or board the place up."

"Bruna!" one of the brothers yelled from a front room.

Bruna scanned the cupboards. "James's wife is going to want that china. Can you help me bring it out to the dining room?"

They picked the house cleaner than a chicken carcass. The silver, the jewelry, the jade figurines, and assorted other curios that Ruth had not realized were worth a mint—all of these were wrapped in newspaper, hauled out in wooden crates, and loaded on one of the brother's trucks.

After bringing out Steadfast's gold-rimmed china and stacking it on the dining room table, Ruth retreated to her room and sat on her bed, eyeing the keyhole where she'd dropped the coin. Waiting for one of them to discover its absence. Finally, she heard the expected commotion, voices in the front hall, and braced herself.

"The little vagabond's stolen it!" one of the brothers shouted.

"She did no such thing!" said Bruna. "I know Ruth Davidson, and she's as honest as the day is long. He hid it, just like the others."

"But all the others are in the jar, Bruna. The Flowing Hair is the only one missing . . ."

Their voices lowered and Ruth couldn't make out the words. She kept her eyes trained on the brass keyhole. She could never tell Bruna's family that Steadfast had given her the coin. Even if they did believe her story—which seemed unlikely—they'd say the old man was muddled in the head and didn't know what he was doing. They'd demand she return it and that would be the end of that.

Ruth set her jaw. Steadfast had given her the coin, and he'd known exactly what he was doing. Whether it was the most valuable thing on earth or just a worthless piece of tin, it belonged to her now.

She would say nothing. The coin would stay safely tucked in the door until she decided it was time to fetch it. That time could be now if she chose. She could find Dell, get the tarnation out of Alabama, and start a new life. But if she left, there was no doubt in her mind Arthur would track her down and kill her just like he killed Steadfast.

"Ruth. Could you come here, please?" It was Edith.

When Ruth entered the front hall, the two strapping brothers directed two sets of nearly identical, accusing eyes at her. Bruna looked angry.

Edith directed her imperious profile at Ruth. "Ruth, my father had a somewhat valuable coin collection. Error coins, some of them dating back to before the Revolutionary War. You know of them?"

Ruth twisted her hands. "Yes, ma'am."

"Well, I'm afraid one of them is missing. Actually, the most valuable coin in the entire collection. It's called the Flowing Hair." Edith's gaze bore into her, cold and accusing. "Have you seen it?"

Ruth stammered. "No, ma'am. I mean, yes, I saw it once, when Mr. Coe showed it to me, in his wife's bedroom . . ."

They all stared at her.

"But I didn't steal nothing," she said, her voice low and steady and strong. "I wouldn't do that to Mr. Coe. Or to his family."

The brothers huffed and stamped and rolled their eyes like a pair of bulls in a pen, but Edith nodded.

"Bruna, you and Ruth look again. Tell us if you come across it."

"Yes, ma'am," Ruth said. "I'll give all the rooms a good going-over tomorrow first thing."

"I bet you will," grumbled one of the brothers. "Gleanings from the field."

"You shut your trap," Bruna snapped, and with that, they were out the door and down the porch steps to the waiting truck. Bruna caught Ruth's hand. "I'm sorry. They're a couple of stupid brutes."

Ruth thought it better not to say anything. She might give herself away. Confess, and then they'd take the coin from her. But she wouldn't. It was hers, fair and square. And she wasn't giving it up.

Chapter Thirty-Three

Florence, Alabama
Present

I was too restless to sleep, so I decided to find a place where I could have a quick beer and fine-tune my statement on behalf of the foundation. I threw on a clean pair of jeans, a white blouse, and flip-flops and was on my way out of the hotel when I ran into Griff.

"Hey, do you have a second?" he asked.

We sat at one of the tables in the breakfast area and he pulled out his phone. "I didn't want to bring it up at dinner because I thought you deserved to know first, but I did find something today."

I felt a ripple of anxiety. Not more bad news. *Please.* "What?"

He handed over his phone, showing an article from an archived website. "It's from 1934, an interview with the husband of Magdalene Kittle, the woman who killed her seven-year-old son."

I scrolled, summarizing. "He blamed the Hawthorn Sisters for his son's death. He said Ruth Davidson told his wife that God would only answer her prayers if she was blameless as a mother and wife. Obeying her husband and bringing her unruly children to heel." I looked up. "No matter the cost."

I skimmed farther down, slowing when I saw the quote from Kittle's husband. "'As long as she lives may God never give that charlatan a night's rest. It's sure as hell better than I'd do for her.'" I looked at Griff. "Wow."

Griff looked almost sorry he'd shown it to me. "I know it's a stretch, but do you think somebody in that man's family, like maybe one of the other kids, might've held a grudge against Ruth because of what happened? Do you think they could've killed Dove and attacked you to get revenge?"

My shoulders slumped. "It's possible, I guess. Hard to believe that someone could hold on to that kind of hate for so many years."

We both fell into agitated silence.

"Now I feel like an asshole," Griff said after a while.

"No, it's fine. We're all grasping at straws."

"Do you want a drink?" He met my eyes. "In my room?"

"Yes," came my answer, unhesitating. "I absolutely do."

In his room, he poured me a glass of wine he'd picked up earlier. I lay on the bed and took note of his room. His clothes were not folded but heaped messily on top of his suitcase. Laptop and camera, hard drive and noise-canceling headphones along with a mess of cords and chargers piled in a jumble on the desk. Coins, wallet, and watch. Phone charging on the nightstand. The mundane items of his life and job brought me comfort in a strange way. And gratitude. This man had put his life on hold to help me. I wish I could tell him he was doing the right thing.

I stared at the ceiling, waiting for something, I didn't know what exactly, to overtake me.

Was it relief? Dismay? A kind of zen understanding that would impart some insight into what was going on? Even with the wine to help, it really was impossible to say. I just felt like I should be able to explain what spending the day in Steadfast Coe's house had meant to me.

Combing through the place had been a strange experience, that was for sure. While no divine force had descended like Ember had hoped, no holy pillar of fire directing us to the coin's location, I'd still felt the place held some kind of special meaning. With every room I entered, every drawer I opened, every loose board I tried to pry up, I'd felt something sharpen inside me. Just a sliver of familiarity. The subtlest knife-edge of a sense that I'd been there before.

No, not been there.

Knew the place. Yes, that was it. In an inexplicable way, I was familiar with the patterns of the wallpaper in the upstairs hallway, the weave of the bed hangings and rugs in the upstairs rooms. I expected the musty odor of the basement. The sticky slick of the polished wood banister. The seasick tilt of the oak plank floors under my feet.

Or maybe it was just my subconscious yearning to understand Dove. To really, finally know the woman who was my grandmother.

At any rate, one thing I was absolutely sure of was that our motley search party wasn't going to find the coin. But we'd had to search, that I knew as well. We had to exhaust all of our options.

Isn't that the way stories went?

You exhaust all options and then, in the third act, the miracle.

I wanted to laugh hysterically. Or cry hysterically. Either would be a relief at the moment, instead of this vague sense of impending doom. But here I lay on Griff's bed, sipping wine in a not unpleasant haze and watching him futz with the remote control. I was no third-act heroine, figuring out a way to save the day. I was just a person who wanted to protect her family but couldn't. A failure.

But God, did it feel nice to be slightly drunk in a hotel room alone with this man. Watching him move, studying the way the muscles in his arms flexed and bunched. The way his hair fell over his eyes. The way his jeans moved with his body as he found a silly movie on cable and then grinned at me.

I liked pretending that I didn't have any cares in the world. I liked pretending that my mother wasn't two thousand miles away, making her way closer and closer to the cliff's edge in my absence. I liked, I liked, I liked . . .

He came to the bed in one fluid movement and pushed me down, suspended over me. I reached up to run my fingertips down his cheek and checked the TV.

"Ah," I said. "*The Fast and the Furious: The Fate of the Furious*. The best of the franchise. Directed by the guy who directed *Friday* and *Straight Outta Compton*."

"Exemplary film knowledge, Eve. I'm impressed."

"Pssh. Girls know movies too." My fingers drifted down one arm. I saw the name *Anna* again.

"You know," he said, "you've never asked to listen to those tapes of Dove and Charles, the ones Margaret Luster gave us. If you want, I could cue them up for you."

I focused on Griff's arm. "I'd rather talk about this tattoo. You sure are committed to your ex."

"She's not an ex. She's family, my great-grandmother. I never knew her, just heard stories from my great-aunts. They said she was a little badass. A survivor."

A little lower down, I found another name. I traced the letters. *J-O-Y.*

"That's my Gram. Total sweetheart. Put up with a lot. More than she should have had to. Wound up with kidney cancer for her trouble."

"I'm sorry." I ran my fingers over the next name, *Helena*. I had a feeling who she was, but I wanted to hear what Griff had to say. This man was more complicated than I'd expected. He paid attention. He saw the people around him and cared deeply about them.

"My mom," he said. "She's smart, tough . . . the worst kind of persistent sometimes. But sweet about it. You never see the storm coming." He laughed. "Half my life, I wanted to kill her, but ultimately her qualities paid off. She's the one who convinced me to go to film school."

"She sounds great."

"Well, she's a caretaker. All of them were, which is probably why they stuck with their men longer than they should have."

I turned my head and studied the nondescript beige polyester curtains.

"I got the tattoos because I wanted to honor them. And to remember that, for me and whoever I end up with, we'll be on equal footing. I don't want one person propping up the other. It's not healthy. Not what I call love."

I gnawed at the inside of my cheek, discomfited. He was pretty much describing my relationship with my mother, stem to stern—and in almost the exact terms Althea had used just moments ago. And they weren't that far off. I'd spent the last half-dozen-plus years keeping secrets that I was scared might upset my mom. I'd gone to work for a company I didn't believe in for her. I put my desires and plans on hold so that I could keep tabs on her.

I'd lost myself.

"Which reminds me," he continued, "I have some bad news."

I frowned. "Oh, no."

"I made the mistake of letting it slip to my parents that I was up here, and they rented a house on the river . . . so they could maybe meet us for dinner or something."

Relief washed over me. And then a different kind of feeling. One that felt suspiciously like happiness. Did he consider us together now? We hadn't had time to talk, and things had moved so quickly.

"Don't worry," Griff said. "I told them it was impossible. That we were too busy with the documentary."

I grinned in spite of myself, relief turning into a different feeling altogether. Sure, disaster loomed just around the corner, but Griff wanting me to meet his parents was . . . an interesting twist. Maybe it was the booze, but I felt buoyed by the thought. Which was a welcome change from the constant gut-churning dread I had been experiencing.

"I'd love to meet them," I said. "We should go."

His eyebrows shot up. "You would? We should?"

"Why not? Otherwise, I'm just going to be sitting around here, twiddling my thumbs, waiting for the end of the world. I might as well keep myself busy." I tried to wriggle my way up, but he gently pressed against my chest, pushing me back to the bed. But he was smiling.

"No, Eve. Just rest. You'll need every ounce of strength for the interrogation. Remember when I interviewed, I told you they followed Dove and Charles's ministry for years? They're fans."

I laughed. "You told me all this. Your dad was calling you for updates?"

"You don't understand."

"Oh, come on, Griff, it's no big deal. Really. I'm used to it. Why are you so bugged?"

He sighed. "My dad ran up some debts in my mom's name. Substantial debts. Anyway, he says it's all paid off, and Mom says they're trying to work it out. Which is good, I guess. But part of getting my mom back means he's got to make nice with me. So, dinner."

I patted his arm. "Think of it this way. If we find the coin, we won't be able to go anyway."

"Good point," he said, looking glum. "Now we've really gotta find that coin."

I laughed. "But I'd really like to meet your family as well. I would. What are Mr. and Mrs. Murray like? Kind and beautiful and talented, like their son?"

He smiled. "I'm Murray, remember? They're Singley. That's my father's name. Bobby Singley."

The way he said it, he almost seemed ashamed. But I didn't want that, not at all. I wanted him to know I didn't judge him by what his father was like. I wanted him—I realized with a jolt—to love me.

My fingers found his chest and then his stomach. I hooked them in the waistband of his jeans. He got very still. I smiled up at him, suddenly nervous. "It's good you can choose the name you want. You can be whoever you want, Griff Murray."

He kissed me, lips soft. "Right now? I just want to be the guy who makes love to you."

Chapter Thirty-Four

Florence, Alabama
1934

When the truck carrying Steadfast's most valuable possessions rumbled off, Ruth locked every door and window. She double-checked that Steadfast's pistol was still safely stowed in the ice cave where she'd hidden it the night after Arthur had left, then sat on the edge of her bed.

She couldn't stop thinking about poor dead Steadfast, his body wedged into the crevice of the cave. What did he look like now? Had the cold air in the cave slowed the process of decay? Had the skin stayed firm? The organs turned to jelly yet? Maybe he'd never rot, but be preserved forever, his milky eyes always open and staring. The mottled skin of his face forever frozen in a death mask, the last expression on his face when he saw his murderer.

Maybe this was how a ghost was made. Murder, the body secretly stashed away in a cave. A con to make money for the one who did the deed. Maybe this was what troubled a soul so deeply it could not leave this earth, but stayed, hovering and swirling, infecting the minds of the guilty. He would come back, Ruth thought, to his home, where he'd last been alive. He would find her here and haunt her. And she would go mad, locked up in this house alone. Just her, this black pistol, and a coin hidden inside a door.

She was woken sometime in the middle of the night by the sound of tapping. She struggled up, bleary and confused. But then she saw Dell's face appear in the window and he motioned for her to let him in.

She unlocked the window, and he climbed through, sweating from exertion and the warm spring night. She didn't wait for an explanation as to where he'd been or why the job in Texas had taken so long. She just pulled him onto the bed and kissed his face all over.

He kissed her back, his lips and tongue ardent, but he did not touch her like last time. He was being a gentleman this go 'round, trying to do the honorable thing. The strange thing was, she wished he wouldn't. The one thing she longed for, the very thing she needed tonight, was to lose herself in him.

He pulled loose from her arms. "I heard your old man went off. That's bad luck."

Her eyes dropped to study his lovely mouth. She didn't dare tell him what she suspected Arthur of doing and what he planned for Ruth to do at the fair. She had no doubt Dell would find the boy and beat the stuffing right out of him, then and there. And word would get out, putting Ruth herself under suspicion.

"Yes," she finally said. "They haven't found him. They think he might've died."

"That's bad news." He took her hands. "Ruth, I got some bad news of my own. Texas was a bust. The job went sour and two of the boys got caught. They're on their way to the penitentiary."

She went cold. "You got away?"

He nodded. "But they saw me. One of the cops, I'm pretty sure."

She opened her mouth.

"And a clerk. And maybe a girl on the street outside the bank."

"Dell!"

"I know, I know. I shouldn't have even come back here—there's plenty of folks around here who'd be tickled pink to see me locked up—but I couldn't leave you in the lurch. I had to tell you what happened." He hesitated. "I ain't got no money, Ruth."

She touched his face, then held it between her hands, drinking in the sight of his beautiful angled cheek, the ruddy skin and golden fuzz that covered it. "I got money," she said. "Lots of it. As a matter of fact, I've got more money in this here room than was in that whole bank in Texas."

He bolted upright. She couldn't help but delight in the sight of him—the way his collar gapped, showing the hollow in his neck and then the rise of his hard chest. The curve of his stomach, his strong legs and what rose between them. What she liked most was the way he looked at her. It was everything wonderful and warm, that mixture of boyish admiration and manly lust.

"Stop joking," he said.

"I'm not joking." She scrambled out of the bed and over to the door, where she seductively turned the knob and swung open the door. She struck a pose against it, vamping.

"What? How?"

"You ever hear of the Hawthorn Sisters?"

"Sure. I worked a meeting they were at. So many folks they couldn't fit 'em in the tent, so they stood outside. While they sang "Turn Your Eyes upon Jesus," I lightened a few folks' burdens myself—"

"Dell." Ruth gave him a wry look. A look she knew he'd understand.

"Hold up. That was you in that tent singing?" he said.

She pursed her lips and lifted an eyebrow. He blinked and shook his head like an overgrown puppy, then smiled with delight.

"I got more than just the money from the Hawthorn Sisters," Ruth said. "I got something big. Something Mr. Coe gave me. A coin, and it's worth a whole year's wages or more."

His eyes drifted back up to her face. "Good goddamn gravy."

"What's wrong?" she demanded.

He hesitated. "It's just that I heard something about that coin. Some fellas talking in town."

She paled. "What? What did they say?"

"That the coin went missing with old Mr. Coe. That . . . somebody most likely stole it."

She frowned. "Who?"

Dell put his hands in his pockets. "Maybe a vagrant. Maybe the maid."

"I didn't steal it," she protested hotly. "He gave it to me."

"I know. I believe you. But listen. Forget that old coin. I can do another job, better than that one in Texas. I'll get us situated and we'll be all set. Besides, the husband is supposed to provide for his wife."

She smacked her forehead. "What does it matter who does it? It's done! He gave me the coin and now we got money and plenty of it."

"If we try to sell it, they'll come after you for stealing, I guarantee it."

"We'll go to Tennessee to sell it. To New York!" She moved back to him and tucked his straw-gold hair behind his ear. "I'll tell you where I hid it."

He put a finger to her lips. "No. Tell me later, after I've got us situated. Okay?"

"Oh, Dell." She huffed and turned her back to him. He was going to hang on to that silly notion of providing for her all by himself, no matter what she said. Stubborn son of a gun.

"After I get us set up," Dell said, "we'll take your coin and sell it. Put the money away for later. For when we got kids or decide to take off to parts unknown." He plucked at her nightgown, pulled until she relented and let him take her face in his hands. He kissed her tenderly and looked deeply into her eyes. "I want to take you to parts unknown, Ruthie. I want to see the world with you."

She traced a finger along his cheek. "Well, the Hawthorn Sisters got a big show in July. At the fair."

He kissed her again. "How'm I gonna wait till July, huh, Ruthie?"

"I'll tell you how. Lay low and stay out of trouble. Then come back the last night of the fair. We'll leave then."

The way he stared at her, like she was the cleverest, prettiest girl he'd ever laid eyes on, made her believe it. She was clever and she was pretty, and when she and Dell were together, why, they could handle just about anything this nasty old world threw at them.

She had another thought too—that there was no reason in the world for Dell to act like a gentleman when they were alone in her tiny room, not if she didn't want him to. After their first night together, she knew what she wanted. And that was to touch Dell's skin, to feel his mouth, his hands, and more on her. So why on God's green earth should she pretend otherwise? As a matter of fact, what reason was there to wait on Dell to get things rolling? She had two hands of her own, didn't she?

She gathered up her nightgown, pulled it over her head, and tossed it aside, enjoying the look that came over Dell's face.

"Let's do what we did the other night," she said. "But this time, let's take our time."

Chapter Thirty-Five

Florence, Alabama
Present

The next morning, I woke with knots in my stomach. For good reason. It was Monday. Day three. The day the asshole was due to call in his chips.

If I hadn't found the coin in roughly—I glanced at the clock radio beside Griff's bed—twelve hours, the foundation was toast. Mom was in danger of another breakdown and my future was . . . well, it was going to look identical to what I'd been doing for the past eight years.

At some point today, I was going to have to call Danny. Tell him everything and get him to sign off on the official statement for the foundation for Pam and Martin in the communications department. And then we'd have to call Mom.

I slipped out between the covers, and felt a hand grab my arm.

"Come back."

His grip was light but insistent. I wanted to. Wanted more than anything to crawl back into bed with Griff and repeat the night over and over again. But I couldn't. I had work to do.

"I'll see you tonight." I kissed him and tried not to melt into his arms as they circled around me. "Dinner with your parents at six-thirty.

Asshole calls around seven-thirty or eight. From there, I guess we just figure it out."

"You're going to survive this. I know it."

"Thanks."

Griff reluctantly let me go, and I showered, then headed on foot to the library. I spent a couple of hours in the reference room looking for something—anything—regarding Steadfast Coe's personal coin collection. There wasn't a single article. I did stumble across the same advertisement Margaret had shown us, the one touting the Hawthorn Sisters' three-night appearance at the North Alabama State Fair. Once again, I stared at the grainy black-and-white photo of Dove and Bruna holding hands onstage, unable to tear my eyes from the pair.

Two more articles caught my eye—one in the *Florence Times* about Edith Faulk's election as president of the Florence Women's Auxiliary and one in the *Tri-Cities Daily* that mentioned Steadfast Coe's disappearance. Also, I found a brief summary of Jason's TV interview that Margaret Luster had mentioned. And then something more interesting: Steadfast's obituary, tucked in the back pages of the March 1936 issue of the paper, the date the family must have decided to have him officially declared dead.

> *Founder of Coe Lumber, a member of First Presbyterian Church, and an important figure in the building of the city, Mr. Coe was widely known to possess a rare coin collection. The most valuable coin was supposedly stolen by the outlaw Dell Davidson. Davidson is currently believed to be running with a gang in Baton Rouge . . .*

Somehow the story had changed, at least the official one. If Steadfast's family really suspected Ruth, they had certainly kept the matter quiet. At least to the point that local journalists were speculating about Dell Davidson's involvement.

Throughout the day, Griff had been updating me on the others' second search of Jason's house. The news wasn't good. They'd come up empty-handed again. Now it was five o'clock. I wasn't supposed to meet him and his parents for dinner for another hour and a half, so I decided to take a walk. I needed to breathe, to take some time alone and prepare myself for the coming storm.

I headed downstairs and out of the library, doubling back down a side road. A block or two along, I found myself before a Gothic-style redbrick church. First Presbyterian, which was over two hundred years old according to the placard on the lawn. I crept around the side, spotting a cemetery.

I saw the granite obelisk, towering above every other marker, before I even reached the gate. **STEADFAST ORILLION COE September 6, 1847–April 11, 1934**. Next to it, **LUCETTE RAMEY COE** and another set of dates. Steadfast's wife.

I sighed heavily, studying her stone. "He'll be home soon, Lucette. Just a matter of time."

I dialed Danny's number, getting his voice mail. "Danny, there's something we need to talk about. Something important. Call me when you can." I paused, hoping something comforting would come out of my mouth, but it didn't. All I felt was hopelessness.

"I love you," I said and hung up.

A horn made me jump. The window of a gleaming black Lexus rolled down, and Jason Faulk's handsome face peered out from the cool confines of the sedan. He was dressed in another suit, this time spotless ivory linen. "Need a ride?"

I climbed in and Jason pointed the car toward the river.

"I see you found Steadfast's grave," Jason said.

I sent him a glum look. "Won't be empty for long, the way things are going."

"You got a minute to spare? Or am I interrupting your plans to wander morosely around town?"

I ignored his sarcasm. "I've got dinner at six-thirty." I gazed out the window at the quiet street. "But yeah, basically just killing time until then."

He stopped at a light. "Today, while we were searching my house, Ember had one of her psychic moments, and we practically destroyed the original, old-growth chestnut flooring in one of my upstairs bedrooms," he said genially. "All we found were a couple of very startled spiders."

I sighed. "I appreciate you letting us into your home. I appreciate your help."

"I'm sorry it turned out this way, Eve. I really am."

"Can I ask where we're going?" I said.

"I have to go down to Birmingham for a couple of meetings, but I was hoping to find you so we could talk, just the two of us, before I left. I'm taking you to the best spot in north Alabama. Where I go when I need to get my head right. You okay with that?"

"Sure, why not?"

We sped over the bridge and headed up the opposite bluff. The winding road was shaded by old elms and oaks, the houses set far back from the road and mostly obscured from view.

"Forgive me if I'm talking out of turn," Jason said. "But I got to thinking about your predicament and it occurred to me that you might actually benefit from my experience." He turned between two broken-down split-rail fence ends and wheeled down a long single-lane drive. "As you may imagine, it's no cakewalk for a gay man to announce that he's going to run for governor in this state. But after the flurry of attention died down—including the charming social media posts suggesting I be run out of the state and/or imprisoned—I realized nobody could stop me from doing what I wanted to do. What I was born to do. So I picked myself up and got back to work. People may not like it, but I'm still here. And still going."

"I admire you for that."

"It wasn't easy. But I really love this place and the people, most of them."

"Yeah." I sighed. "People can be a tough crowd."

He parked at the end of the drive, where the beginnings of a narrow path snaked into the woods.

"You're not luring me out here to beat the crap out of me and shove my face in a pile of bones, are you?"

He looked at me with a disturbed look. "Jesus."

"Last time I went for a walk with a guy, I got the crap beat out of me."

Jason shook his head. "I swear, Eve. Alabama is not that bad of a place."

He beckoned me forward and we walked through a small orchard of old pecan trees, then came upon a small grassy area with a spectacular view—a sweeping vista of the thundering river below, the quaint town, and rising hills beyond. I walked to the edge and peered over. The view was dizzying.

"Gorgeous, right?" The voice sounded familiar.

I turned to see my brother standing beside Jason. He lifted a hand. He was dressed in dark jeans and a blue dress shirt, and the hand he lifted was like a white flag of surrender. When I got closer, his mouth dropped open. "Eve! Your eye!"

"Looks worse than it is, I promise. Now somebody better start talking, fast."

"Let's sit." Jason pointed to a bench made out of artfully bent twigs situated at the very edge of the bluff. Danny and I sat, but Jason remained standing. I jiggled my knee nervously, adrenaline shooting through me.

Jason folded his arms. "So, Eve. Long story short, Danny contacted me a couple of days ago, looking for you."

I gaped at both of them.

Jason nodded at Danny. "He had called Margaret Luster, and she told him you'd come to Florence to see me."

"And then you told him what was going on," I said flatly.

Danny waved his hand in dismissal. "I knew something was wrong when you didn't fly back home with us. It just took me a while to get the details straight." He clenched his jaw. "You didn't have to hide the truth from me, Eve. I could've taken it."

"Could you? I don't know."

He looked offended. "Nobody ever knows that kind of thing for sure. That's what trust is."

I averted my eyes from his gaze, wounded. I hated to admit it, but he wasn't wrong. I always thought I was so different from Dove, that I was doing so much better for my family. But he was right. I'd been shutting Mom and Danny off in my own way.

"Would you mind if we talked business, Eve?" Jason asked.

"Do I have a choice?" I said.

He ignored my sarcasm. "How bad do you think it's going to be? I mean, really? You know, the world's come a long way since Jimmy Swaggart in the hotel with prostitutes. So who do you expect will pick up the story? What publications?"

I leaned back, the twigs digging into my back. "Honestly, I'm not sure. These scandals might be passé, but people still like to see their idols fall."

Danny nodded his assent. "More likely, though, it'll just be *Charisma* and *Christianity Today*. Maybe *World*. The big guns in conservative religious circles. But sometimes other outlets do pick up the story and it ends up going mainstream, and when that happens, you're finished."

Jason absorbed this. "You'll put out a statement, though, correct?"

"We will," I said. "Though I doubt it'll make much difference. Faith-based corporate sponsors are notoriously skittish. We'll lose at least half of them right away, if not more."

Jason pursed his lips. "That's what Danny and I wanted to talk to you about."

I let out an exasperated sigh.

Danny touched my shoulder. "Just listen to what he has to say."

"I want to make you an offer," Jason said. "You and Danny." He squinted out over the river. To our left, the sun was sinking, warming the surface of the water, saving its best rays for the last hour of the day. "I'd like to go to the authorities myself. Tell them what's happened to you, what this guy, this asshole, is doing to you. And tell them what I know."

I blinked at him. "What you know? I don't follow."

He nodded. "That my great-great-grandfather, Steadfast Coe, actually wandered off willingly—because he intended to end his own life."

I shot Jason a look, then Danny, but both their faces were unreadable. "Wait, you're telling me you knew this all along and you—" Jason's look made me pause. The insouciant curl of his lip, and the smug lift of his eyebrows. "Oh." I laughed at my gullibility. "Okay, I get it. You're saying you would lie."

He tilted his head to one side. "I am a politician, after all."

"Not funny. So not funny, Jason."

"Eve, it would be so simple," Danny said. "It's the perfect solution."

"I have reams of his papers," Jason said. "Letters, notes, his will, typed on a 1926 green Corona, which, it so happens, is still in my possession."

I shook my head. "Wow. Okay."

"I mean," Jason went on, "who's to say Steadfast didn't type a suicide note on, let's say, the back of his will?"

Danny leaned forward. "It would be nothing, Eve. He could just say his family was embarrassed about the suicide and wanted to keep the story quiet. He could put a stop to this guy accusing Dove and we could all move on."

"It's not nothing, Danny. Lying is never nothing." I glanced over the bluff. It would be easy; he was absolutely right. And probably nobody around Florence would care enough to debunk a letter like that, not even the police. Most importantly, it would immediately quash the asshole's attack on the foundation.

Mom and Danny and the foundation would all be safe. And I'd be free to go on with my life. I'd finally feel free enough to let them go.

But it would make me more of a liar than I already was. And Danny and Jason would be complicit in the lie. Worst of all, it would turn me into everything I despised. I would be just like Dove.

But wasn't I like her already? I'd been lying by omission to Mom and Danny since I was fourteen. Not telling them that Dove was a fraud. I was already following in my grandmother's footsteps, so what was one more lie? Who even cared? Maybe we were all doomed to run away from the truth until the day we died and let those left behind pick up the pieces.

Jason stood. "Don't give me your answer now, but you should know the letter is ready to go." He looked at his watch. "You've got a few hours left. I'll drop you at your dinner on my way out of town. I'll be waiting for your call."

He strolled back to the car and Danny took my hand.

"Don't be mad."

"I'm not," I said. "But now that we're being honest . . . I should probably tell you the rest."

"The rest about Dove, right?" Danny said. "What happened that time you flew to see her when you were a kid?"

I nodded.

"I'm ready." Danny stood, pulling me up with him. "Tell me everything in the car."

Chapter Thirty-Six

Florence, Alabama
1934

It was up to Ruth, and Ruth alone, to pry Bruna loose from the clutches of Arthur Holt. She'd arrived at this dismal, thoroughly inescapable realization the night of the Doves of Hattiesburg meeting.

The Doves were a ladies' church group that organized charity drives and soup kitchens for farmers in the area who found themselves down on their luck. This particular meeting was a benefit for the children—a fund to keep the school open for a few more hours a day—and they'd invited the Hawthorn Sisters. The girls were scheduled for singing and healing and then the president of the club, a Miss Evergreen Smith Staples, was to preach. For some reason, the whole arrangement seemed to put Arthur in a sour mood.

They rode to the meeting grounds in his newly purchased Hudson truck, but he grumbled the whole way. "I told them I'd do the preaching for a discounted fee. But they said no. The love offering'll be next to nothing with a bunch of ladies there."

"You don't know that," Ruth said.

"I do. Husbands may send their wives out the door with pocketbooks full of cash for Billy Sunday or John Lake, but not for anyone named Miss Evergreen Smith Staples." He punctuated this declaration with a sneer.

Later, Ruth would understand there was a deeper root to his foul temper.

Tupelo was a pretty town, and rather than being on the outskirts, the meeting tent was right in the middle of Main Street. The tent was bright white canvas with pots of palms and gardenias set out at every corner and swarmed with ladies and children. All of the Doves were dressed in white with corsages of lilies or azaleas at their collars.

Ruth ran her scales outside the tent at half past four, just before the meeting was to get underway. She kept a sharp eye on the lines of ladies in lacy white dresses filing into the tent. They looked like they may prove Arthur wrong and drop plenty of cabbage in the pot. Arthur and Bruna were off somewhere, getting up to their usual who-knew-what. Her friend had seemed quieter lately, pale and distracted. Ruth knew she was grieving the loss of her grandfather, but she wondered if it was something more. Some private matter Bruna didn't think it proper to discuss with Ruth.

She wanted to be miffed, but what could she expect? She'd kept plenty from Bruna—and her secret was a gracious plenty more serious. If Bruna wanted to keep something to herself, who was Ruth to complain?

She was getting ants in her pants. She always did before they went on. It wasn't the singing, it was the rest of it that didn't sit well with her. The way the people rushed to her and Bruna, their faces drawn in sorrow or pain, and fell at their feet. The desperate way they grabbed the hem of her dress or her sleeve. Part of it she understood. She'd been cold and hungry and lonely at one time in her life, but she'd always had her pride and more than a little fight in her. She'd never groveled. But what did she have to offer them?

She was just a bastard born in a lunatic asylum. A runaway, a thief and grifter. And now—if you wanted to get right down to it—a fornicator as well.

And yet . . .

When she laid her hands on people, things happened. They trembled and sweated. Raised their hands and wailed and cried. They fell down, in waves sometimes, like a giant, invisible hand was sweeping chess pieces off a board. And then they declared themselves healed—of their headaches and backaches and neuralgia and internal bleeding, breast cancer, rheumatism, even blindness.

But had these illnesses really been healed? Or were the people mistaken? At times, Ruth had felt something strange—a sort of electric charge hit her, then coursed through her body. But was the charge related to the healings, or did the healings cause the charge? She didn't know.

The long and short of it was, the whole thing had begun to frighten Ruth and she wanted loose of it.

The piano started up, whoever was working the pedals going at it like an especially determined soldier on a march toward battle. She could hear the corresponding thrum of the women inside the tent, clapping and stomping their feet. This one was going to be a humdinger.

She scanned the sidewalks, hoping to spot Bruna and Arthur. Down a ways, she saw one of the Doves, who'd cornered a man. The fellow was standing partly behind a parked car so she couldn't see his face, but he was tall and dressed entirely in black. She could only see the top of his oiled black hair.

The poor rube must be getting chewed out for trying to sneak into the female-only affair. That struck her as unusual. Most fellows used the occasion of ladies singing to slip down to a local juice joint and tie one on. But there were the odd ducks here and there. The types that felt the need to supervise in case the womenfolk imbibed too much of the Spirit and got up to no good.

"Miss Davidson?" It was one of the Doves, a helper running the meeting. "Five minutes."

Ruth smiled. "Thank you."

She trotted around the other side of the tent, hoping to get a glimpse of Arthur and Bruna. She spotted them a half a block up the street, standing on the steps of a bank. Their heads were bent close and their hands clasped. She didn't much fancy busting up a romantic clinch, but work was work. It was best if they got their fannies up on that stage before all that hand-clapping, foot-stomping fervor lagged. More excitement meant more healings, and that meant more money.

She started toward the bank. But as she drew closer, she realized Bruna and Arthur weren't kissing at all but praying. Well, Bruna was praying, her soft voice carrying down the sidewalk.

". . . and forgive me my trespasses as I forgive those who trespass against me."

"What are your trespasses?" Ruth heard Arthur say.

Ruth stopped and there was a beat of silence.

"Standing on a stage before men and God," Bruna said.

"And?"

"Preaching and instructing from the scriptures."

"And?"

She hesitated and when she spoke again her voice was small and careworn. "Vanity of appearance. Love of self. Jezebel spirit."

There was a pause. "All right, then. Finish up."

"Almighty God," Bruna said in a small voice. "I humbly repent of these sins and any others I commit tonight. I ask for your gracious forgiveness in the name of your son, Jesus Christ, and commit myself fully to you, body and soul."

"Amen," said Arthur.

"Amen," Bruna echoed.

Ruth turned and ran back to the tent.

Chapter Thirty-Seven

Florence, Alabama
Present

I told Danny he was welcome to come along with me to dinner with Griff and his parents, but, with his typical deadpan humor, he insisted he desperately needed to catch up on whatever happened to be on the hotel TV in the next couple of hours. Jason dropped him at the hotel, then me at the Cajun restaurant outside town.

"Call me," Jason said, but I just sighed and shut the car door.

Griff and his parents had gotten us a booth by the window, a red-leather and brass-trimmed setup. Helena Singley, an elegant hippie, wore her hair twisted into a loose bun, dangling stone earrings, and a worn denim shirt. Bobby, Griff's father, was handsome, white-haired, and barrel-chested. Basically, an older version of Griff.

Everyone stood when they saw me.

"Don't mind the bruise," I said preemptively.

"Shower door," Griff said.

"Tree branch," I said at the exact same time.

There was a brief moment of silence, then Helena darted forward to hug me. She smelled like coffee and organic shampoo. Bobby offered me a wide, bright white smile in a sun-weathered face. He wasn't as big as Griff, rangier, but just as solid. He wore stiff jeans and a starched collared shirt. Bifocals hung on a lanyard that proclaimed *War Eagle*.

"Bobby Singley." He stuck out a large square hand and I shook it. "Glad y'all could make it so we could get a look at Griff's girl." He winked and my face reddened. "And whether it was the shower or a tree, she's still sure enough a beauty." Another wink in Griff's direction. "Not unexpected. The men in this family have fine taste in women."

"Okay, Dad," Griff said. "Dial it back about a hundred clicks." But his hand didn't move from where it rested lightly on my back.

"Bobby, you're embarrassing her," Helena said.

But Bobby wasn't to be dissuaded. He smiled at me conspiratorially. "She's tough. I bet she can take a compliment. Can't you, Eve?"

"I can," I said. "Nice to meet you, Mr. Singley. Mrs. Singley."

"Call me Helena, please."

Bobby winked. "My apologies. I get carried away when I'm starstruck."

We slid into the booth, opposite the Singleys. Griff put his hand on my leg under the table and I did the same. His leg was warm beneath the jeans.

"I thought we might be overstepping," Helena said, "coming up here to see you. But we're so proud of Griff, working on a movie about such an inspiring woman."

I nodded. "He's doing a fantastic job. The film's going to be great."

Bobby signaled the server. "Helena and I saw Charles and Dove back in '78, I think it was?"

"No kidding," I said.

"That's right," Helena said, "1978. It was May. The National Day of Prayer at the capitol building in Montgomery."

"Pat Dye was there," Bobby said.

"Football coach," Griff said to me. "A god, basically. Little *g*."

Helena nodded. "And that Miss America, I think. Whatever her name was."

The server came and we ordered beer. Then Bobby turned to me, his eyes bright and laser- focused. I instantly recognized the look. It was the super-groupies look, the one they got when they were recounting an interaction with Dove. *She laid her hands on me. I went right over—and poof! When I went to my doctor, he said I didn't have diabetes anymore, praise the Lord!*

"I'll never forget that Montgomery meeting." Bobby sipped his water, thoughtful. "Dove was older—in her fifties, at least. But a clock-stopper, just like you. But it was more than the way she looked." He grew serious. "She had a kind of air about her. Like she possessed some kind of secret wisdom. When she took my hand and looked into my eyes, I swear, she could see the blackness of my soul." He held my gaze. "You know what she said to me?"

I shook my head. Griff had found a toothpick from a dispenser and was gnawing on it ferociously. Helena was sitting very still.

"She said God saw my suffering—and He wanted to relieve me of it."

I watched him. Bit my lip nervously.

"How about that?" His face softened, even though his voice stayed gruff. "I've had my vices, there's no doubt. I've had some anger management issues. Some financial things that have caused suffering for the people I love." At this, he reached for Helena's hand and squeezed it. "But she saw me. How at the bottom of it all, what I was doing was really hurting myself. Isn't that something?"

I swallowed. I felt Griff beside me, still like Helena. I wondered if he was embarrassed.

"She was so kind, Dove," Helena chimed in. "I remember, she stayed until almost midnight, until the very last person got prayer."

"Yes, that was definitely my grandmother," I said. "She was tireless."

"Do you have any good Dove stories?" Helena asked. "From the old days?"

I lifted one eyebrow. "Oh, too many to tell here."

"That reminds me." Griff helped himself to a basket of biscuits. "Y'all ever hear any stories about Dove ministering with another young girl around this area? They were kind of a big deal back in the early thirties. Called themselves the Hawthorn Sisters."

Helena's face grew thoughtful. "I don't think so."

"No," Bobby said. "Not that I recall. What kind of ministry did they have? Prophecies? Healing? Or just plain old preaching? Those folks, those traveling preachers, were a dime a dozen around here back in the Depression."

My phone rang. "Eve," Margaret Luster drawled into my ear with her honey-sweet accent. "Do you have a minute?"

"Sure." I glanced at Griff. "I'm sorry. I need to take this." I slipped out of the booth and fled the dark restaurant for the humid, still bright parking lot.

Margaret apologized for interrupting, then launched into her spiel. "I've been listening to Charles's old sermons again. And, like I said, all Dove usually does is sing a few songs here and there. Occasionally pray for people in the audience. But there's this one tape. I've heard it before, but this time—knowing what I know about the missing coin—it sounds entirely different. May I play a segment for you? It's from one of their earlier meetings. In Memphis, I believe, 1938."

I felt my stomach clench and flutter by turns. "Please."

She fumbled with her electronics, and then I heard the scratchy whir of the old magnetic recording mechanism. I was instantly transported to an old tent, musty and hot, on the grounds of some centuries-old church. Adjacent to a cemetery, probably. Surrounded by sawhorses loaded down with covered dishes.

"My wife used to know a very rich man," Charles Jarrod said on the tape. Even in the tinny recording his voice was deep and sonorous. "Isn't that right, Mrs. Jarrod?"

"That's right, Mr. Jarrod," came Dove's chipper reply.

"This wealthy man thought he could hide his treasure from the Lord, didn't he?"

"That he did, Mr. Jarrod."

A chorus of voices shouted out their disapproval.

"Tell the people, Mrs. Jarrod, where did this man hide his treasure?"

"Well, sir, he hid it under stairs, under floorboards, and behind drawers. Why, I do believe he even hid money inside the leg of the piano bench!"

"Because God can't see inside the leg of a piano bench?"

Dove giggled. "Mr. Jarrod, the Lord can see everywhere at all times, you know that. He can see inside that piano bench just as well as He can see inside that man's heart."

Someone started banging away at a piano, and Margaret Luster paused the tape. "I've heard this tape dozens of times. I can't believe I never picked up on this part."

My God . . .

"Is there one still in the house?" Margaret asked me. "A piano? Because you may find what you're looking for there."

Chapter Thirty-Eight

Florence, Alabama
1934

Three days later, Ruth sat at the table in Steadfast's dark dining room. The room, stripped of its china and silver, felt dismal and cold. The previous night, Arthur had announced to the girls that he'd persuaded Bruna's father to let her skip the family vacation and attend the state fair. He'd claimed the governor was planning on attending the Hawthorn Sisters' show and it was impossible for Bruna to bow out.

Another lie, Ruth knew, without even asking.

She stared at the dented silver pitcher, back in its place on the table and holding a single camellia branch, and weighed her options.

She could go for broke and try telling Bruna everything: that she suspected Arthur had killed Steadfast in his bed, and that then he had cajoled Ruth into hiding him and agreeing to the whole sham about revealing a fake revelation from God at the fair.

But would her friend believe her? There was no proof that Arthur had actually murdered Steadfast. She hadn't actually seen him touch the old man. And Steadfast was old. Very old. Maybe he really had died in his sleep, the way Arthur had claimed.

And Bruna would believe him. Because inexplicably, the lovely, upstanding young girl with the rich family and the prettiest singing voice Ruth had ever heard believed whatever Arthur Holt told her. Bruna would definitely think Ruth was lying, possibly even trying to turn her against Arthur. She would be furious. She might end their friendship forever.

There was only one solution she saw.

And that was Charles Jarrod.

The renowned evangelist had appeared before all sorts of important people. He knew President Roosevelt and even a few kings and queens, Ruth had heard. He was rich, connected, and if the instincts she'd developed in the past four years were any indication, he was one of the smartest people she'd ever met.

He didn't have a choir or regular music director traveling with him, not like Billy Sunday. He might be willing to hear Ruth's proposal. Because that's what she'd decided to do, sitting there at Steadfast Coe's long cherry table in the dark, staring at the silver pitcher.

She'd gone down to the post office and asked Melva Caldwell to help her find an address in California. Then she went back to the house, rifled through Steadfast's drawers, and found a letter that just might work. It was dated thirty-five years before, but Ruth liked the turn of phrase the fellow had used. And besides, it was written to Coe by someone seeking a job.

Which was exactly what she planned to do.

Chapter Thirty-Nine

Florence, Alabama
Present

After I hung up with Margaret Luster, I made a quick apology to the Singleys, then climbed into a waiting Uber. Griff leaned into the open door.

"I'll wrap up dinner, then check back in with you. Call me, no matter what you find. Good luck." He shut the door.

Jason Faulk's house was locked tight, windows curtained and shuttered. In the softening light of the day, the grand antebellum facade showed its age in crumbling mortar and missing bricks in the front steps. I noticed for the first time that the whole house seemed to be listing to one side, shifted slightly off its foundation.

I couldn't believe I was doing this. That I thought for one second there could still be a chance . . .

But you do, Eve.

I did. As much as it pained me to admit it, I still had this feeling down in the deepest part of me that the coin was there—at my fingertips, close enough to touch, but just out of reach. I couldn't just walk away. I couldn't give up.

And yes, maybe I wanted to give Dove's gift one last chance to reveal itself, helping me find the coin. It might mean I'd lost my mind just a little bit.

On the front porch, I retrieved the key from under the brick like I'd seen Ember do. Once inside, I eased the door shut behind me. I hoped the neighbors were too busy or far away to notice my low-key breaking and entering. Or maybe they'd assume I was one of Jason's coterie of staff, just dropping by to polish the chandeliers or inventory his paper towels while he was on the road.

Only one lamp was burning in the wide hallway, a small silk-shaded porcelain mermaid that threw just enough light to see vacuum marks on the rug. The doors were all sensibly shut, every drawer slid neatly back into place. No sign of Althea and Griff's day of ransacking. I put the key on a long glass table.

"I'm back," I said aloud.

The house seemed to swallow my voice. Strangely, also the sounds of my breathing and heartbeat. *That was odd.* The old houses I'd been in had always creaked and groaned and sighed. Dove's house rattled in the night wind, like an old lady who'd forgotten her cardigan. But this place . . . this place was deathly quiet. It seemed to suck away sounds instead of making them. Maybe it was because this particular house was too full. Of the past, of other lives—their fears and foibles, loves and labors.

In the parlor, I found the burled, baroque piano. I flipped the bench over and unscrewed one of the legs, but when I peered inside, the hollow space was empty. I pulled off the next leg. It was empty too. And the next. When I gripped the fourth and last one, it felt different, screwed in tighter.

I braced the bench against the floor and twisted with all my strength. It finally loosened, and I shook it, but nothing came out. I upended the leg and peered into the cavity. There was something. A piece of paper maybe? It was hard to tell. I dipped two fingers in, but whatever it was had been pushed down too far to reach.

I grabbed a poker from the hearth and, carefully maneuvering it into the cavity, managed to hook the tip on something. I drew it out. Two pieces of yellowed paper, which turned out to be brittle and water-spotted hundred-dollar bills. I stared at them, then broke into laughter. They may not have been what I was looking for, but I couldn't fault Margaret Luster's detective skills.

I tossed the bench leg and the bills on the sofa and let my eyes shutter closed. *What had we missed?*

Maybe we shouldn't have assumed the coin was in the house. Maybe we should've thought bigger. In truth, it could be anywhere. It could be back at Dove's house in Pasadena, tucked beneath a floorboard or hidden behind a false drawer. Dove could've taken it on her travels with Charles. Maybe she'd hidden it in a hotel in Tennessee or a boarding house in Iowa.

Or maybe, like Jason had said, Dove had never had the coin in the first place. Maybe Steadfast, OCD raging, really had hidden it, just like the other error coins—but at some special place of his in town or down at the river.

But as much as I wanted to believe it, I didn't. I didn't feel it, in my gut or my heart . . . or—and I couldn't believe I was thinking this—my arm.

The coin wasn't in Pasadena or Tennessee or Iowa. It was here.

Here in this house.

I stayed there for a long time, eyes closed, wondering if the sound-swallowing rooms would speak to me. The idea was ridiculous; part of me—no, most of me—knew it, but maybe . . . maybe, if those old voices wanted to make themselves heard badly enough, they would speak. My arm had started to ache with a sort of dull, rhythmic throb. Like the beating of a heart. Maybe that meant something.

And then I heard a sound. Or sounds. The faintest sounds, coming from the back of the house. Murmuring voices. Or singing. Yes, it was singing. That hymn, the one Ember had sung. *There's a land that is fairer than day . . .*

I closed my eyes. Stayed as still as I dared, listening, listening. But then instead of singing I just heard a whooshing sound. Like wind or water crashing over a fall. But that wasn't real either, was it? Just like the singing, it was my imagination, my exhausted, overwrought mind playing tricks on me. But still, I stayed there, standing in the hall, letting the sounds of the house—real or imagined—surround me.

This place . . . there was something so strange about it. Almost like it was a passageway to another time. To another person. A small, shadowy tunnel to the girl my grandmother had been . . .

The jangle of my phone made me yelp. "Mom. Hi."

"Eve? Eve? The reception's bad."

"I can hear you." I rubbed my forehead, trying to wake myself up from the strange trance I'd fallen into.

"I'm on my way to Phoenix for the trafficking summit, but there's some issue with the electrical system and we're still sitting on the tarmac at LAX, if you can believe it."

I raked my fingers through my hair. "Oh, Mom. That's the worst."

"I'll admit, I did drink a mimosa." She let out a little rueful tongue cluck. "What's going on? Are you okay? Is something going on with the documentary? I haven't heard from you in a few days and I was getting worried."

I pressed my fingers against my lips. "Let's talk later, when you get to Phoenix."

Her voice was soft, hesitant. "I know you're working hard on this film. And I can see how much you care about it. About getting it right. I'm just . . ." She trailed off.

"It's okay, Mo—"

"No, Eve. I need to say this." She hesitated. "I've known there was the chance that along the way you might uncover some . . . stories . . . about your grandmother that might not show her in the best light."

I made a noncommittal sound, but my heart had started thumping painfully.

"I've heard rumors through the years. But they mostly came from unreliable sources so I never believed them. People are jealous. Obsessed with discrediting people who do good."

I stayed quiet.

"I know it may be tempting to believe them because . . . well, because of what happened with your arm. How she couldn't heal you."

"Mom. Don't worry. It's all good. I'm good. You know that."

"I just wanted to say that no matter what you may hear, Dove loved you. Loved us. And she tried her very best to follow the Lord and do what He wanted her to do. And now we have the chance to carry on her work. It's an honor. A blessing. I hope you feel that way."

I could hear the squawk of the captain's voice in the background. It was all I could do not to scream and throw the phone. She had no idea what Dove had done to us. How, in just hours, her mother's precious legacy was going to turn to rubble unless I did something. Because I was the one who'd started all this. I was the one who'd agreed to keep the lie going to protect everyone, and instead, I'd signed them up for humiliation and heartbreak.

"I don't know what I'd do without the work," Mom said. "I just don't know—"

I gritted my teeth. "Mom. Listen to me. We'll talk soon. Now enjoy your flight and have another mimosa, okay?"

This was my fault, perpetuating Dove's lie. But I couldn't help remembering Althea's words. *Some people might even call it abuse.* I couldn't think straight, feelings of love and anger clashing inside me.

"Mom, I've got to run. Call me when you land."

I walked into the hallway and looked up the shadowy stairs to the room that held the case of dusty error coins. We'd already searched it, multiple times, and hadn't found the Flowing Hair. So why was I still so drawn there? What more did I think I could learn in that room?

I didn't have an answer, but time was running out and there was nothing left to lose. "Mom, I've really got to run. You going to be okay?"

"I will, Eve. I'm going to be okay."

Chapter Forty

Muscle Shoals, Alabama
1934

Singley lay on his bed in Mrs. Ezra Ennis's boarding house in Muscle Shoals, Alabama, sleepless and raging. He clasped his hands behind his head and muttered a string of epithets at a set of cobwebs that gently swayed from the ceiling.

He'd been so calm the last few weeks, so at ease after that upset at Billy Sunday's tabernacle. A month ago, he'd seen Ruth at that meeting, and her appearance on the stage had troubled him greatly.

Ruth was going by a new name, Davidson, and she was a part of an evangelist duo, this tasteless Hawthorn Sisters outfit. She looked like a harlot up on that stage. The lipstick, that filmy plum-colored dress with the ruffled collar that dipped below her creamy neck. She swayed when she sang, and oh how her eyes flashed and winked as she swung the hand of the girl next to her. She wasn't the unblemished girl he'd met at Pritchard—not even the poor mite he'd pictured being helplessly ravished by hooligans—no. She was a common whore now, obviously.

But after he'd trailed her and her cohorts back to Florence, the Lord had spoken to him. Ruth's descent into depravity wasn't her fault.

She'd been forced into it—by the hardships and the loneliness and the brutish men around her. And she still needed rescuing, still needed a Hosea to save her, now more than ever.

He had devised a plan. He couldn't simply snatch her off the street. She'd run or her friends would fly to her rescue—and he didn't fancy spending any time whatsoever in jail on charges of kidnapping. It was clear he had to be smart about it. He must plot his steps deliberately so that when he took possession of his intended, there would be no chance of losing her.

He committed himself to a new routine of waiting, which had begun to feel like a game to him. A delicious, drawn-out game, which involved the first move of procuring a place to stay near Ruth. He'd found this boarding house and concocted quite a story.

Mr. Robert Shallowford, ma'am, lately of Birmingham. I sold all that I had, save a small rental house in Tuscaloosa, to follow the Lord. I've been carrying on charity work amongst the needy children of the mills, but now I'm following the call of the Master to find myself a wife.

The woman to whom he'd told his tale swung her door wide open then, offering her cozy attic room. On the way to show him his new accommodations, she tittered on about how nice he smelled, how clean, like oranges and clove. He imagined himself strangling her.

He spent his days wandering the quaint town of Florence, asking about Ruth, hoping for a glimpse of her. He was told by the postmistress that she had cared for an elderly gentleman who'd wandered off and died most likely, a Mr. Steadfast Coe. He strolled past the great house a few times, nerves taut. Once, he thought he saw her step out onto the front porch, but he was so overcome that he hid behind a mimosa tree. He heard rumors of a young man about town. A vagabond who'd robbed a bank or two and said he knew Ruth. He saw the boy once, down at the ferry. Golden hair and broad shoulders. Handsome face and easy laugh.

His jealousy inflamed him and he fantasized about killing the boy, but he resisted the urge and continued to sniff around. He learned a few things. Namely that the boy had been involved in some bad business over in Texas. He found one of the boy's cronies and told him the cops were hot on their tails. That they all better cut out of town if they wanted to stay free men.

Knowing Ruth was only a few miles away gave him a surprising sense of well-being. Nights, Singley—now Shallowford—spent at the boarding house. He smoked with Mr. Ennis and the other men in the backyard and, to their amazement, whistled in mourning doves. As the days passed, Singley reckoned he finally understood what it was the scriptures talked about, that *peace that passeth understanding*. He'd actually come to relish the leisurely hunt, the plotting of his next move. He dreamed of the shock on her face when she finally saw him.

And Mrs. Ennis made a delicious sage pot roast.

And then all that had changed. He decided to attend one of Ruth's meetings—one smaller than Mr. Sunday's—in Tupelo. A meeting where he could actually see her. He took a bath. Had Mrs. Ennis press out his good suit. Then, after shaving and splashing his face with witch hazel, he snuck into Mr. Ennis's bathroom to splash a bit of Florida Water in his hair.

But, just after his arrival, that evil old witch in a white lace dress had gone and wrecked it all. Sticking her mannish finger in his face, she told him he wasn't allowed entrance. Accused him of lascivious intentions. What right had she, that miserable cow of a female, to look upon him with the eye of judgment? Did not God judge a man Himself? Was He not the knower of all the secrets of a man's heart—and not a hysterical woman bound by her limited scope of imagination and experience in the world? How dare that whore!

He threw back his tearstained face and lifted his bony hands to the ceiling. The moon cast a shadow against the ivy wallpaper, casting his fingers as a thorny thicket of brambles.

"'Blessed are ye,'" he proclaimed to the ceiling. *"'When men shall revile you, and persecute you, and shall say all manner of evil against you falsely, for my sake. Rejoice, and be exceeding glad: for great is your reward in heaven: for so persecuted they the prophets which were before you.'"*

There came three thumps on the wall beside him from the lodger next door. "Lay off in there, you chucklehead. Or I'll come in there and give you a wallopin'!"

He dropped his hands and rolled to his side.

The burning was back now. A relentless, almost intolerable pain in his body. He wanted to strangle something. Tear skin from flesh, flesh from bone, and bone from socket. He yearned to pound, to slice, to bludgeon until he was blood-soaked and spent. But because he couldn't creep downstairs and throttle the bright Mrs. Ennis, he would have to settle his urges another way.

He took the pink ribbon from the brim of his hat and wound it round and round his wrist, pulling it tighter and tighter until his hand felt large and blue and disconnected from his arm. Until it felt like it was not a part of his body at all.

In the morning, he woke late to an empty house. There was a plate for him on the kitchen table, a warm tea towel draped over it, and a copy of the *Florence Times* beside his coffee cup. He opened it and saw the photograph on the lower corner of the third page. Two young girls, one plump and brunette, the other like a bird—all sleek, simple lines and tantalizing eyes. *Hawthorn Sisters Healing Revival!* the ad above the picture proclaimed. *Holy Ghost Preaching, Prayer for the Infirm, Word of Knowledge in Operation.*

Singley's heart soared and he nearly burst into holy praise right there in Mrs. Ennis's kitchen. The Hawthorn Sisters were appearing at the North Alabama State Fair.

Ruth had called to him, he had come, and she would soon be his.

Chapter Forty-One

Florence, Alabama
Present

I was pouring sweat. And it wasn't because it was June in Alabama—the AC on Jason's second floor was humming away. It must have been my nerves.

I looked around the open second-story landing. All the doors were shut. But I could smell the mildew and mothballs. The old scent of coal dust and propane. And maybe a whiff of something sweeter. Lavender or rose water. Did old desires, unsatisfied needs, have a smell? Fear supposedly did. Maybe other emotions did too.

I ran my hands along the banister. Steadfast had lived here with his family. Then Dove. And Bruna had walked these floors too. But now they were all dead and gone.

Dust to dust.

Whatever the case, I didn't hear any murmuring voices or music on this floor. Only the dead, dead quiet.

I arced my toe along the worn red-and-blue-patterned carpet, then pivoted to face the front of the house. I hadn't really noticed anything the first time I'd been up here. Ancient wallpaper covered the front wall, a fuchsia-and-plum concoction of grapevines and foxes. There was a delicate fan-shaped window below the ornate molding, but I couldn't see the street outside, only white sky.

I squeezed my eyes shut and steadied myself on the banister. It wasn't just me. It really was hot. The heat, along with the smell, was making me lightheaded. But I needed to get on with it.

The mint-green bedroom was just as I remembered—the case of coins on its pedestal near the window. I lifted the lid and pressed my finger into the center, that depression in the blue velvet reserved for the Flowing Hair Dollar. I felt a jolt. The smell of silver melting. The metallic tang filled my nostrils and tightened my jaw.

Made with a fine silver by the US mint director. Pressed with lettering around the planchet that was irregular, the weight of the silver inexact. They plugged the center to make the weight match, then distributed them.

Had Jason told me all that?

No . . . Griff must have read it to me. Something he found on the internet.

I lowered the lid and scanned the room. Canopied bed, dresser, wardrobe, and door. All opulent in their day—done with heavy silks and taffetas—now gone threadbare. But there was nothing new to see. We'd already gone through this room, Jason, Griff, Ember, and I, and come up empty-handed.

I turned back to the case and lifted the lid again. Carefully, I removed one of the coins from its velvet slot, hardly even realizing what I was doing. I felt the weight of it between my fingers. Thicker than a modern coin. Heavier. I liked the weight of it in my hand. And I had just a spark of a thought, an idea that I could feel forming in the back of my mind . . .

I went to the bedroom door, and there, my fingers traced the ornate plate and keyhole. The whorled pattern was a vine just like on the wallpaper out in the hall. My gaze traveled up the door. Just a simple six-paneled piece of solid oak, worn smooth from decades of hands pushing and pulling, slamming or throwing open. I touched the mechanism again, the metal smooth and cold under my fingertips. The keyhole, a perfect coin-slot size.

I examined the coin. It was copper, laced with a bluish-green patina that hadn't been polished off. On this one, a penny, the letters were doubled, making me feel like my vision was blurred. It was hard to believe something so small, so simple, could be desired by so many people.

I held the coin to the slot, at the same time holding my breath. I'd started to tremble, but I ignored it and pushed the coin into the keyhole. It disappeared, clinking through the mechanism, and a second later, hit the bottom. I stepped back, observing the door as if for the first time, trying to order my thoughts. Every door in this enormous house could have a whole collection of coins stuck in their locks. But if Dove had hidden the coin, and hidden it in a door, there was only one that would be.

I ran downstairs, through the hall to the kitchen and into the maid's room.

I grabbed a hammer from the metal shelves bursting with household detritus and went to work prying the bronze lock off the oak door. Eventually, I managed to separate the metal face from the wood. I shook it, peering down into the recesses of the door.

Nothing inside. Nothing that I could see. I threw the hammer across the room, and it crashed into a file cabinet and clattered to the floor. I rubbed my arm. It was throbbing. But what did that mean? Nothing. Other than the fact that one time, long ago in my mother's womb, a clot had formed and blocked the flow of oxygen to my brain, killing the cells that controlled the muscle memory to my right arm.

That was it.

It didn't mean I was going to find the missing coin. I wasn't.

The search was over. Now all I had to do was go back to the hotel and call Danny. Get ready to clean up the mess Dove had made.

Then I heard something behind me. A voice, twangy, with that hint of hillbilly.

"Good to see you again, darlin'."

Chapter Forty-Two

Muscle Shoals, Alabama
1934

The Hawthorn Sisters were scheduled to appear on the grandstand the last three nights of the week-long fair.

Arthur grumbled when he'd gotten word of their start time. "Six o'clock's when God-fearing folks eat supper, not when they pray." He said they should start at eight, or even later, but Ruth was secretly relieved. She was growing more and more uneasy with Arthur's plan. The fewer people in the crowd to witness their charade, the better.

She'd received a short note typed on a thick sheet of creamy vellum from Charles Jarrod's secretary in California telling her that the evangelist was ministering in South Africa, but that she'd certainly forward the correspondence on to him. It had not been the assurance Ruth had been hoping for.

She thought of the alternative. If she did really go through with Arthur's scheme. Would the audience buy that some spindly girl was hearing, direct and clear as day, from the Spirit of God about where Steadfast Coe had wandered off? Could she pull off the acting required to convince the people?

All she'd ever really done was tell people what they already wanted to hear. *Your headaches are healed in the name of Jesus . . . Lumbago, I rebuke you in the name of the Lord! I feel that rheumatism lessening . . . yes, indeed I do!*

This was altogether a horse of a different color. Life and death. Surely, people would see that Ruth's prophecy was only a stunt. They'd see right down to her black heart, and then they'd think she'd killed Steadfast.

Charles Jarrod was her only way out.

On Wednesday, Ruth planned to set off early for the grounds to get the lay of the land. She had thought she might hitch a ride on a hay truck across the railroad bridge to Muscle Shoals, but before Ruth was down the steps of Coe's house, Bruna appeared in her father's car.

The whole drive down, Bruna kept biting her lip, her hands gripping the steering wheel like she was wringing laundry. Once they parked, then entered the fair, she hung on to Ruth's arm.

Ruth jostled her. "Let's walk down the midway. I reckon you could win a watch for Arthur. I mean, they're a bunch of junk and the hands don't even move, but it'd be fun."

"Why should I spend good money on Arthur?" Bruna tilted her chin up at a defiant angle. "He takes a third of everything we make, remember?"

More than a third, Ruth thought, but she didn't say it. It was the first time she'd heard Bruna speak that way about Arthur. She took hold of Bruna's elbow. "Let's get some cotton candy."

They strolled down the crowded midway, past the concessions of watered-down lemonade and hot dogs, the wheel of fortune tents and hoopla games promising safety razors or Kewpie dolls or pearl-handled revolvers for a ten-cent toss. Toward the end of the thoroughfare they came upon the show tents advertising whatsits and freaks of every shape and sort. Mostly two-headed creatures—calves and chickens and goats—and the odd assortment of mermaids and unicorns, which Ruth guessed were just gruesome fish and poor horses with paper-mache horns.

Beyond lay the Ferris wheel and the roller coaster and the grandstand where the vaudeville acts performed. That's where Ruth and Bruna would sing and preach later that evening. Opposite that was the exhibition hall and stock pavilion.

They paid a nickel each for fluffy cotton candy and continued on to the pavilion, a pole barn the town had built for the occasion with rows of crates for all the hogs and sheep and horses. Inside, a cacophony of snorts and snuffs and grunts and bleats greeted the girls. And the smell . . . Ruth thought she'd gotten used to it back at Dr. Asloo's outfit, but she must've gotten soft working in Steadfast's fancy house. The stench of manure and piss and creature was overpowering.

Bruna took her hand. "Let's go look at the lambs. I love the lambs."

They picked their favorite, a docile rambouillet from Scottsboro with a silky white face, white hooves, and the cleanest, softest pelt Ruth had ever felt. His name was Solomon.

Bruna looked wistful. "Isn't he just the sweetest? I always did like the twenty-third Psalm the best. *'The Lord is my shepherd; I shall not want.'* What could be nicer than that? To have someone always looking out for you?"

Ruth nodded. The way Daddy Warbucks picked Annie out of the orphanage and took her home. That *had* happened to her—with Steadfast. He'd given her the coin, and despite nearly getting blown to kingdom come with a shotgun and chased with an ax, living with him had turned out to be a pretty wonderful setup.

Bruna had gotten quiet again. "You don't believe, Ruth, do you? The promises of the hymns? The things we preach at the meetings?" She hesitated. "God."

Ruth kept her voice light. "Of course I do. Don't be silly."

"No, I don't think you do. I don't think the people can tell. But I can."

A moment of uncomfortable silence yawned between them.

"It doesn't matter to me," Bruna hastened to add. "I just wanted to know because we're friends. I wanted you to trust me enough to tell me the truth."

Bruna's words hit Ruth like an arrow in the chest.

The truth.

There was so much of it she hadn't told Bruna. About Steadfast and Arthur, Charles Jarrod and her plan. Already, she'd lied more to Bruna than she'd ever lied to anyone. If her friend found out now, before Ruth was ready to tell her, Bruna might never forgive her.

"Don't be sore," Bruna said. "It's just that you have this way . . ." She struck a pose, chest out, hip cocked coquettishly. "The Spirit says someone in this room has a *splinter* in their *spleen*." Bruna raised her hands in the air, inhaling theatrically. "That there is Satan's splinter, the Lord God Jehovah says."

Ruth flushed. She did put on a bit of a show. And she liked to get a jump on the audience and call out her own infirmities. She felt there was less room for error that way.

Bruna broke into song, winking seductively at Ruth and shimmying her shoulders. "Satan's splinter, Satan's splinter, Satan done put a splinter in your spleen . . ."

Ruth shook her head, but she snorted with laughter in spite of herself. "Stop it!"

"Admit it. That's you to a tee!"

Ruth slapped her shoulder. "Well, you're just as bad!"

"You girls cut out that racket or I'm gonna call the cops!" a man shouted from the other side of the pens.

They smothered their giggles with their hands and walked on, past the fat, snuffling hogs and the assortment of goats and calves.

"Didn't you believe just a little bit, though?" Bruna said. "When the woman over in Nauvoo with the bent leg got it straightened out? Or what about that little boy in Leighton whose spots cleared right up?"

Ruth pressed her lips together. She'd seen those things a few times. She called them "lightnings," the strange electrifying bolt that came from nowhere and hit her—but she'd also seen the shams, like Bug's shell games and Dr. Asloo's flea circus. Did it make a difference whether the miracles were real or lies? The important thing was the money kept coming in.

Bruna persisted. "You don't believe that God works miracles through the touch of your hands?"

"You know as well as I do," Ruth said. "That we got our cappers, same as every fellow out there on the midway. We're not that different from them, in a way."

"We are, though. We're selling the Gospel of Jesus Christ, which is better than a celluloid doll." Bruna had a look of such earnest confidence that Ruth had to look away, but Bruna grabbed Ruth's hand. "Oh, come on, Ruth. You don't really think we're hornswoggling all of them, do you? You have to believe at least some of it. There are accounts of real signs and wonders out there. Maybe we don't have enough faith to do them, but I've read about them."

"John G. Lake's disappearing bullet? Is that what you're talking about?"

Bruna lifted her chin. "Well, good golly, Ruth. If God is God, making one thing disappear or move to another place would be nothing for him. Just a wiggle of His pinky finger."

Ruth didn't answer.

Bruna pulled her to a stop. "You're telling me you don't ever feel it? That thing that goes through your body when you sing or prophesy or pray? When you put your hands on them? Don't you feel them trembling? Don't you tremble too? Feel it like a fire all over, just under your skin?"

Ruth wanted to say yes. Because she had felt it. But even when that lightning feeling coursed through her, a part of her wasn't sure if that wasn't anything more than her mind playing tricks. Hadn't she cried herself into a headache plenty of times? Drunk herself to sickness? Felt a boy's touch lift her to euphoria? If the things she felt when she laid hands on people and prayed for them were miracles, then maybe everything was. She just didn't know.

Ruth gently loosened Bruna's grip. "Don't be mad at me. I can't help it that I don't have the faith that you do."

"You think I'm a dip, don't you? A real dumb Dora?"

"No—"

"I suppose you'll have a good laugh when I tell you I'm marrying Arthur, too."

Ruth stared at her friend, her eyes wounded.

Bruna's cheeks went pink and she plucked at the neck of her dress nervously. "I just couldn't tell you, Ruth. I knew you wouldn't like it. I haven't told my parents either."

Bruna looked so lost, so sad, Ruth almost couldn't bear it. "Oh, Bruna."

Bruna burst into tears.

Ruth took her by the shoulders, then pulled her close. "You don't have to do it, you know."

"But he's done so much for me. For us."

"That may be true, and I appreciate it all. But you don't belong to him. You belong to yourself." She inhaled. "You know, if you marry him, he'll never stop thinking he owns you. Is that what you want?"

Bruna just wept.

Ruth cleared her throat and spoke carefully. "Bruna, tell me. Do you want to be his wife?"

Bruna paused for a very long time. "I don't believe I do," she finally answered and gasped out a small, ragged sob.

Ruth gathered her friend in a fierce hug. "Then you don't have to be."

She considered telling Bruna, then and there, about what Arthur had planned for the final night of the fair—about the revelation she was to have concerning Steadfast—but she was too scared. Bruna would be angry, understandably so. But then she might fly off the handle and confront Arthur, which would ruin absolutely everything. This whole operation demanded delicacy and care. Ruth couldn't afford to make a mistake now.

But what she could do was tell Bruna about the letter she'd sent to California.

Ruth released Bruna. "I have a plan to keep the Hawthorn Sisters in business without Arthur."

Bruna's eyes widened. "You do?"

Ruth nodded. "I do. And it's a doozy."

Chapter Forty-Three

Florence, Alabama
Present

Bobby Singley stood in the doorway of the maid's room, tall and broad, lit from behind by the kitchen light like some modern-day angel in disguise. My heart slammed against my chest. What was Griff's father doing standing in the middle of Jason Faulk's house?

I took an involuntary step backward, my brain ticking through explanations. Griff had asked Bobby to follow me from the restaurant for some reason. He'd been passing by, seen the lights, and I had forgotten to lock the front door behind me, so he wandered in to check if I was safe.

But none of those reasons made sense, and I knew it. Fear crawled up my throat. My mouth had gone so dry I couldn't swallow.

He leaned casually against the cased opening, his arms folded over the War Eagle lanyard, and shot me that blinding smile again—so much like Griff's and yet, somehow, not. "Fancy house, ain't it? I always wondered what it was like to grow up in a mansion like this. Admired and respected . . . envied by everybody you know."

"What are you doing here?" I asked.

"Oh, just saving myself a phone call."

I shook my head, not understanding.

"Don't worry," Bobby said. "I told Helena and Griffin that I needed to take care of some business and to finish up without me. They're having a high old time, mother and son. Without Dad, the old buzzkill, around."

He'd said it in a pleasant enough tone, but there was a barb there, buried beneath his words. "I . . . I'm sorry I had to leave," I said. "There's some stuff going on with my family. Business stuff."

"Dove's business?" He flashed the smile again, blinding white with a dedicated golfer's sun-cracked lips. "And you're taking care of it here, at the future governor of Alabama's house?"

"It's a long story."

"I love long stories."

I smiled uncertainly at him.

He produced a photograph from his vest pocket. "That's for you. A little visual aid for the lesson I'm about to impart."

It was a sepia-faded picture of three people posed in the yard of a wood house. A boy, a dark-headed toddler in short pants. A man beside him, bearded, a stocky bull in overalls and a bandanna tied around his neck. A few feet away stood an older man, tall and thin in a full suit, a dusty black hat pulled low over his face. None of them were smiling.

With a calloused finger, Bobby pointed at the man in the middle. "That's my father, Robert Singley Jr. His father, Robert Sr., the one in the hat. The baby's me." He chuckled. "Bobby the third. What do you think of that, Eve? Three generations of Singleys, just fellowshipping on the farm. Ain't that nice?"

I couldn't speak. My mind was reeling with too many pieces of disparate information. Griff's father . . . that country accent . . . the zealous gleam in his eye at the restaurant when he talked about Dove. I'd mistaken him for a super-groupie, rather than a man who'd been nursing a grudge for decades. A man who'd waited a lifetime, planned carefully, thoughtfully, how he would rain vengeance down on those he held responsible for his misery . . .

But I'd known. Somewhere in my deepest consciousness I'd known it the minute I'd seen him. I'd just ignored it. Ignored that little warning bell inside me. And now . . . now I was going to pay the consequences.

Bobby continued. "My grandmama Anna—she ain't in the picture, but let me tell you what. That woman was a saint. She sure was. Because, Lord, did Robert Sr. beat the stew outta her."

I still couldn't make a sound. The words were stuck in my throat, blocked by fear. My brain wasn't functioning correctly either. Not to make sense of what he was telling me. Not to formulate any plan of escape.

I was Bobby Singley's captive audience. Which was exactly what he wanted.

"Well, now that wasn't his fault," Bobby was saying. "They say he was heartbroke over a woman. Sick in his soul, from way back, over a lying, thieving, murdering whore named Ruth Davidson."

Chapter Forty-Four

Muscle Shoals, Alabama
1934

Somebody had arranged for a Salvation Army band to play with the Hawthorn Sisters, and when the girls lit into their first song—*"Blessed assurance, Jesus is mine"*—the sound of the cornet, piano, and trombone nearly made Ruth shoot right out of her skin. That and the big slatted microphone in the center of the grandstand platform that shrieked and hummed and sent their voices bouncing through the crowd, then back home to their ears, was enough to send her reeling back into the canvas backdrop.

It was strange, too, to be set up on the grandstand. She could only see the tops of people's heads, their straw panamas and jaunty white berets, sedate cloches above tweed and serge suits, silky dresses, and overalls. But it was all too clear—everyone, even the farm folk, had donned their best for the Hawthorn Sisters show.

The girls sang the new songs they'd practiced: "In the Sweet By-and-By," "It Is Well with My Soul," and "His Eye Is on the Sparrow." The crowd clapped and swayed and sang along. Ruth even saw a few ladies dabbing at the corners of their eyes with handkerchiefs.

During the songs, Ruth scanned the crowd for that shock of light-brown hair, film star face, and broad set of shoulders. But Charles Jarrod was nowhere in sight. Had his secretary really sent her letter to South Africa? Would he have even read it? And would he travel all the way to Alabama just to help a couple of girls out of a jam?

There was no reason for him to do such a thing. The Hawthorn Sisters might be popular in one tiny corner of the world, but when you got down to it, they were small potatoes. If Jarrod agreed to take them on, it would only be out of his generosity of spirit. *But there was a chance.*

During Arthur's preaching, there were the regular sightings of angel wing feathers and smears of holy oil appearing out of nowhere on people's foreheads at Wednesday night's meeting. A few folks spoke in tongues and one fainted, then several shouted that they saw glints of gold dust appearing on their fingertips. Afterward, Bruna called out ailments, inviting the crowd to come to the stage for healing. Migraines, diabetes, cancer, palsy, neurasthenia, and lungs burned by chlorine gas. Crooked spines and necks and legs and arms. Drunkards who wanted off the drink and smokers looking to quit.

It was overwhelming. People clawed at the girls' dresses and sobbed into their chests, as Bruna and Ruth prayed and laid hands, declaring the healing of the Lord until they were hoarse. At last, thankfully, they got pushed off the stage so the next performers, an acrobat troupe from Memphis, could go on.

"We'll be the last show on Friday," Arthur assured them backstage. "We'll rake in the dough then. You wait."

Ruth collapsed on a wood crate and gulped cold lemonade from a thermos. Elation buzzed through her. She had felt what Bruna had been talking about earlier—the *fire*. She'd felt it pass between her and every single person she'd touched. Was that the Holy Ghost? That spark of divine connection between a mere human and the Most High? Or was she just hysterical with nerves because of what lay ahead?

She couldn't tell.

She glanced over at Bruna. Her friend was pulling at the knuckles of each finger, cracking them slowly, one right after another. If only Ruth had seen Charles Jarrod in the crowd, why then she could give Bruna some reassurance. But all she could do was keep hoping.

"Be right back." She leapt up and headed down the alley, intending to hit the outhouse. Just beyond the row of animal pens, she hit an immovable wall of musty-smelling black wool. She backed up a few steps.

"Sorry, mister."

But large, strong hands gripped her and held her still. It was a tall man dressed in a scratchy wool coat and vest, and for a moment—one terrible, electrifying moment in time—she thought it might be the ghost of Old Steadfast come to swallow her soul.

"Ruth," he said in a deep, melodious voice that made her insides quake and her blood chill. The smell that clung to him, oranges and cloves, made her feel sick to her stomach. She pulled away, but he held her fast and leaned closer. He was thin, angled, sallow. If the devil had a face, she thought, this would be it.

"You remember me, don't you?" The man's voice shook. "Reverend Robert Singley, at your service. At your pleasure. We first made our acquaintance at the asylum, although I've followed your career since."

She turned away, searching frantically for Bruna and Arthur. But they were nowhere in sight. No one was. The area behind the grandstand was now deserted and barely lit.

"I have to go, mister." Ruth tried to wrench free, but Singley locked her arms in his grip.

He pulled her so close his face pressed against hers. He let out a moan—a horrible combination of craving and loathing that raised goose bumps on every inch of her skin. She remembered him. The preacher. Jimmy Singley's uncle.

"I really do have to go," she said again, twisting this way and that.

But he shook her, then closed his eyes, inhaling deeply. "Ah, yes. My Ruth. My harlot."

Fear engulfed her—a burning, all-encompassing sensation she'd never felt before, not even when she'd been locked in the cage with the lion. This was the glitter of a lion's eye and the gleam of his teeth. A predator sizing up his prey, but with the prudence and cunning of a man.

"I've seen the boy," he said. "Your young man. I told his friends that the police had their sights on him, and I expect by now he's somewhere in Kentucky. Now it's just me and you, nobody else between us." He leaned his face closer. "I'll find him later, don't you worry. Maybe gut him like a fresh-killed deer. Let him cry for his mama and die with his innards spillin' out every which-a-way."

She let out a gasp, so strangled with fear that it was barely audible.

He warmed to the sound, his eyes burning with fervor. "I tell you, Ruth, nobody will come between the two of us. We're bound to each other for life with the ties of duty and affection and blood."

She felt faint. God had sent the man here, to punish her. She'd played with fire. She'd pretended to be the voice of God and now He was demanding retribution.

"Hey, look-a-there!" came a voice a few yards off. "Look at them turtledoves."

Singley startled and loosened his grip the slightest bit, but Ruth was too lost in horror and panic to notice who the voices had come from. She could only see the Reverend Robert Singley. As she looked into his gaunt face and black eyes, a fragment of an old memory drifted into her mind.

"Sittin' by the roadside," she said faintly to herself, *"on a summer's day . . ."*

He gave her a quizzical look. "How's that?"

She didn't quite know why the song had come to mind, but it had and now it was bolstering her courage.

"Talkin' with my comrades to pass the time away . . ."

The reverend looked down at her, nostrils flared, lip curled. "Well, now. What are you—"

Her head lolled to one side, then the other, and her hips swayed. She felt her voice grow stronger. She offered him a little wink. *"Lyin' in the shade underneath the trees. Goodness how delicious, eating goober peas."*

He darkened, then gripped her arm again and shook her. "I said hush! Hush up, you nasty whore!"

She moved closer to him, whispering the last words, slowly and seductively, relishing each word. *"Peas, peas—"* Ruth hit him hard, a savage elbow jab to his belly. *"Peas, peas . . ."* Another shot with her knee, swift and sharp to the softest part of his groin. *"Eatin' goober peas!"*

He doubled over, wheezing and whimpering. Ruth slipped out from under his arms, losing him in the crowded midway. She didn't slow or look behind her until she was all the way past the animal pavilion. And by then, he'd vanished.

Chapter Forty-Five

Florence, Alabama
Present

"My grandpa was in love with Ruth Davidson, your beloved grandmother. What do you think about that?"

I glared at Bobby Singley, focusing the weight of all my disdain on him. "I don't think anything about it."

"You should. Robert Sr. was quite the character. Word was, he killed his own sister. How d'you like that? Choked her with her own housecoat tie and threw her down a well." He chuckled again, wry and weighed down with what seemed like a kind of grudging admiration. "Now that's a man who goes after what he wants."

The mountain twang struck like a particularly ear-splitting bell in my head, and his words from the other night—*we always known who that bitch was.*

My attacker was Griff's father. Griff's father wanted revenge on my grandmother, Griff's father had killed Dove, and he was about to enact his final revenge on her because I'd failed to get him the coin. The facts were all out in the open, as simple and straightforward as they could be, but I still couldn't wrap my head around it.

"The tie was never found so there was some doubt as to who might've done it." Bobby shook his head. "So Robert Sr. went free. Free to terrorize more womenfolk . . . and a few kids along the way too." He winked at me, a horrible replay of earlier this evening. "Some folks might say Miss Ruth Davidson dodged a bullet, and I'm inclined to agree. But what was lucky for her was certainly unlucky for the rest of us, wouldn't you agree?"

I handed the picture back and tried to walk past him, but he caught me by the arm.

"It's passed down, you know. The meanness. It's in the DNA, in the bones and the blood. It's in Griff, even if you haven't seen it yet. Oh, yes ma'am, that boy has got himself a temper. I don't guess you've seen it yet. You don't with him, not right away."

I jerked my arm away. But I didn't run or push him. Was Griff in on this too? Had he orchestrated this whole thing along with his father?

"He loved her, you know that?" Bobby purred into my ear. "From the minute he first saw her. Never got over it. In fact, I do believe it made him meaner, if you can imagine it. A man who'd strangle his own sister getting meaner?"

He neatly maneuvered my arm behind my back. I caught my breath at the sharp stab of pain that shot through it. Panic made my skin prickle.

"It made sense to me, though. He had to live his life without the one woman he loved, even though she was a murderer and a thief. And then on top of that, he had to deal with the fact that she was onstage beside Charles Jarrod. That she was making all that money for the wrong preacher man. Not to mention sleeping in his bed."

I tore free, my shoulder wrenching painfully, and pushed past him, through the kitchen and out into the hall. I faltered, the fear throttling me now.

"You want to leave, but you can't, can you?"

I turned.

Bobby stood in the dimly lit hallway, serious now. "I'll tell you the story, if you really want to hear it."

I didn't answer him. But I didn't move.

"You want to hear it, don't you, darlin'? You want to know every dirty deed your sweet Dove did."

I hated myself for it, but he was right. I did want to know. Because of all the lies Dove had told me. Because of everything I'd lost on account of her. "Tell me."

He sauntered closer. "My daddy took off, and then my mama died. Lucky me, I ended up living with my grandma Anna and grandpa Robert Sr." I could smell his minty tobacco breath mixed with the smell of beer. "He nearly beat the life right out of me. He'd get me in a corner, pin me with one hand so the other was free to swing. When I was twelve or thirteen, he started something new. He'd put his hands around my throat and choke the life out of me good and slow."

I felt all the breath leave my body.

"He'd go into these rages. Break tables, smash dishes. He'd chase me around, pin me down like I told you."

He put out a hand and fingered a lock of my hair. His voice was a rasp.

"He made me say my name was Ruth and that I was sorry for running from him. And then, he'd beat me."

Tears slipped down my face. "I'm so sorry . . ."

"Yeah. Me too. Me too." He picked up the key and the two hundred-dollar bills from the table. He slipped the money in his pocket, then bolted the front door with the key. "Look at that. Double cylinder deadbolt. Handy. Keep you from running." He slipped the key in his pocket.

"I won't run. We can talk this out."

"No. No, we can't. I thought Dove might feel bad about all the abuse I suffered at my grandpa's hands, when I saw her that last time.

But she acted like she wasn't the least bit responsible for making old Reverend Singley the monster he was. But she was. She was."

"Please—"

"Then I found her written confession to killing Steadfast Coe in a deposit box after Robert Sr. died. Don't know where he managed to pick up such a thing, but it got me thinking that there might be a way to make things right for me after all. I tried to find the coin myself at first. Looked everywhere on God's green earth for it, for eight years."

"You killed her. And then you searched her house for the coin." I could hardly believe the words even as they came out of my mouth. "And you broke in other times too, didn't you?"

He nodded. "Never no luck, though. Couldn't find that coin no matter how much I looked. Then, all these years later, I hear about the documentary and *bingo*. I realize my boy, my very own Griff, can work on this thing and feed me info from the inside. He got in, all right. But he wasn't much help. When I'd call him, all he wanted to talk about was Dove's granddaughter. The *interesting* and *attractive* Eve Candler. So that gave me a better idea."

I glared at him. If I'd been able to kill him with my eyes, I would have. With no shame.

"Funny thing, ain't it? Robert Sr.'s great-grandson falling for Dove Jarrod's granddaughter. Like I said, some things are just in the DNA." He shrugged.

"You should just get on with what you've got to do. And I should go." I made another move toward the door, but he sidestepped, blocking me with his bantam boxer's body.

I reached into my back pocket for my phone, but he grabbed it and pried my fingers loose. Then he sent it sailing across the room into the opposite wall. He grabbed my arm, the weak one, and twisted it just enough that I gasped out loud.

"You ain't calling nobody, darlin'. You're staying right here and giving me what I'm owed."

"Listen, Bobby." I held out my hands. "I know you're angry. But I'm telling you the truth. I can't find the coin. I tried, but I don't know where it is."

"You did try, Eve, but you went about it the wrong way. You can find it, you just gotta believe." He pulled me across the hallway into the dim parlor, where he yanked me to a stop.

I heard a soft rustling and then on a chaise near the fireplace, Ember sat up. She stretched drowsily.

The sight of her gave me a jolt. "Ember. What are you doing here?"

She sent me a sunny, stoned smile. "I'm here to see you."

I whirled on Bobby. "What did you give her?"

"I gave myself something." Ember stood, listing slightly to one side. "Three or four somethings, in fact. And then this guy, the bones guy, stopped by the shed and said I should come with him."

I looked back at Bobby. He was smiling triumphantly.

"He said the Hawthorn Sisters were going to perform one last miracle."

Chapter Forty-Six

Muscle Shoals, Alabama
1934

On their second night at the fair, the Hawthorn Sisters were winding up their opening hymn when a young man in the back waved his hand, then cupped it around his mouth.

"Steal Away to Jesus!" he shouted. The crowd clapped their encouragement, and a few people started in on the chorus. Then the band picked up the toe-tapping beat.

Ruth winced. Arthur was not going to like them singing the spiritual again. But Bruna giggled and leaned into the microphone. Her sweet soprano voice filled the cooling twilight, stilling the ruckus.

"Steal away . . ." Her voice was no more than a purr. *"Steal away . . ."*

A hush fell over the crowd.

"Steal away to Jesus." She made a face at Ruth, then sidled up to the microphone and cocked one hip, then an eyebrow. She belted out the last line, long and low. *"Steal away home!"*

The crowd leapt to their feet, stomping and clapping and whistling as the girls started on the first verse. It was good fun and a lively start to a meeting. It also gave Ruth a chance to search the crowd. She sauntered around the stage, scanning the crowd for Reverend Robert Singley or Charles Jarrod, but there was no sign of either.

Just as her nerves started to settle, Ruth spotted the woman from the St. Florian meeting, the wrung-out one with nine children. She was standing behind the last row of benches, but this time she had a little boy with her, and both were dressed for the occasion. She wore a simple dusty-rose dress with a pretty straw hat, and the boy, a freckle-faced imp, had on a clean, starched shirt.

Brimming with unease, Ruth hurried toward the microphone, and tried to fall into step with Bruna's easy swaying. As if Ruth didn't have enough fraying her nerves, with Arthur, Steadfast, and the horrible reverend's threats about Dell. Now this woman, whose husband had the look of a bruiser if she'd ever seen one, was back without him.

They sang another two songs, then Bruna called the people down for prayer. People streamed to the stage, but the woman in the rose dress hung back.

"Only them who haven't gotten prayer yet," Arthur shouted at the people. "If you came last night, step to the rear of the line!"

Ruth laid hands on as many of them as she could, praying until her throat was raw, but still the lines seemed to go on forever. Where had these people all come from? Her spirit was flagging, legs buckling beneath her, when she felt a tug on her arm. She turned to see Arthur shooing the remaining people back.

"Backstage," he ordered her.

She didn't move. The woman in the rose dress hadn't made it to the front of the line yet. In fact, Ruth couldn't see her at all. Had her husband snatched her away? Or maybe she was just hanging back, following Arthur's instructions.

Ruth pressed her mouth close to Arthur's ear. "I can keep going. Please, Arthur."

"No way. Got to leave them wanting more. And I've got to make the announcement."

She felt her skin go clammy. He was talking about Steadfast.

Goddammit!

"Ruth." Arthur's eyes held a clear threat.

But then Ruth spotted her—the woman in rose pressing her way past all the bodies. Ruth ran to the woman, grabbing hold of her hands.

"I'm so glad to see you again! Maggie, right?"

"That's right." The woman gave her a tremulous smile. "I can't believe I'm here."

Arthur had stepped in front of the microphone. "Evening, ladies and gentlemen. Beloved children of Almighty Jehovah!"

The crowd burst into applause.

"Well, I can," Ruth said. "I'm looking right at you. And in such a pretty dress too." Ruth's eyes swept the crowd behind her.

"He went to his brother's in Nashville. My sister's got the kids. Well, all except Jasper here. I brought him so you could pray for him. He's got a stubborn streak, this one. Picks at the others. Teases the baby."

Ruth squeezed her hands and smiled down at the little boy. "Pleased to meet you, Jasper."

The little boy sent her a sullen look and twisted away.

"I want to tell you I feel something," Arthur went on from the stage. His voice echoed through the tinny microphone, then he paused dramatically. "A heaviness in the Spirit that I just can't shake. And I tell you, you're not going to want to miss this."

Everyone on the floor was staring at him, hushed and attentive.

"After Jasper, would you pray for me too?" Maggie snapped her back to attention. Her eyes were dark, troubled in a way that made Ruth even more nervous. "I know I don't have the faith. Not the right kind. I'm weak and lazy and sometimes downright mean-spirited, but I believe He can help me . . . if I don't stumble."

Ruth didn't know what to say. This woman, this downtrodden woman with nine kids, was coming to her for a blessing. But Ruth didn't have that to give. She didn't have anything for such a woman.

Maggie drew herself up. "You can say if it's the kids, blocking the will of God. I swear I don't know why, but I got a pack of bad kids, and I been trying hard as I can to point 'em the right way."

"Well, that's good," Ruth said.

Jasper let Ruth lay her hand on his shoulder. Then Ruth rested her hand, lightly, on Maggie's head as well. The woman's chin tilted up to the sky, her eyes closed. Ruth's eyes fell on Maggie's hair. It was soft, finger waved along the side. Beautiful.

But Maggie's wholesome country beauty hadn't won her love. It hadn't kept her safe from the cruelty of the world or the savagery of a man whose heart was so small he would abuse the mother of his nine children. Was this the end of all girls? To marry men who they believed loved them, only to become the object of their husbands' disappointment and rage?

Ruth opened her mouth to pray, but at that very moment, Arthur appeared at her side.

"Let's go." He took hold of her arm.

She shook him off. "Arthur, no."

Maggie blinked in confusion, as Arthur gently disconnected the two women.

"Come back tomorrow," he told Maggie. "The Spirit of the Lord has a mighty word for everyone."

Maggie turned a pleading face to Ruth. "My husband will be back in the morning."

Arthur cut in. "Get on home. Fast and pray that the Lord will speak to us all."

He whisked Ruth away, past the grandstand and right to his waiting truck. Bruna was already there, hands folded on her lap. Ruth climbed on the bed and they drove back to Florence in silence.

They ate a late dinner at Trowbridge's—fried eggs, cornbread, boiled ham, and coffee. Ruth's voice was froggy, so Arthur told her to gargle salt in warm water and go straight to bed. She agreed. She was too tired to argue. Besides, Bruna looked like she might be on the verge of tears.

But she wanted to fight. She wanted to tell Arthur that it was wrong that he'd sent the people away, that he'd sent poor, downtrodden Maggie Kittle back to her nine kids and her glowering husband. That he was wrong to lord it over Bruna, making her confess her sins and pray for forgiveness before she went onstage.

The waitress appeared at their table. "Gent at the counter paid y'all's ticket. Snazzy one, with the face."

The three of them swiveled toward the counter, and for once in her life, Ruth felt sure she was going to faint. The man, sitting by himself at the counter, the one with the head of chestnut curls and crisp white shirt, lifted his hand. And then he directed a dazzling smile straight at her.

At last. Charles Jarrod had come.

Chapter Forty-Seven

Florence, Alabama
Present

I wanted to run straight to Ember, but I knew I couldn't. I had to play this smart. Bobby had already shown me how dangerous he could be.

He spoke behind me in a quiet voice. "That's right, Eve. The Hawthorn Sisters are back in business and the show's going to be one night only."

I turned to him, disdain and fury making my voice unsteady. "We're not the Hawthorn Sisters."

He raised his eyebrows, a sneer twisting his lips. "Well, see now that's the thing. When I saw you at the restaurant and realized you hadn't found the coin, I got to thinking. You probably hadn't exhausted all your options."

I laughed, but it was really more of a crazed-sounding, high-pitched shriek. "How many times do I have to tell you? If my grandmother did take the coin—and there's zero proof she did—she didn't clue me in on where she put it."

"You aren't listening to me, Eve." He pointed at Ember. "She's a fortune teller. Someone who communes with spirits. So I'm of a mind to believe that she's got the raw materials to find out." He stepped closer. "And I think you've got raw materials too. If you two get together and do that Hawthorn Sisters thing your grannies used to do, maybe we could solve the mystery."

I wanted to cry. To scream. More than anything, I wanted to punch him in the nose. Instead, I spoke calmly. "I have no idea what you're talking about. There is no 'thing.'"

He pointed to his eyes, blazing with barely controlled fury. "With these very eyes I seen Dove Jarrod pray over people. I've seen her heal 'em, give 'em a new lease on life. And then I saw with these same eyes all the money people threw at her for it. Now it's your turn and I don't want to hear excuses."

I lifted my chin, matching his anger. "I'll tell you exactly what I got from Dove. I got her red hair and her great skin and her ability to lie to everyone's face." The knot in my stomach loosened and unwound and I suddenly felt a wild, feral flash of freedom. "But here's some truth for you. I will never help you find that coin."

I spit in his face. He jerked back, wiping his face with his sleeve and sending me a reproachful look.

"My God, ain't you a shrew. I don't know what my son sees in you." He snapped his fingers at Ember, and she straightened to attention. "Sit down."

She obeyed but fixed me with a pleading expression. "I'm sorry, Eve. I knew I shouldn't have taken the pills. I wanted to stop. I swore when you showed up that I was going to stop." She started to cry.

Bobby turned to me, his face now placid, lips stretched in that genial grin, white teeth flashing.

"You too, darlin'. Sit down. We're about to have church."

Chapter Forty-Eight

Muscle Shoals, Alabama
1934

"At the Cross," Arthur shouted from the wings over the pounding piano and squawking cornet. *"At the Cross!"*

Bruna leaned toward the microphone, her face wreathed in a bright smile. "Hello, children of God! '*This is the day that the Lord hath made*'!"

Ruth jostled her shoulder and winked out at the people. "Or the night. At any rate, let us '*rejoice and be glad in it*'!" She snuck a glance at Arthur. His arms were folded, and he was pouting.

The girls smiled out over the crowd, giving the band a chance to catch up. They were dolled up—curled hair, bright lipstick, and matching slate-blue dresses with tulip-puffed sleeves and soft coral piping that Arthur had bought at Rogers Department Store. Earlier that day when they'd tried them on, Ruth had to keep straightening hers so it wouldn't slip off one shoulder or the other. Arthur had gotten the smallest size they had, but it was apparent it was too big.

"There's no time to take it in." Bruna pulled at Ruth's collar, then the waist. The dress swam around her.

"I'll wear the green one," Ruth said. "I like it better anyway."

Arthur put his hands in the trouser pockets of his new tweed suit and shot her a disdainful grin. "You won't wear the green. You'll wear the dress I bought you."

"With our money," Ruth retorted.

"What do you mean by that?" he shot back.

"You know you've been cutting into our shares. I see how much goes into those plates, and the math don't add up."

"Like you can add worth two toots," Arthur sneered.

"You two," Bruna said.

"Excuse me," Ruth said. "I don't remember the Hawthorn Sisters making you costume mistress of this production."

Arthur regarded Ruth for a few moments, then spoke in a measured tone. "Tonight, everything changes for us. Do you hear what I'm saying? Do you understand what I'm telling you, my dear, cheeky, impertinent Ruth? Tonight the Hawthorn Sisters are finally going to make a name for themselves. To prove to the people that they're a bona fide professional outfit, even slicker than Billy Sunday and Aimee Semple McPherson."

Bruna cut her eyes at Ruth, then looked away.

"No more pole barns and dirty old canvas tents full of mud puddles and rats," Arthur went on. "We're going to New York. To California and Boston and Chicago. They'll build us our own tabernacles with real paneling and velvet curtains and a backdrop painted with real gold. Why, Charles Jarrod is a world-renowned evangelist and he came to Alabama to see you! I'm the one who did that! I made that happen for you!"

A bead of sweat trickled down along Arthur's hairline. Ruth and Bruna watched him, their mouths both pressed in grim lines.

He leveled a cold stare at Ruth. "So you'll wear the dress, and you'll sing the songs I tell you. When I say preach, you'll preach. And when I say prophesy . . ." His face twisted as he let out an almost animal snarl. "You goddamn better prophesy."

Ruth clenched her fists at her side. "I'll do everything you say, Brother Holt. Sweet as you like, just as soon as I see every last bit of the money we've made."

He didn't answer her, just walked to the sideboard and pulled a cigarette from a pack.

"Is there a problem, Brother Holt?" Ruth asked. "You still got it, don't you, Brother Holt? That little extra you skimmed off the top and didn't give to us? Or did you spend it all on hooch and whores?"

She laughed, and he swept in and issued a stinging slap across her cheek before she realized what was happening. She leapt forward, claws out, ready for battle.

"Stop!" Bruna screamed. "Ruth, stop! There's no need."

Ruth knew Bruna was right. There was no need; they were leaving tonight and she was just picking a fight. But she'd been angry at Arthur for a long time now. And she was in no mood to let this go. She snagged a fistful of his suit jacket, and then a fistful of curly hair, but he shook her off and grabbed her wrist. She swung with the other hand, a wide arc that he intercepted as well.

She spit in his face. "Coward. You're nothing but a lily-livered, corn pone–eating coward!"

"Jezebel!" he growled at her.

"Arthur, please, please!" Bruna wailed.

He released Ruth, threw his cigarette on the floor, and stalked out of the room.

"You'll never hear me confess no sins!" Ruth screamed after him. "Not in your presence. Not like she does. You hear me? No man tells me when I'm sinning and when I ain't!"

The front door opened, then slammed shut.

Bruna blinked rapidly, like she was on the verge of breaking down. "Leave him be. It doesn't matter anyway."

"But it's our money," Ruth said. "We earned it."

Bruna's face was pale. "He's losing everything tonight, Ruth. Let him have his consolation prize. Let him have the money."

Bruna scurried back to her bedroom, and Ruth swallowed a scream. She was sick to death of keeping her and Arthur's secret from Bruna. Sick with worry about prophesying tonight. If something went wrong tonight—anything at all—she could be blamed for Steadfast Coe's murder.

And so many things could go wrong. She could freeze up and not be able to speak. The crowd might think she was lying. And then it would just be a matter of calling the police and having her hauled into jail. They'd put her in handcuffs, force her to break down and confess everything . . .

And then there was Dell. What had that old preacher done to him? If she and Bruna did successfully escape with Charles Jarrod after tonight's big show, would she be able to contact him? Would she see him again?

Her stomach heaved and even in the oversized dress, she felt unbearably hot. Everything was too far gone now. She had no other choice. She had to stick with the plan. She returned to the Coe house and in her room, jimmied the brass plate off the door. She dug out the Flowing Hair and hid it in her sock, then sat on her bed. She took one last look at the narrow room. She suspected she'd never see it again.

"At the cross, at the cross, where I first saw the light . . ."

Ruth snapped back to the present. To the tent, the music, the enthusiasm of the crowd before her. Lost in her thoughts, she'd stopped singing, and Bruna had elbowed her, sharp and pointed.

Ruth caught up, harmonizing with Bruna. *"And the burden of my heart rolled away . . ."*

They clasped hands as if the move had been choreographed.

"It was there by faith I received my sight. And now I'm happy all the day!"

Another lie. Another stone to add to the altar of untruths she was building.

And then she saw him—well, them. They were both watching her, both slicked up and scrubbed down. Charles, in the middle section, three-quarters of the way back, and Dell, lounging at the very back like a pool hall cat. Her voice thinned to nothing.

Again, Bruna dug her elbow into Ruth's side. Ruth jumped and came in with her line, but she was fit to be tied. Between Dell and Charles, she didn't know who to keep her eye on.

Goddamn, goddamn, goddamn . . .

Bruna poked her hard, and Ruth realized she'd cursed out loud, right into the microphone. A hush fell over the people. Children stopped squirming and the night air seemed to gather around. A few of the ladies in the front row had fixed her with dubious frowns.

Arthur broke in between them, seizing the microphone. The thing shrieked in his grasp as he spread his arms toward the crowd.

"I feel the heaviness of the Spirit in this place," he said. "I feel it like the world must've felt it, the very moment before God sparked all things into being. *'And the earth was without form, and void; and darkness was upon the face of the deep. And the Spirit of God brooded upon the face of the waters.'* The Spirit's speaking tonight. I feel it in my bones."

He turned to Ruth and flashed his teeth. It wasn't a smile. More like how an animal bared its teeth at an adversary. "The Spirit's speaking to you, isn't that right, Ruth?"

She didn't move. She just looked into his eyes, feet rooted to the stage.

"Go." Bruna gave her a gentle push.

But Ruth shook her head. Bruna just thought it was like all the other times. That Arthur wanted Ruth to call out healing for some sickness. Bruna had no idea what he expected Ruth to do.

"Come on up here, Ruth," Arthur said.

It was an order. One she had to obey.

She did. In the glare of the lights, Arthur's arm snaked around her waist. "Folks, Ruth hasn't been right tonight. Have you, sweetheart? Tell me what you're feeling right now."

She swallowed and glanced back at Bruna. She knew it was a bad idea, but she wanted her friend beside her, holding her hand. Helping her do this awful thing she'd promised to do.

Arthur jostled Ruth. "Folks, she's trembling. I can feel it. Trembling under the hand of God. Ruth, can you tell me what the Spirit's saying to you? Why are you trembling?"

She craned her neck, seeking Bruna out again, but was blinded by a light shining from someplace beyond the crowd. Someone had turned a spotlight on. The nausea returned, slamming into her with such force that she had to cling to Arthur for support. Arthur liked it, thought it was part of the show, she could tell. He held her even tighter.

Ruth squinted against the light. She found Charles—he'd moved forward in his seat, back straight and lips parted in rapt attention—but Dell was nowhere in sight. Had he left? Or had Singley shown up and done something terrible to him? Had that man called the police, reported that he was wanted by the law? She felt a wild desperation cloud her mind. She couldn't think for the fear.

"Bruna?" she said. Her voice, which had started low and unsure, rose to a scream. "Bruna!"

Bruna appeared on her other side, taking her arm. "Hush, Ruth. I'm here."

Arthur leaned to the microphone. "Folks, Ruth here is sore burdened with this word." He put a hand on Ruth's head. "It's about a man in this town. A man we all know, Mr. Steadfast Coe. Isn't that right, Ruth?"

Ruth felt Bruna disconnect from her. Felt her friend's gaze bore into her. Ruth kept her eyes on her feet. She couldn't bring herself to look back.

"Ruth, the Lord's spoken to you about Mr. Coe, hasn't he?" Arthur said. "He's revealed to you where he wandered off to. Where he laid his head in his final rest. Where he came face-to-face with his Maker."

A gasp traveled through the crowd. A few souls cried out amens.

"Ruth?" Bruna whispered.

Arthur lifted an arm. "I say prophesy, Sister Ruth. Prophesy to the people."

But Ruth couldn't. Not with Bruna staring at her like that. She lifted her eyes to meet Bruna's, to see her friend's were welling with tears. Ruth went to her.

"I'm sorry I didn't tell you. I'm sorry, Bruna, I'm so sorry . . ."

Bruna grabbed Ruth's wrist. Her tone was fierce. "What's he talking about? You know where Grandy is?"

"Bruna, listen," Ruth said. "Toward the back. Did you see him? Charles Jarrod."

Bruna looked pale and distracted. A sheen of sweat along her temple glistened in the lights. "How long have you known?"

Arthur cast an annoyed glance at the girls. "Bruna, let her go. Ruth . . ." He motioned impatiently.

Ruth ignored him. "You have to trust me," she whispered to Bruna. "Right after they leave to find Steadfast. That's when we go. Okay?"

"I don't understand." Bruna's eyes were wild, her voice rising in volume. "How do you know? How's Arthur know—"

Arthur leaned to the microphone again. "Fear not, sayeth the Lord. Speak His word for the people and you will see your reward in the land of the living!" He turned to the girls. "Ruth!"

Ruth touched her forehead to Bruna's. She was trembling. "I'll tell you later. When we're gone. I promise I'll tell you everything."

Bruna pressed her lips together. Tears spilled down her face.

"What is it?" Ruth wasn't whispering anymore. She had the horrible, sinking feeling that something outside her realm of understanding had occurred. When she wasn't paying attention, everything had changed.

Bruna wiped her face with her sleeve. "I can't go with you."

Ruth frowned. "What?"

"Not here," Bruna said. "I can't tell you here."

"Tell me now," Ruth said fiercely. "Or so help me, I'll never forgive you."

"I'm pregnant," Bruna said.

Ruth told herself to breathe, told herself that she would faint if she didn't, but her body would not comply. Somehow, she'd known this was how it was going to end. With Bruna staying behind, choosing Arthur over her. But she'd never imagined the emptiness she would feel, the certainty that a hole had been torn in her gut.

"I was afraid to tell you before," Bruna said. "And I thought I could still go away with you, that it didn't matter . . ."

The crowd was riled up, clapping and calling out, "Praise Jesus!" and "Glory!" and "Hallelujah!" Arthur covered the microphone and yelled over the din. "Ruth! Get over here! Now!"

"But it does," Bruna said. "It changes everything. I can't leave, Ruth. I just can't."

She studied Bruna's tearful face, her mind a blank, her body empty now of all warmth, of life and hope.

Her best friend was going to marry Arthur Holt. And have his child.

Ruth was alone. She wasn't Little Orphan Annie—she wouldn't even be a Hawthorn Sister for much longer. She was nothing.

Finding Charles in the crowd, she cleared her throat.

She inhaled, threw her head back, and let out a long guttural shriek. It sounded like it might have come from some small hunted animal . . . or, conversely, a human possessed by a thousand tormenting devils.

Chapter Forty-Nine

Florence, Alabama
Present

I sank down on the sofa beside Ember and she reached for my hand. Her pupils were large—the expression in her eyes fearful and disoriented. I realized I was scared for her, maybe more than for myself. Bobby didn't appear to have a weapon, but he was built like a tank, and had made it abundantly clear that night at Pritchard that he wasn't reluctant to use violence to get his way. I could try to make a break for it, but it would mean leaving Ember behind. No way was I doing that.

Bobby walked to the piano, its bench now upended, legs severed, and dropped one finger on a key. The sound reverberated through the room.

B-flat. Of course. The sound of a black hole singing.

The note faded and he spoke in that twangy, fake-folksy voice. "Look at you two, like you just stepped out of a picture. So much like Bruna and Dove." He rubbed his hands gleefully. "The Hawthorn Sisters. Back for their final show."

"Motherfucker," I whispered under my breath. "Lunatic."

Bobby sent me a patient look.

Ember leaned back against the chaise. "I told you, she doesn't believe."

"You still don't see it, do you, Eve? Dove had the fire. The anointing of a prophet."

I snorted. "Just because she claimed to heal people doesn't make it true. Just because people said they were healed doesn't make it true."

He furrowed his brow.

"That's right, Bobby," I said. "It was all a lie. Dove couldn't perform miracles."

"Bullshit. I saw it."

"You saw a show. Smoke and mirrors. Here's the truth. A long time ago, when I was just a kid, I asked her to heal my arm. But she couldn't. Because she'd never healed anybody. Not one single person. She told me that."

Bobby struck another key. The note hung in the air. "Maybe she wouldn't heal you because you didn't deserve it. Maybe you were a spoiled little princess, and she thought you ought to earn your salvation, like the rest of us regular folk. Ever think about that?"

I had thought about that—I'd thought about it all my life. I'd always been torn between a desire to believe in childhood fairy tales and cold, hard reality. But I'd rather throw myself into a flaming pit than admit it to Bobby Asshole Singley.

"Play a song," Ember said to Bobby in a dreamy tone. "And she'll see." Her eyes were still glassy, pupils dark and dilated. "It's how the girls connected to the fire. Through the hymns."

"Ember, stop," I said quietly. "You're high."

She looked hurt. "I know you think I'm just a waste of space. That I use because Jason got all the money and I got nothing. But you don't know anything about me. What I've had to deal with. They taught me this stuff was real. That Bruna, one half of the Hawthorn Sisters, my grandmother, had a connection to God, and if I was just holy enough, if I could just be nice and quiet and obedient enough, I would hear the voice of God too. And I do. I hear things. I know things. I tell people their futures—"

"Ember—"

"I may be high, but I'm not stupid!" she yelled.

Bobby clapped out a loud, discordant applause. "She's right, praise God. She's a child of the Lord. And you are too, Eve, whether you want to admit it or not. Now I said we were gonna have church, and by God we're gonna have church. Lead us in a hymn of worship, Eve."

"No." I stood. "We're not doing this."

She spoke in a plaintive voice from her chaise. "Come on, Eve. Just try." She cleared her throat. *"Savior come, abide with me . . ."*

"Ah, one of the old ones." Bobby pushed me down on a chair and hurried back to the piano. "You don't hear those much anymore." He played the intro.

Ember continued, her voice unsteady. Then a loud bang of discordant keys broke the spell.

"Sing, you stubborn bitch!" Bobby yelled at me.

I shot him a scowl.

"Eve, please," Ember said.

I sat again and took her hand. My voice was thin and faltered on certain notes, but like last time, we harmonized perfectly, like we'd been singing together for years. *"I am longing, I am praying, for a closer walk with Thee . . ."*

Bobby's eyes lit with an otherworldly fire, and he played on as we sang the next lines. His face glowed above the ivory keys of the piano.

"You feel it, don't you?" he crowed. "My God, I do! I feel every hair on my body standing up!"

I had begun to shake. This man was not well, and there was no predicting how far he would go to get what he wanted. So I did what he demanded. I sang, all the while frantically trying to make sense of what was happening.

If Griff was in on this with Bobby, even if I managed to get away, he might be out there waiting for me. Was there anyone else out there along with him? Althea? Could she have hitched her wagon to Bobby and Griff's star? Maybe I was the fool in this scenario.

But how far did they plan to take this?

What would they do to get what they wanted?

Bobby banged on the piano keys, jolting me from my thoughts. He strode across the room and yanked Ember up by the arm.

"Now give me a word, girl," he hissed. "Speak the word of the Lord and for once do something in your useless life." In the dim light of the room, I could see his eyes glitter. They made him look unhinged.

"Let go of her!" I yelled at him. "It doesn't work that way! You don't sing a song and think happy thoughts and get a secret message from God."

I pulled Ember away from him, but she turned to me, a pleading look on her face. "Eve, you're wrong. You're wrong! I know there are miracles. I *know* it. It's that believing that keeps me going. In spite of everything they say."

"Fine! Believe what you want, Ember. But don't let him use it for his own personal gain. You own your belief."

A bolt of pain stabbed through my arm. I clutched at it and without even realizing what I was doing, let out a whimper.

"What?" Bobby barked. He let go of Ember and raced to me. "What happened?"

I angled away from him. "It's nothing."

"Bullshit. You're sensing something. Just say what's in your head, Eve. Whatever it is, just say it!"

Our eyes met.

There was so much in my head, I doubted I could put it into words. Images of Dove and Bruna holding hands onstage. A letter to Charles . . . *singing and ministering here and there, managed by Mr.*

Arthur Holt . . . The sound of a misstruck penny, clinking down into the lock of the door.

Dove's house, too, the small one across the highway from Pritchard Hospital.

I'm not the one who can give you your miracle, she'd said to me there, running her fingers so lightly down my right arm.

All I can do is tell you the truth . . .

But was what she told me that day really the truth? Or was there something more that lay beyond her words . . . something bigger and brighter and so confounding that Dove herself didn't know whether to call it the truth or a lie?

I tore my gaze from Bobby to face Ember. "Has God spoken to you, Ember?" My voice came out harsh, unyielding. "Has He told you where to find the coin?"

She stared at me, then looked away. "No."

"He hasn't told me either." I addressed Bobby. "So that's it, okay? Yes? We did what you wanted. We sang and nothing happened. Let her go."

"Your arm was showing you," Bobby spat. "You just didn't listen. Maybe you need some encouragement. Maybe this'll help."

He strode past me, pulled Ember by her shirt and swung her toward the chaise. She gasped and stumbled over her feet, but he didn't stop. He pushed her down and closed a hand around her throat.

I sprang toward him. "No!" I screamed. "Stop!"

She barely struggled, barely even moved beneath his weight. Then, with his free hand, he drew back and punched her, a sharp, well-aimed jab to the nose. I screamed as I heard the air whoosh out of her lungs.

I clawed at his back, but he swung around, deflecting me easily, and I fell back against an ottoman.

In a flash, his hand around Ember's neck. Then I heard the sickening sound of flesh striking flesh. I jumped up and pulled at his shirt, trying to capture his free arm, trying to stop him from hitting her again. But he was so strong. I couldn't seem to contain him.

Time slowed and I felt immobile. Then Ember grunted and Bobby leapt awkwardly away from the chaise, nearly stumbling over me as we both toppled to the floor. I scrambled up, and so did Bobby, breathing hard and thumbing at his nose.

"You scrawny little cunts always go for the jewels, don't you?" he snarled.

She sat up. Blood poured from her nose, and her mouth looked swollen and bloody. But she was conscious. And looking at me. I nodded, once, just the slightest movement so Bobby wouldn't see, then as if we shared an internal signal, we simultaneously launched ourselves at him.

She got there first, pushing him backward into a polished marble cocktail table. He flipped over it, and she grabbed him by the shirt and pinned him with an elbow to the neck.

"You know, I could see your future the minute I laid eyes on you," she said, her voice low and fearsome. "Your family's going to leave you and you're going to die alone. You're going to die, weeping for all the good days your family's going to have when you're gone at last."

She twisted back to me, her blood-smeared face making her look like some terrible, battle-frenzied goddess. "Go."

Chapter Fifty

Muscle Shoals, Alabama
1934

Ruth screamed and screamed until the veins stood out along her temples and her neck was corded. Until saliva dripped from the corners of her mouth, her hands bent to claws, and she felt like a woman who had lived a hundred lives.

As she screamed, she imagined her body lifting up and away from the grandstand, flying back to her old room in the east wing of Pritchard Hospital. That putrid yellow room had stunk of all the bodies who had lived and died there. It was where her mother had laughed and sang to her and then, at the end, swung from the doorjamb, the restraining strap from the cot looped around her neck. Ruth had cried for days, tears falling and nose running onto the dirty, broken-glass floor, a rope connecting her leg to the cot, until her head throbbed and she thought the world had ended.

She screamed for all that had followed those horrible days. For the steam from the washers in the laundry that singed off the first tender layer of skin on her face. For when Jimmy Singley breathed his hot, damp words into her ears and left the imprint of his fingers on her arm.

She screamed for when the Major sang his song and when Dell shot his marbles and when Eunice and Ethel laid their cards on the scarred wooden table. She screamed through the broiling heat and unbearable cold and the stink of shit and piss and vomit, mildew and rot and despair. She screamed until her throat was raw and all that came out was a croaking, gasping sound. And then she quit.

The people below stared in stunned silence. Ruth dully registered a man in the audience step into the aisle and lift his hat. It was a magnificent black homburg with a pink satin ribbon tied around it.

"I know her," he announced in a formal voice, nodding genially, deferentially, at Arthur. "She ran off from the insane hospital down in Tuscaloosa."

Arthur squinted into the light. "Who are you?"

"I'm the Reverend Robert Singley, chaplain of the hospital and emissary of the superintendent, sent to fetch her back on home." He ambled down the aisle toward the stage. "She's a loon. And not a harmless one. She's a danger to herself and all who dare to enter her circle."

"You have documentation, I assume?" Charles Jarrod edged his way down the row of bodies into the aisle behind Singley. Ruth didn't look at him.

Singley turned back. "May I ask who's inquiring?"

"Charles Jarrod, a friend of Miss Davidson's." The crowd let out a ripple of admiration, which Charles acknowledged with a wave of his hand.

Singley ducked his head in deference. "Hello, Mr. Jarrod, and a hearty welcome to the state of Alabama. I acknowledge that you are a man of God. A man of rectitude and charity. But all the same, the law's the law. The girl's a runaway. She should be locked up before she does any further damage."

Ruth searched the faces she could see, looking for Dell, but it was Charles Jarrod's eyes she found. They were kind and trusting, and instantly she saw that he was waiting for her. Waiting on her next move before he did anything else.

But she didn't know her next move. She'd come tonight planning to tell the crowd that Steadfast had gotten lost in Key Cave like Arthur wanted. But Bruna's news had changed everything. Her best friend was going to have a baby. She would stay in Florence and make a family with Arthur; Ruth couldn't tell this terrible lie about her grandfather, then leave. She just couldn't.

She looked into Charles's eyes, bolstered by the calm way he looked back. Just a moment before she'd been terrified and alone and trapped like the lion in his cage. Out of options. Out of friends. But now . . .

Now she knew what she must do.

She ran to the end of the stage, and, stopping just short of flying off the edge, seemed to hover above the crowd. The audience gasped, and for a moment, there was crystalline silence. Then she caught herself and curled into a ball. She let out another ear-shattering scream and the people stared. She clawed at the air then, contorted her face into a fearsome expression, and shrieked so shrilly some covered their ears.

Bruna seemed frozen in horror and confusion. Arthur too. Only Charles appeared unperturbed.

"See?" Singley hurried toward the stage. "Just look at how she suffers! She must be locked up!"

"No!" Charles Jarrod shouted, thrusting his hand to the stage. "You'll do no such thing. The girl isn't insane."

The people quieted, then turned their faces toward him.

"Anyone can see, she's tormented with a demon. She needs deliverance, not a hospital."

Low exclamations rippled through the crowd. Ruth whimpered and sobbed.

"The Lord's spoken to her," Arthur interjected quickly. "She knows where Mr. Steadfast Coe has gone, and she's got to prophesy."

"She can do that after she's been prayed over," Charles said curtly.

"I'll handle that." Singley leapt onto the stage with lightning speed. He grabbed Ruth's right arm, twisted it behind her, and forced her to the stage floor. She went down easily, no match for his strength and fervor. Charles sprang toward the stage, but Arthur caught him, and Singley, emboldened, twisted her arm. Ruth's vision went spotty, and she cried out, this time in real agony.

"Come out! Come out, foul spirit!" Singley bellowed.

Ruth struggled in his grip to find some purchase on the worn floorboards, but there was not a chink to be found. Her face pressed against the smooth wood, and she squeezed her eyes to shut out the blinding pain.

She thought she heard someone calling her name—Bruna, maybe—but it felt like it was coming from underwater. A voice in a dream.

Where was Charles?

Singley yanked her arm farther back—"In the name of Jesus, I command you to leave her!"—and she heard something crack. An electric jolt shot through her and she swayed, body arching in an effort to escape the pain.

Oh God, dear God. Had he broken her arm? Had he . . . had he?

"Get her!" someone shouted. A smattering of applause rippled through the crowd.

Singley wrenched her up by the shattered bone. "Speak, foul spirit!"

She screamed, this time an unearthly sound, even to her own ears.

"Listen to that!!" Singley bellowed. "The demonic spirit speaks to us from the fiery pit of Hell itself!"

He twisted the arm again, but she was beyond sensation at that point, only hazily aware that Charles Jarrod and maybe a few others had finally reached the stage. She heard an outraged voice yell out a string of colorful curses—*Dell?*—then she felt a pleasant blanket of fog descend. She was slipping away, her consciousness telescoping until all she could see was a small pinpoint of light. Then she heard Charles's voice ringing out above the rest. It drowned out everything—the heat, the pain, the fear—and she willed that voice to fill her physically, if that was such a thing. And she welcomed it.

"I said get your hands off her," Charles said. "Before I relieve you of them both."

Chapter Fifty-One

Florence, Alabama
Present

I ran to the front door but pulled up short a few feet away.

Shit. I'd forgotten. Bobby had locked it and still had the key.

I changed course, tearing down the hall toward the back of the house. When I got to the kitchen, I looked wildly around. I could leave. Run out the back door and see if I could find someone with a phone, or run to the police department. But that would mean abandoning Ember, and I couldn't leave her alone with Bobby.

The gun . . .

The one Griff found the other day.

I pushed open the mangled door, now stripped of its hardware, and crept to the center of the maid's room. Surely Jason had put that old Colt 1911 back into the lining of the ice chest. Ember had said it wasn't loaded.

Hadn't she?

I pulled the chest down from the top of the old wooden fridge and plunged my hand inside.

"Eve."

I jumped. Bobby was standing in the doorway, still slightly hunched in pain. His face was a repulsive combination of fanatic zeal and unmitigated hatred.

"Where's Ember? What did you do to her?"

"You know where it is, don't you?" he barked. "The coin. You saw it just a minute ago when you were singing. I know you did."

My fingers closed over the cold metal, I drew out the pistol, and with my right arm, aimed it at his chest. I felt a tremor roll through my arm, and, for a split second, I worried it wouldn't be strong enough to hold it steady.

Don't you fucking move, I ordered my arm. *Not one inch.*

"You monster," I said. "You lying, murdering piece of shit. You actually think I'd tell you if I did? You think I'd let you touch what doesn't belong to you? Where is Ember?"

"Out like a light." Bobby put his hands up, but he was smiling. "That thing's a hundred years old. Hasn't been oiled in forever."

"Whatever you say." I was trembling with fear and adrenaline and I knew he could see it.

Hold still. Hold still.

"It's not loaded." But he wasn't sure and I saw it in his eyes. But the problem was, I wasn't sure either. Ember had said it wasn't loaded. But she hadn't checked the chamber, had she? I was no gun expert, but wasn't it possible that a bullet could be loaded there?

"Is Griff helping you?" I asked.

Bobby shifted his position in the doorway, hands still up, obviously still feeling the effects of Ember's knee.

"Answer me!" I yelled.

He grinned through his pain, enjoying mine.

"Does he know you attacked me? Did he help you plan it?" I couldn't help it. My voice cracked and Bobby offered a sympathetic smile.

"Don't you worry about Griff, darlin'. It's just me and you here right now. Just us two"—he waved his arms like an old-time preacher—"and the Flowing Hair. I can feel it's in this house, like the Spirit coursing through my body. Can't you feel it?"

I held the gun steady. Did I need to pull back the slide if there was a bullet in the chamber? I had no idea. I'd never shot a gun. I'd never even held one.

God help me. What am I doing?

"I know you felt it a minute ago, Eve. Don't be afraid to admit it," he said.

"I didn't feel anything. Except disgust and pity for you."

His hand went to his chest. "Oh, darlin', you wound me. I thought we might be family one day. Keep that circle unbroken."

"I don't want any part of your fucking circle."

He cackled, his face shining with deranged fire. "Look, I'll split it with you, the money from the coin. Eighty-twenty. I think that's pretty generous. Don't you? And I'll give you the old man's bones, too. Then I can pay off my debts and get Helena back. And you . . . you can marry that pussy son of mine and the two of y'all can move out to Hollyweird. Make all the movies you want. I'll keep your secret. Dove's secret."

"Your son is a great man."

"No. He's soft. Weak." Bobby shrugged. "It was easy to get him to take this job. He's always been so desperate for my approval."

"Which you couldn't be bothered to give."

"Who needs approval," Bobby said, "when they can have money? Right? I think even Dove would see what a good deal I'm offering you. She was a hustler. She'd tell you to take my deal and run."

My arm shook. I fought to hold the gun steady.

"I have no doubt," I said, evenly, "if my grandmother was here right now, exactly what she would tell me to do."

He straightened, turned as if ready to leave me and this conversation behind. "Okay, then. Have it your way. I've got the psychic. What do I need you for?"

With an ease and control that surprised me, I pulled back the slide on the pistol and lowered the weapon approximately two feet south, aimed right at the center of the zipper on his jeans. He smirked in response. He didn't think I would do it.

But he didn't understand how coming to Alabama had changed me. How I'd found a side of my grandmother I never knew existed. And that because of it, I now understood that I had to fight—really fight, not just worry and fret and prepare—for my family. They were what was most important. I was going to defend them. I was going to do whatever it took to keep them safe. And now, that family included Ember.

"Now you're nothing but a goddamn complication," Bobby said, then coiled and lunged at me.

I pulled the trigger.

Chapter Fifty-Two

East Alabama
1934

Ruth bolted upright, woozy and disoriented, screaming Bruna's name.

A voice shushed her. "It's okay. You're safe now. You've been sleeping."

The car smelled new to her, all polished leather seats and shiny burled-wood panels. And the seat was soft. Very soft. And Charles, still in his starched white shirt and tie, one arm over the seat, was driving down a dark road.

The hot July air blew in the windows, and Ruth lay back and closed her eyes. Her arm was wrapped in some kind of contraption, secured tight to her chest. It still hurt, but it was better than before.

"How's the arm? I was worried it might be broken."

Ruth shifted, trying to get comfortable. "Don't know. Never had a broken arm before."

"I'm sorry I didn't get to you sooner. I wasn't sure if it was part of the show." He shook his head. "You know that fellow? The one who did it?"

"Kind of. A long time ago." She was too tired to explain, and thankfully, Charles didn't pry.

"When the ruckus kicked up, the police arrived and he ran. Off to do more deeds of darkness, I assume."

"Where are we going?"

"Greenville, South Carolina. We have a tent meeting starting Friday." He glanced at her. "That agreeable to you?"

She stared at him. When was the last time anyone had asked if she agreed to anything? She couldn't remember. Maybe never.

"It is," she said quietly.

They rode in silence for a while longer, then she spoke again.

"Did you see my friend? Bruna?"

"She left with the young man I believe."

"Arthur."

"Arthur," Charles repeated. "But not before he had a few words with the preacher fellow that broke your arm."

She contemplated this, but unable to imagine what Arthur and Singley would have to discuss, put it out of her mind. She wanted to ask about Dell but didn't want to risk Charles's questions. Instead, she pressed her cheek against the smooth leather of the seat and let the wave of wishing crash over her. Wishing that things had gone differently. That Bruna hadn't fallen in love with Arthur. But things had gone how they'd gone, and now Bruna was lost. Which made her think of something else . . .

"You expected the two of us," she said quietly. "You wanted both the Hawthorn Sisters."

He kept his eyes on the road. "Well, we'll see. Fact is, I could use a soloist. Or if you just want to help out with meals and cleaning. There's plenty to do. You have a place with me. I mean to look after you for as long as you want or need. Or until your friend changes her mind."

She swallowed back the tears that threatened to spill over. "Thank you."

"There is something, though . . ." He cleared his throat. "Something to address along those lines. My team is going to wonder why I've brought you along. They'll have questions." He took a deep breath. "I decided, if you're agreeable to it, I will tell them that you're my wife. That we're married."

Ruth glanced at him. "Are *you* agreeable?"

He nodded and gripped the steering wheel. "How old are you?"

"Seventeen. Eighteen soon."

"It's not ideal, but you're legal. I'm twenty-nine."

"And no wife?"

"There was one." He managed a smile. "And then there wasn't."

She was glad he didn't say any more. She couldn't bear any more sad stories. Not right now. She leaned her head back on the cushioned seat. "I reckon you shouldn't call me Ruth. In case that preacher gets wind of us."

"Good thinking. What would you like to be called instead?"

She thought. She used to be called Annie, a lifetime ago. But she didn't want to be that girl again. She didn't want to be a girl at all. She wanted to be a woman. She remembered that first day in Steadfast's parlor, sitting with Bruna. *You have a pretty voice. Like a dove. And you look like a dove too. Soft and delicate. And gray.*

"Dove," she said at last. "Dove Davidson. Half sister of the outlaw Dell Davidson."

It was another lie. But one that felt more real than anything else in her life.

He chuckled. "Okay."

She closed her eyes. "How far is Greenville?"

"We'll drive all night. Should be there before dawn."

She looked out over the flat cotton fields, thick with the fluffy bolls. In a couple of months the harvest would come and go. And she would miss it. Would anyone miss her?

"Mr. Jarrod—"

"Charles."

"Charles. Are they real? The signs you see, the wonders you perform?"

There was a long silence before he answered.

"I don't know. Some days I'm sure of it. Some days I doubt everything."

"Have you ever done a real miracle? I don't mean heal arthritis or a headache. I mean a real, honest-to-God miracle?"

He laughed. "I would like to think those qualified. But it's clear you're getting at something specific."

"Have you ever moved an object with the power of God?"

He laughed outright, like she'd told a bawdy joke. "I'm a preacher, not a spiritualist. You're talking about psychokinesis. Moving things with your mind."

"With the power of God," she corrected. "Well, have you? Or has anyone you know done it?"

"Ruth, if you need a package delivered, just say so and we'll make a trip to the post office."

Gingerly, taking great care not to jostle her arm, she reached into the pocket of her dress. She drew out a small coin, copper laced with green, and laid it on her knee. She rested her head against the door and watched it balance there, the promise of a life with the boy she had always loved. Her hope for a future. "I can't mail it."

Charles sighed and focused on the thin ribbon of road before the car. "I've never moved a physical object with my mind. But on the scientific side, I have heard of a doctor, one J. B. Rhine over in North Carolina, who says it can be done. Only, like I said, he's talking about using the power of the mind, the fifth force."

"But God could do it," Ruth said, her eyes locked on to the coin.

"I suppose He could," Charles said. "As He's God."

Ruth barely moved. Her arm hurt, but she was determined to see this through. "Tell me what to do. The right words to say."

"I certainly don't claim to know that kind of prayer . . ."

"Just tell me what you think." Her voice was edged with frustration and fear.

He went quiet. "Just tell Him what you need. That's all. That's all I ever do, just tell Him what I need."

She did as he said, right there in the car. She told God what she needed Him to do with the coin. Where she wanted it to go, who she needed it hidden for. She prayed and prayed—the request looping through her brain, coming out on her lips in audible words—until the darkness, the rattling of the car, and the hum of the tires ushered her into the oblivion of sleep.

When Charles woke her, they were parked at a motel outside of Rome, Georgia, the sun rising through a ridge of pines.

The coin was gone.

Chapter Fifty-Three

Florence, Alabama
Present

Ember's house was actually rather charming once you got the hungover, unshowered college students out of it. She'd cleaned it top to bottom for us and lit candles on every piece of battered secondhand furniture she had. It felt cozy.

She'd also made a peppery salmon and quinoa salad and opened a bottle of icy sauvignon blanc that must've blown her monthly budget to pieces. She looked pretty in a simple yellow sundress, the skin of her shoulders dewy and pink. Her black hair was shiny and smoothed behind ears lined with small, sparkling studs. The bruises and split lip hardly showed at all.

"Totally clean," she said, pulling me aside. "Six days."

I hugged her. "Good on you, Em."

"I'm going to do this, I swear." She gripped my hands and I squeezed back.

"I know you will."

We ate around a coffee table made of wooden pallets—Althea beside me, then Griff, then Ember, Jason, and Danny. Then after the meal, Ember leapt up to gather our dishes.

"I can do that," Althea protested, but Ember waved her off and bustled back to the kitchen.

"Sit tight, guys." Griff disappeared into one of the bedrooms.

My arm twinged, and I tried to ignore the drumbeat of anxiety rolling through me. I shouldn't be worried. Thanks to Alabama's stand-your-ground laws, I'd only gotten a slap on the wrist for shooting Bobby Singley. It helped that I was a terrible shot and only grazed his hip. But it created enough shock and pain for me to leap over his writhing body, find Ember in the parlor, and tell her I was going for help.

After the ambulance took Bobby and Ember away, Griff, Althea, and I found Steadfast Coe's bones in the toolbox in Bobby Singley's F-250. They were now safe and sound in the Lauderdale County ME's drawer, awaiting their resting place under the marker in the First Presbyterian cemetery. Dove's signed confession was with the police, but they seemed to think it was some kind of forgery.

On the home front, Mom had agreed to check herself into a facility in Palm Springs to rest, she said, and sort through things. I had a ticket to fly out and see her the following week. We would finally have the heart-to-heart we needed, and I was feeling optimistic. Danny was sitting and eating with my friends, holding his own. And my application to Colorado was still active.

But I couldn't shake the feeling that a cloud was still hanging over me. So many areas of my life were up in the air.

Just yesterday, the cops had marched into the hospital and arrested Bobby, charging him with Dove's murder, my assault, and various counts of kidnapping. At the moment, he was sitting in the Lauderdale County jail, probably cursing my name.

It was a lot for Griff to deal with and had made things awkward between us. We agreed that he would finish the documentary and then move on to the next gig. He had a lot to work through, but I'd be lying if I said I was okay with never seeing him again. I just didn't know how it was going to work.

And then there was the coin, the last remaining loose end. After all this, the Flowing Hair Dollar was still missing. I couldn't help feeling frustrated that we'd uncovered so much but failed to fully clear Dove's name. It was still possible that she'd taken it.

Interrupting my thoughts, Griff reappeared in Ember's living room. He was carrying a small cardboard case edged with tarnished brass under one arm and a bigger cardboard box balanced on his hand. He dumped everything onto the coffee table and went to work, snapping open the brass buckle on the box and lifting a bulky metal object out.

"What the hell," I said.

"A projector?" Ember exclaimed.

Goose bumps rose on my arms as I watched him plug in the long black cord. "Where did you get it?"

"Margaret Luster found it on eBay, if you can believe it," Althea said.

Griff pried open one of the cans, lifted out the film and expertly threaded it through the antiquated machine. He flicked on the motor. A beam of light shot through the aperture and an image appeared on the opposite wall.

My hand rose slowly to my wide-open mouth.

Dove—or Ruth—and Bruna were standing on a makeshift stage, clasped hands swinging, smiling and singing energetically. Bruna had dark eyes and hair, a Rubenesque body, and a megawatt smile. Beside her Dove looked diminutive, a waif with a sheet-straight bob and delicate but angular features.

No one made a sound. We were enchanted, struck speechless, by the sight of the girls, these girls we'd chased so desperately.

Bruna and Ruth were perfectly matched, impossibly pretty, and magnetic. They carried themselves like seasoned performers, executing smooth choreographed moves as they sang. A shoulder shimmy, perfectly timed dips, a pert series of handclaps. I felt like I was watching a homegrown version of the Andrews Sisters. I could see why they'd created such a stir in tiny Florence.

The scene cut again. Now Bruna stood on the stage, wearing a simple skirt and blouse, eyes closed, hands raised. Dove stood beside her in a plaid dress with a Peter Pan collar, one finger lifted to heaven, addressing the crowd. People swarmed toward them, blocking the camera, but whoever had been shooting shifted to a better angle in time to catch a wave of supplicants collapse in a heap on the straw. The girls climbed off the stage and crouched over the worshippers, laying hands and working their way through the crowd.

I felt Ember's hand on my back, and my skin rose with goose bumps. My eye fell on the stacks of film cans, small rusty discs that held hours and hours of footage of the Hawthorn Sisters. Their singing and praying and preaching. It was a window into the past, sure, but what would watching them tell me in the end? What would it change?

A bolt of pain sliced through my arm and my hand jerked.

Griff glanced over at me. "What? What is it?"

I couldn't say. I just held my arm and did my level best not to moan out loud.

"Eve. Tell us," Ember said. The others gathered, forming a protective circle around me.

"I'm—" I didn't know how to explain what was wrong with me. I knew that I felt tired and confused and scared to face life. That I was being bombarded with strange thoughts and images. That I felt massively uncomfortable being the center of their concern and my arm hurt like hell.

In my mind, I saw the tree again, that gnarled old hawthorn tree. I don't know why my brain had gotten stuck on that particular image, but there it was again in all its white-blossom glory, burned into my mind. I looked at the box of film cans at my feet, and the vague pictures in my head began to shift into subtle patterns. It was so close, a meaningful picture, but I couldn't put all the pieces together.

I lifted one cardboard flap and peered inside. "Are they all film, I wonder?"

"I assumed so," Griff said. He jumped up and started prying apart the cans. Film spilled out all over the table, unspooling and snaking across the surface.

"This one." I reached into the box with my good arm and drew out a can.

He grabbed it and twisted apart the sections. But instead of film, a packet of worn envelopes fell out. I sat up straight, every nerve ending in my body screaming.

"Holy shit," Ember blurted. "What's that?"

"You don't know?" Althea said.

"I told you, I've never opened the cans until today."

"They're letters." I grabbed the packet, tore off the narrow black ribbon holding them together, and flipped through the envelopes. "They're all from Dove Jarrod to Bruna Holt. Dated 1934 to 1939."

"Oh my God," Althea said. "Oh my God. I can't believe it."

"Read them," Jason and Danny urged at the same time.

I unfolded the first letter with shaky hands. *"Dearest Bruna, my heart, my soul . . ."* I stopped, overwhelmed.

"Keep going," Ember said.

I inhaled.

> *"As you know, I have secured us a fine arrangement. Charles Jarrod will harbor us as long as need be. He's given me his word. Room and board and gainful employment provided, not to mention protection from Arthur Holt and the despicable preacher from Tuscaloosa who attacked me. I will stay with Charles indefinitely, until such time as you come to me. Until we can be reunited and make plans of our own. I eagerly await that day and can think of nothing but your safety and happiness. Have you by chance seen Dell Davidson or heard of him about town? If so, please tell him I have something for him. Regardless, please*

write and let me know when you will be able to come to us. There are no restrictions. Children are welcome. Everyone is welcome. I await your reply. Your sister, Ruth."

"Something for Dell Davidson?" Ember practically screamed. "That's got to be the coin, right? She was concerned for Bruna's safety, but she hid the coin for Dell!"

"Looking out after the people she cared about most," Althea said.

"Read another one," Danny said.

I opened the next envelope, dated 1935.

"Dearest Bruna, I won't scold you or barrage you with tales about how delightful life on the road with Charles's outfit is, but you must know, this life would far surpass your life with Arthur. We travel on trains often and stay in the best cabins. We eat roast duck and chicken every day. Charles is generous and kind and the work, cooking and washing mostly, is light.

"Everyone is anxious to meet you and Arthur Jr., as I've told everyone about you and him and the Hawthorn Sisters. (And, of course, your wonderful soprano voice.) I've not heard from Dell and, I must admit, I fear for his safety. Have you read anything in the newspapers? Charles and I do live as man and wife for the benefit of his organization, but I still love Dell with everything in my heart. Sometimes I fear he has heard I am married to another man, and I will not have the chance to explain myself. If you see any acquaintance of his, will you please tell him about our plan and where to find me? I can't bear to think of him angry or aggrieved . . ."

I faltered, dropping the letter on my knees.

"She stayed with Charles for Bruna," Ember said. "Because Arthur Holt was bad news."

I flipped through the rest of the letters, skimming and reading aloud in turns, the story finally taking shape, piece by piece. A while later, I put the letter I'd been reading down and stared at the pile.

"So Dove married for convenience," Althea said. "Only it was Bruna's convenience, not hers."

Ember sighed. "But even after all that, Granny Bru never left PawPaw Arthur."

"And Dove never left Charles," Danny said.

"Dell Davidson must never have shown up either," Griff said. "So they all just stayed where they were. Waiting for something to change."

We were quiet, the somber reality settling over us. Ember reached for her water glass. I picked up my glass and touched hers. More glasses clinked.

"To Dove," Ember said.

"Dove," everyone echoed.

There was one last letter in the stack, the only one still unread. I unfolded it as the rest of the group finished their wine.

"Oh guys," I breathed. "You're not going to believe this."

Ember and Althea straightened. Griff, Jason, and Danny leaned closer.

"It's dated 1940." I took a deep breath. *"I know you've asked me not to write again, but I had to, one last time. It is important. Charles confessed to me last night, dearest Bruna, a sin . . ."*

A wave of dizziness hit me. And my arm began to throb.

"Eve?" Griff said.

"Ball up, girl," Danny snapped. "Keep going."

I did.

". . . a sin of omission," I read.

Chapter Fifty-Four

Tupelo, Mississippi
1934

It had been exactly five and a half weeks since Charles Jarrod introduced the beautiful young redhead as his new wife. They'd been crisscrossing the southeast since, from church to church, town to town, leading revivals, and Dove Davidson had certainly turned out to be quite a help. She was a natural, leading the singing and getting the people to come down for prayer, and everyone loved her.

Fingers templed, Charles watched Dove sleep in the room at the motor lodge they'd gotten just outside Tupelo. He chided himself for the hundredth time. As much as he might like her to be, this young woman was not his wife. It was just a story he told everyone. A necessary lie.

But she was lovely, so lovely. The way she lay on her back, soft white arms flung to the side, perfect, delicate face lifted to the ceiling as if lost in a dream. It nearly incapacitated him. He wasn't sure what she would think, but he could see a version of the future where the lie they'd been telling became truth.

Her beauty might overwhelm his, but even more arresting was the effect of her presence. She was like a balm to his soul. An unexpected oasis in a life that had begun to feel more and more like wasted wilderness. A lonely trip through towns he couldn't tell apart and didn't care much to remember. But then Ruth had come. Dove. She was more healing than any prayer.

Just watching her sleep, he felt his soul finally at rest.

He thought back to her prayer that first night in the car. It had not been as silent as she'd meant it to be. In her exhaustion and delirium, she'd spoken of someone named Dell, someone she clearly loved. Someone she wanted to have the coin. He had felt an unreasonable pang of jealousy and then chided himself again. If Dove loved this man, then he must be worthy. And besides, he was only here to help the girl. Nothing more.

But still—being a man of weak flesh—he'd held on to the coin.

Tonight's meeting had been a good one, well attended, and it brought in a nice offering. For the first time since Dove joined, folks had come down front during the singing, lining up at the stage. They were waiting for prayer from her, not him, and it brought a smile to his lips. Like him, they saw the light that surrounded her, a nimbus of joy and good humor and fire, and found themselves helplessly drawn to the warmth.

He couldn't blame them, but he couldn't lie to himself; his motives were not completely pure. He did, quite honestly and truly, care about helping Ruth and her friend escape their situation with Arthur Holt. But there had been an additional motivation as well. He'd found himself thinking of her, dreaming of her, ever since their first meeting in Florence. When her letter had come, it had felt as if he'd somehow conjured it up through the sheer force of his desire.

And lately, the more time he'd spent with her and gotten to know her, he'd become more than slightly attached to her. At the oddest times, he would catch himself wondering what the delightful redhead looked like under her clothes. Imagining the feel of her skin under his hand. He dealt with these carnal thoughts much as he did any other carnal thought—he ignored them. Not just because they didn't befit a man of God, but because he valued her company above anything else. The last thing he wanted was to scare her off.

On this night, after he and Dove arrived at the motor lodge, he'd let her use the bathroom and settled in the chintz chair by the window to wait his turn. He'd made a promise to himself and to her, and he intended to keep it. She would not be touched. And he would not scare her away with his feelings. She was too precious for that. Too important.

And he'd made his decision.

Leaving Dove sleeping in the narrow bed, he carefully backed the car out of the gravel lot and headed east. He drove for hours, sipping from a thermos of coffee and smoking Lucky Strikes, finally crossing into Alabama just as the sun warmed the pine-studded horizon.

Pritchard Insane Hospital's brick and limestone facade was laced with rot and mold and thick fingers of angry ivy that looked as if it'd made a blood vow to never release its hold on the stalwart walls. Many of the windows were cracked or missing altogether. The trim needed painting, and if there had been a sidewalk leading to the yawning front entrance, it had long ago eroded.

There were trees—two regal magnolias anchoring the wings of the hospital, and a lovely hawthorn just to the left of the building. An ancient man, emaciated and still, sat on a chair beside the hawthorn. He looked as old as the building, a sort of kindly Cerberus, guarding the gates of Hades. Charles approached and the man doffed his cap.

"Young man." He spoke in a thin, gravelly voice. "Here to see a friend?"

"No," Charles answered. "No friends here."

The old man laughed, a wheezy, phlegmy sound. "Me neither. Not anymore."

Chapter Fifty-Five

Tuscaloosa, Alabama
Present

> *Charles confessed to me last night, dearest Bruna, a sin of omission that he committed against me. Against, he says, the Almighty . . .*

Dove's final letter to Bruna explained almost everything. Between that and the insistent throbbing in my arm, I'd realized our search was not over. Which was why we were headed back to Pritchard.

Althea drove her SUV down the oak-shaded drive, the Alabama sun knifing its way through the thick branches and protective tent of leaves as it set. Jason followed in his Lexus. This time the drive to Pritchard felt less like a scene from a horror movie, and more like the fulfillment of a promise made long ago. That fulfillment—the answer—that started with Dove's final letter to Bruna.

> *. . . there are things I must tell you. Your beloved grandfather and my dear employer, Steadfast Coe, gave me a coin, the Flowing Hair Dollar your family accused me (and then Dell) of stealing. The night Steadfast gave*

> *it to me he was in possession of his good mind, I swear to you. He fully intended it to be mine . . .*

Althea drew into a space in front of the old hospital and the five of us piled out. Jason parked his car nearby and joined us by the fountain. I shaded my eyes and surveyed the fortresslike building. Stalwart and dignified against the blue-and-pink-striped sky, Pritchard's red bricks and granite seemed to defy the battering they'd taken through the years. Surely the hospital held its secrets, but there was only one I was interested in. Dove's.

> *. . . tonight, Charles has confessed. He heard my prayer that night, the night we left the fair, that God would take the coin. That He would miraculously transport it to a particular spot that only Dell and I knew of. Charles heard my prayer and took the coin himself . . .*

Althea touched my shoulder. "Eve. I just wanted to say, thank you for not . . . kicking me out of the search party. Thank you for letting me stay."

I smiled. "You helped me find my grandmother. For that I'll never be able to repay you." I hugged her and she gripped me so hard I nearly lost my breath.

"I know how you can repay me." She cocked an eyebrow. "You could pray for Jay."

I smiled at her and shook my head. "I don't suppose you'll listen when I say I don't have any special powers."

"Nope." She shook her head. "You believe your way, I'll believe mine."

The lines of Dove's letter ran through my head again. I'd read it so many times on the way down from Ember's, I'd practically memorized it.

. . . oh, Bruna. Fool that I am, I convinced myself that God had taken pity on me, that He'd forgiven me all the playacting I'd done in his name and granted me a true miracle. But I was young and frightened and wanted to believe . . .

I turned in the direction of the old, gnarled tree that crowned the velvet lawn, a survivor of decades and storms and droughts. When I reached its blooming canopy, I ducked under and was enveloped in an enchanted leafy world. I ran my hands over the thin bark, its knots and whorls. A line of fat black ants scuttled along a branch on some urgent errand.

And now for the sin. It seems Charles held on to the coin for a full five weeks, contemplating what to do. Perhaps turn me in as a thief? Sell the coin for himself? But he resisted temptation and, resolving to be a man of honor, decided to honor my prayer and leave it for Dell . . .

"Eve," Griff said from somewhere behind me. But I was too lost in my thoughts to answer him. I felt like I'd entered a different dimension, protected from the outside world. It was strange, but I could feel my grandmother's presence in this place. All around this tree.

He drove to Alabama and hid the coin—where, I dare not write in this letter. Then, by what means he wouldn't reveal, he sent word to Dell . . .

I parted the branches to see Griff holding out a pocketknife, its serrated edge gleaming. I reached for it, but he held it back and caught my hand.

"Wait," he said.

"What?"

"I just want you to know. Whatever happens, whether you find the coin or not, I . . ." He faltered.

My gaze stayed steady. "I know. Me too."

His face went a little red and he let go of my hand. "Okay. Careful. It's sharp."

I nodded and ducked back under the tree.

> *. . . but today, an end to that story. And the reason for Charles's distress. Finally, news of Dell Davidson has arrived. He was shot down in a lonely French Quarter alley, between a feed store and an abandoned warehouse. Gunned down by police officers in pursuit of a man suspected of robbing the Banque de L'Etat de la Louisiane . . .*

The trunk of the tree was knotty, some of the knots filled with tar. But farther down, just at the base of the bole, I noticed one large protrusion that looked different.

> *My soul, my heart, my love. He's gone, Bruna . . .*

I dropped to my knees and felt the bump. It was a type of blister, a short, swollen scar running across the trunk around which the bark had grown. Gripping the knife, I began to hack at the blister. I chopped and chopped, gouging out chunks of bark and wood.

As I dug, I exposed the tree's core—raw sapwood or the heart; I wasn't sure what it was called. But it was redolent with the same sickly sweet smell of the blooms. I'd almost cut away the entire surface of the blister, when I saw something. A flash of blue-green . . .

> *Dell never retrieved the coin, but Charles has no doubt if he'd left it earlier, if he hadn't entertained his*

temptation, Dell might not have felt compelled to rob the bank . . .

I pried the object out using the tip of the blade as a lever. It rolled into my palm and I stared in a state of surprise. A marble.

What I do know is that Dell never accepted the gift I offered—that was mine to offer. He made his choice and now I make mine.

Beneath it, I found a second treasure. An amber marble.

I stabbed again at the wood, digging and gouging into the heart of the tree, and then finally the blade hit metal. After chipping carefully around the edges, I saw copper laced with a green patina. I pulled at it.

The coin is yours, Bruna. I give it to you. Think back to our first meeting, that first day at Steadfast's house, when you interviewed me for the job, and I told you about Dell. In that conversation, I told you where to find the coin. Remember? I know you do. So then find it and start a new life, any life you choose.

I brushed enough of the rotted wood away that I could see the engraved image. A woman encircled by stars, hair streaming behind her, face lifted to the sky. *Liberty 1794*, it read. I stared at it, not believing what I was seeing, not wanting to move in case this was a dream that I would wake up from.

Now's your chance, my sweet Bruna. Sell Steadfast's coin, buy yourself a piano, and sing to the children all day long if you like. Sing the old hymns, the happy ones, and when you do, tell the children about your old friend Ruth.

I have loved you, Bruna, with all my heart and soul. And I loved Dell. Now, I find that I love Charles too, in a way—and what can be wrong about that? It's a marvel, isn't it, when the lie becomes the truth?

I dropped the knife and stumbled out from under the tree. I held up the coin, still partially encased in wood, for the rest to see.

"I found it," I said, my voice shaky. "I found it."

Althea put a hand to her mouth. Griff and Danny and Jason stood very still. It was only Ember who approached me, her face glowing in the red-orange sunset.

"The Flowing Hair." Her words came out in a fevered rush. Her eyes were dancing fires, her face flushed pink. "You knew, didn't you?"

"I guessed," I said firmly. "Dove told us once about how she and a boy used to leave presents for each other in this tree. She must've told Bruna that too. And I just put it together."

She shook her head. "Or maybe it was your arm. Maybe Dove was somehow telling you through your arm."

"No—"

"Stranger things have happened. Dove and Bruna healed people."

I wasn't going to win this argument with Ember, but what did it matter? No matter who was right, the Flowing Hair Dollar was in my hand. And now I knew its story.

Charles had hidden the coin for Dell, and then later Dove had told Bruna where it was, and that it was hers for the taking. But when neither Dell nor Bruna came for it, Dove must've intended it for someone else. That must've been the other reason she'd left all her money for the hospital's restoration. She'd wanted to safeguard the coin in this old hawthorn tree. Maybe, I couldn't help thinking, Dove thought I'd be able to solve the riddle. Maybe she suspected all along that I had a trace of her gift.

Maybe, in a way, Ember was right.

It was almost too much to wrap my head around.

I dropped the coin into Ember's hand. "Split it with me?"

"No." Ember looked taken aback. "Steadfast gave it to Dove. And you and your mom and Danny are her heirs."

"But Dove left it here for Bruna. She said so in the letter," I countered.

Ember gave me a conspiratorial smirk. "All right, so we split it. But what the hell does a person do with . . ."

"Seven million dollars?" I said. "Roughly."

"Seven million dollars." Ember breathed the words. Then our eyes locked and we both burst into giggles. When we gained our composure, we just stared at each other, wide-eyed.

"What do you think Bruna would've done with it?" I asked.

Ember's eyes went dreamy. "She would've taken her kids and left Arthur. Left Alabama. Traveled maybe . . ." She shook her head. "She used to tell me about going with her parents to Palm Beach. And the Greenbrier. If she'd had the courage."

"You have courage, Ember, so much of it. So go to Palm Beach and the Greenbrier. For her. Then come home—back to your house—and buy it from Jason if you want. Then do whatever you want to do next."

Her eyes were wet, her voice soft and serious. "Okay, but first, I'm going to throw a big-ass party. And you better come."

I threw my head back and laughed. A laugh brimming with expectation and hope. Oh, I'd go to Ember's party. I'd be the first there and the last to leave. I'd throw caution to the wind, let my hair down. I'd embody all the clichés. I'd celebrate and drink too much and not worry about secrets ever again.

And I'd dance with Griff Murray. Hell, yes. I would definitely dance with Griff.

He was walking toward me now, and when he reached me, he swept me into his arms and kissed me. I breathed him in, and the kiss, and the words of Dove's letter rang in my head.

> *. . . I hope to see you again, dear Bruna. I've planted a hawthorn in my yard just for you. I won't cut blooms from it until you come to me. When you're set up in your new life, bring Artie and Deborah for a visit to California and we'll dance around it.*
>
> *Do come . . .*

Dove

That chilly October night, after a dinner of vegetable soup and a slice of sourdough, Dove settled onto the peeling wrought iron divan on her stone terrace to watch the warm California day darken to night. And to consider calling her granddaughter one more time.

This time, Dove wouldn't bother trying to lure Eve with afternoon tea at a fancy hotel. No, she'd tell the girl the whole story while she had her on the phone. She'd tell her the truth that had been locked away for so many years, so Eve could decide for herself how she would face her future.

But as the night deepened from purple to blue to black, she just continued sitting on the terrace. She admired how well her hawthorn tree had adapted to the silty clay soil in her yard. It had become quite a tree, sturdy and fine. She'd never cut a single bloom from its branches. Dove threw back her head to search for the Big Dipper and savored the feel of the autumn air as it wrapped its smoky cloak around her.

She was procrastinating, she knew. It made her marvel at the magnitude of her cowardice. Ninety-five and still behaving like a scared jackrabbit! She couldn't even call her granddaughter and talk the stuff of life. But she'd always been this way, hadn't she? Reluctant to admit when she didn't fully understand. Reluctant to tell the truth when it was complex. Then reluctant to face those she'd lied to.

Ah, yes. She'd procrastinated another time, years ago, when Eve showed up on her doorstep. Procrastinated then copped out altogether, sending poor Eve off with some cryptic excuse. But she had her reasons. She wanted to protect her granddaughter. From confusion, from doubt. From the pain that came when faith was disappointed.

So she'd told Eve that it had all been a lie. Of course, that, too, had been a lie. But now lies wouldn't do. Now it was time for the truth . . .

The whole truth, which was simply this:

The great evangelist Dove Jarrod had not faked all of it.

There had been a few, just a handful, of true miracles. A sick baby in Huntsville. A woman with kidney stones. And Old Steadfast, that day when she'd brushed his hair and he came back to himself. Others, too, the memories of which she'd tucked away in the back of her mind . . .

She had never been able to predict when the miracles were going to occur. Because the gift—or the fire, or whatever the thing was—hadn't come from her. It had come from the outside, *out of nowhere in fact, striking her like a bolt of summer lightning when she least expected it.*

It was as if she were overtaken, suffocated in light and heat and a brief, intense knowing. *She was completely wrung out when it was over. But just as in the dark as ever. She couldn't parse these experiences. All she could do was ready herself for when—if—it happened again. And that's what she needed to tell Eve. In case the girl had the same gift. In case she still had some belief left in her.*

In the smoky dark, Dove bid good night to the constellations, rose heavily, and walked back into her house. She'd only left on a few lamps, so the rooms had a twilight glow. She decided to leave them as is. Maybe it would be easier to talk to Eve in the shadows.

She'd left a window open in her bedroom, and the room felt as cool as the terrace. She picked up the receiver from the nightstand, then put it down again. She removed her hairpins and lay on the bed, hands clasped across her chest. She was scared, she realized. To finally admit all the murky lies. To admit, at last, to a truth she didn't fully understand and couldn't fully explain.

She closed her eyes to rest. Maybe the lightning would visit her one last time.

She was still pondering this when she felt a hand on her arm. She opened her eyes to see her dear old friend Bruna, sitting on the edge of the bed. She was the plump, pretty girl with dimpled cheeks Dove remembered so well, and Dove's heart swelled with joy.

"Aren't you going to telephone the girl?" Bruna demanded matter-of-factly.

Dove blinked, not expecting the scolding. "She doesn't like me much."

"You haven't allowed her to like you or not. That's not her fault."

"Bruna, my dear Bruna." Dove's eyes filled. "I'm sorry I couldn't save you."

"That wasn't your job. It was mine. But I was too afraid. Afraid of so many things."

Dove was quiet, enjoying the feel of Bruna touching her hair. No one had touched her in such a long time.

"Just call the girl," Bruna instructed. "Tell her the truth. That's all you need to do. That's all you've ever needed to do."

Dove nodded. That was what she wanted, after all. Not only for Eve, but for Diane and Danny too. She wanted them to know the truth, no matter how difficult or confusing it might be, so each of them could choose their own path and follow it with a courageous heart.

She must've drifted because when Bruna spoke again it seemed like hours later. "I have to go now, Ruth."

"No," Dove said. "Please don't."

"I came with a message and now it's delivered."

So she had, Dove thought. The lightning had indeed hit once again, just like Dove had hoped. Her old friend. A miracle.

"I love you, Bruna," Dove said. "I always have."

But Bruna had stopped stroking her hair. She already felt farther away. "Someone's here," she whispered and then disappeared.

Dove sat up, awakened by a dream she couldn't remember. She looked at the clock, but she'd left her glasses outside and couldn't see the time. She could see the shadow man who sat motionless in the slipper chair beside her dressing table. He watched her with eyes that glittered.

"You," she said.

Acknowledgments

Thanks to all my readers, for making it possible to continue the story of the original Honeysuckle Girl. Without your support, I don't get to do what I love, and I'm grateful for you every day.

Thanks to my agent, Amy Cloughley, and the rest of the team at Kimberley Cameron and Associates, as well as Mary Alice Kier and Anna Cottle at Cine/Lit Representation. Lake Union is a fantastic place to publish a book, and I've been lucky enough to work with Alicia Clancy on my past three books. Laura Chasen is a dream developmental editor and Sabrina Dax makes publicity a breeze.

Thanks to M. J. Pullen for telling me whose story this actually was, to Chris Negron and Shannon Kirk for early reads, and M. J. Pullen, Kimberly Brock, and Katherine Scott Crawford, who helped come up with the title. Thanks to Julia Dahl for her brilliant editorial input and for understanding what I was trying to do. Charlene Kurkjian, Brittany Koch, and the Lake Union team guided me in properly representing Eve's hemiplegia. Any aspect of the condition I missed is purely an oversight on my part.

As always, a shout-out to my hometown Erratica crew, colleagues, and friends: Becky Albertalli, George Weinstein, Chris Negron, and M. J. Pullen. Also one for the Tall Poppy Writers, who encourage me to get out of my introverted writer shell and don't get mad when I post controversial memes.

Finally, thanks to Rick, Noah, Alex, and Everett for your support and love.

A Conversation with Emily Carpenter

What inspired you to return to the world of *Burying the Honeysuckle Girls*—and what made you decide to write Dove's story?

I've missed the Honeysuckle Girls the minute I finished writing that book five years ago. Those women really stuck with me. After my previous book, *Until the Day I Die*, which was truly an adventure-thriller, I was hankering to get back to my Southern gothic roots where I started. I wanted to tell spooky stories about generations of families discovering secrets and hints of the supernatural. From the beginning, I always felt Dove in particular had a fascinating story—and I knew in my gut that she had probably lied to everybody in her life about the details of that story. I couldn't wait to dig up those lies. It was such an adventure.

Did you know Dove's backstory when you were writing the original book?

Not at all. I only knew she'd been born at the asylum in Tuscaloosa, Alabama, and had somehow escaped when she was a teen. What I did know was that she had secrets. And that she'd had to have been an extraordinarily tough person to survive alone on the streets during the Depression. But that was it.

What was your inspiration for the Hawthorn Sisters?

I drew a lot from the real-life tent evangelism and healing ministries of John G. Lake, Aimee Semple McPherson, and Billy Sunday, all of whom were extremely successful during the early to mid-1900s. Those folks raked in a lot of money, became huge celebrities, and had some fascinating scandals swirling around them.

All your books blend family drama, secrets, and suspense with a distinct streak of Southern gothic. Does living in the South affect how you write? What do you think is unique about the Southern gothic books being written now?

There's a sort of thickness of history down here; it's hard to push your way through it sometimes. Living in Georgia and Alabama, you can't escape the sins of the South's past—the specter of slavery always hovers. And you can still find a strain of that longing for the "old days" from a certain subset of people. But romanticizing the South's violent past isn't what I do. Even though I don't take these very important issues head-on in every book, I don't ignore them. I'm more interested in looking in a clear-eyed way at how things have changed in the small towns and big cities of the South. And I'm fascinated with the direction of the new Southern gothic tradition of literature. As a white woman especially, I'm always interested in how white society still clings in certain ways to a past that isn't real, that's a mirage their ancestors created for them.

Half of *Reviving the Hawthorn Sisters* takes place in 1934. How did you go about researching that period of time?

Years ago I wrote a screenplay set in the thirties in north Georgia, so when I wrote *Honeysuckle Girls*, I already had all that homework in my back pocket. For *Hawthorn Sisters*, there were some particulars that I wanted to understand better, so I watched movies and read books produced or published in 1934. I found this wonderful book of photographs of children in the Great Depression. The pictures were absolutely stunning, heartbreaking, and communicated more clearly than any dry, stuffy reference book could.

Are there any other characters from this book whom you might be interested in writing about in a future book?

I'm completely in love with Dell Davidson, Ruth's childhood best friend from her early days at the hospital and later, her love interest. I think exploring his outlaw career, and who he crossed paths with, would be so much fun. I wonder too, if there might not be more to the end of his story.

You explore issues of inheritance in *Honeysuckle Girls*—the possibility of a curse—and in *Hawthorn Sisters*. Ruth inherits the coin, Jason inherits the rest of Steadfast's fortune, and Eve seems to have inherited Dove's knack for attracting people and maybe even her "gift." What do you think you've inherited from your ancestors?

As far as I know, I'm the first writer in my family, but not the only one. Both my sister and brother write as well. My maternal grandmother was a really talented artist. I have portraits she painted of my mother and me hanging in my house. I do think I inherited a measure of discipline and dedication to pursuing a goal from my ancestors. I also think I inherited an interest in family histories and the history of the South. And, from my father, a love of architecture and old houses.

This novel explores the sacrifices a person may decide to make for love. What part of that theme do you hope will resonate with readers?

The idea that we can never really judge the decisions a person makes, or who they love, because we don't know the intricacies of their lives and relationships and circumstances. People do what they do because they must; I've learned this lesson more and more the older I get.

Is Dove's gift real?

I leave that for the reader to decide, but I happen to believe. I think. Mostly.

What are you working on now?

I'm strangely superstitious about talking about my ideas before they've taken shape, so I'll just say I've got a million ideas bouncing around in my head. A couple of supernatural suspense stories, and another historical novel—"not quite true, but could've been true"—set in the 1950s. And an un-ghost story. How's that for answering without answering?

About the Author

Photo © 2018 Ashley Taylor

Emily Carpenter is the bestselling author of four thrillers: *Until the Day I Die*, *Every Single Secret*, *The Weight of Lies*, and *Burying the Honeysuckle Girls*. A graduate of Auburn University, Emily has worked as an actor, producer, screenwriter, and behind-the-scenes soap opera assistant for CBS television. Raised in Birmingham, Alabama, she moved to New York City before returning to the South, where she now lives in Atlanta, Georgia, with her family. Visit Emily at www.emilycarpenterauthor.com.